THE VELLHOR SAGA VOLUME 1

ELVEN BLOOD

MARK STANLEY

DRAGONTALE
PUBLISHING

First published by Dragontale Publishing Limited 2024

Copyright © 2024 by Mark Stanley

All rights reserved. No part of this publication may be reproduced, stored or transmitted in any form or by any means, electronic, mechanical, photocopying, recording, scanning, or otherwise without written permission from the publisher. It is illegal to copy this book, post it to a website, or distribute it by any other means without permission.

This novel is entirely a work of fiction. The names, characters and incidents portrayed in it are the work of the author's imagination. Any resemblance to actual persons, living or dead, events or localities is entirely coincidental.

Mark Stanley asserts the moral right to be identified as the author of this work.

First edition

ISBN: 9798327790117

Cover art by David Leahy

To my incredible wife, whose hard work and tireless dedication have sustained our home and business whilst I have delved into crafting fantastical realms! Your love and encouragement fuel my every success. I'm endlessly thankful for your balance in my life. When I'm low, you lift me with your unwavering support, and when I fly too high, you ground me with wisdom and perspective. Your presence is a guiding light, keeping me steady on my journey.

I love you to the moon and back

Mark x

Contents

ᚠᛟᚷᚾᛋᛋ (Glossary)   I

1   A Father's Burden   1
2   One Last Patrol   5
3   Outcast in the Woods   19
4   A Mage's Journey   35
5   Traitor in the Midst   51
6   A Daughter's Despair   67
7   The Road to Lamos   82
8   Escape!   88
9   Shadows of Loss   99
10   A Potential Ally   109
11   Prophecy Unbound   124
12   The Sandaran Flower   138
13   The Hostage Situation   153
14   Parting Ways   165
15   The Olive Tree   179
16   Between a Rock and a Hard Place   194
17   Friendship with a Fae   210

18	Herald of the Gods	226
19	A Journey with the Enemy?	232
20	A God Amongst Dwarves	247
21	Moonlit Strife	259
22	A Timeless Tomb	270
23	A Story of Stonesprites	281
24	Friend or Foe?	291
25	Bonded in Stone	302
26	Alliances Forged	314
27	Betrayal	325
28	The Forgotten Realm	338
29	Battle for the Sacred Tree	343
30	Dark Places	353
	Afterword	361
	About the Author	366

ᛚᚩXᚾᛏᛁ (Glossary)

ᚱᚩRᛁᚾR ᛏ (Races)

Dwarves - Renowned for their discipline, training, and superior craftsmanship, Dwarves are a formidable race. Their society is steeped in traditions of hard work and bravery, governed by a complex political structure involving clan chiefs and their elective council. They are characterized by their short stature and robust builds.

Elves - They are known for their mastery of magic. Elves stand no taller than five feet and have slender, elegant features. They are known for their deep-rooted traditions and connection to nature, in particular the Great Elven Forest.

Humans - Humans in Vellhor have the ability to practice magic, although they are not as adept at magic as the Elves are. They are integral to the world's dynamics, contributing through various trades and participating in significant conflicts and alliances.

Drogo - The Drogo Mulik are a fierce and chaotic race of lizard like people, feared across Vellhor for their brutal nature. Standing at over seven feet tall, Drogo warriors have scales and an intimidating presence. Their appearance is dragon-like, with a muscular build and a savage demeanor. The Drogo are known for their aggression and lack of discipline, making them unpredictable and dangerous enemies.

ᛏᛆᚱᛏᚺᛦᚱᛁᛊ (Main Characters)

Gunnar - dwarf - heir to Clan Draegoor, Gunnar is a stalwart figure among the Dwarves, Gunnar's leadership and combat prowess are legendary. As a seasoned warrior, he navigates the treacherous political landscapes and defends his kin against relentless threats, including the fearsome Drogo Mulik.

Anwyn - Elf - outcast by Elven society, Anwyn lives with her parent in the great Elven forest, outside of Stromyr. she is a graceful yet formidable Elf, whose role will become crucial in the united front against her adversaries.

Kemp - Human - a mage of rare elemental affinity, stands as a beacon of magical prowess within the human kingdom. His journey is a balance of honing his natural talents and navigating the societal expectations of a young mage.

Ruiha - Human - once a feared assassin and a former member of the Sand Dragons gang, Ruiha's life is a testament to resilience and transformation. Trained by Faisal, a dangerous and manipulative figure, Ruiha executed his murderous commands for eight long years. However, a moment of moral awakening led her to defy Faisal, putting her own life at risk.

ᛊᛖᛚᛆᛏᚺᛦᚱᛁᛊ (Supporting Characters)

Dakarai - Drogo - Dakarai is a character who struggles with familial and societal pressures. His devotion to his people and his internal conflict about his son's path are putting him in a difficult position.

Lorelei - Lorelei, a Fae of the forest, is Anwyn's steadfast companion and guide. Her ethereal presence and magical abilities significantly bolster Anwyn's own powers.

ᚠᛟᚲᛋᛏ (Glossary)

Havoc - Havoc, a newly bonded Stonesprite to Gunnar, possesses remarkable control over earth and stone despite his infancy. His chaotic and unpredictable nature is balanced by Gunnar's steady influence.

Karl - Karl is a jovial dwarf known for his loyalty and bravery. He is a close companion of Gunnar.

Magnus - Magnus is Gunnar's younger brother, also a seasoned Dwarven warrior. He often engages in light-hearted banter with his comrades.

Laslo - Laslo is a fierce and determined Dwarven warrior, known for his bravery and agility in battle. His fearless nature often puts him at the forefront of danger.

Hansen - dwarf - provides guidance and aid to Gunnar and Karl during a critical time.

Laoch - Laoch is a revered Elven warrior and the father of Anwyn. Known for his mastery of the katana and his unwavering dedication to his family.

Eira - Eira, the mother of Anwyn, is a master of magical arts. Her wisdom and grace are evident in her teachings and the way she cares for her family.

Alden - Alden, Anwyn's grandfather on her mother's side, is a figure shrouded in mystery and wisdom. An academic genius with the rare gift of prophecy, Alden has spent many years traveling and gathering knowledge.

Thalirion - an Elf who stands by Anwyn, plays a critical role in the efforts to unify Elves and Dwarves.

Harald - Human - Harald's story is marked by suspicion and complexity. A former professional guard, his disciplined bearing and intense focus hint at a deeper, possibly sinister agenda.

ᛚᛟᛏᚨᛏᛁᛟᚾᛋ (Locations)

Dreynas - A realm of snow-covered mountains, home to the Dwarven clans. Each city within Dreynas, such as Draegoor, Braemeer, Uglich, and Hornbaek, has unique characteristics that contribute to the rich tapestry of Dwarven culture.

Draegoor - Gunnar home city, known for its strategic importance and the elite Draegoorian Snow Wolves. It stands as a testament to Dwarven resilience and martial prowess.

Braemeer - A bustling mining metropolis, Braemeer is distinguished by its deep connection to the earth and its uniquely brown-skinned Dwarves. Its proximity to the Drogo city of Claw often stirs tensions.

Uglich - Known for its coppery-skinned Dwarves, Uglich adds to the diversity of Dreynas with its distinct cultural and physical traits.

Hornbaek - A city noted for its shorter Dwarves who share the pale skin of Draegoor's inhabitants, reflecting the varied heritage within the Dwarven realm.

Luxyyr - An Elven realm situated on the Great Elven Forest, home to cities like Stromyr, Gwydir, Coetyr, Sylvestyr, and Kyrwode. Luxyyr is a place of magical elegance and deep-rooted traditions, central to the Elven way of life.

Stromyr - A forest city in Luxyyr, where Anwyn's parent's once lived

Gwydir - A forest city in Luxyyr

ᚱᚢᚾᛏᛏ (Glossary)

Coetyr - A forest city in Luxyyr

Sylvestyr - A forest city in Luxyyr

Kyrwode - A forest city in Luxyyr

Fenmark - Fenmark is a human kingdom known for its rich history, diverse landscapes, and three prominent provinces: Tempsford, Lamos, and Fenchester. The kingdom is a tapestry of verdant forests, rugged mountains, and bustling towns, each with its own unique charm and character. The three provinces each house a prestigious academy of magic.

Tempsford - Kemp's home city. It is the northernmost province of Fenmark and is home to the Lakeview Academy, situated on the serene Alghari Lake.

Lakeview Academy - Situated in Tempsford, the Lakeview Academy is a renowned institution for magic. The academy's rigorous training and serene location make it an ideal place for scholars and mages.

Lamos - a province that tells a tale of conflict and cultural fusion. Located just north of the Al Asita Pass and the Sandaran capital of Ostium, Lamos was annexed by King Luthar of Fenmark approximately three decades ago. This region has a history of civil unrest due to its divided loyalties between Fenmark and Sandarah. Over time, however, the tensions have eased, and Lamos has become a blend of Sandaran and Fenmark cultures.

Fenchester - A province known for its rugged terrain and hardy inhabitants. It is the northwestern province of Fenmark and is characterized by its harsher climate and resilient people. Fenchester is home to many soldiers and mercenaries, and the Fenchester Guard is renowned for its disciplined and skilled warriors.

Sandarah

Gecit - Gecit is a city known for its sprawling slums and the dangerous criminal underbelly. It is where Ruiha, a former member of the Sand Dragons gang, honed her skills as an assassin. The city's harsh environment and ruthless gangs reflect the more sinister aspects of Sandaran society

Ostium - Ostium, the capital city of Sandarah, is located just north of the Al Asita Pass. It has a rich history of conflict, especially with neighboring regions like Lamos, which was annexed by Fenmark. Ostium's strategic location has made it a center of political and military activity, deeply influencing its culture and governance

Porta - Porta is a coastal city in Sandarah.

Atea - A city known for its strategic importance and its bustling port. It serves as a major gateway for trade and travel, linking Sandarah with other parts of Vellhor. The city's vibrancy and economic significance make it a crucial part of Sandaran life.

Giris - Giris is a coastal city in Sandarah.

Agilis - Agilis is a coastal city in Sandarah.

Drogo Mulik - Situated in the heart of the Scorched Mountains, Drogo Mulik is the home of the Lizard race known as Drogo. Many of the homes were built by Dwarven architects centuries ago.

Claw - Claw is a city known for its brutal strength and its inhabitants' savage reputation.

Strong - Strong is another prominent city within the Drogo Mulik territories. Its name reflects the Drogo's obsession with

ᚱᚢᚾᛁᛋ (Glossary)

physical power and dominance.

Death - Death is a city that embodies the Drogo Mulik's dark and ruthless nature. The name itself strikes fear into the hearts of their enemies and symbolizes the lethal force that the Drogo wield.

Fang - Fang is known for its warriors' ferocity and their deadly precision in battle. The city's name reflects the sharpness and lethality of its fighters, who are trained to be both ruthless and efficient.

Hammer - Hammer is a city where the Drogo Mulik are known for there strength and unyielding nature.

Skull - The city is a grim reminder of the Drogo's connection to death and their unyielding pursuit of power through any means necessary.

Aerithordor - The heavenly Dwarven realm where gods and fallen warriors reside. A place of deep spiritual significance to the Dwarves. Believed to be situated amidst the craggy peaks of an impossibly high, unknown mountain range, this ethereal realm is a testament to both the Dwarven craftsmanship and their unwavering connection to the divine

ᚠᛚᚪᚾ ᛏᚺᚱᛖᛖ (Map)

COETYR
SYLVESTYR
GWYDIR
LUXYYR
STROMYR
KYRWODE
TEMPSFORD
LAMOS
ATEA
GIRIS
GECH
ACILIS

1

A Father's Burden

'A father toils to carve a path of security, yet shadows lurk where his light cannot reach.'

Dakarai

Dakarai's weary footsteps whispered through the dimly lit corridor of his home, each soft sound a reminder of the relentless toil he endured in the mines. Despite the weight of exhaustion pressing upon him, he moved with a certain grace, a testament to the inherent strength and agility of his lizard-like heritage.

Standing over seven feet tall, Dakarai navigated the familiar stone halls with practiced caution. The ancient abode, meticulously crafted by Dwarven hands centuries ago, stood as a testament to their artistry. Yet, its dimensions were tailored to their stature, presenting a constant challenge for the towering Drogo Mulik who now called it home. Thus, Dakarai trod carefully, ever mindful of low-hanging beams and doorframes that threatened to deliver a painful blow if he dared to let his guard down.

Despite the longstanding animosity between the Dwarves

and the Drogo, Dakarai couldn't help but acknowledge the awe-inspiring craftsmanship of the Dwarven architects. As he traversed the corridors carved deep within the bowels of the Scorched Mountains, he marvelled at the meticulous precision evident in every stone. The buildings stood as enduring monuments to the skill of their creators, their sturdy frames weathering the passage of centuries with stoic resilience. Even though the towering Drogo dwarfed their stature, the Dwarves crafted structures of grandiosity and magnificence, enabling even the hulking Drogo to navigate their halls with relative ease.

As Dakarai crossed the threshold into the living room, he found his wife, Melagai, seated by the hearth. Her weary countenance was unmistakable, the lines etched into her leathery face reminiscent of weathered stone. The dancing flames cast flickering shadows across the room, accentuating the fatigue in her reptilian eyes. With a heavy sigh, she looked up as Dakarai entered, managing only a small, forced smile.

"Dakarai, you're home," she said.

Dakarai nodded, his own weariness reflected in his gaze. Though he yearned for nothing more than to collapse onto his bed and surrender to sleep's embrace, he knew there were duties demanding his attention first.

"How was your shift?" Melagai asked, though her tone held little interest. It was a question asked out of habit rather than genuine curiosity.

"Long," Dakarai replied with a sigh, stripping off his heavy work boots and setting them aside. "But fruitful. We struck a rich vein today."

Melagai nodded absentmindedly, her gaze fixed on the flames dancing in the hearth. "That's good," she murmured, though her mind seemed elsewhere.

Dakarai frowned, sensing the distance that had grown between them in recent months. Ever since their son, Drakamor, had fallen in with some of the younger Drogo from the warrior class, Melagai had become increasingly distant. She seemed preoccupied, her usual warmth replaced by a tense reserve, consumed by worry for their son. While Dakarai and his family hailed from mining stock—a position not as esteemed within Drogo society as that of the fighting warriors—he understood the importance of the Fang clan's role in mining the mountains. He could endure the disdain of the warrior class as long as his family had food on their table and a comfortable cot to sleep on. However, Drakamor, young and impressionable, possessed a mischievous streak and an insatiable desire to become a warrior, a dream he'd held since his fifth birthday.

Thinking of his son, Dakarai turned his attention to the corner of the room where Drakamor usually sat, his brow furrowed in concern. Drakamor, now a young adult, exuded an air of restless energy and ambition, but lately, that energy seemed to be directed towards questionable pursuits. Dakarai knew he needed to have a conversation with him, to help guide him back onto the right path, but finding the time amidst his demanding work schedule proved to be a challenge.

"Where's Drakamor?" Dakarai asked, trying to keep the concern from seeping into his voice.

Melagai's expression darkened at the mention of their son's whereabouts. "Out with his friends again," she replied bitterly. "Nergai only knows what trouble they're getting into."

Dakarai's brow furrowed at his wife's words, a flicker of discomfort passing through him. He had never been one for the fervent devotion to Nergai that Melagai exhibited. While he respected the traditions of their people, he couldn't help but feel a pang of unease whenever Melagai invoked the name of their Draconic god, who valued strength and power above all else.

Instead of bringing it up, Dakarai sighed, running a hand over his scaled head, his fingers tracing the small horns that adorned it. He hated seeing the strain that Drakamor's choices were putting on their family, but with his long hours in the mines, there seemed to be little he could do to intervene.

"I'll talk to him," Dakarai promised, though the words felt hollow even to his own ears.

Melagai said nothing, her silence casting a heavy weight that hung between them. Dakarai understood mere words wouldn't mend the growing rift in their family, but for now, it was all he had to offer.

As Dakarai settled in for a troubled sleep, the weight of stone pressed down upon him, both physically and metaphorically. He knew the challenges facing his family were far from over, but he also knew he would face them head-on, as he always had, with strength and determination born from the depths of the Scorched Mountains.

2

One Last Patrol

'In the forge of preparation, our mettle is tested. It is the well-prepared who emerge as the true architects of victory.'

Gunnar

Gunnar sat among his fellow Dwarven warriors in the dimly lit cavern, their makeshift sleeping quarters for the past six months. The chatter and laughter of his comrades filled the air, but thoughts of his anticipated return to his home city, Draegoor, consumed his mind.

"Two more days, Gunnar, that's all we have left before we get to go back to Draegoor as heroes!" proclaimed Magnus, his younger brother and fellow warrior.

Standing at a sturdy five feet, Gunnar commanded attention, towering over the rest of his unit who stood no taller than four and a half feet. His broad, muscular frame spoke of years spent training in combat and enduring the challenges of the underground world.

With his long blonde hair tied back into a neat ponytail and a thick, well-kept beard adorned with intricate braids and tiny trinkets reaching down to his chest, Gunnar presented a striking figure. His square jawline and chiselled cheekbones accentuated his rugged appeal, while his clear blue eyes sparkled with intelligence.

Gunnar couldn't help but grunt in response to Magnus's proclamation of heroism. The notion didn't sit well with him. Reflecting on the past six months spent on the Dreynas-Drogo Mulik border, he found the period uneventful compared to the tales of valor spun by his brother.

The bulk of the Draegoorian army was currently stationed within Fort Bjerg, an immense underground stronghold crafted by their ancestors centuries before Gunnar's time. This colossal fortress served as their base of operations, its sturdy walls echoing with the whispers of history. Three days' march away lay the Dwarven city of Braemeer, nestled deep within the recesses of Braemeer Mountain. A sprawling mining metropolis, it bustled with life, inhabited by the sturdy and resourceful Braemeerian Dwarves. These Dwarves were not merely defined by their customs but also by their physical traits. Gunnar and his kin from Draegoor boasted pale skin, while the Dwarves of Uglich bore a coppery tinge to their complexion. However, the Dwarves of Braemoor had a unique bark-like brown tone to their skin, a testament to their deep connection with the earth. The only other clan to share their pale skin were the Hornbaeks, though they were notably shorter than the towering figures of Draegoor. Each clan, with its distinct features and heritage, added layers of richness to the tapestry of the realm of Dreynas.

Unfortunately for Braemeer, its nearest neighbor was the Drogo Mulik city of Claw. Gunnar couldn't help but find the name Claw somewhat absurd, but he understood its significance in Drogo culture, where strength held paramount importance. In fact, the Drogo Mulik even boasted a city named 'Strong,' a fact that never ceased to amuse the Dwarves. Gunnar often mused that if someone had to incessantly proclaim their strength, it might suggest an underlying insecurity or the need to overcompensate in some way. Despite such musings, Braemeer's proximity to Claw often stirred tensions, with the Drogo often venturing unwelcomed into Dreynas' territories.

In truth, Gunnar was more than ready to bring his tour with the Snow Wolves to an end. Over the past six months, he had endured the bitter cold of Dreynas while stationed at its remote border, tirelessly ensuring that the Drogo Mulik did not encroach further into Dwarven territory. Although, unlike his younger brother Magnus, Gunnar carried the weight of responsibilities that awaited him upon his return to Draegoor. Thus, the prospect of heading home was a bittersweet one, as it came laden with the burdens of being the eldest born son and heir of Erik the Blood, clan chief of the Dwarves of Draegoor.

Gunnar understood the necessity of the Dwarven Army's presence on the border, given the escalating raids by the Drogo Mulik on Dwarven resources. This concern resonated deeply with every dwarf in Dreynas along with the Dwarven Council.

Dreynas, a land of snow-covered mountains housing four proud Dwarven clans, spanned the Frost Mountain range. Each clan resided in a great city, hewn into the mountain centuries ago by skilled craft smiths. These mountains bore the names of the Mountain Goddess Dreyna's four sons: Braem, Draeg, Lich, and Baeka. True to Dwarven nature, they named their cities after these mountain deities, reflecting their straightforward and pragmatic disposition.

The Dwarven Council consisted of representatives from the four clans, including clan chiefs and clan priests. It was a democracy of sorts, with no single ruler; instead, a council vote made decisions. With the surge in Drogo raids, the four clan chiefs had convened and voted, and the Council had acted swiftly. The Dwarven Army, including Gunnar's Snow Wolves, had been mobilised to defend the Dwarven lands from the relentless Drogo Mulik, yet a state of war had not been declared.

Gunnar reflected on the gravity of the situation, well aware that any confrontation with the Drogo Mulik should not be underestimated. These formidable adversaries, standing at an imposing seven feet tall, were a truly intimidating sight to behold. Small, tough scales covered their bodies, and they had a strange hairless appearance. Bony horns protruded from their heads and shoulders, and their faces bore a horrific snarl, making them hideous to look at.

Nevertheless, Gunnar's stoic demeanor remained unchanged, a testament to the resilience ingrained in the heart of every dwarf. Like his kin, he harbored no excessive fear of the Drogo Mulik that haunted the fringes of their realm. In his seventy-five years of life—a mere blink in the vast expanse of Dwarven existence—he had weathered his fair share of skirmishes with these relentless foes.

With a grizzled resolve born of experience, Gunnar had come to understand the nature of the Drogo Mulik. Though undeniably formidable in strength and ferocity, a glaring lack of discipline and training marred their prowess. They wielded their weapons with reckless abandon, their blows fueled by raw aggression rather than honed skill. Clad in scant armor, if any at all, they relied on primitive swords, hammers, and axes, their arsenal devoid of the craftsmanship that defined Dwarven weaponry.

But it was not merely their crude weaponry that marked the Drogo as inferior foes. Gunnar had witnessed firsthand their penchant for chaos and discord, their ranks often descending into disarray in the heat of battle. Fueled by anger, confusion, and frustration, they were as much a danger to themselves as they were to their adversaries.

In comparison, the Dwarves were a model of discipline, boasting extensive training, and were adorned in top-tier armor. The outcome of any conflict was evident: it was no contest. Gunnar, a formidable combatant in his own right, was confident in the strength of his race and remained steadfast in his belief that they were more than capable of defending their lands against the Drogo Mulik.

Key to the Dwarven defense was the elite Draegoorian Snow Wolves. Upon Gunnar's initial arrival at the Snow Wolves, a renowned unit notorious for harboring the finest warriors within Draegoor, he had encountered a mixed reception. The seasoned veterans, those grizzled warriors who had shared the battlefield with Erik the Blood and had seen his courage firsthand, were the first to extend a begrudging nod of acknowledgment to Gunnar. In their eyes, the respect Erik had commanded had trickled down to his son, bestowing upon Gunnar a modicum of goodwill.

Yet, amongst the rest, that goodwill was lacking. The fact that he was the rightful heir of the clan chief for the City of Draegoor bore no sway among these stubborn dwarves. Dwarven culture, steeped in a tradition of relentless hard work and bravery, dictated that respect was a prize hard-won and never gifted by virtue of one's birthright. Gunnar understood that he was tasked with proving his mettle, for his kin, as well as his fellow warriors, and he, himself, held little patience for titles unearned.

Over the span of a decade, Gunnar had ceaselessly toiled to wrestle from his soldiers the respect that had initially eluded him. He devoted himself to a grueling regimen of training and education, honing his skills until he stood unrivalled within his unit. While his slightly above-average height and muscular frame certainly played to his advantage, it was the relentless grind of unyielding discipline and unflagging effort that catapulted him to the top and continued to keep him there. Through relentless study, Gunnar delved into the intricacies of his craft, learning about weaponry, battles, tactics, the different races on Vellhor and the magic systems used by those races. He refused to cut any corners in his pursuit of mastery.

With his ascent to the rank of Section Leader five years ago, Gunnar had assumed leadership with an unwavering sense of purpose. His command was firm yet fair, ensuring that his unit followed him not out of obligation, but out of genuine respect for the leader he had become.

He was brought out of his reverie by Karl calling his name, "so, has Gunnar *the Fair* got any Draegoorian lassies waiting for him?" Karl joked. He was a jovial dwarf with a wild mane of red hair and a bushy red beard. He had a contagious hearty laugh and a penchant for smoking the Elven tobacco known as broadleaf. His amusement echoed through the chamber like a bell. With a playful glint in his eye, he couldn't resist teasing Gunnar, who bore the nickname of 'Gunnar the Fair' owing to his striking good looks.

In Dwarven culture, names held significant weight. They were more than mere labels; they reflected one's essence and heritage. The naming ritual was a sacred tradition, passed down through generations. Gunnar understood this well, having been named after his grandfather, a revered warrior of old. Yet, the nickname 'Gunnar the Fair' had been bestowed upon him by his comrades, a title that teased his deviation from traditional Dwarven aesthetics. As Gunnar pondered the origins of the moniker, a fleeting thought crossed his mind - did it truly matter? In the grand scheme of things, the name held little sway over his actions or his sense of self. While he appreciated the camaraderie it represented, the question of whether it was born out of respect or jest held little significance to him. After all, he was Gunnar, grandson of a legendary warrior, and ensuring that he honored that legacy was all that truly mattered to him.

Magnus, Gunnar's brother, joined in the joke, his massive hand scratching his bulbous nose as he chimed in, "Aye, you can bet your last ale that there'll be a few lasses throwing punches over who gets the honor of sharing a drink with Gunnar the Fair!"

Gunnar attempted to silence their banter with his swift reply, his tone heavy with a sense of responsibility that overshadowed any playful exchanges. "Enough of that, you two! You both know that I won't be having fun. Unlike you two, I'll be kept in endless meetings with father and the council, wrestling with the momentous decision of whether we should recklessly plunge into a cursed war with the bloody Drogo!"

Magnus shook his head at that, his unkempt brown beard swaying in front of his large barrel chest, "I'll be honest with you, brother, better you than me. I can't stand those old bastards—the city chiefs and their bloody priests—all pretending to know what's best for us!"

At that, Laslo, one of Gunnars most distinguished warriors, raised his head and stared at Magnus, "thank the Mountain Goddess that you're not next in line to become chief, Magnus. What a sorry state of affairs that would be. You'd be more interested in chasing skirt than ruling properly!"

Magnus responded with an easygoing shrug, raising his hands nonchalantly. "Well, not all of us can boast the handsome looks of my dear brother here. Some of us need to put in the effort to charm the lasses. They don't exactly throw themselves at the rest of us, you know!"

With the desire to steer the conversation away, Gunnar swiftly interjected, his tone becoming more serious. "In any case, those council meetings are as tedious as one might expect. Half the clans clamor for war, while the other half yearns for the status quo, unwilling to invest too heavily in the Drogo. It's a relentless cycle of deliberations, and it often feels like no one actually listens to me, anyway."

"And what is it you've got to say then, boss?" Laslo asked, peering over at Gunnar.

Gunnar let out a heavy sigh, his shoulders drooping under the weight of his concerns. "We're already dedicating a substantial portion of our resources to contend with the Drogo," he remarked, his voice tinged with a note of exasperation. "Adding further strain now, especially with winter looming, could prove disastrous for the clans. The overground farms haven't yielded well at all this season, and embarking on a war with the Drogo in our current state would be rash and unwise. Let us exercise some patience, a virtue that Dwarves are notoriously poor at, may I add! We should focus on replenishing our reserves in the coming seasons before broaching the subject of war again."

Karl looked through his bushy red eyebrows, and across the smokey cavern they had turned into their sleeping quarters. He turned to Gunnar, his tone tinged with curiosity and a hint of provocation. "Tell me, Gunnar, are you not excited by the prospect of war? I assumed you'd relish the chance to escape the confines of our city. See yourself in some real combat. Perhaps even carve out a name for yourself like your old man did."

Gunnar stroked his beard for a minute, "I agree, we need to keep an eye on the bastards, but declaring war?" Slowly shaking his head, he continued, his voice measured, "like I said, I think it's too early. All we've seen so far is an increase in minor raids, troubling, but not catastrophic. They haven't done worse yet."

"*Yet*, is right", a gruff voice rumbled from the cavern's entrance. Startled, the three Dwarves turned their heads, their eyes locking onto the stocky figure that stood there. Instinctively, they rose from their seats, ready to show respect to their general.

General Wilfrid, whose malevolent smile lurked beneath his

thick black beard, fixed them with a withering gaze. He had a face that appeared to relish the misfortune of others. "Unfortunately, lads," he declared, his tone lacking any semblance of sympathy, "I come with some bad news."

Curiosity and mild apprehension lingered in the air as Magnus, half in jest, ventured, "So, what's the bad news then, boss? Has our tour been extended or something?" His words carried a hint of humor, but beneath it, there lay a genuine worry.

"No, no, nothing so drastic as all that. But you lucky bastards will be going on patrol in the morning. One final patrol to see the end of your tour through!".

"By Draeg's holy balls, boss!" Magnus exclaimed. "We're set to depart in just two days. Can't you dispatch another unit instead?"

The very mention of Draeg, the revered Mountain God of the Dwarves, seemed to hang heavily in the air, as if invoking the deity's wrath.

General Wilfrid, however, offered no reprieve. With a solemn nod, he turned stiffly and made his exit from the cavern, a smug smile still etched across his face. His words were final and left no room for negotiation. "No, lads, this mission is for the Snow Wolves," he affirmed, before disappearing into the shadows beyond.

Gunnar heaved a weary sigh at the thought of yet another patrol. Admittedly, he was more than a little surprised that his unit had been selected, knowing of several other units who had been resting longer and still had several weeks of their tour left. Perhaps one of the lads had pissed someone important off. He'd have to double check that when they got back tomorrow.

"Why's your uncle being such a prick?" Karl huffed.

Gunnar, maintaining his composure, responded calmly, "Mind your tongue, Karl." Then, with a wry smile that betrayed a hint of familial exasperation, he added, "He may be a prick, but he's also the General of the Draegoorian Army, and, let's not forget, the Chief's little brother..."

As he rose and stretched his tired back, the satisfying cracks breaking the silence, Gunnar prepared his gear for the impending patrol. The uncertainty of what awaited them on this final mission gnawed at the edges of his thoughts.

Gunnar

At the break of dawn, Gunnar stood before a formidable assembly of fifty of the finest warriors in all of Draegoor. These Dwarves were a breed apart—toughened, meticulously trained, and possessed of keen intellect. They bore the distinct mark of professional soldiers, individuals who had not merely served, but excelled during their mandatory eight years of military service, a rite of passage for every male dwarf across Dreynas.

Upon completing their military service, most Dwarves would typically return to their respective clans to pursue a trade. Yet, the fifty Dwarves who now stood before Gunnar were no ordinary soldiers. Each one had distinguished themselves as an exceptional warrior, recognized by their superiors, and personally selected to remain within the military fold. Together, they formed the illustrious and fearsome elite unit known far and wide as the Snow Wolves.

Each of these elite warriors donned the finest Dwarven armour, meticulously crafted to encase their entire bodies. From head to toe, they were enveloped in layers of protection, donning pointed barbute helmets that veiled most of their faces, leaving only a distinct T-shaped opening for vision and communication purposes. Their formidable presence was further heightened by the long oblong shields they bore, which offered a steadfast defense.

In addition to their defensive gear, each dwarf was armed with a weapon suited to their individual combat style—whether it be a sword, axe, mace, or some combination thereof. They also carried a crossbow and a quiver brimming with bolts, ready to unleash precise and deadly ranged attacks when needed.

The weapons and armor were not mere creations; they were masterpieces meticulously forged by the most highly skilled Dwarven smiths in Dreynas. Crafted from Frosteel, the strongest metal found on Vellhor and sourced exclusively from the Frost Mountains, these arms and armor boasted unrivaled strength and durability. Frosteel was a metal so resilient that only the dwarves could work it, for its melting point far exceeded the capabilities of ordinary furnaces. Only through the application of Dwarven craft magic, an art unique to their race, could Frosteel be shaped and manipulated. In the realm of magic, Dwarves were unique, excelling specifically in craft magic.

Although both the Dwarves and the Drogo lived underground, most of the Drogo that had been spotted in Dreynas had been above ground. This meant that today's screening patrol was going to be outside in the freezing cold, treacherous terrain of the mountain passes.

"Listen up, lads," Gunnar's voice boomed with authority, his words cutting through the crisp mountain air with a commanding presence. As he addressed his elite unit, he couldn't help but notice the undercurrent of anticipation rippling through their ranks. Many of them, he knew, had been eagerly awaiting their return home tomorrow, their thoughts already drifting to warm hearths and hearty meals.

Yet, as the weight of General Wilfrid's orders settled upon them, Gunnar saw the resolve harden in their eyes, the anticipation giving way to steely determination. They were warriors, forged in the crucible of conflict, and they would meet whatever challenges lay ahead with unwavering resolve.

"General Wilfrid has issued orders for us to conduct a patrol from checkpoint eighty-four all the way down to checkpoint sixty," Gunnar continued, his tone firm and unwavering. "That's a staggering forty miles of treacherous mountain terrain we'll be traversing. You've done this before, so you know the drill. Keep your senses sharp; the gods damned Drogo are bound to be lurking out there somewhere, and I won't have us caught unawares."

As Gunnar spoke, his breath billowed into the cold air, forming a sizeable cloud of fog that hung like a shroud around them. He surveyed his unit, his gaze flickering from one face to the next, gauging their readiness before proceeding.

"Alright," he continued, "to cover that amount of terrain, we will need to form four squads within the unit. Axel, you and Magnus take your squad and cover from eighty to eighty-four, then head back. That's mainly high ridges you'll be walking, so keep an eye out below you."

Despite the chill in the air and the looming threat of danger, a surge of pride swelled within Gunnar as he looked upon his comrades. In their unity, he found strength, and in their determination, he found reassurance. Together, they would face whatever lay ahead, their bond as unbreakable as the mountains themselves.

"Leif, take Otto and your squad up to checkpoints eighty and head down to seventy-two before heading back. It's flatter there and you'll be able to cover more ground."

"Arne, you and Sigurd will cover seventy-two right down to sixty-five, that's a bastard of a trek, but it's nice and open so you shouldn't encounter any problems, and even if you do, you'll see them coming a mile away."

"Karl and I will cover the rest. I know it's not as far, but there's two chokepoints, which'll cause us some issues. When we're all done, we'll meet back here and your squad leaders will buy you a well-deserved ale!"

The squad let out a half-hearted cheer at that and started getting into their formations.

"Squad leaders, on me," ordered Gunnar as his unit was preparing themselves.

"I know I don't need to tell you this, but the terrain's a bitch out there. If the bastards are coming for us, it'll be from above and it'll probably be on the flank, so stay organized, and stay vigilant. Ensure your squads are covered on all sides."

"Lastly, keep lines of communication open at all times. Use your SLS to communicate. I want to respond to an attack as soon as possible. Questions before we set off?"

Karl deftly removed his SLS from his gear and meticulously ensured that it was in perfect working order. These devices, officially known as 'Sympathetic Link Systems,' were an invaluable asset employed by the Dwarven military for long-distance communication. Crafted by the skilled hands of the Dwarves, these hand-sized stone tablets were etched with intricate, enchanted runes. These enchantments bound them together in a complex network, establishing a secure and reliable line of communication that allowed the Dwarves to stay connected across great distances.

Following his address, Gunnar locked eyes with each of his squad leaders, a deliberate and intense gaze that conveyed both the gravity of the situation and the unspoken assurance that he would be right there beside them. He wanted his squad leaders to fully grasp the seriousness of the mission but also to recognize his unwavering commitment to sharing in the risks they would face.

As he surveyed the expressions of his squad leaders, Gunnar's expectations were met with a silent understanding. There were no questions, no uncertainties; they were a seasoned unit, well-acquainted with their duties and well-versed in the dangers that awaited them. In that moment of shared determination, the Snow Wolves were ready to face whatever challenges lay ahead.

3

Outcast in the Woods

*'In the shadowed boughs of the forest, the outcast finds solace.
Yet, beware the whispers of the leaves, for in the silence of exile, a
forgotten melody stirs.'*

Anwyn

"Focus, Anwyn, you're not yourself this morning!" Laoch's words cut through Anwyn's distracted thoughts, and she couldn't deny their truth. She struggled to concentrate on her sword practice, her mind drifting to other concerns. Despite her father's reassurances, Anwyn couldn't shake the feeling that she had reached a plateau in her training. She had surpassed what she knew was the standard level for an elf her age, and she suspected she was close to mastering the art. Yet, living isolated in the woodlands outside of Stromyr, with a former warrior as her father, Anwyn knew that swordsmanship held far more importance than mere art in Elven society.

Though Anwyn modestly regarded herself as unremarkable, she knew her father saw her differently. Laoch often praised her appearance, pointing out her high cheekbones and finely shaped nose inherited from her mother. He frequently spoke of the captivating power of her eyes, comparing them to pools of liquid honey that revealed the essence of her soul. With each glance exchanged, her gaze revealed a glimpse of her pure and unspoiled spirit, a soft reminder of the enduring innocence she possessed.

As Anwyn swept her straight, long blonde hair out of her eyes, a sense of anticipation bubbled within her. Setting her katana aside, the blade, a symbol of her skill and determination, gleamed in the dim light of the morning. Turning to face her father, she couldn't contain her excitement for their impending journey to Stromyr.

"Apologies, father," she began, her voice bubbling with eagerness. "I'm just so excited about our trip tomorrow. I can't stop thinking about it!"

Beneath her words simmered a longing, a yearning to break free from the boundaries of their familiar world and dive into the promise of new adventures and discoveries. Despite her usual modest demeanor, in this moment, Anwyn's heart pulsed with anticipation.

Every three months, Anwyn's parents embarked on the two-day trek into Stromyr to replenish their essential provisions, necessary for their life in the wilderness of the Elven Forest. Anwyn herself hadn't set foot in Stromyr since infancy, with no memories of the city whatsoever. Her knowledge of Stromyr, and Elven society in general, was limited to what her parents had imparted to her and what she could glean from the books in her mother's collection. Laoch shifted uneasily, unable to meet Anwyn's gaze. Anwyn's heart sank at his discomfort, but she composed herself, taking a slow breath to steady her nerves. "Now who can't focus, father? Is there something you are not telling me?"

Laoch, with his towering figure and sinewy muscles, commanded a presence that spoke of years of disciplined training.

His hair, a glossy black mane, was habitually tied into a tight ponytail, a practical choice for a warrior accustomed to swift movements in battle. His eyes, a warm and deep brown, held a wealth of experience and wisdom, a testament to the countless battles he had faced. Renowned throughout Luxyyr for his mastery of the katana, Laoch was a legend among his kin. Stories of his prowess echoed through the halls of Elven society, a testament to his unparalleled skill and unmatched dedication to his craft. Anwyn often found herself captivated by tales of her father's valour, a legacy she hoped to one day emulate. Despite his fame and the reverence afforded to him, Laoch had chosen a different path. Instead of seeking glory on the battlefield or pursuing a prestigious position within the High Elven Council, he had devoted himself to his family. For him, the greatest honor lay in protecting and providing for his beloved wife, Eira, and their daughter, Anwyn.

She knew her father, and she could tell by the way he was acting now that he was uncomfortable with what he was about to say.

"Look, love," He began, uneasily, "me and your mother have been speaking. We're just not sure it's the right time for you to head into Stromyr."

Although Anwyn had thought this might happen, she still hadn't prepared herself for the reality of it, and a crushing hopelessness washed over her.

Seeing the impact of his words on his beloved daughter, Laoch moved to embrace her. Initially, Anwyn hesitated, considering the impulse to pull away and retreat, but instead, she leaned into his comforting embrace. In her heart, she understood that her parents' intentions were rooted in their desire to protect her.

Laoch, now able to look his daughter in the eye again, mumbled, "it's just with the increase in trade with the humans, bandits and bands of rogues have been seen wandering the forest, and they'll likely see you as easy pickings."

Anwyn let out a derisive snort in response to her father's words, and her father barely suppressed a small smile, quickly averting his gaze. Although there may have been an element of truth in what her father had told her, he wasn't truly concerned about the humans.

Anwyn had never met a human before, but she knew, just like her father did, that although she was just over four foot, and much smaller in stature than a human, she could still handle more than a dozen of their best warriors, alone, without her magic.

Yet, she knew the real concern lay not with the humans but with her own kin. "Father, you must realize, humans pose no threat to me, even if they were to catch me unaware! It's not about them, it's about me! You and mother are ashamed of who I am!" Her words hung heavy in the air, cutting through the tension like a blade. Anwyn recognized the injustice in her accusation, sensing the hurt reflected in her father's anguished expression. At just fifty years old, she was considered young among the long-lived Elves, yet she yearned to break free from the confines of the forest that had sheltered her all her life, longing to reveal her true self to the world beyond.

Regret gnawed at Anwyn as she softened her tone. "I'm sorry, father, that was unfair of me. I know you and mother love me. But the truth is, it's not my fault that the Elves in the city are so closed-minded that they can't accept me for who I am." In Luxyyr, Elven twins were deemed a gift from the forest, cherished by society. Anwyn, however, stood alone as the sole elf in Luxyyr born without a twin in centuries, condemned to rejection and solitude within Elven society's rigid structure. Bound by archaic rules and traditions, Anwyn found herself barred from utilizing Elven resources to pursue her magical studies. The path of a warrior Elf, like her father's, was forever closed to her, and the idea of starting a family was forbidden, lest her perceived "curse" taint future generations. Yet, bitterness lingered, as Anwyn doubted that anyone within the Elven community would have desired her companionship, cursed as she was.

Anwyn's unwavering determination and focus had driven her to excel in both magical and combat skills, despite the restrictions imposed by Elven society. She practiced diligently each day, honing her skills and engaging in sparring sessions with her father using the katana. Her mother guided her through the intricacies of harnessing the forest's magical aura, teaching her to meditate and channel the energy into her spirit. Anwyn was determined to prove Elven society wrong, showing them she could achieve greatness despite their prejudices.

For an incredibly intelligent and advanced race, Anwyn thought the Elves were being extraordinarily archaic in their belief that the forest had cursed her family.

"Listen, love. Let's finish your training session, and when we get back to the house, we can have a talk with your mother. Sound fair to you?" Laoch, who adored his daughter, had broken. Now it was time to work on her mother. Anwyn hid her expression of triumph as she unsheathed her curved katana. As she held the sword in a two-handed grip and conducted a few practice swings, she watched the morning sunshine glinting off of the impossibly sharp blade.

"Fair enough, father," Anwyn replied, a subtle hint of triumph in her expression. "But be prepared, since I wasn't focused during practice earlier, now I'm not only unfocused but also quite upset, and I might make a mistake…" She smiled mischievously as she assumed her stance, watching her father, the most renowned warrior Stromyr had ever seen, gulp and mutter, "Bloody Eira, making me have this conversation with her." With a sigh, Laoch drew his blade and readied himself for their sparring session.

Anwyn

Nestled within the embrace of the Great Elven Forest, Eira, Laoch, and Anwyn, called a charming cottage their home. Built by Laoch and Eira shortly after Anwyn's birth, the cottage sat beside a serene stream, its waters whispering secrets to the surrounding woods. Inside, two bedrooms contained two large beds, a cosy kitchen offered warmth, and a sitting area embraced tales by the hearth's flickering flames, which doubled as both fireplace and oven. Adjacent, a modest storeroom safeguarded essentials: weapons, books, and memories. Nearby, a diminutive outhouse stood, offering privacy for personal needs. The cottage served as a humble yet cherished refuge, and it was the only haven Anwyn had ever known. Close by, a small stable sheltered Honey, the family's horse. Named for her coat's honey hue, which mirrored Anwyn's captivating eyes, Honey was acquired after Anwyn's birth and had remained a loyal companion throughout her Elfling years. Unlike horses of Fenmark's human lands, Elven steeds boasted remarkable longevity, spanning over a century, echoing the timeless bonds woven within the forest's embrace.

As Anwyn strolled past Honey, the beautiful mare let out a soft snort. Anwyn chuckled to herself and gave her a gentle rub between the ears, eliciting another soft snort and a graceful swish of her tail. Always prepared, Anwyn reached into her pocket and withdrew the apple she had saved for Honey, igniting the horse's excitement even more as she began to gently paw at the ground in front of her.

"That's a good girl," Anwyn soothed as she continued to stroke her ears. "We'll go for a ride later, okay?" With a final pat, she turned and joined her father as he approached their cottage.

Eira, engrossed at a small, handcrafted table, delved into the pages of a substantial tome on magic. Her golden locks framed her porcelain face, allowing one of her pointed Elven ears to peek through. Her nose flowed seamlessly into elegant cheekbones, imparting a regal air to her visage. Her lips bore a subtle, rosy hue, hinting at a gentle disposition.

Her mother's collection comprised roughly two hundred magical books, all used to educate and train Anwyn. Glancing at her mother and the book, "Advanced Magical Healing," Anwyn recognized it as a familiar text they often explored together. Sighing inwardly, she suspected her mother was preparing another lesson for her. Watching her mother flip through the pages with focused intensity, a mixture of anticipation and resignation welled up within Anwyn. While she cherished the opportunity to learn, a part of her longed for a break from the relentless pursuit of the arcane arts. Yet, beneath her apprehension, lay a flicker of excitement, recognising the privilege of being mentored by someone as skilled and experienced as her mother.

"Morning mother" Anwyn called from the doorway.

Eira looked up. Smiling, she greeted her daughter, "Anwyn, you're back! How did your training session go?"

"Well enough, mother," Anwyn responded, not sure how to bring up the topic of going to the city.

Smiling, Eira asked, "and where is your father?"

Laoch shuffled past Anwyn and nodded to his wife. "Eira, how's things going?"

"Just lovely dear" Eira responded, then as Laoch fully emerged into the room, she gasped, "what in all of Vellhor happened to your shirt!"

Laoch glanced down at his disheveled attire, his shirt now adorned with rips, dirt, sweat, and leaf remnants from their morning training session. He cast a glance at Anwyn, who wore a sly grin. "Why don't you ask Anwyn..." he grumbled.

Eira turned her gaze toward her daughter, who continued to smirk. "Anwyn?" she inquired, her slender arms folded.

With as much innocence as she could muster, Anwyn replied, "Father and I were engaged in a spirited sparring session, and, well, I might have let my enthusiasm get the better of me..."

"Brilliantly understated, my love," Laoch chuckled. "I think she was teaching me an important lesson, Eira. Always bring reinforcements when delivering bad news!"

"Ah, I understand," Eira remarked, her tone calm as she continued, "now that reinforcements have arrived, it seems prudent to delve deeper into the matter." It was evident she was already aware of the dire news Laoch had alluded to.

Anwyn had been uncertain about what she was going to say the whole way home. She had tried to come up with an argument that might persuade her mother, fully aware of Eira's unyielding nature compared to her father's more receptive disposition. As they had walked, her thoughts had churned, each possibility turning over in her mind like leaves caught in a whirlwind. She knew she needed to tread carefully; emotional pleas or simple logic rarely swayed her mother's decisions.

Anwyn had searched her mind for the right words, hoping to find a path through her mother's resolve and into understanding.

As Anwyn crossed the threshold into their home, her rehearsed arguments crumbled like ancient parchment. Despite her attempts to summon courage and address her mother rationally, uncertainty clouded her words. Was she coming across as assertive, or merely as a petulant Elfling?

"Mother, you can't just cancel the trip to Stromyr," she pleaded, her voice trembling with a mixture of desperation and frustration. "Not only have I been preparing for the trip all week, but we're nearly out of essentials. Father himself told me that!"

Though her words carried a sense of urgency, Anwyn couldn't shake the nagging doubt that they fell short of conveying the depth of her feelings.

She glanced over at her father, hoping for some form of support, but he remained silent, his expression unreadable. A pang of disappointment pierced her heart, a stark reminder of the divide between her parents when it came to matters of decision-making. Despite her best efforts to sway her mother's stance, Anwyn couldn't shake the sinking feeling of her heart that her pleas would fall on deaf ears.

Eira's response carried a softness, her words laced with tenderness as she addressed Anwyn. "I understand your disappointment, Anwyn, my love. However, our main concern is your safety. You are fully aware of the sentiments the Elves of Stromyr harbor toward us. Let your father go tomorrow, and he can speak to some of his old friends. See if it's a good idea first. Then, if he's content that you'll be safe, we can all go together next week."

Anwyn's voice quivered with a mix of frustration and sadness as she poured out her thoughts. "Thank you, mother, for your understanding. I truly appreciate it. But I cannot fathom why they harbor such animosity toward me. I've never harmed them. They discriminate blindly, without knowing who I am or what kind of elf I am. They readily accept the humans into the city, even though the humans neither respect our traditions nor our culture. They brandish their blades on innocent Elves, seeking to intimidate and exploit them, and then have the audacity to lament when our warriors retaliate for the dishonor they've caused. Father has recounted the stories to me, mother. We've tried to explain to the humans countless times that life holds immense value to an Elven warrior, and they are strictly forbidden from unsheathing their katana in anger. If they do, honor demands they must use it to kill. They don't take us seriously. Instead, they mock us and provoke us into drawing our blades, forcing our warriors into a position where they must take a life."

Anwyn sensed her mother's heartache as she listened to her argument. They had shared many conversations about their sentiments, but Anwyn knew the weight of tradition and politics weighed heavily on her mother's decisions. Despite her own frustrations, Anwyn understood the complexity of the situation. Her father had explained the Elven Council's perspective: allowing humans in with 'minor infractions' was a calculated move to maintain control and surveillance over them. Yet, Anwyn couldn't shake the belief in the compelling nature of her argument. A surge of determination rushed through her, fueled by her conviction that there had to be a better way.

Laoch, noticing his wife's pained expression, intervened to support her. "Anwyn, my dear. The last time we took you to the city was a catastrophe. Shortly after we left, the groves around the city withered from a dreadful disease. Even though we had gone nowhere near them, they blamed you—uh, us," he quickly corrected himself. "They dispatched warriors to apprehend us and subject us to interrogation. You were just a babe, by Vellhor's grace! And your so-called crime? Being born without a sibling!" Laoch's anger was getting the better of him now, and Eira decided it was her turn to steer the conversation.

With a gentle hand resting on Laoch's shoulder to soothe him, she continued, "Yes, my love, it was a dreadful time, but it eventually resolved itself, and we made the decision not to take you into the city again."

"That we did," Laoch agreed, his voice laden with pain, "but look at her. She's like a prisoner here, locked away for a crime she didn't commit. It's hard for me to see her like this and have to be the one who shatters her dreams. Sometimes I wish we'd sent her off with your father." He stared into the distance, a cold, faraway look in his eyes.

Eira's father, Alden, was an exceptional elf; by all accounts, he was an academic genius, teaching complex magical and theoretical studies at Elven educational institutes, and his extensive collection of books was a significant part of Eira's personal library. It was also said that Alden had the gift of prophecy. A unique and rare form of magic, which was almost impossible to control, and even harder to comprehend. Shortly after Anwyn was born, Alden went to lecture at human academic institutes across Fenmark, earning him a name of defector and traitor to the High Elves of Luxyyr.

Unfortunately, Alden had not been seen by anyone since he left almost fifty years ago, and in the past, Anwyn had overheard her parents speculating about where he could be. Her father believing him to have died on his travels somewhere. Her mother, however, clung to the hope that he was still alive and planning for something important. The mystery surrounding Alden's whereabouts weighed heavily on their family.

Eira, hearing the pain in her husband's voice, gave him an understanding look. She knew how much Laoch loved their daughter and that it hurt him deeply to see Anwyn confined to their forest home. Gently, she said, "I know, my dear, I know. I wish things were different too, but you know how stubborn the High Elves can be. They won't change their ways easily, and it's our duty to protect our family. Perhaps in time, we can revisit this issue."

Anwyn had been a part of this conversation many times. Her parents hadn't ever lied to her, wanting her to understand the risks and their reasons for keeping her away from the city. Nevertheless, with each discussion, the weight of it all didn't lessen. As she sat there, absorbing their words once again, a familiar sense of frustration mingled with a growing determination within her.

She longed for a sense of freedom beyond the confines of their secluded home, yet the gravity of the dangers outside loomed large in her mind, a constant reminder of the careful balance her parents sought to maintain.

Holding back the tears that threatened to stream down her soft cheeks, Anwyn spoke up, attempting to keep her voice steady. "Mother, father, it's okay. I know the reasons, and I understand your decision. Let us enjoy our lunch, and then I'd like to go out and hunt for dinner. It will help take my mind off things."

Laoch and Eira exchanged glances before Laoch strode over to Anwyn, wrapping his muscular arms around her, and Eira joined the embrace. They held each other in silence for a moment, their love unspoken, before Anwyn pulled away and offered them a weak smile.

Walking off to her room, Anwyn decided she would meditate before lunch. She always liked to do this before a hunt. It helped her to connect to her surroundings and filled up her spirit with the magic of the forest. All Elves needed to meditate in order to connect their spirit to the forest. Without doing this, their magic would be weaker than that of a human mage.

The process was simple in theory; meditate, connect one's spirit with the forest, and absorb the surrounding aura into their own spirit. This not only strengthened the spirit, but also made practicing magic easier and enhanced an individual's own magical power.

Taking a deep breath, Anwyn began her meditation. Inhaling for five seconds and exhaling for five seconds, she repeated this rhythmic breathing technique. As she did, she opened her awareness to feel, or rather, sense the aura of the surrounding forest. It was unmistakable once she felt it—like it had always been there—a feeling of hazy euphoria that seemed to resonate within her core.

While maintaining her steady breathing, Anwyn extended her consciousness and connected with the surrounding aura. This part had been challenging when she was younger, as the overwhelming euphoric sensation often flooded her senses. However, now it came naturally to her.

Once the connection was firmly established, Anwyn focused on drawing the aura into her spirit, filling it up like a bucket slowly being replenished with small, regular splashes. It was a time-consuming process, and it would have taken Anwyn approximately ten hours to fill her spirit completely if it were ever entirely empty.

Her mother had always told her it was dangerous to let her spirit run dry, so usually, she would simply meditate for an hour at a time, multiple times throughout the day, since this would generally top up anything she had expended. As she concentrated on replenishing her spirit, Anwyn couldn't help but wonder whether she had let it run dangerously low. Thoughts of her upcoming journey weighed heavily on her mind, and a wave of guilt washed over her. She reminded herself to be more mindful in the future, to avoid letting distractions pull her away from her mother's teachings.

Once Anwyn had finished, she felt much better. Not quite happy, but she had a feeling of peace and invigoration. The sensation of being replenished was akin to a comforting embrace, wrapping her in a cocoon of renewed energy and vitality. With a contented sigh, she made her way through to the kitchen where the aroma of a rabbit roasting on the hearth and delicious vegetables freshly picked from the forest attacked her senses, and hunger struck her anew. She smiled and sat down next to her parents, grateful for their comforting presence and the nourishing meal before her.

Anwyn

After lunch, Anwyn set out from the cottage to hunt. Hunting had always been her solace, her sanctuary from the confines of her small, sheltered world. From childhood, it had been her only refuge, where she felt a semblance of real freedom and a natural harmony with the Elven forest that surrounded her.

Despite her father's insistence that the forest had bestowed its blessings upon her, Anwyn was acutely aware that the High Elves of Stromyr regarded her as cursed.

Unlike other races, the Elves didn't believe in gods or goddesses. Instead, they revered nature itself as divine, attributing sacredness, magic, and spiritual power to it. Their goddess was the vast, enigmatic forest, a provider of abundant resources and a wellspring of spiritual magic that flowed through their spirits.

To the Elves, natural calamities, such as the blight that had stricken the groves near Stromyr, were perceived as nature's retribution. It was this belief that had led them to seek Anwyn out when she was an infant, and it was the reason her parents forbade her from venturing beyond the confines of the forest.

The forest had always thrived around their cottage. It teemed with wildlife, with natural beauty, and even the mystical Fae, magical beings no bigger than her palm, lived around their home.

Her father's wisdom resonated with her deeply. He had always reminded her that if the forest harbored any curse upon her, the surroundings would be barren, devoid of life. Yet, Anwyn remained uncertain about it all. What she did know, however, was the profound connection she felt when alone in the heart of the forest. There, her spirit merged seamlessly with the natural world. With every breath she drew, she could sense the forest in her lungs. Placing her palm upon the mossy ground, she felt the vibrations of the creatures around her, an intuitive awareness of their presence. If she pressed her ear against the ancient trunk of a tree, she could hear its inner core pulsating with the rhythm of life. Amidst the tranquility of the woodland, Anwyn found solace and a sense of belonging that she rarely experienced elsewhere.

Anwyn often sang to the forest, her melodic voice weaving song spells that could coax a tree to flourish or encourage a flower to bloom. These memories of practicing song spells with her mother during her childhood always brought a warm smile to Anwyn's face.

Anwyn continued to walk amongst the tall pine, yew, and oak trees, listening to the forest speak to her. The rustling of the leaves in the canopy above her, the odd thump of a nut or seed falling on the forest floor in the distance, the shuffling feet of animals in the undergrowth, the distant trickle of a stream, a far-off bird chirping its sweet melody. She relished all of it.

Anwyn spread out her awareness, looking for the perfect opportunity. Her father had taught her to be selective and patient regarding her quarry.

Then, she sensed it—a mature stag, bearing the signs of age and injury, making its way through the forest about a hundred yards from her. This was the perfect choice. Anwyn would never consider hunting a robust, healthy creature in the prime of its life; such an act would be an injustice, an affront to the forest and the creatures that called it home. Her father's lessons had left her with a profound respect for both the forest and its inhabitants.

Anwyn assumed a low stance, her dagger at the ready, as she stealthily closed in on the injured stag. Her controlled breaths synchronized with her deliberate steps, maintaining her focus on the creature before her. She waited patiently until the stag turned its gaze toward her. In a gesture of reverence for the animal, Anwyn established eye contact and quietly uttered the words her father had passed down to her many years ago, "Grant me wisdom and respect in my pursuit. Embrace the spirit of this creature." Then, with perfect precision, she released her dagger. It struck true, finding its mark between the stag's eyes, piercing its brain and bringing about an instantaneous, painless death for the majestic animal.

Anwyn approached the fallen stag with utmost reverence. She carefully retrieved her dagger, ensuring it was pristine before returning it to its sheath. With each step, Anwyn followed the traditional Elven rituals for preparing the kill, honoring and blessing the spirit of the noble animal.

With the meat safely stored in her pack, Anwyn made her way back to the cottage. She had been gone for more than three hours now, and the sun was beginning its descent, drawing long shadows across the forest floor.

As she drew nearer to her home, a sudden sense of danger sent a chill down her spine. Anwyn halted in her tracks, instinctively opening her senses to the forest. She could feel it—an undercurrent of pain and distress.

Without making a sound, Anwyn gracefully sprinted through the forest, her footsteps expertly navigating the terrain as she raced toward the cottage.

4

A Mage's Journey

'A journey of a thousand steps begins with a single decision.'

Kemp

The rain battered against the windowpane violently, its relentless rhythm a haunting accompaniment to the mournful howl of the wind outside Kemps' seventh-floor dormitory chamber within the Lakeview Arcane Academy.

With a heavy sigh, Kemp turned his gaze towards the rain-swept landscape beyond. On a clear day, he could lose himself in the majestic view that stretched out before him. The distant mountains of the Eldrakar Divide, their peaks glistening with pristine snow, mirrored gracefully in the tranquil waters of the Alghari Lake to the west. To the east, the sprawling expanse of the Elven Forest, an unending sea of emerald green. But today, obscured by the curtain of rain and heavy clouds, the world outside had faded into an indistinct grey blur, robbing him of the enchanting view he so often cherished.

Nevertheless, despite the dreary weather enveloping his surroundings, Kemp's heart brimmed with anticipation. The thought of his impending journey ignited a surge of excitement within him. Though the rain currently obscured the landscape, he held onto the knowledge that it would eventually dissipate, revealing the path that lay ahead. With each droplet that tapped against the windowpane, his determination renewed, fueling his unwavering resolve to embark on the adventure awaiting him. Despite the uncertainty looming on the horizon, Kemp's spirit soared with the promise of new discoveries and experiences that awaited him on his journey.

Still, he fervently wished for a change in the weather sooner rather than later. After months of tirelessly petitioning the Vice Chancellor of the Academy, his request for an excursion to the Scorched Mountains had finally been granted. Tomorrow marked the day he was due to depart from the small island upon which the Academy tower and its outbuildings had stood for centuries.

The Lakeview Academy was one of three prestigious schools of magic in the human Kingdom of Fenmark. Each of the kingdom's three provinces, Tempsford, Fenchester, and Lamos, boasted its own distinguished Academy, with Lakeview, situated on the Alghari Lake in the Province of Tempsford.

Seldom did students venture beyond the borders of their native province to enroll in a school from another domain. The kingdoms, engaged in their relentless pursuit of the most formidable mages for their individual territories, usually ensured such exclusivity.

Kemp was an elemental mage from the Tempsford province. Most mages across the Kingdom of Fenmark had a natural affinity for at least one of the elements, making elemental magic the most common magic for humans to possess. Kemp had a strong affinity for all the elements, making him somewhat of a rarity at the Academy.

This meant that his innate gifts lay in commanding the very elements themselves, endowing him with a connection to all of the natural elements. This mastery flowed through him more effortlessly than it did for those who could practice other forms of magic, take, for instance, a time mage, capable of manipulating the passing of time (albeit without the power of true time travel, which was impossible), or a battle mage, who harnessed the destructive forces of magic, heightening their senses in tandem with their surging adrenaline.

That's not to say that a mage could not practice magic which wasn't in line with their natural affinity, of course. It just made it significantly harder. For example, Kemp could slow down time for a minute or two, but the effort required to expend that amount of energy would be double or maybe even triple that of what it would cost a natural time mage.

The Lakeview Academy spent a significant portion of a student's first year teaching them how to align their spirit with their natural affinity. Kemp, therefore, had spent a long time meditating around large fires, or up on the upper platforms in the wind, or submerged in water, or sometimes, actually buried in earth. After successful completion of the first year of study, students were required to select additional subjects to study. Kemp, being in his final year, was currently studying Dragon lore and Divine Magic as part of his final thesis, before he could finally graduate.

Eight years of relentless study had sculpted Kemp's path, leading him from the simplest cantrips to a profound understanding of the intricate laws of thaumaturgy. Graduation from one of Fenmark's most esteemed Academies loomed on the horizon, promising a certificate, and sparking lofty aspirations for his future career.

Standing just shy of six feet tall, Kemp possessed undeniable attractiveness. His features were chiseled, his build lean yet muscular, an ensemble that should have drawn eyes in any room.

Yet, as he navigated the corridors of the academy, he couldn't shake the feeling that his profound lack of confidence and shyness dulled this potential allure to the girls around him.

"Kemp, you lazy git... coming for dinner or what?" Ellis's voice shattered Kemp's reverie. Startled awake, Kemp wiped the drool from his cheek, where it had dribbled onto his workbook, and glanced up in confusion at his friend.

Ellis had been Kemp's closest friend from the minute they had both arrived at the Academy. With his neatly cropped dark brown hair, a sturdy build that stood a few inches shorter than Kemp's towering frame, and a perpetually mischievous grin, Ellis was difficult not to like.

Ellis possessed an innate affinity for enchantment, a rare gift that allowed him to imbue objects, and occasionally, even living creatures, with a temporary alteration of their will and nature.

One memory etched in Kemp's mind involved Ellis, and a prank they had played on a professor. She was a battleaxe of a professor, with dark-red hair, whose disposition seemed to harbor an odd resentment toward her students, despite her role in educating the kingdom's young minds. Ellis, in an act of impish brilliance, had harnessed his enchantment powers to manipulate a colony of ants, using them to disrupt her lecture on dream magic. The outcome had been uproarious, albeit fleeting, as Professor McArdle swiftly discerned the culprit behind the antics.

"Huh... Ellis... what time is it?" he croaked, his voice laden with drowsiness.

Ellis chuckled and ventured deeper into the room. "It's dinnertime, mate. Feeling a bit worn out, are we?" His tone bore a hint of teasing in it.

Kemp unfurled himself to his full height and stretched. He ran his hand over his head, his fingers threading through wavy chestnut brown locks, and then yawned before responding, "Yeah, I must be. Last thing I remember, I was gazing out the window, hoping against hope for better weather!"

"Well, it's still hammering it down, and, if you don't hurry, there'll be no food left for us!" Following Ellis's lead, Kemp made his way out of the door and, together, they made their way through the complex maze of corridors and stairways to the main canteen.

Kemp

"So, what time are you leaving tomorrow?" asked Addy through a mouthful of mashed potatoes.

Kemp had known Addy for the past two years, when they both enrolled on the same rune reading course. "Well, I was planning on getting the dawn ferry first thing in the morning." Kemp responded.

Addy looked up, his eyes hungry for information. "What will the journey be like? I've never left Tempsford before!"

"Well," Kemp began, "once I reach Redbourne, I'll be joining a caravan bound for the southern lands. It'll probably take about a week to get to Lamos Province, and I plan to look for a guide to take me into the mountains once I get to the City of Lamos."

Addy's eyes widened with excitement. "Are you nervous? The Scorched Mountains! They're almost mythical! I remember hearing stories about them as a child."

Ellis, seated next to Kemp, chuckled warmly. "Nervous!" he exclaimed, a slight grin on his face. "Look at the size of him, he's big enough to handle himself!"

Kemp felt his cheeks flush slightly at Ellis's words. He paused, gathering his thoughts before responding. "Well, I've planned the trip meticulously. I've also explained each stage to the Vice Chancellor, who grudgingly approved. It'll be fun. I'm really looking forward to it."

"And what, exactly, are you planning on doing when you get there, may I ask?" scoffed a haughty girl with an upturned nose, a familiar face from Kemp's theurgy classes.

With a composed tone, Kemp responded, "Well, Becca, as part of my thesis, I aim to substantiate the theory that the dragons, last known to inhabit the Scorched Mountains, practiced a form of divine magic or ritual that bestowed them with immortality."

As laughter erupted from the two girls seated near Becca, Kemp could feel the heat of a blush creeping onto his cheeks. Despite his efforts to maintain his composure, the ridicule stung, causing a knot of discomfort to form in the pit of his stomach. He silently chided himself for allowing his classmates' reactions to unsettle him, reminding himself of the importance of staying focused on his research goals.

Noticing the tension, Ellis interjected with his trademark cheeriness, "Come on, Kemp, we'd better leave if we're to enjoy your farewell drinks tonight!" He rose from his seat, and Kemp quickly followed suit, picking up his food tray as they made their way to the exit, leaving the awkwardness behind at the table. As they walked, Kemp couldn't help but mull over the exchange, his mind racing with a mix of embarrassment and determination to prove himself in his academic pursuits.

Kemp

The next morning, a low, persistent vibration stirred Kemp from his slumber. "*Prohibere,*" he muttered drowsily, invoking the spell to silence his magical alarm clock. After rising and stretching, he made his way to the washbasin. He scrubbed his face and hair vigorously, then rinsed his mouth with a minted water he had enchanted to keep his teeth clean.

Feeling more awake now, he hastily donned his undergarments, trousers, and shirt before selecting a warm jacket and gathering his pack. With a sense of purpose, he left his room.

The morning was clear, though the lingering rain from the previous night had left its mark. Kemp had to navigate the path to the ferry slip in a serpentine fashion, strategically avoiding the many puddles that obstructed his way.

Upon reaching the ferry slip, Kemp noticed only one other person—a middle-aged gentleman, patiently waiting and puffing on a pipe. As Kemp walked over to sit beside him, an inexplicable sense of serenity washed over him. There was something intriguing about the stranger, an air of mystery that piqued Kemp's curiosity. Was it the way he held himself with quiet confidence, or the enigmatic gleam in his eyes that hinted at depths beyond mere surface appearances?

Seated across from the stranger, Kemp glanced up to offer a polite greeting. As his gaze lingered on the man, he noticed the intricate details of his attire—the fine embroidery on his waistcoat and the silver cufflinks gleaming in the soft light. The man's piercing blue eyes flickered across the pages, his bushy brows furrowing in deep thought.

Kemp couldn't help but wonder about the world contained

within those pages, the secrets and knowledge that captivated the man's attention so completely. An uncanny feeling coursed through him, as though he'd encountered this man before, but the sensation passed as quickly as it had come. Despite the fleeting sense of familiarity, Kemp found himself drawn to the man's presence, unable to shake the feeling that there was more to him than met the eye.

A gentle breeze rustled the pages of the book, carrying the faint scent of ink to Kemp's nostrils. It was an intoxicating blend of curiosity and anticipation, mingling with the aroma of Elven tobacco. The familiar smell added to the mysterious allure of the moment, deepening Kemp's intrigue about the stranger seated across from him.

The man nodded in response, then returned his attention to the book he was reading, puffing thoughtfully on his pipe filled with the renowned Elven broadleaf tobacco. As Kemp observed him discreetly, a nagging sense of intrigue gnawed at the edges of his mind.

Kemp did not have to wait long for the ferry, and soon, he could spot the vessel approaching in the distance. The ferry journey lasted a mere half an hour, and as Kemp disembarked, he found Redbourne to be a bustling hub of activity, abuzz with traders, merchants, dockworkers, and artisans. Kemp had to navigate through the crowd, pressing onward through the throngs of people engaged in their daily transactions. After about an hour of weaving through the lively streets, he finally arrived at the Merchants' Guild House, situated at the heart of the bustling city.

Kemp knocked loudly on the brass doorknob adorning the grand, ornate golden door and waited. Just as he was about to make a second attempt, the massive door swung inward.

"Good morning... Sir," the gentleman in the foyer called out.

"Sir?" Kemp replied, his tone colored with a touch of embarrassment. "No, I'm not Sir. Well, my father, I suppose, would be Sir..." Kemp's rambling was kindly interrupted by the doorman, who inquired if he'd like to step inside.

"Sir, if you'd like to wait in the lobby, one of our attendants will be with you shortly."

"Thank you, much appreciated," Kemp responded, settling onto the plush leather sofa. As he glanced around the lobby, he observed pristine white walls contrasting beautifully with various shades of gold decor. The opulent furniture, of a quality seldom available to the common folk, exuded an air of elegance that added to the Guild House's grandeur.

"Sir, how can we assist you today?" inquired a charming female voice. Kemp lifted his gaze and beheld a strikingly beautiful woman with vibrant crimson locks cascading halfway down her back. She appeared to be in her early forties, nearly two decades Kemp's senior.

With awkward movements, Kemp stood and smoothed down his clothing, inexplicably feeling a touch insecure about his attire. He proceeded to explain his identity and his intent to journey south, expressing his desire to join a merchant caravan if one was departing today.

"Ahh, I understand, Sir," she responded, her tone warm and understanding. "While we do have caravans bound for Lamos departing daily, as you're likely aware. I do regret to inform you that today's caravan has already set out at dawn."

Kemp's disappointment must have been evident on his face, for the lady's features softened, and she offered him a warm smile. Though her words were practical, Kemp couldn't help but feel a twinge of frustration at the missed opportunity. He had hoped to catch the caravan heading south and begin his journey without delay.

"Sir, I would suggest spending the night in the town proper, not on the outskirts. Not only will you be safer there, but the journey to the caravan departure point will be much closer in the morning. You'll find a fine inn in the heart of town. I can recommend the Old White Horse, situated next to the Engineers Guild House. They serve exceptional food and ale, and their prices are quite fair."

Grateful for her advice, Kemp managed a polite smile, though it felt somewhat forced. He appreciated her concern for his well-being, yet he couldn't shake the disappointment of missing the caravan.

As he turned to leave, he couldn't shake the feeling of being observed. Glancing back, he caught the lady regarding him with a peculiar expression, her head slightly tilted and her lips pursed, a playful strand of her red hair between her fingers. Was it curiosity or something else that lingered in her gaze? Feeling somewhat self-conscious under her scrutiny, Kemp hurriedly left the establishment and made his way to the Old White Horse, his thoughts swirling with frustration and the need to make the most of the situation.

As Kemp approached the inn, he once again had that strange feeling of calm wash over him. Baffled by the feeling, he glanced around briefly, but could only see people getting on with their day. Shrugging the sensation off, Kemp walked through the doors and into the Old White Horse Inn.

After leaving his pack in his room, Kemp went down to the common room to get some dinner. Having spent most of his life effectively stranded on an island with no escape, Kemp had spent little time in taverns or inns, so coming down to the commotion of the common room was an entirely new experience for him.

A haze of smoke hung in a lazy drift around the ceiling of the room, causing Kemp to cough a few times before he grew accustomed to it. On one side of the large common room, a man was playing an intricate tune on a lute, while a buxom lady stood before him, regaling the audience with a comedic ballad. Her song recounted the tale of a sailor she had once met, one who had promised her the world but had vanished mysteriously by the time morning came. The entire room, including Kemp, erupted in bouts of laughter and applause in response to the whimsical tune.

As the night wore on, Kemp found himself happily sipping ale after ale, immersing himself in the various forms of entertainment unfolding around him. He was engrossed in a captivating tale recounted by a bard, detailing a heroic knight seeking revenge against his treacherous brother for a past crime, when a slender hand descended softly upon his shoulder. Startled, Kemp turned to see who it was, and to his astonishment, he found the lady from the Merchants Guild smiling warmly down at him. Her presence caught him off guard; he had given little thought to their earlier encounter. Now, as he looked upon her in the dim, flickering light of the tavern, he noticed the delicate features of her face and the warmth in her eyes, the true extent of her stunning beauty hit him.

Leaving her hand upon his shoulder, she positioned herself beside him and leaned in close, whispering into his ear. Kemp nearly sprayed his ale across the room at the view she presented, his cheeks flushing crimson as he resisted the urge to glance downward at her revealing attire. She flashed him a seductive smile, sweeping a rogue strand of crimson hair away from her face as she continued to lean closer, inquiring if she could join him at his table.

Kemp, momentarily rendered speechless, managed only a nod of agreement. It took him several awkward moments before he mustered the courage to offer a witty and charming remark. "Do you, um... frequent this place often?" he stammered.

She laughed softly, her beauty accentuated by her mirth. "Oh, my sister and brother-in-law own the establishment, so I do come here quite a bit. But tonight, I couldn't resist the opportunity to converse with a mage from Lakeview! I'm curious about your *unique powers*."

Kemp awoke the next morning ensnared in a tangle of arms and legs, his head thick from the ale he had drunk the night before. He blinked groggily, his mind struggling to clear the fog of sleep. As he glanced over, he saw the woman from the merchants' guild lying beside him, completely naked and snoring gently. Despite the haze of his thoughts, Kemp couldn't help but smile as he looked at her. She truly was beautiful.

The events of the previous night seemed surreal, like a dream he couldn't quite grasp. Ellis wouldn't believe him if he told him what happened on his first night out of the Academy. With a confusing mix of embarrassment and secret pride, Kemp quietly gathered his clothes and prepared to leave for the caravan. He gently nudged the woman awake, her eyelids fluttering open as she glanced around the room.

"I have to leave now," whispered Kemp, a pang of guilt tugging at him for the sudden departure.

The woman smiled and sat upright, her long red hair draping around her shoulders in a cascade of vibrant waves. Kemp couldn't help but admire her poise, even amidst their awkward situation. Her whispered question sent a shiver down his spine, her hand lingering suggestively on his thigh, inching upwards. "Are you sure?"

Despite his determination to depart, Kemp felt an irresistible surge of temptation enveloping him. As she held him in her slender arms and guided him onto his back, his resolve crumbled completely. A smile played on his lips—he didn't even know this woman's name.

Kemp

As Kemp sat in the back of the wagon, he tried not to focus on the tedious bumps in the road which were causing a jarring pain, starting somewhere in his lower back and ending somewhere close to his neck.

Despite their efforts to make the interior of the wagon as comfortable as possible with thick blankets and padded cushions lining the seats, Kemp found that he still had to inject a little healing magic into his sore back now and then to numb the pain. He didn't know how he would have coped had he not long ago learned the magical art of healing. He couldn't help but feel a profound gratitude for his magical abilities during those moments.

Of course, every so often, he'd think back to just a few days ago in Redbourne, a smile gracing his lips as he reminisced about the mysterious, red-headed beauty from the Old White Horse. But then a wheel would smack against a stubborn rock, or drop into a large hole, and he'd come rushing back to the present.

Despite the discomfort of the journey, Kemp remained genuinely excited about being on the road and venturing beyond the borders of Tempsford. He had been travelling south for five days now, and the change in climate was already evident. The air was warmer, and the once lush landscapes, dense woodlands and verdant plains had gradually given way to an arid terrain dominated by hues of brown, yellow, and red, with greenery becoming a rare sight.

Travelling in the company of around thirty merchants, spread across twenty wagons and carts, Kemp discovered they carried a diverse array of goods from the Tempsford region, intended for sale in Lamos. In conversations with one of the merchants on a quiet evening, Kemp learned that many among them were also eager to buy southern delicacies to bring back to Tempsford, with hopes of reaping substantial profits.

He couldn't deny that the life of a travelling merchant seemed exciting, and he would have been envious, were it not for the constant pain in his back, an ever-present reminder that he was not made for travelling long distances on the back of a wagon.

The merchants had wisely hired a score of mercenary guards, comprised of ex-soldiers who had left or discharged from the military for one reason or another. Their presence provided a feeling of security amongst the group, who had no doubt seen some of the worse the road south could offer. Bandits and thieves were known to attack weary travelers who didn't adequately protect themselves.

Lamos had gained notoriety as a province divided by history and conflict. Approximately three decades ago, King Luthar, ruler of Fenmark, had launched an invasion into Lamos, annexing the province, which had previously been part of the Kingdom of Sandarah. Located just north of the Al Asita Pass, home to the Sandaran capital, Ostium, Lamos had proven notoriously challenging for the Sandarans to defend.

King Luthar's intervention had deeply split the population of Lamos. While half of the populace welcomed the new rule, the other half remained staunchly Sandaran in their loyalty. This division had led to two tumultuous decades of civil unrest, marked by frequent riots and coup attempts. Over the past decade, however, tensions had somewhat subsided, with no significant efforts to overthrow King Luthar's authority in Lamos.

Despite the recent lull in hostilities, the historical divide had rendered Lamos a dangerous region to travel without proper protection. Robberies and attacks on travelers had become commonplace, serving as the primary motivation for Kemp to journey with a merchant caravan and guard.

Over the past five days, Kemp had been repeatedly graced by the same serene feeling he had first encountered at the ferry slip near Lakeview Academy and then again in Redbourne. Ordinarily, such an inexplicable sensation might have unsettled Kemp. Considering his extensive study of magic over the past eight years, he would have pondered whether it resulted from a spell or enchantment. Yet, every time he began to dwell on it, that profound sense of calm washed over him again, reassuring him that all was well, ultimately soothing his concerns.

A smooth, well-educated voice brought Kemp out of his reverie then, "Kemp, lad. How is the back feeling this afternoon?" Kemp turned to look at Theodore, an older merchant with short grey hair and a grey stubble. Theodore had been travelling this route for the past twenty-five years. He had befriended Kemp on the first day, and Kemp had learned more about timber, Theodore's main commodity, in the past five days than he thought he ever needed to know.

"Hello, Theodore. Thanks for asking. I'm managing well enough, I suppose," Kemp replied, hesitant to admit that he had been employing his magic to alleviate the discomfort, as if it might somehow be considered cheating.

"Well, that's good to hear! I remember when I first started this game, it took me months to acclimatize to the pain! You mages are made of sturdier stuff, it seems!" The old man quipped, with a knowing glint in his eye, as if he were privy to Kemp's secret.

With a small smile, Kemp responded, "I'd hardly say that I'm-"

A scream of agony abruptly interrupted Kemp's sentence. Kemp's gaze darted around nervously to find that the guards surrounding the convoy had stopped and were brandishing weapons. Those within his line of sight were either crouching behind carts and wagons or standing ready.

Kemp could see that up ahead, the man who had been driving the front wagon lay slumped to the side with an arrow protruding from his neck. His wife had jumped off the wagon and was screaming hysterically, her arms flailing.

Kemp's heart sank as he watched another arrow materialize and pierce the woman's chest, sending her collapsing to the ground, her anguished screams abruptly silenced.

5

Traitor in the Midst

'In the heart of the mountain, where trust is forged like steel, a traitor's axe echoes louder than a thousand pickaxes'

Gunnar

Gunnar had been on patrol for two hours when a panicked voice pierced the air, crying out, "CONTACT - FRONT - RIGHT - UP ON THE RIDGE - TAKE COVER!" In an instant, the entire squad dropped to the ground and assumed a defensive position behind a cluster of boulders scattered just a few meters away.

Gunnar recognized the terrain they were in – the first chokepoint. They had entered a vast oval-shaped valley, resembling a colossal bowl. The valley stretched for approximately two miles, flanked by steep mountain cliffs on both sides. At each end of the valley, it narrowed significantly. They had already passed through the first narrow entrance; now, at the opposite end, lay the exit—a similarly constricted passage.

"Karl, get the SLS and contact the other squads, get one to provide backup, and get the others to stay put until further notice." Continuing with his orders, Gunnar faced Laslo. "Laslo, go check the forward positions. Make sure the two lads are still with us. Do not get seen. Go."

"Yes boss," Laslo immediately responded, no fear visible in his cold eyes.

Gunnar's heart pounded in his chest as he led the remaining members of his squad to a large boulder, its imposing presence offering a semblance of safety amidst the chaos of battle. His grip tightened on his axe, his fingers tracing the familiar grooves of the haft, seeking comfort in its weight. With a quick glance around, he assessed their surroundings, noting the other boulders that dotted the landscape, each one a potential refuge.

From their chosen vantage point, Gunnar's eyes scanned the terrain ahead, his gaze sharp and focused. He watched as Laslo moved with calculated precision around the jagged rock formations, his silhouette a shadow against the fading light. It was a dangerous maneuver, navigating the treacherous landscape under the threat of enemy fire, but Gunnar trusted in Laslo's skill and determination.

In the distance, a pang of concern gripped Gunnar's chest as he spotted Oleg and Franz, their figures lying motionless near the passage's exit. His breath caught in his throat, a surge of adrenaline coursing through his veins. Were they injured? Or worse?

Despite the chaos unfolding around him, Gunnar forced himself to remain calm, his mind racing as he weighed their options. Every decision weighed heavily on his shoulders, the lives of his comrades resting in his hands. With a silent prayer for their safety, Gunnar steeled himself for what lay ahead, knowing that their survival depended on his ability to lead them through the storm.

"Karl, any luck with the SLS," he called back.

"Nothing boss, the damn thing isn't working," Karl responded, frustration heavy in his voice.

"Draegs balls, what's going on," Gunnar muttered under his breath as he kept a vigilant eye on Laslo's progress toward the exit of the 'bowl'.

Scanning the ridgeline to his right, he discerned dark figures moving about. Gunnar continued surveying the area, carefully weighing his options and assessing the situation.

Suddenly, a low rumbling reverberated through the ground beneath him, jolting Gunnar's senses back to the present moment. With a quick pivot, his eyes honed in on the source of the disturbance, a cascade of rocks tumbling down the rugged mountainside in the distance. The landslide unfolded before him, each rock and clump of earth a testament to nature's relentless force. As he surveyed the scene, a sense of foreboding crept over him, realizing that the very path they had just travelled now lay sealed off by this formidable barrier.

"Bollocks," Gunnar cursed inwardly, a knot of apprehension tightening in his gut. The realization dawned on him with chilling clarity - they were trapped, hemmed in by nature's unforgiving hand. His mind raced, grappling with the implications of their predicament. Panic threatened to claw its way to the surface, but Gunnar pushed it down, his jaw set in grim determination.

In the face of adversity, Gunnar's resolve hardened like tempered steel. He knew that despair was a luxury they could ill afford in this unforgiving terrain. With a steely glint in his eyes, he turned to his comrades, his voice steady despite the turmoil raging within.

"We press on," he declared, his words a solemn oath. "There's no turning back now."

Gunnar

An hour later, Laslo finally returned to the squad, his expression grim. "Sorry, boss, but Franz and Oleg didn't make it. Crossbows got 'em," he explained, his voice heavy with sorrow.

"Drogo don't use crossbows, boss," Karl said with a frown. "What are they doin' with bloody crossbows now?"

Gunnar's eyelids fluttered shut as he sought refuge in the darkness behind closed lids, a brief respite from the harsh reality unfolding around him. His fingertips traced the contours of his weary face, a gesture weighted with the burden of grief for the comrades lost in the chaos of battle. Each fallen soul weighed heavily on his heart, their absence a gaping wound in the fabric of their camaraderie.

With a heavy sigh, Gunnar's thoughts turned to the present, the weight of responsibility pressing down upon him. For the past hour, they had strained to establish contact with the SLS, their efforts met with nothing but silence. The void left by the absence of communication loomed large, a stark reminder of their isolation in this unforgiving wilderness. As the gravity of their situation settled over him like a suffocating blanket, Gunnar knew that they stood at a precipice, teetering on the edge of uncertainty.

"I don't know, Karl," Gunnar sighed wearily. "Maybe they've learned how to use them. Regardless, we need to get closer to the exit. With the path behind us blocked off, we'll have to break through them." His words ignited a flicker of determination among the squad members, their resolve solidifying in the face of the tragic loss of Franz and Oleg.

Cautiously, the squad made their way to the exit of the

chokepoint, knowing that the Drogo Mulik were watching their every move.

The first crossbow bolt landed short of the squad. They were a hundred yards away from the bodies of Franz and Oleg, and apparently out of range. Gunnar halted his squad. They spent a while dragging boulders over to fortify their defensive position somewhat before trying the SLS one last time. Nothing happened.

"Right lads, we're going to form a shield wall in a testudo formation. We need to be ready to punch through anything waiting for us when we're through that pass. They're on the ridge on the right, so I need you all to remember that's where they're going to hit hardest. Keep your shields high and your heads low. Remember, we've also got Dwarven armor on. Those bolts won't be getting through."

Forming the testudo formation, the Dwarves interlocked their shields and got ready to set off. The formation was designed to protect them from bolts, arrows and other projectiles coming from all directions, including from above. The Dwarven soldiers formed a tight, impenetrable shell, with shields held overhead as well as in front and on the flanks, ready to face whatever lay ahead.

The Dwarven squad advanced slowly, moving forward twenty paces before locking their formation in place. Gunnar's voice resonated through his helmet, praising their work and checking on their well-being.

"Strong work, lads! Everyone okay? We're not in range yet, but we'll be there by the next time we stop. We'll start feeling them when we're on the move, so stay alert and maintain the formation. Ready. As one. Let's move!" Gunnar's command echoed across the pass.

As expected, the first bolts came from the right flank. Gunnar could discern the distinct sound of crossbows firing, accompanied by the metallic thuds and scrapes as the bolts struck their thick metal shields. Gunnar couldn't help but wonder where their assailants had managed to get the crossbows from.

Another ten paces, and Gunnar ordered another halt. He addressed the squad, his face glistening with sweat. "Next time we stop, we'll be through the pass. Keep your eyes open. We don't know what in the name of the five gods is waiting there for us, but it's not going to be pleasant."

As the Dwarven squad resumed their advance, drawing nearer to the pass, the onslaught of bolts intensified dramatically. Amidst the barrage, a stroke of luck favored a Drogo bowman who fired his crossbow. The bolt found a small gap within the formation, between the armor and helmet of an elderly dwarf named Jakob and struck with fatal precision, killing him instantly. Tragically, the opening created by Jakob's fall allowed more bolts to penetrate, claiming the life of another two Dwarves.

In response to this dire turn of events, the remaining dwarves swiftly closed ranks and pressed forward, their shields once again forming a barrier as they cautiously proceeded towards the exit of the pass, their resolve unwavering despite the losses they had suffered.

As the Dwarven squad advanced further into the narrow pass, they passed the lifeless bodies of Franz and Oleg, It was apparent that the attackers had lain in ambush, waiting for Franz and Oleg to reach the pass before launching their deadly assault. After a few more paces, they halted once again, and Gunnar took a moment to survey their surroundings and to his bewilderment, the pass seemed completely devoid of any immediate threats—no enemies in sight, just scattered piles of rocks and stones.

Just as the squad was preparing to continue, the earth beneath them trembled ominously. The piles of rock and stone littering the area began to vibrate and shift, gradually converging into a massive amalgamation of rock and stone. With one final tremor and a deafening thunderclap, the rocky mass settled into a menacing form, standing at an imposing twenty feet in height, complete with rudimentary arms and legs. Horrified, Gunnar recognized the creature towering before them.

Gunnar's mind raced as he grasped the dire situation. "Shit!" he exclaimed, his voice quivering with urgency. "Golem! Everyone, stand ready!"

Gunnar had heard of golems before, but he had never truly believed they were real. His studies had taught him that these colossal stone constructs were brought to life through powerful magic, often requiring a blood ritual or a blood sacrifice. Once awakened, they were bound to a specific mission, which usually involved destruction or defense, until they were summoned to cease their actions. Gunnar was also grimly aware that stopping a golem without magic was virtually impossible.

The squad quickly assembled in a defensive formation, their shields raised, and their weapons ready. The giant golem creaked and cracked as it shifted its weight and Gunnar could see the thing slowly rotating and moving its body as if it were warming up for a training routine. Its head twisted and faced the Dwarves, before its giant foot crashed forwards, shaking the ground around them violently. Slowly, the other giant foot followed.

Gunnar's booming voice cut through the cacophony of the golem's slow, grinding movements. "Attack!" he roared, his voice carrying above the deafening sounds of the massive creature shifting its colossal feet. The Dwarven squad responded immediately, surging forward as one cohesive force, charging headlong toward the formidable golem. Gunnar couldn't be certain if his comrades had any prior knowledge of golems, and he briefly wondered how their morale might have wavered had they been as informed about the creature as he was. He banished the fleeting thought immediately, knowing well that his unit of seasoned warriors would not have hesitated.

Gunnar, determined and fearless, led the charge and reached the golem first. With a mighty swing of his axe, he struck what he believed to be the creature's knee. Shards of stone splintered off, but to Gunnar's dismay, the golem remained unfazed. The rest of the Dwarves joined the fray, hacking and pounding at the colossal beast, breaking off substantial chunks of stone. Yet, the golem continued its relentless assault, stomping its massive feet and swinging its boulder-like fists at the Dwarves with unyielding determination.

The brutal battle with the golem claimed its first victim when one of the dwarves, caught off guard, misjudged a swing from the creature's stone hand and was crushed. Gunnar couldn't help but notice that the sturdy Dwarven armor offered little protection against the relentless force.

The tragedy continued to unfold as two more comrades met their grim fates. One was fatally crushed beneath the golem's colossal stomp, which shattered every bone in his body. Shortly after, another fell when the monstrous creature clapped its massive stone hands together, and he couldn't evade the deadly blow in time. The loss of his comrades weighed heavily on Gunnar's heart, but he knew there was no time for grief; the battle raged on.

Gunnar, Karl, and Laslo regrouped, their grim expressions revealing the futility of their attacks against the colossal creature. The three Dwarves exchanged knowing glances, acknowledging that if they couldn't find a way to escape, this would be the end of their journey.

As the golem slowly closed in on them, Laslo suddenly stood to his full height of four feet and three inches, a determined fire burning in his eyes. "I'll be fucked if I meet my end here, boys! Cowering like a bairn!" he bellowed, his battle rage fueling his resolve. With an earth-shaking roar, he charged toward the creature. Gunnar and Karl watched their comrade's fearless charge with a mix of admiration and disbelief through the visors of their helms.

As Laslo surged forward, his face etched with a fierce determination, the golem swung its colossal fist down toward the earth. In a display of incredible agility, Laslo swiftly dived to the side, executing a series of nimble rolls before rising back to his feet. His eyes blazed with anger as he charged toward the stone behemoth, battleaxe unsheathed and poised for action.

With a deafening roar that echoed through the rocky pass, Laslo closed the gap between himself and the golem. As the creature prepared to deliver a devastating blow with its mighty fist, Laslo leaped into action. His battleaxe cleaved through the air in a thunderous arc, striking the golem's stone form with tremendous force. The impact created a swirling cloud of dust and debris, obscuring Laslo from view entirely.

When the dust finally settled, the battlefield revealed a grim scene. All that remained of Laslo was his battered and lifeless body, lying motionless on the ground beside the golem's towering foot.

Gunnar and Karl exchanged a meaningful glance, a silent understanding passing between them. In Karl's eyes, Gunnar glimpsed true fear, a chilling acknowledgment of the dire circumstances they faced. Gunnar braced himself, fully convinced that these were his last moments in the mortal realm. Stepping forward, he faced the stone creature, his knuckles white as he tightly gripped his battle axe—a weapon of last defiance..

As the seconds ticked away, Gunnar's gaze remained fixed on the approaching golem, his determination etched in the lines of his face. He muttered a brief prayer to Dreyna and wished desperately for more time, for another chance, as he braced himself for what was beginning to look like the end of his time on Vellhor.

Then, an inexplicable serenity washed over him, and the world around him began to slow, time itself seeming to grind to a halt. Gunnar's eyes darted around, trying to make sense of this strange occurrence. To his astonishment, he saw Karl behind him, his expression frozen in fear, and before him, the golem, moving at an excruciatingly sluggish pace, as though a day would pass before its colossal foot descended.

With his heart pounding, Gunnar took a deliberate step toward the golem, realizing that whilst everything else had slowed down, his own movements remained unaffected. Approaching the golem, he tentatively reached out and touched its coarse stone surface.

Upon contact, Gunnar experienced a peculiar sensation, like tendrils of energy coursing through him. It was such an unfamiliar force, yet Gunnar instinctively knew how powerful it was. Perplexed, he withdrew his hand, and the sensation ceased.

Circling the stone monstrosity, Gunnar cautiously reached out to touch its leg once more. The strange feeling returned, and this time, he decided to explore it further. Focusing his thoughts, he envisioned himself squeezing and shattering the stone leg of the golem. In an instant, the creature erupted into countless minuscule shards of rock, scattering in all directions. Gunnar couldn't help but gasp in astonishment at the extraordinary outcome.

However, this newfound power came at a significant cost, it seemed. Overwhelming weakness coursed through him, and his legs gave way beneath him. Falling to his knees, he noticed Karl sprinting toward him, a clear indication that time had once again resumed its natural course. Then he passed out.

Gunnar

A stinging slap snapped Gunnar back to the realm of the conscious. He attempted to lift his hand to his throbbing face, only to be met with a surge of agony coursing through his forearm and bicep. Wincing, he abandoned the idea and instead allowed his bleary gaze to wander, his mind clouded by confusion.

"Alright boss, how are you feeling?" a voice inquired from nearby, its source eluding Gunnar's hazy perception. It seemed close, just out of reach, as his eyelids drooped again, lulling him back into unconsciousness.

"Boss, boss, we really need to get out of here. Wake up!" The urgency in the voice grew louder, accompanied by vigorous hands violently shaking him. Gunnar's eyes fluttered open once more, and he tried to raise his hand once again. He was relieved to notice that the searing pain which had gripped him earlier was no longer there.

Opening his eyes, he experienced a blinding pain lance through his skull, nearly incapacitating him once again. However, much to Gunnar's relief, as swiftly as the pain had come, the agony quickly subsided, allowing him to shift into a seated position. Almost immediately, nausea welled up within the dwarf, and he attempted to recline again, but the same robust hands that had roused him now held him upright, denying him the retreat of rest.

With his efforts to lie down thwarted, Gunnar took in his surroundings. An expanse of rocky debris stretched in every direction, littered with the bruised and broken bodies of his unit. His senses heightened instantly, and he snapped to high alert.

"What happened?" He croaked, his mind racing to piece together the events leading to their current predicament.

Karl's voice cut through the haze of confusion. "What was the last thing you remember, boss?"

A waterskin came to Gunnar's lips then, and he drank deeply. Gunnar looked up and noticed Karl. He was so close; it shocked Gunnar that he only just realized he was there.

"Going on the patrol."

"And do you remember what happened on the patrol?"

Gunnar's brow furrowed, and he shook his head. "No, but it doesn't look good."

Karl's tone grew urgent. "It wasn't... Listen boss, we need to get out of here. You've been on your arse for an hour or so, and the gods dammed Drogo will be here any moment. Can you move?"

Gunnar didn't have a clue whether he could move, but he nodded in agreement anyway, realizing he had little choice.

Karl extended a hand, gripping Gunnar's forearm to help him rise. For a moment, Gunnar swayed and relied on Karl's support, but soon he felt steady enough to stand on his own. "Alright Karl, I'm good to go now. Although I want to know what in Draeg's holy ballsack happened to us."

"That makes two of us," muttered Karl under his breath.

The two Dwarves slowly made their way away from the carnage and started walking towards a small crevasse in the mountainside. As they entered the fissure, they both stopped to take on some water. Although they had only been walking for twenty minutes, Gunnar was desperately glad for the respite.

"Alright Karl, so tell me what happened out there?"

"You really don't remember, do you?" Karl was shaking his head slowly.

Ashamed that he'd let his squad down and got them killed,

Gunnar stared down at his boots, unable to meet Karl's gaze. "Look Karl, I don't have a clue what happened, but I'm sorry. I let everyone down. I got the whole squad killed."

Despite his efforts to gain the approval of his unit, Gunnar had never aspired to bear the burden of leadership. The role of clan chief was not what he had ever wanted; rather, it was thrust upon him by his birthright, and now he found himself having failed in the most drastic way. His father, who had held high expectations for him, would be consumed by anger and disappointment, adding another layer of guilt to the weight already crushing his heart.

Sighing, Karl looked up at Gunnar then and, for the first time, stared intently into his eyes. "Boss, what you did back there, I mean, what happened back there, shouldn't have happened."

"I know Karl, I'm sorry…"

"No, Gunnar. Listen to me. It shouldn't have been able to happen. I don't know how you did what you did back there, but by everything that is logical in the world, it should not have been possible."

Gunnar looked at Karl, his brow furrowed in confusion. "What are you talking about, Karl?"

A glimmer of fear surfaced on Karl's stern face before disappearing again. He responded grimly. "A golem attacked us. A fucking golem, Gunnar! Straight out of one of the stories my old man used to tell us to scare the shite out of me and my brothers."

Gunnar raised his eyes at that, knowing that Karl wouldn't be joking at a time like this, but unsure of what to say in response.

"That's not even the strangest part, either." Karl said, clearly still shocked. Gunnar stayed quiet and let the dwarf continue with his story.

"Aye, the strangest part, the part I can barely wrap my head around, was when you moved like a blur, Gunnar. I can't even describe it properly. One minute, you were there, stood twenty paces in front of that giant bastard, and the next you were right next to it and the thing just... exploded!"

"And all of this happened after it had killed the rest of the squad?" Gunnar asked slowly, shaking his head.

"It was our last stand, I suppose you could say. It had already annihilated the others like it was swatting flies. I thought we were done for Gunnar. You should've seen Laslo though, that crazy bastard." Karl chuckled humorlessly. "If I have anything to do with it, the bards will sing his name in taverns across Dreynas for millennia."

Gunnar's brow furrowed in deep concentration, his mind a whirlwind of conflicting thoughts and emotions. Karl's account of the events sent shockwaves through his senses, each word a jarring reminder of the precariousness of their situation. Fear, like a specter, crept insidiously into the corners of his mind, its icy tendrils threatening to paralyze him.

A fleeting doubt crossed Gunnar's mind, a whisper of skepticism amidst the tumult of uncertainty. Was Karl embellishing the truth, spinning tales to feed his penchant for mischief? But even as the question lingered, Gunnar dismissed it with a certainty born of years of camaraderie. Karl might be a jester in lighter times, but in moments of gravitas, his words held the weight of experience and authenticity.

"I need some time to think, Karl," Gunnar finally spoke, his voice tinged with urgency. "Let's make a move, and we can discuss this further on the way."

With a silent nod of agreement, they retraced their steps through the rugged terrain, their movements swift yet deliberate. The mountain loomed overhead, a silent sentinel bearing witness to their clandestine journey. But their progress was soon interrupted by the unmistakable sounds of marching soldiers, the rhythmic cadence of boots echoing off the stone walls.

Instinctively, Gunnar and Karl sought refuge in the shelter of a narrow crack in the mountainside, their bodies pressed against the cool rock as they waited in tense anticipation. With each passing moment, the clamor of approaching footsteps grew louder, mingling with the murmur of unfamiliar voices that echoed through the cavernous expanse. And as the shadows lengthened, and the dusk deepened, Gunnar knew that whatever lay ahead, they had to be ready to confront it head-on

The harsh accent of the Drogo Mulik, the sound like rocks scraping together, reached their ears. Gunnar glanced at Karl, knowing that he would have the common sense and skills to remain quiet and unseen.

The marching Drogo soldiers approached. There must have been at least twenty of them, in ranks of three wide. They were all equipped with rough iron swords and, to Gunnar's astonishment, each soldier had strapped to their back a Dwarven crossbow with a quiver full of bolts.

After the soldiers had passed, Gunnar and Karl waited for several moments before leaving their hiding place.

"They're on a search for something," Gunnar declared. "It sounded like they had some trouble to resolve first, and then they planned to comb through the Frost Mountains."

"What exactly are they searching for?" Karl inquired.

"I don't have the faintest idea, Karl. They didn't disclose that," Gunnar responded.

"And I'm curious about this 'mess' they mentioned," Karl remarked knowingly.

"Aye, I wonder," Gunnar replied, his voice dripping with sarcasm. "What I truly want to understand is, how those bastards got a hold of Dwarven crossbows?" Gunnar pressed on.

"That's what they used to attack us during the patrol. I don't know how they got their hands on them, boss, but it's not a good sign, if you ask me."

"You're right there Karl. We need to get back and report this."

"Boss, I've been thinking about that. I'm going to be honest with you. I don't know how, in Draeg's name, you are going to explain to General Wilfrid what happened with the golem. I'm not convinced we should tell him the whole truth."

"Aye Karl, I doubt he'd believe us even if we did."

Gunnar chose not to share his suspicions about his uncle, but he couldn't help but connect some dots that pointed to the possibility of the Draegoorian Army General being involved somehow. As they started their journey back, the weight of their discovery settled heavily upon them. The Frost Mountains loomed ominously in the distance, a silent witness to the secrets and dangers that lay ahead.

With each step, Gunnar's resolve hardened. They would uncover the truth behind the crossbows, the golem, and the mysterious search. But for now, they needed to survive the trek back and face whatever awaited them upon their return. The path was uncertain, but one thing was clear: this was only the beginning of a much larger, darker journey.

6

A Daughter's Despair

'Heavy hangs the crown, burdened with the weight of choices and the echoes of responsibility.'

Anwyn

As Anwyn approached the cottage, she could feel a palpable surge of magic lingering in the air, a tingling sensation that felt like a subtle hum. The tranquil forest was marred by the unmistakable sounds of clashing swords, the sharp metallic reverberations cutting through the usually serene forest. As she drew nearer, the noises intensified, marked by frantic shouts and a heart-rending scream that seemed to tear through the very fabric of the woods. It was a voice she recognized all too well – her mother's.

Without a second thought, Anwyn raced toward the source of the chaos, her heart pounding in her chest. A sinking feeling of dread settled like a heavy stone in the pit of her stomach, but she pushed it aside, focusing on the urgency of the situation. In her mind, a whirlwind of thoughts raced—fears for the safety of her family, the potential danger lurking ahead, and a determination to confront whatever awaited her head-on. As she sprinted forward, her breaths came in ragged gasps, each step fueled by a mixture of adrenaline and resolve.

Emerging into the small clearing, Anwyn's eyes widened with horror. A dozen Elven warriors encircled the cottage, their gleaming katanas poised for battle. In the center of the clearing, where laundry typically hung to dry, lay her father, surrounded by the lifeless forms of seven Elves, their dismembered limbs strewn haphazardly like discarded rubbish.

Her mother was being held a dozen paces away by two of the Elves. They were clearly twins, being identical in every way. Tears streamed down her face, and her anguished cries pierced the air. "Laoch," she wailed, her voice strained with grief, "Laoch, no, my love... Get up, Laoch," she sobbed, her pleas wrenching at Anwyn's heart.

Anwyn approached the scene, still sprinting at full pace. Swiftly and silently, she withdrew her set of daggers and released two of them, killing the two Elves holding her mother captive before anyone even knew she was there. Still sprinting, she withdrew another dagger and struck an elf standing a dozen paces away from her through her eye. She stopped then, looking at her mother, who was on her hands and knees, tears still streaming down her face, desperately crawling towards her father.

As the nine warrior Elves closed in on her, Anwyn sensed the expertise in both combat and magic emanating from their every move. They encircled her like hunters stalking their prey, their Elven grace and precision on full display. Amidst the tension and danger, Anwyn couldn't help but briefly question her own lack of fear. Perhaps it was the adrenaline she thought.

She drew a long, deep breath, waiting for one of them to make the first move. A destructive spell flew towards her. If it had hit, it would probably have annihilated her. Instead, she held out her hand and summoned a small containment spell to hold it, before releasing it into the ground, letting the magic contained within fizzle out to nothing. With her slender hand still outstretched, she gently flicked her wrist, releasing a tiny ball of condensed wind which shot into the Elf's midsection. It left a hole the size of a marble through his heart.

Eight assassins remained, and Anwyn pivoted to confront them, her icy gaze unwavering. She inhaled, raising her hands above her head, allowing the raw emotions of anger and sorrow over her father's death to surge forth. With a thunderous scream, she lowered both her outstretched hands, directing her rage at the elves. Two streams of destructive magic erupted from her fingertips, killing three of the Elves, reducing everything it touched to utter nothingness. No smoke, no debris, just a void of emptiness left in their wake.

Five Elves remained now. Anwyn withdrew her katana, holding the curved blade by its two-handled hilt. Her father had taught her how to use the katana like a true warrior, with honor. "One strike, one kill." He had lectured, time and time again. "This weapon is not designed for exchanging blows, it was made for delivering a swift death. That is why we only ever draw it when we intend to kill," he had said each time they sparred together.

With memories of him fresh in her mind, she stepped toward the five warrior Elves. She had five strikes to avenge her father.

Strike one – a muscular elf with long, straight black hair approached her first. He moved like a dancing snake, weaving this way and that, hoping to distract her. Her father had been faster, quicker. This elf wasn't half the fighter he had been. He brought his blade down towards Anwyn's head. Gracefully, she stepped to the side; the blow missing her by several inches. Her katana moved in a blur. She sliced the elf from his right hip through to his left shoulder, cutting him in half with an upward strike.

Strike two – Using her momentum from her previous strike, she maintained her spinning motion, her katana extended straight before her. The sweeping arc of her blade found its mark, decapitating a blonde female elf who was charging toward her. Her head rolled several paces away, blood soaking the ground as it tumbled along the dirt.

Strike three – Standing still, her icy gaze fixed upon the three remaining elves, their hesitation palpable in the aftermath of their comrades' swift deaths. She didn't give them an opportunity to surrender or run. Her katana had been drawn. She could not stop until all of her opponents were dead. That was her code of honor. But more than that, she wanted her revenge. She deserved it. She needed it. Closing the distance like a cornered viper with her katana raised above her head, she brought it down and cut the third elf in a diagonal slash starting at his left shoulder. He fell, his torso slowly sliding apart, a testament to both the strength of the blow and the impossible sharpness of the blade.

Strike four – Both attackers advanced on Anwyn together, in a hope that they could divide her attention. She allowed the first elf to swing his katana, stepping casually backwards and avoiding the strike. She pounced like a tiger, knowing that he had fully committed to the swing and could not recover quickly enough. She crashed the blade of her katana vertically down the center of his skull, splitting it in two.

Strike five - Immediately after landing her pouncing strike on opponent four, Anwyn dodged a well-placed blow to her head. Had she not instinctively rolled to the side, she would have been decapitated. Instead, however, she was now stalking her opponent. Holding his katana in one hand, he raised his free hand and launched a fireball made of pure magic at Anwyn; she watched it as it flew past her side, missing her by inches. After he had realized that he had missed his chance, the elf panicked, and he ran away from Anwyn and toward the tree line... *coward*. She could have ended his life in multiple ways by using her magic, but her father deserved a warrior's revenge. So, with her katana raised above her head, she launched. It went spinning, end over end, through the air until it lodged in the center of his back, skewering him through his spine. She walked over to him and dislodged her sword, before wiping the elf's blood off on his robes.

Although exhausted after her battle, Anwyn sprinted over to her mother, who had crawled over to Laoch and was weeping inconsolably over his dead body. Anwyn looked down at her father, his blood-stained katana by his side, still gripped in his hand. Scanning her eyes over his body, Anwyn realized the cowards had shot him with arrows, a weapon viewed with disdain among her kind. They couldn't defeat him with their katanas; that much was clear given the limbs strewn over the place. Resorting to arrows spoke volumes of their cowardice and desperation.

Kneeling by her father's side, Anwyn's heart ached with an intensity she had never known. She tenderly cupped his smooth and weathered face, her fingers tracing the familiar lines etched by time and experience. His presence, so strong and unwavering throughout her life, now lay fragile before her, and the weight of it pressed heavily on her chest. She pressed a tender kiss to his cheek, feeling the warmth of his skin beneath her lips, a stark contrast to the cold reality of the moment. Another kiss followed, this time to his forehead, a silent farewell to the man who had shaped her world. Tears blurred her vision as grief consumed her, her sobs mingling with her mother's, forming a symphony of sorrow that echoed in the stillness of the clearing. In that moment, all Anwyn could do was hold on tight, clinging to the memories of her father and the love that bound them together.

Anwyn's mind drifted back to the book her mother had been reading before lunch. She had learned about healing, and even though she understood her father was gone and beyond any true healing, her sorrow overwhelmed her reason. She couldn't bear the thought of not trying something, anything, to change this grim reality.

Rising to her knees, she positioned herself over her father's lifeless body, her hands firmly pressed against what she thought were his most serious wounds. With unwavering determination, she channeled her will into the act of healing. She sensed the magic in the air resonating around her. Evidently, so could her mother, because her head shot up, and she looked curiously around.

"Anwyn, what are you doing? He's gone. You can't bring him back," her mother cried out in despair.

But Anwyn didn't listen to her mother's desperate pleas. Instead, she intensified her concentration on the wound, pouring even more of her will into the effort. She sensed his spirit lingering within, feeble and almost imperceptible, but undeniably present. To her, this tiny glimmer of hope was worth everything. She would cling to the slightest chance, no matter how faint, to bring her father back. With determination, she opened her own spirit and pushed it into her father's, a desperate attempt to bridge the gap between life and death.

After what seemed like an eternity, Anwyn finally sensed a spark of life within her father's spirit. It was a glimmer of hope, but it came at a great cost. She was utterly drained, her own spirit nearly depleted. Her father required more. His spirit yearned for more, but she had nothing left to offer.

In an act born of pure desperation and instinct, she opened herself up once more. This time, she somehow managed to tap into the latent energies around her. She could feel the vibrant life force residing within the trees, coursing through the animals of the forest. She sensed the power inherent to the very heart of the forest itself. If only she could harness that power to aid her father, she thought, her determination to save him pushing her to explore this newfound connection to the natural world.

In that moment, she heard a mesmerizing whisper in the wind. It sounded like the chiming and tinkling of bells.

"Seishinmori, you must rise and stand strong in the midst of the oncoming storm, for this is your first test," it spoke, a whisper in her mind.

Desperation welled up within her as she gritted her teeth and implored, *"I need more power."*

"Seishinmori, you have everything you need. Use it wisely," the ethereal voice replied.

Anwyn's connection to reality wavered; she couldn't tell if she had blacked out or not. She had lost all sense of time and reality. Amidst the chaos, one thing remained clear—she had a purpose, an unrelenting need to save her father, to gather more power. In desperation, she urged the forces around her to obey her will.

Then, like a hurricane slamming into her very soul, she could feel it—a tremendous force enveloping her, surging violently into her being. She screamed in agony, and then, as suddenly as it began, it ceased. Once again, she sensed the lush grass beneath her knees, felt her father's shirt between her trembling fingers, heard her mother's cries beside her, and noticed her father's chest faintly rising and falling.

As she dared to open her eyes once more, she realized her father was actually breathing! The arrows had been drawn out of his body, and they lay strewn around him, still coated in his blood. Her heart skipped a beat. She had achieved the impossible. Overwhelmed by her emotions, she burst into tears. Her mother, sitting beside her in awestruck disbelief, had tears streaming down her face. Her father coughed and slowly opened one eye. Anwyn, consumed by joy and relief, embraced her father. Her mother crawled over to join the embrace, and together they wept.

Anwyn

With great effort, Anwyn and her mother assisted Laoch in hobbling toward the cottage. Despite the short distance, the journey seemed to stretch for an eternity. Anwyn's gaze continually flitted to the devastation and loss that now marred the once-peaceful clearing, each glance filling her eyes with more tears.

Finally, the three of them made it into the cottage. Laoch slid gingerly into his homemade chair, which was covered in blankets, while Eira begun preparing herbal tea. The familiar aroma of white willow bark wafted through the air, a scent Anwyn recognized from her lessons with her mother; it would help ease the pain and discomfort her father was surely enduring. She also detected the sweet, soothing scent of chamomile, known for its wound-healing properties, capable of reducing inflammation and swelling, another welcome remedy for her father's injuries.

Eventually, her mother brought over three mugs of steaming hot tea, along with Laoch's old smoke pipe. Laoch hadn't smoked broadleaf tobacco for years, and Anwyn glanced at the pipe in confusion and then looked at her mother quizzically.

"This is for me, dear. I think I am in need of something slightly stronger than tea today. Although, should your father also like some, I would be more than happy to oblige him as well."

Anwyn remained silent, exhaustion weighing heavily upon her, her spirit utterly drained. She had never allowed herself to reach this point of complete depletion before, and the fatigue she now experienced was almost incapacitating.

"Drink the tea, Anwyn." Eira urged. "It will take some of the edge off of how you are feeling. We need to come up with a plan. We are not safe here and we all need to be at full strength as soon as possible so that we can leave."

Anwyn sipped the tea, the warm liquid working its way down her throat and into her stomach. The sensation was strange. Although she had regularly drank herbal tea in the past, she had never before noticed how the liquid was absorbed by her body and its healing properties processed. But now, in her depleted state, she felt every drop working to mend both her body and her spirit, revitalizing her from within.

She helped her father take several sips from his mug while her mother finished packing the pipe and lit it with a simple thought. Her mother sat back and sighed, blowing out a long stream of grey smoke.

Anwyn looked at her mother then, looked at her for the first time since the battle had finished. That's when she first witnessed the cracks in the porcelain picture of perfection she had always known as her mother. She saw what the grief, the fear, the despair had done to her innocent, beautiful, perfect mother and her rage threatened to flare once again.

Burrowing her head into her hands, she sighed loudly, earning her a glance from both her parents.

"Mother, father, who were those Elves, and why were they here?"

After glancing at each other briefly, Laoch went to speak, but his voice cracked and he had a brief fit of coughing before drinking some more tea. Eira took over the conversation instead.

"Those Elves, Anwyn, were here to arrest you. When they arrived, they didn't believe you weren't at home. They came in and tried to search for you."

Anwyn's gaze swept across their usually organized and tidy cottage, and for the first time, she took in the disarray. She wondered how she had failed to notice the chaos earlier, chalking it up to her exhaustion and her recent battle.

"They then attempted to arrest your father," her mother continued, her voice tinged with a mix of sadness and frustration. "When he questioned their motives, they unsheathed their blades."

Anwyn knew that in doing so, those Elves had effectively sentenced her father to death. Once blades were drawn, there was no alternative. Her father had to kill them, or he would die.

"Your father, as was his absolute right, defended himself in the most honorable way a warrior could."

Anwyn looked at her father then, whose face remained blank. "And the cowards shot him with arrows when they realized how skilled he was," she remarked with indignation thick in her voice.

Her mother managed a small smile. "Yes, Anwyn, the cowards did just that."

Her father's deep, raspy voice broke the conversation, then. "How did you heal me, Eira? I had passed. I felt my spirit leave me."

"Anwyn healed you, my love. And I too would like to know the answer to that. You had indeed passed. I scanned for your spirit many times, looking for a spark." Her mother's voice quivered, a brief sob escaping her lips as the recollection of that painful moment resurfaced.

Anwyn's parents both fixed their gaze upon her, curiosity and gratitude etched into their expressions.

"I don't know how I did it," Anwyn admitted, her tone uncertain. "I was so upset that I wasn't thinking properly. I knew you had passed and that it should have been impossible for me to heal you. But I didn't care. I tried anyway. Then I felt it. I felt the spark in your spirit, so I pushed my spirit into you and healed you."

With a look of contemplation and her hand gently rubbing at her chin, Eira slowly started nodding. "I see, yes," she murmured, "that part does make some sense, I suppose, in theory. An elf who was strong enough, and by that I mean, an elf who had a strong enough connection to their spirit, but also had a strong enough bond to the forest, could, and I mean, *theoretically,* could sense the fading spark of someone who had recently passed. But what I am truly struggling to comprehend is how the actual healing occurred?"

Laoch looked at Eira then, his brow furrowed in confusion. "When you say healing, Eira, do you mean reviving?"

Eira contemplated the question for a moment before responding. "Well, yes and no, I suppose, love. It's true that you were revived, in a sense, since you had indeed died. But your spirit had not left our world. It was still here, albeit faintly, connected to your body. So I believe the more accurate term would be 'healed', since it was the healing of your spirit that led to your revival."

Both of her parents turned their gaze to Anwyn, their expressions expectant. Laoch gestured with his hand, encouraging her to elaborate. "Well, Anwyn, tell us what else."

Although it had only just happened, Anwyn struggled to recall the details accurately. She was still exhausted, and although the soothing effects of the tea had helped settle her somewhat, it could not help replenish her depleted spirit so quickly.

As she contemplated her drained spirit, a realization dawned upon her, causing her head to snap up from where she had been fixated on the table. "I know!" She cried. "I remember! I connected to the forest. I knew my spirit alone wasn't enough, so I opened myself up and harnessed the power of the forest. I used its energy to heal Father!" Anwyn relayed this information eagerly, as if it were the most natural thing in the world, expecting her mother, at least, to grasp the significance of her words. However, upon observing her mother's perplexed and shocked countenance, Anwyn realized that her mother did not understand at all.

"Anwyn, dear. The forest and your spirit... they don't, they just don't work like that." Eira was speaking slowly, as if talking to a child.

"But mother, I distinctly remember the forest whispering to me. She was helping me!" Anwyn exclaimed.

Her mother gasped in astonishment at Anwyn's revelation, while her father remained still, eyes wide and mouth agape.

"What?" she asked them both. Hoping for an explanation.

Her father, who still hadn't moved, remained silent, so her mother responded. "Are you telling us that the forest spoke to you, Anwyn dear?"

"Yes, she spoke to me. She told me I was *Seishinmori*, and I must weather the storm."

Laoch had found some of his composure now and turned to Eira. "Then the prophecy has come to pass, and the forest in her wisdom has chosen our daughter as the savior."

Eira shook her head in disbelief. "No," she said, "it cannot be. Anwyn is too young. She's never even left the forest before. How is she Seishinmori?"

"What prophecy are you talking about, father? You've never mentioned it to me before." Anwyn pressed.

"We can discuss it further once we've made some decisions," Laoch replied, casting a glance at his wife. "No we must rest and recover. Remaining here is no longer an option. Those Elves were not from Stromyr, they were from Gwydir in the west. We probably have three days, at the most, before whoever sent them realizes they failed and sends more after us."

Although desperate for answers, Anwyn could barely keep her eyes open and had to admit to herself that she agreed with her father. Rest was imperative now.

Still shaking her head in disbelief, Eira prepared another pipe and lit it. "I'll stay awake for a few hours to keep an eye out."

Anwyn helped her father to his bed. She helped lay him down and pulled a blanket around him to ensure he was comfortable; she bent at the waist to kiss his forehead, telling him that she loved him. As she turned to leave the room, he took hold of her hand and squeezed.

"As a warrior, they taught me always to be prepared for death, Anwyn," Laoch began, his words carrying the weight of a lifetime's experience. "Whether that death was to be my own or someone else's, I never feared it. And today, when I died, it was no different." A wistful smile graced his lips, and a solitary tear welled up in the corner of his eye, slowly tracing a path down his cheek.

"Today, though, a new fear took hold of my heart," he continued. "When they came to arrest you, I feared for you, my dear. I feared that because I could no longer protect you, I had failed. However, I now realize that I have nothing left to fear. Your skill is unparalleled, surpassing even my own. You have far exceeded my wildest expectations, mastering all the disciplines of a warrior. I am immensely proud of you, my love," he said, his eyes moistening with pride and affection.

Moved by her father's words, Anwyn drew closer, and he tenderly cupped his hand to her cheek, brushing away a tear that had snaked its way down her soft cheek.

"Thank you, father," she replied, her voice filled with heartfelt gratitude. "That means more to me than you could ever imagine."

Pausing for a moment, Anwyn decided to address a question

that had been lingering in her mind. "Father, why did they come to arrest me?" she asked.

Laoch sighed and spoke with a heavy heart, "Anwyn, my love, they fear you. That is why. They fear you because you were not born with a sibling. Fear has led them astray from the virtues and honor of our people. It has fanned the flames of anger and hatred, and it has paved a path marked by bloodshed and death."

Anwyn let out a sigh of her own. "I've never even been near Gwydir before," she lamented, the injustice of it all weighing heavily upon her.

"I know, dear," Laoch responded with a sigh. "And now, because the trees around Gwydir are withering and rotting, they attempt to hold you responsible. For some, it's easier to seek someone to blame than to seek the truth. But now that you've been named as Seishinmori, I'm uncertain how the cities will react."

"What is Seishinmori, father?" Anwyn inquired, her curiosity piqued by the unfamiliar term.

"Seishinmori," Laoch began, "was the title we bestowed upon our kings and queens millennia ago. The forest itself would choose an elf to rule our people. However, a Seishinmori has not been selected in over a thousand years. Your grandfather, before he left, prophesied that a Seishinmori would once again be chosen to lead our people in the most significant war ever witnessed on Vellhor."

"Why me, though? I mean, why did the forest choose me, father?" Anwyn probed further, seeking understanding.

"I do not know the answer to that question, Anwyn," Laoch admitted. "What I do know, is that a Seishinmori is only selected if they possess a pure spirit. The name Seishinmori means 'Spirit of the Forest' in the ancient language. You now bear the power of the forest within you. But remember, my love, with great power comes great responsibility." His words carried a weight of wisdom and caution.

Anwyn sighed and kissed her father one last time before turning and leaving him to rest, the weight of his words weighing heavily on her.

7

The Road to Lamos

'Courage is not the absence of fear, but the triumph over it; embrace your fears and let them fuel your journey.'

Kemp

As the horrifying spectacle unfolded with the deaths of the merchant and his wife up ahead, Kemp found himself locked in a paralysing fear. His muscles refused to respond, and he remained rooted to the spot, a helpless witness to the violence unfolding before him. In the distance, he heard someone screaming his name.

"Get down, Kemp! Get down now!" Theodore's frantic cries pierced the chaos. "Kemp. Kemp! Get down, lad!" The desperate shouts continued to reach Kemp's ears, but they seemed to register only vaguely.

Then, suddenly, Kemp was yanked from his seat with a violent force and pulled down onto the ground by Theodore, who was dragging him under the wagon for cover.

As Kemp was dragged unceremoniously across the dusty ground, he felt a warm, damp patch spreading through his trouser leg. He was so consumed by fear that he didn't even register the humiliation of what had just happened.

Lying there in the dirt, Kemp felt a chilling numbness seep into his bones, paralysing him as he watched the chaotic exchange of arrows unfold before him. His mind screamed for action, for escape, yet his body remained frozen in place rendering him powerless. With each life taken in the violent clash, a sense of dread coiled tighter around his heart, weighing heavily on his chest. Despite the chaos raging around him, Kemp found himself lost in a haze of terror, unable to tear his gaze away from the nightmarish scene unfolding before his eyes.

The deafening screams and incoherent shouting assaulted Kemp's ears, rendering him incapable of making sense of the chaotic turmoil around him. He knew that he should do something, anything, to help his companions, but a paralysing fear held him firm in its grip. All he could manage to do was shake involuntarily as his body quivered with dread.

Tears blurred Kemp's vision as he watched Theodore, the man who had extended a hand of friendship to him on his first day, fight desperately for survival. Each movement Theodore made, fueled by determination and fear, pierced Kemp's heart with a profound sense of helplessness. As Theodore reached for the fallen guard's bow and quiver, Kemp's chest tightened with dread, knowing the perilous gamble he was about to take.

With a mixture of admiration and dread, Kemp witnessed Theodore emerge from beneath the wagon, his motions deliberate yet frantic as he sought cover behind the rear wheel. The air crackled with tension as Theodore unleashed a flurry of arrows toward the source of the chaos, each shot a testament to his courage in the face of overwhelming odds.

But Kemp's heart shattered as he saw an arrow pierce Theodore's thigh, eliciting a heart-wrenching cry of pain. Despite the agony etched across his face, Theodore summoned the strength to fire another arrow, his determination unwavering. However, the cruel hand of fate intervened, as Kemp watched in horror as another arrow found its mark, lodging itself in the center of Theodore's chest.

A choked sob escaped Kemp's lips as Theodore crumpled to the ground, the weight of his injuries evident in the frothy bubble of blood that escaped his lips. In that moment, Kemp felt a profound sense of loss, knowing that Theodore's unwavering bravery had cost him his life.

Blood began to dribble down Theodore's chin as he turned his gaze toward Kemp one last time. In that fleeting moment, the light faded from his eyes, leaving them vacant and lifeless.

At that moment, the world around Kemp seemed to come to a standstill, even though the sounds of battle continued to echo in his ears. The screams, the clashing of metal against metal, and the thudding of arrows into wood still assaulted his senses. The metallic tang of blood hung heavily in the air, intermingled with the sickening stench of spilled entrails. Overwhelmed by the horror of it all, Kemp vomited, and darkness overtook him.

When Kemp regained consciousness, he found himself being gently pulled out from under the wagon. Initially seized by fear, he was soon comforted by a sense of recognition as he looked at the man who held his leg. An unusual feeling of calmness washed over him once more, and he relaxed.

"The mage boy still lives, Kris," the man dragging him out shouted over to another man.

Despite the sweltering heat in the southern region of Fenmark, the man who had pulled Kemp from under the wagon was clad in a long black coat. His short, neatly combed blonde hair was slicked to the side, and his face appeared utterly unremarkable, the kind of visage that you'd probably forget as soon as your gaze shifted away from it.

Another man, presumably Kris, approached. He stood tall and broad, his light hair shaved very short. His pockmarked face bore a rugged, muscular countenance, and his deep, intense brown eyes fixed upon Kemp. With a simple nod, Kris acknowledged the young man.

"Hello, son. You're okay now," the man addressed Kemp with a reassuring tone. "We fought them all off. Lost over half of our convoy, and there are only eight guards left, but you're safe enough now." His speech carried a slight northern accent, likely from Fenchester. However, Kemp noted that the accent was not nearly as rugged as that of a typical person from the north-western province of Fenmark.

Kris called over to the man who had pulled Kemp out from under the wagon, "Harald, go get a healer's kit over here, please, mate. He's got a few scrapes and cuts I'd like to see to."

Harald cast a quick, judgmental glance toward Kemp, and for a fleeting moment, Kemp saw the disdain in the man's eyes. With a tut and a roll of his eyes, Harald turned away and left to search for a healer's kit, his head shaking in apparent disapproval. Inside, Kemp's self-critical thoughts continued to gnaw at him. He berated himself silently, thinking, *You've hidden under a wagon and lost control of yourself while the real men did all the fighting. Of course, he thinks you're a coward.*

Apparently, Kris had also noticed Harald's actions because he turned to Kemp and offered some words of comfort. "The first time I saw a man die, I vomited and passed out as well, mate. Don't worry about it. That guy's new, only been with our team since Redbourne. He doesn't realize that a lot of the folk we protect down this road haven't seen combat. They're merchants, not soldiers, that's why they employ us. He should remember that."

As Kemp's gaze drifted over to the spot where Theodore had

met his tragic end, a heavy weight settled in his chest. Though the guards had already removed Theodore's lifeless body, the crimson stains and dusted ground served as haunting reminders of the violence that had unfolded there.

Grief and guilt clawed at Kemp's heart, threatening to overwhelm him. He turned to Kris, his eyes brimming with tears, the weight of his confession pressing down on him like a leaden burden.

"I froze," he admitted, his voice thick with emotion. "I saw people fighting and dying, and I froze like a coward. Harald is right to scorn me. I was useless. I let my friend die because I was too scared to help him."

In that moment of raw vulnerability, Kemp grappled with the crushing weight of his inaction, his mind tormented by the knowledge that he had failed his friend when he needed him most.

Kris responded with a compassionate and understanding tone, trying to console him. "My father used to tell me that 'courage is the mastery of fear and not the absence of it.' So, how can a man such as you, who has never been in danger before, know how to master his fears? Harald told me he was a professional soldier in the Fenchester Guard. If he tells anyone he didn't shite himself the first time his life was in danger, then he's a liar."

As Kris's words sank in, Kemp found a fleeting sense of solace in the man's understanding. Yet, beneath the surface, a tempest of guilt and shame raged within him. He couldn't escape the crushing weight of responsibility that bore down on him like a heavy shroud.

The truth was stark and unforgiving: Theodore had faced his fate with bravery, sacrificing himself in the heat of battle. What tormented Kemp was the agonising realization that he held the power to alter their fate, to save them all with his magic, yet he had faltered in the face of fear. He had watched, paralyzed, as his friend fought valiantly to protect him, and that knowledge haunted him like a relentless specter.

The fear of repeating his failure loomed ominously in Kemp's mind, casting a shadow over his thoughts with each passing moment. Despite Kris's well-intentioned attempts to offer comfort, the sting of embarrassment and shame persisted, like a dagger twisting in his heart. Each pang served as a bitter reminder of his own perceived cowardice, a burden he knew he would always carry with him like a heavy chain.

8

Escape!

"Leaving behind a past life is like sailing away from a storm; the waves may be turbulent, but the horizon promises calm and clarity."

Ruiha

The sandstorm swirled violently around Ruiha and the group of travellers she was with as they attempted to wait it out, huddled together in the ruins of an old wagon, which had been abandoned in the middle of the Sandaran desert.

Ruiha had her long dark, almost black, hair tied back, and she could feel it whipping against her back. And, in a bid to prevent herself from being torn to pieces or from choking on the sand which was blowing all around her, she had also covered her dark, olive-toned face and skin with rags and cloth.

Ruiha briefly wondered whether the original occupants of the wagon had perished here in a similar sandstorm, but quickly banished the negative thought from her mind. She knew there was no point in dwelling on what she could not change. Her training, if you could describe learning how to murder in the slums of Gecit, as training, had taught her to make the most out of any situation, and Ruiha had been in far worse situations than this.

"Ruiha, if the boat isn't there, what will we do? We'll surely die out here. Our rations will only last a few more days!" shouted Ari, a dark-skinned man with a cloth wrapped around his face, his voice barely audible over the relentless storm.

As Ruiha's patience wore thin amidst the howling storm, her frustration bubbled to the surface in a fierce outburst directed at Ari. Her words were laced with urgency and a hint of menace as she shouted over the roaring winds, her voice barely audible above the tempest.

"Listen, Ari," she snapped, her tone sharp with irritation. "I'm not telling you again. The boat will be there. You ask me one more time, and panic the rest of them, and I'll break your godsdammed neck. Gottit?"

Though her words carried a threat of violence, deep down, Ruiha knew she couldn't follow through with such a drastic action. Despite Ari's incessant complaining and worrying, she actually liked him, and generally appreciated his company... when he wasn't voicing his concerns so loudly, anyway.

Ari nodded, his face obscured by the cloth but his agreement clear in his tone. "Okay, okay Ruiha, apologies. I'm just worried, is all. We're so close to the coast now, after this blasted storm calms down, we'll practically be able to see it!"

Ruiha went to glance over at Ari, but the fine sand blowing all around her made her change her mind. "And that, my dear Ari, is why we shouldn't start worrying yet. We won't know either way until at least tomorrow, so... stop crying over something you can't change!"

Although she wasn't worried about the boat being there or not. She was confident in her ability to survive, boat or not, she was certain of that. But she did want out of this desert. It was the threat she aimed to leave behind that drove her urgency. She knew who was coming for her, and escaping Sandara was her only chance at freedom. And even that was a slim chance.

Leaving the slums of Gecit seemed like a reasonable aspiration, but the Sand Dragons, her former gang, had a different plan in mind. They had discovered her intentions far too soon, and Ruiha seethed with anger at the thought of betrayal. If she ever found out who had exposed her plans, they wouldn't know what hit them, that's for sure. Although, knowing what Faisal was like and capable of, she doubted the snitch would still be breathing.

Faisal had become a figure of dread in Ruiha's life. Once her protector, confidant, and even lover at one point, although she couldn't help but regret that romance.

He was a dangerous man; a truth she knew from firsthand experience. He was a narcissistic sociopath and was single-handedly responsible for turning a small, inconsequential criminal gang into an organised empire that ruled the criminal underbelly of Gecit, with its reach extending the entirety of Sandara and even into Fenmark.

For eight long years, Faisal had meticulously groomed and honed Ruiha into his personal instrument of death. She was his relentless enforcer, carrying out his murderous commands without question, until that fateful mission, the one she knew would take her past the point of no return.

In some ways, it was a moment of relief for Ruiha. She had numbed herself to her emotions for so long; at points, she had worried that she'd lost her humanity completely. Yet, when the order came, she realised that she still possessed the capacity to feel, to care. It was a reminder that she hadn't entirely sacrificed herself for the Sand Dragons, and she couldn't carry out that order without destroying what was left of her.

For the first time in eight years, Ruiha had disobeyed a kill order. Disobeying Faisal was a risk she had never imagined taking, yet in that moment, it felt like the only choice she could make. And despite her fear of Faisal, she couldn't bring herself to regret it. Screw Faisal, she thought defiantly, a surge of defiance coursing through her veins as she stood firm in her decision.

The next day, when the sun rose, and the sandstorm had turned into just another bad memory, the small group of travellers made their way north. Her contact in Gecit had assured her that the boat would be there, and the slimy toad was far too scared of Ruiha to lie to her.

As they approached the makeshift port, where contraband items were already being loaded onto a small boat, Ruiha smiled. Turning around to gloat to Ari, her smile vanished. On the horizon, a dust cloud approached, carrying a dozen horses and as many thugs. They were coming for her.

"Ruuuuuun" she screamed, taking off without looking behind her. She could make it. She was only half a mile away from the boat and the horses, although fast, could surely not catch her now.

As she approached the boat, she drew her scimitar and waved it threateningly at the two men loading the illicit cargo. "Get that boat moving... Now!" she screamed.

Looking up and seeing the armed horsemen, the two men dropped the box they were carrying and started getting the boat untied.

Reaching the boat, now just a few meters into the water, she leaped on board and couldn't resist turning to look at her pursuers. It was a decision she immediately regretted. They had lost their target, but their fury had been unleashed on the small group she had travelled with for the past week. The last image etched in her memory before a club struck the back of her head, plunging her into darkness, was Faisal's sinister gaze fixed upon her as Ari's head was severed from his shoulders.

Ruiha

Ruiha gasped and then proceeded to choke on the freezing cold salty water, which had been dumped into her face. Spluttering, she looked around at her surroundings. Still disoriented, she tried to recollect what had happened to her. Ari... she remembered, and it all came flooding back.

The room she was in was gently rocking, and the contents of Ruiha stomach began swishing along with the room. Forcing herself to keep it all safely inside her stomach, she swallowed and took shallow breaths.

In her peripheral vision, Ruiha noticed two men standing next to her. She also noticed that they had tied her hands behind her back with a thick, rough rope.

"You better start talking, darlin'. Why were those men chasing you?" Ruiha looked up at the fat man who was talking to her. He was missing plenty of teeth, and the ones that remained looked like they were hanging on for dear life.

"Who wants to know? And why in all that is holy did you hit me?" Ruiha responded to the man, irritation thick in her voice.

"We'll be asking the questions, love. Now answer my friend here's question, and maybe we can talk about what we're going to do with you," the man next to the fat man said. He looked like a cross between a rat and a weasel, with a couple of generations of inter-breeding thrown in for good measure.

"Listen fellas, I know you *think* you have me, a poor defenceless woman, all tied up in a..." Ruiha looked around the room then, seeing nothing but wooden cladding all around her, "where the fuck even are we? Anyways, I'm going to give you one chance here, lads. Let me go, apologise for hitting me on the back of the head, maybe sort me out with some form of compensation for my troubles, and then take me to Lamos, and I won't kill you both." Ruiha asserted with a hint of a dangerous smile.

Chuckling, the inbred rat man brandished a dagger, whilst the fat, toothless man smiled with a sick, perverted glint in his eye. "This is gonna be fun," he said, licking his lips.

At that point, and to the utter astonishment of the two men, Ruiha, who had already untied the pathetic knot tying her hands together, stood up and slowly shook her head. "I gave you bastards a chance," she muttered. "I'm trying my godsdammed hardest to turn over a new leaf. Then you had to go and ruin it for me."

Sighing, she dodged the stabbing thrust from the inbred man's dagger, using his momentum to bring him closer to her. She could smell stale tobacco and alcohol on his breath. As he reached her, she twisted his arm and grabbed the dagger before it hit the ground. With an upward thrust, she pierced his chest at an angle she knew would have also reached his heart. Pulling the bloodstained dagger out, she then threw it at the fat man, lodging it in his neck. His eyes went wide, as his hands reached up and grasped the hilt, before he hit the deck, unmoving. The fight, if you could call it that, was over in a matter of seconds.

Opening the door, Ruiha could see out onto the main deck of the small boat; she looked around but couldn't see anyone.

The boat was around forty feet long, and fairly narrow. Other than the small room that she had just come out of, the entire deck was open to the elements. The boat was sat unmoving, bobbing up and down in the middle of the ocean. That explained her brief period of sickness earlier, she thought.

Walking up to the front of the ship, the prow, or something she thought it might be called, she looked around again. Finally, she saw someone. A man lay slumped against a coil of rope.

Hoping he was alive, she kicked him with her foot. He jumped up crying out, "owww... what in Vellhor's name was that for?"

Looking at the man and deciding whether he was a threat, Ruiha cautiously asked, "who are you, and do you know how to get to Lamos?"

The man looked at her in surprise. "You're that girl they took to question."

"Clever one, aren't you?" Ruiha responded, her statement thick with sarcasm.

He continued to gawk up at her, confusion etched across his simple face, and asked, "how'd you get out here?" He paused briefly, glancing at the door Ruiha had just made her way out of. "And where are Omar and Xavier?" he asked, perplexed.

"I wouldn't worry about your friends. They're having a nice long *rest*." Ruiha explained, still on her guard.

"Friends," the man scoffed. "Those bastards don't have friends. They make me sail this boat for them. I'm hardly better than a slave!" Realising what he'd just said, he panicked and cautiously looked around. "Having a rest, you say? You don't reckon they heard me, do you?"

After seeing the genuine fear in his face following his misstep, Ruiha felt a little more at ease with the man. She went on to explain, "those two fools won't be bullying anyone again. Don't worry about that. What's your name?"

Gulping, and still not looking much at ease, the man said, "I'm Samir, but everyone just calls me Sam."

"Well, Sam, I'm Ruiha and I want you to take me to Lamos, please. I've got coin that I can pay you with, but you're also welcome to take anything from the bodies of Omar and Xavier as payment, and if this ship isn't yours already, consider it yours now. Deal?" she asked.

She knew the offer she'd just put on the table was more than likely far too generous, but she really was trying to turn over a new leaf, and she didn't want anything from the two brutes lying dead downstairs. She just wanted to forget them both and move on.

With his mouth opened in an 'O' shape, an astonished Sam nodded but struggled to remember how to speak the Vellhorian language, "erm, ah... erm. It's a boat..."

Ruiha furrowed her brow. "What in Vellhor's name are you talking about?" Ruiha responded.

"Erm, miss, it's not a ship, it's a boat. You called it a ship." Sam stammered.

"Listen Sam, I'm hungry, tired and I've got a blinding headache. I'm going to eat, and then I'm planning to sleep for the rest of the journey. Get me there safely, and our deal stands, okay?"

Not even waiting for Sam to respond, Ruiha turned around and started her search for food and sleep.

Ruiha

Ruiha knew that Sam had been contemplating waking her for some time now. He kept walking up to her sleeping form and hesitating, then he would turn away and carry out some chore instead. At some point during her sleep, he would have ventured into the small storage room and seen the aftermath of what she had done to Omar and Xavier. She wondered what his true feelings about that were. In her experience, those who engaged in illicit activities like smuggling often operated by their own moral code, one that didn't always align with conventional notions of trustworthiness.

Sam's occupation as a smuggler had already cast a shadow of doubt in her mind, but it was his response to the two thugs she had dispatched that offered a glimmer of reassurance. His fear of them hinted at his gratefulness, yet she couldn't help but shake the lingering shadows of doubt which always accompanied her when she met someone new.

As he reached out to nudge her awake, her hand shot out quicker that a viper, and grabbed his wrist in a vice like grip, causing him to freeze in fear. She opened one eye lazily and gazed at him. Finally, she released his trembling hand, and he stumbled backwards.

"We better be there, Sam, otherwise I'll be inclined to think you were trying to rob me... or worse," Ruiha looked at him with her eyebrow arched in suspicion.

"No.. no.. miss, nothing like that," Sam stuttered. "We'll be approaching the shores of Lamos in a few hours, and I thought I'd wake you to make sure you're ready to depart!"

"Good Sam, I knew I could trust you. Now tell me, have you got any coffee on this ship?"

"Sorry, but no coffee. Got nothing to heat the water with. And, err, miss, this isn't a ship, this is just a boat."

"What's the difference?" Ruiha enquired, "No, wait actually, I don't really care. Urgh, no damn coffee, that's a shame, I haven't had a proper coffee in weeks. Tell me then, where will we landing?"

"Unfortunately, we can't go to the city direct. The authorities check the vessels, and I'm assuming the reason you're on this boat is that you don't have any papers?"

"That's right Sam, I'm an illegal immigrant now." Ruiha sighed at the thought. "Well, how long will it take for me to get into the city from where you drop me?"

"Not long." Sam assured, "It will more than likely take you

a day or two. The road that leads from Lirate to Lamos along the coast is well travelled and in good order. I would suggest waiting at a tavern or an inn along the road and joining a group of travelers or merchants heading into the city. The authorities will be far less likely to question you if you're in a large group."

"Thanks for your advice, Sam. I won't forget it if we ever meet again," Ruiha expressed her gratitude, her words tinged with a sense of finality.

Sam regarded her with a furrowed brow, a silent question lingering in his gaze. Instead of responding immediately, he inquired, "What are you planning on doing when you get there, Ruiha?"

"You know something, Sam," Ruiha remarked, a faint smile playing on their lips, "that's the first time that you've used my name. Does that mean we're friends now?" Ruiha's smile faded somewhat before she continued, "honestly though, I have no idea, I just needed to get out of Sandara."

Sam gulped, "those men on horses, they butchered those people, all of them. They were after you." It was a statement and not a question, and Ruiha felt the guilt rise in her over witnessing Faisal decapitate Ari. She just nodded.

"Ruiha," Sam said, "I'd suggest heading to an inn called 'the Olive Tree,' my uncle owns it. He's a hard man to work for, and the inn isn't the nicest, but he'll be able to give you work and help get you on your feet. You helped me out with Omar and Xavier, I'd be working for them for the rest of my life, if you hadn't, erm,. sorted them out for me."

Smiling, Ruiha responded, "thanks Sam, I think I'll do that." They both sat there in silence, looking at the approaching shoreline of Lamos inch closer and closer. Eventually, Sam walked away and began preparing for their arrival.

As the boat's hull settled onto the sandy shores of Lamos,

Sam disembarked and skilfully secured the ropes in various places. Ruiha observed patiently, waiting for him to complete his tasks. Once satisfied that the small vessel wouldn't drift back to Sandara, Sam approached Ruiha. He pointed toward the north and said, "okay, walk north for a mile or so. You'll come to a large gravel road. Head west for another mile or two until you come to an inn. You'll be able to wait there for a company of travelers passing through."

    Reaching out her hand, she clasped his wrist. "Thanks Sam, I mean it. If you're ever in trouble, come find me at the Olive Tree." With that, she turned away and began walking northward.

9

SHADOWS OF LOSS

"In the darkest depths of grief, even the strongest heart can become enslaved to sorrow."

DAKARAI

*F*ire... somewhere, a part of Dakarai's senses registered the acrid, pungent odour of smoke. Distantly, he could also hear the faint sounds of screams too. Despite the fog clouding his mind, he automatically realized that there was danger around him. He opened his eyes and, in a panic, jumped out of his bed, all traces of the sleep he had been enjoying long forgotten.

On his way outside, he could feel his heart pounding against his ribcage. He could also feel a knot in the pit of his stomach. Unsure what the danger was, exactly, he went to grab his hammer and a knife from his tool cupboard, in case he needed them.

Because he had been working last night, he had no clue where his family was, amplifying the gnawing pit of anxiety in his gut. With worry for his family weighing heavily on his mind, he gingerly opened his front door, bracing himself for whatever awaited him on the other side.

The cloying smoke immediately stung his eyes, making them water. Rubbing them with the back of his scaled, clawed hand, he stepped out further into the underground street, which was dimly lit by light shafts which opened up, letting some weak natural light through. When he looked around, it shocked him to see the utter carnage which awaited him.

The air was thick with the deep grey smoke of distant fires, casting an ominous pall over the landscape. Bodies lay strewn across the scene, each one a testament to unspeakable violence. Some bore the gruesome mark of head injuries, others dangled lifelessly from posts, their bodies swaying gently. But most had met their end through stabbing or hacking.

Surveying the once-familiar surroundings, he couldn't escape the gut-wrenching realization that his neighbors were likely all dead. Many of the houses stood in ruins, evidence of looting and destruction. However, some, like Dakarai's, had been spared, more than likely because the attackers were in a rush to clear the area. Amid the devastation, a question nagged at the back of his mind: How had he slept through such horror?

Dakarai crouched low behind a waist-high stone wall, heart pounding in his chest, as a small band of Drogo Mulik arrogantly swaggered up the street. Each one adorned with a dark red cloth wrapped tightly around their muscular arms, a stark symbol against the backdrop of destruction. The air was thick with tension, and as Dakarai's eyes lingered on the blood-red fabric, a chilling realization took hold. They were from the Claw clan, and the blood-soaked cloth hinted at the gruesome butchery they had unleashed upon the Drogo from the Fang clan all around him.

It took a moment for the gravity of the situation to sink in. This was no ordinary raid—it was a devastating onslaught, unlike anything Dakarai had ever experienced or even heard of before.

Even as the Claw gang continued walking down the street and disappeared from his view, the echoes of their laughter and taunts lingered in the air. The sound of hacking and slashing continued, relentless, as they mercilessly attacked the undefended Drogo from his clan. None were spared from their brutality.

A young Drogo warrior from the Claw clan turned the corner at that moment, his reptilian face contorting into a gruesome smile as he spotted Dakarai. With a rush of blood lust, the warrior surged forward, his eyes widening with a predatory gleam. Dakarai instinctively stepped backward, but an unseen obstacle beneath his foot sent him tripping over.

Dakarai's heart pounded against his ribcage as he scrambled to regain his footing. The young warrior closed in, his sinister grin widening as he approached.

Cursing himself as he tried to regain his feet, Dakarai's hand landed on the thin pole-like object which had tripped him – an unexpected stroke of good luck. It was a spear. Good, he could use a spear, he thought. Grasping the wooden shaft in his large, scaled hand, he swiftly rose into a crouching position, bracing the end of the haft against his leather boot. As the blood-crazed Drogo warrior closed in, sword raised high above his head, Dakarai yanked the tip of the spear upward. The haft remained braced against his foot, but now the tip hovered about four feet off the ground, poised for defense.

As the warrior came hurtling towards Dakarai, his eyes suddenly widened in panic as the realization struck that he was moving too fast to stop in time. The spear, held firmly by Dakarai, met the charging warrior with a resounding impact. A moment of dreadful stillness hung in the air before the warrior's face contorted in agony. The leather armor offered no protection as the spear impaled him through the midsection, its unforgiving tip penetrating flesh and piercing his stomach.

Dakarai, caught in the midst of the unexpected turn, felt a surge of mixed emotions—relief, shock, and a grim determination as he grappled with the consequences of his actions.

Dakarai stood, grappling with the stubbornly lodged spear in his opponent, for a few tense moments. Despite his best efforts, the weapon refused to budge. The once-wailing warrior at the other end of the spear now lay still. Recognising the futility, Dakarai released the spear, letting it clatter to the ground. He cautiously stepped further into the street, his senses on high alert. The absence of both allies and enemies prompted him to scan the surroundings. The eerie silence weighed on him as he made his way up the street, cautiously heading in the same direction the small band of Claw warriors had disappeared, the lingering uncertainty hanging heavy in the air.

Dakarai knew that at the end of the street lay a courtyard, a once-bustling intersection where families gathered to draw fresh water from a small well. In the normal course of events, carts would line the courtyard, selling roasted lizard, fried insects, and other delicacies the Drogo loved. Today, as Dakarai gazed upon the courtyard, he witnessed a grim transformation. The carts lay upturned and aflame, the acrid scent of burning mingling with the stench of death. The lifeless bodies of the cart owners hacked to bits and callously discarded like old trash. A heavy silence hung in the air as Dakarai absorbed the gravity of the scene, his emotions a turbulent mix of sorrow, anger, and shock at the ruthless destruction of a once-thriving community space.

He noticed a commotion at the center of the courtyard. With caution, Dakarai crept up to an upturned cart, using it as cover. Peering over the side, he witnessed a scene that seemed to be drawn from the depths of the underworld.

Suspended a few feet in the air, at the heart of the courtyard, was Dakarai's son, Drakamor. Thick wooden beams and large rusty metal stakes pinned his arms in place. Dark blood stained his pale wrists and forearms, forming two chilling puddles beneath each outstretched hand. The air resonated with his agonized screams as flames from a small fire, kindled beneath him, mercilessly licked at his blackened scaled feet.

Dakarai's heart sank, and an indescribable anguish gripped him as he confronted the nightmarish reality unfolding before him. The courtyard, once a vibrant space, now stood as a stage for unspeakable horror.

Dakarai felt a sharp pang deep in the pit of his stomach, a tear welling in his eye as he looked up at the horrifying scene. A seething rage surged within him, thickening his blood as it coursed through his veins like slow-moving oil. With each heartbeat, he could sense the pulsing of that anger spreading through his entire being.

In that moment, without a plan or a clear idea of what lay ahead, Dakarai knew he would seek revenge for the unspeakable agony his son endured, regardless of the consequences to himself.

Turning away from the screams of his son, Dakarai desperately scanned the area for a way to help, but in reality he was looking for anything to distract him from the harrowing sight. It proved futile; the haunting cries still echoed in his ears. That's when he spotted her—his wife, Melagai—lying on a broken cart, bruised and bleeding from multiple wounds. A leather belt cruelly strapped around her neck held her down, and though she lay limp and unmoving, the laughter of a Claw warrior dismounting her pierced through the cacophony of pain and despair.

The eight warriors who had passed his house earlier were gathered around her, their laughter cutting through the air. Dakarai watched in seething silence as one of them spat at her, unbuckling his belt and lowering his trousers.

After witnessing his son's torture and the rape of his wife,

Dakarai's anger ignited like a red-hot flame. A high-pitched ringing drowned out all other sounds, and the world around him darkened. The vibrant colors of the courtyard took on a darker, more sinister hue, tinged with a deep red. The blood pumping through his veins burned and itched, but Dakarai was beyond feeling.

The vile scene before him pushed him to a breaking point where his own life ceased to matter. He wasn't thinking clearly; he didn't care. All that consumed him was the need to unleash the rage, the anger, and the death within him—for his family, for his friends and neighbors, for his clan.

In an instant, he stepped forward, hammer in his right hand, dagger in his left. A guttural scream of fury erupted from his lips. His rage hung thick and ominous in the air, a palpable force that seemed to defy the very essence of the courtyard.

As Dakarai approached the group, their expressions betrayed amusement rather than fear or concern. Words were exchanged, taunts perhaps, but Dakarai couldn't hear amidst the deafening rush of his own rage.

Without warning, they closed in on him, laughter and teasing filling the air, oblivious to the seething anger within Dakarai. One of them dared to get too close, offering a taunt that was lost on him. In response, Dakarai swung his hammer with brutal force, caving in the offender's head.

Spinning around, Dakarai seized the element of surprise, delivering a crushing blow with his hammer to another Drogo who had ventured too near. The impact splintered bone, blood, and brain matter, casting a gruesome spray in all directions.

His movements felt swifter and more precise than ever, as if his opponents were slogging through thick mud, their every motion sluggish in comparison. Dakarai had dispatched two of the group effortlessly, not even breaking a sweat.

The remaining adversaries closed in cautiously, aware of the threat but unwilling to back down. They hesitated, understanding that weakness could lead to immediate repercussions from their own leaders. Dakarai, fueled by a primal rage, was oblivious to their apprehension. He lunged forward with his dagger, thrusting it into an opponent's chest before stepping back, slashing and hacking in a frenzied display.

A fortuitous swing caught an opponent's arm, blood gushing from the severed artery. Yet, before he could revel in the moment, strong arms seized him from behind, and a club struck his head. The pain was a distant sensation as he retaliated, head-butting the Drogo holding him, teeth flying, and a muffled scream filling the air. Unfazed, Dakarai swung his hammer again, connecting with another opponent's head. The sickening sound would have horrified him under normal circumstances, but in the heat of battle, Dakarai was impervious to such things.

Although he couldn't feel it, Dakarai saw a sword cut through the muscle of his left forearm, and involuntarily, his dagger dropped from his grip. Cursing loudly, he sprinted toward the closest warrior wielding a large club, diving at him, the two grappling on the ground. Dakarai landed on top, hammering the weapon into the Drogo's face.

Quickly getting to his feet, he spotted two Drogo charging at him. Without hesitation, Dakarai screamed in rage, dropping his hammer as he ran straight at them. As he reached the attackers, he lunged into the closest one, hands outstretched and reaching for the neck. Their combined weight brought them crashing to the ground, and Dakarai used his brute strength to crush his windpipe, feeling it snap like a brittle tree branch in his hands.

Despite the blows raining down on him, Dakarai managed to stand again. He turned to the last attacker, roaring in defiance as he stepped forward. A heavy punch connected to his opponent's chin, making him stagger. Dakarai followed up with another punch to the top of the head, then one to the stomach. Eventually, the Drogo was on the ground, and Dakarai stood over him, his foot on the Drogo's neck. Without a hint of remorse, he crushed his opponent's neck underfoot.

A slow clapping brought Dakarai rushing back to reality. As he looked around, the gruesome scene he had wrought met his eyes. He couldn't recall every strike, but the crimson evidence on his hands and clothes irrevocably confirmed his deeds. His son, now silent and unmoving, hung from the wooden beam, and his wife lay limp on the cart.

A wave of fatigue and pain washed over Dakarai. His body was bruised, his head pounded, and he realized his hands and clothes were coated in the crimson blood of his fallen enemies. The rage threatened to bubble again, but he found himself drained, with nothing left to give.

Despite the desolation, Dakarai managed a weary smile. Slowly turning towards the source of the clapping, he anticipated another fight, expecting the sweet embrace of death.

"Well done, boy. I am Junak, chief of the Claw clan. Who are you?"

Dakarai looked at Junak, a colossal Drogo with reptilian eyes that held an amused expression, exuding a patronizing superiority familiar to the strong and powerful. Junak's massive frame, adorned with three small, curved horns evenly spaced on top of his head, loomed over Dakarai. He wore trousers made from a dark animal hide, revealing a bare, muscular torso adorned with a variety of metal piercings. Dark tattoos spiraled and swirled in complex patterns around his arms and chest. Across his back, Junak carried the largest axe Dakarai had ever seen.

Meeting Junak's gaze, Dakarai refused to betray any hint of fear or intimidation in his voice. "I am Dakarai," he responded, his tone steady, though his mind raced with thoughts and emotions in the face of the imposing chief.

"Well, Dakarai, you are strong, I have to admit. You have done well to defend the honor of your weak clan! I have not witnessed such strength in a long time. I feel it warrants recognition!"

Dakarai scanned the courtyard, his eyes falling upon the battered and bloodied women and children of his clan, lined up against the wall. "I want no recognition from you. A murderer of innocents!"

Junak smiled, a wry laugh escaping him. He nodded slowly, responding, "If a clan is too weak to protect itself, then I hold no issue with my actions. I am merely purging the weakness of our people. Today you showed great strength, and you will be rewarded for that."

"As I have already said, I do not want a reward. Kill me now and let me be at peace with the knowledge of a courageous death." Junak barked a sharp laugh at that.

"No, I cannot do that. Nergai has surely seen your strength today and would disapprove of me dishonoring it by rewarding you with death."

So a fanatic then, Dakarai thought to himself. He had known a few of the religious followers of Nergai from his time in the mines. Nergai, the God of the Drogo Mulik people, was said to have been banished to the underworld many centuries ago. Many believed his tomb to be located in the far eastern reaches of the Scorched Mountains, however, Dakarai struggled to believe it. The Drogo had lived in and explored the Scorched Mountains for centuries, and no sign of Nergal's final resting place had ever emerged.

"Do as you will then." He reached down on the floor and picked up a discarded spear. Hefting it in his right hand, he launched it with as much speed and power as he could muster.

It flew towards the Claw clan chief, who watched it with a broad smile on his face. At the last possible instant, Junak calmly moved his head to the side as the spear slammed into a young Drogo who was standing just behind him. Without giving the Drogo, who had taken his place in death a second thought, Junak strode over to Dakarai, a smile still beaming on his face. "Your spirit and strength are strong, Dakarai. You have earned yourself a place in my hall of servants. Congratulations."

10

A Potential Ally

'In the presence of your enemies, an ally becomes the axe which cuts through the darkness.'

Gunnar

Soon after their return to the barracks, Gunnar received a summons to report to General Wilfrid. He had discussed the situation with Karl during their journey back, and he had a fairly clear idea of what to convey to the General after Karl had provided him with the missing pieces from his memory.

"Sir, as you may already know, our patrol squad was ambushed near checkpoint sixty-two," Gunnar began, addressing the General. "Karl and I are the sole survivors of the attack."

General Wilfrid glared at Gunnar; anger etched across his face. Being a few inches shorter, he had to stare up slightly for his glare to reach Gunnar's eyes. Gunnar could see that his uncle's cheeks were a dark crimson behind his thick black beard.

"Explain, Section Leader, how you fucked up so profoundly!" General Wilfrid was shouting now, his voice booming through the room.

"Sir, with all due respect, I'm not sure how you believe we

fucked up," Gunnar replied, maintaining his composure. "We were ambushed in the middle of a chokepoint, and the assailants used Dwarven crossbows, may I add. Despite this, we managed to navigate the squad successfully through the chokepoint until…"

"Ah, yes, I suppose you're about to tell me about the *golem* now!" General Wilfrid scoffed.

Gunnar knew this would be a challenging explanation, especially since he had no personal recollection of the event. He could hardly believe it himself, let alone report it to his General. He had agreed with Karl to mention the golem in the report, but leave out Gunnar's direct involvement.

"Yes sir, however, before that, I was actually going to explain that we also had a serious fault with our SLS communicators and could not contact the other squads." Gunnar thought that reminding him that not only did the Drogo have Dwarven crossbows but also that their SLS had malfunctioned, seemed prudent.

General Wilfrid waved the concern away with a dismissive gesture. "Yes, well, malfunctions with kit are prone to happen when the Section Leader doesn't ensure they are properly maintained."

"Sir," Gunnar growled, his voice thick with aggression and his eyes glaring in fury at his General, "all squad leaders ensured their SLS communicators were in good working order prior to the patrol, as per protocol."

Wilfrid's tone grew cold and menacing. "Section Leader Gunnar. It pains me to have to do this. However, I believe that Sergeant Karl and yourself must have deserted the squad or even been complicit in the deaths of your squad members. I have no other option other than to place you both under arrest until we return to Draegoor and we can organize your court marshal." As he finished his sentence, the doors opened wide and four heavily armed Dwarves entered the room.

"Uncle, are you sure you truly want to go down this route?" Gunnar asked, giving the General an opportunity to change his mind.

"Gunnar, I have been waiting for this day since you were born." The four guards surrounded Gunnar then and drew their weapons.

"Lads, it doesn't have to go like this. Walk away, let me and the General finish our conversation and then we can put all of this behind us," Gunnar urged, hoping to avoid any unnecessary conflict.

One guard grunted at that and stepped forward, his short sword pointed towards Gunnar's face. Gunnar couldn't help thinking it was a bad move. The guard would have to pull his weapon back in order to thrust it, giving Gunnar both a pre-warning of his impending attack and the precious time to decide how to defend.

In a heartbeat, Gunnar swiftly moved to the side, allowing the guard's strike to go wide by several inches. Not wanting to kill the dwarf, Gunnar punched him hard in the side of his neck, just above the collarbone and to the side of his windpipe, hitting his carotid artery forcefully. The guard crumpled to the ground, unconscious but still alive, hopefully to wake later.

The other three guards hesitated for a moment, surprised by Gunnar's agility and decisive move. Gunnar quickly assessed the situation, his mind racing to find a way out of this confrontation without bloodshed.

The second guard, having learned from his companion's mistake, approached cautiously. Gunnar, anticipating the guard's move, remained poised and ready. As the guard hesitated, unsure of how to proceed, Gunnar seized the opportunity. The moment of hesitation was exactly what Gunnar was waiting for.

In a flash, Gunnar struck like a coiled serpent, launching a rapid barrage of blows at the dwarf. His first punch targeted the solar plexus, and despite being protected by his Dwarven armor, Gunnar's formidable strength left the guard gasping for air. The second strike found its mark on the dwarf's knee, shattering it with a sickening crunch. Before the guard could react, the third and final blow landed squarely on his chin, rendering him unconscious.

The final two guards approached together, as expected. Using a pincer movement to corner Gunnar, they approached from either side. Gunnar remained calm and kept an eye on them both as they slowly and cautiously approached.

Gunnar took a measured step backwards, not in fear, but to position himself closer to his uncle's desk, where he could see a large ornate inkwell. Reaching behind him, he took a hold of it and launched it just as the guard charged him. The inkwell shattered on the dwarf's temple, spilling the dark liquid everywhere and the dwarf crumpled to the floor.

The final guard looked at Gunnar and approached cautiously, his knuckles white from gripping the hilt of his axe so tightly. Just as Gunnar was about to attack, the guard's eyes flickered to Gunnar's right and he heard the creaking sound of a crossbow string being pulled back. As fast as lightning, Gunnar dived to the side at the same time as hearing a loud thud as the metal bolt hit the desk.

Looking up, he saw his uncle pointing the crossbow at him, a fierce snarl contorting his face. Gunnar shook his head in disappointment; he had hoped for better from Wilfrid, perhaps a sign of remorse, but instead, he was met with a snarl of hostility. Despite the pang of disappointment, Gunnar charged his uncle, barreling into him and knocking the wind out of his lungs. Wilfrid's head smacked the rock wall behind him before

A Potential Ally

he dropped to the floor.

Gunnar turned on the remaining dwarf then. "Listen, I have no quarrel with you. I'm innocent and have been falsely accused. If you come at me, I'll try not to kill you, but I promise you it will still hurt you. Throw your weapon down and I'll leave you be. You can tell the others that I disarmed you, and they'll believe you."

The dwarf looked relieved before quickly throwing his axe to the ground. "Just so you know, Gunnar, I believe that you're innocent. There's no way that you would've betrayed your squad."

Grateful for the dwarf's sentiment, Gunnar nodded in acknowledgment, though his mind raced with urgency. There was no time to linger on pleasantries; every moment counted in their current situation. With a sense of purpose driving him forward, he swiftly exited the room, his focus fixed on the task ahead.

Gunnar

As Gunnar darted out of his uncle's office, a wave of uncertainty engulfed him. He knew he needed to figure things out, and removing himself from his uncle's influence was his first step toward doing that.

His uncle had all but admitted wanting him out of the picture. It raised some serious questions in Gunnar's mind about how and where the Drogo had acquired the crossbows. It also made Gunnar wonder why the SLS wasn't functioning and why his unit, of all the units available to Wilfrid, had been sent on a final patrol two days before they were due to rotate back home.

"Too many coincidences," Gunnar mused inwardly, his father's teachings echoing in his mind. His father's wisdom had ingrained in him the notion that a single stroke of bad luck might be dismissed as mere happenstance, perhaps even twice, but a third occurrence hinted at something darker—a deliberate betrayal. As he contemplated the unfolding events, Gunnar couldn't shake the feeling that all signs pointed to Wilfrid's treachery.

As Gunnar reflected on his relationship with Wilfrid, he couldn't deny the strain that had always lingered between them. His father, Erik, had appointed Wilfrid as General of the Army, seemingly as a means to placate him and remove him from the city's political landscape. Gunnar had long sensed an undercurrent of jealousy from Wilfrid, a feeling exacerbated by the appointment. Yet, he had never imagined Wilfrid would act upon it. In Gunnar's mind, Wilfrid's resentment had merely seemed like the petty grievances of a jealous dwarf, nothing more.

It had become apparent that Wilfrid had now acted upon his simmering discontent, igniting the flames of rebellion or perhaps a coup. His manipulation of the Drogo conflict to further his agenda branded him a traitor in Gunnar's eyes. Gunnar couldn't ignore the fact that if Wilfrid emerged victorious, he would hold the power to shape the narrative as he saw fit. After all, history is typically written by the victors, and Wilfrid had already made attempts to paint Gunnar as the villain.

While coups weren't entirely unheard of in Dwarven history, they remained exceptionally rare occurrences. Most Dwarves regarded subterfuge and deception as acts of cowardice. In their society, if a dwarf had grievances with the ruling chief, be it Erik or any other clan leader, they traditionally opted for a straightforward approach. Regardless of their station within Dwarven society, they would confront the leader, demanding either change or a satisfactory explanation. It had always been that simple.

A Potential Ally

Dwarves, as a rule, despised the intricacies of politics and the accompanying deceit. However, like in any society, there were exceptions—Dwarves like Wilfrid, who clung to their jealousy and chose a different, more backhanded path.

Gunnar knew individuals like Wilfrid were resolute about tying up loose ends to prevent future complications. This line of thought led him to consider another loose end – Karl. Gunnar couldn't help but wonder about Karl's fate, what Wilfrid might have done to him, if anything at all. Since Gunnar was Wilfrid's primary target, it was possible that he hadn't yet had the opportunity to deal with Karl.

Gunnar recognized Karl held vital knowledge that could help him piece together the events of the past twenty-four hours, particularly the battle with the golem. As far as Gunnar could establish, he had employed some form of magic to defeat the monstrous creature. However, it was common knowledge that apart from craft magic inherent in all dwarves, they couldn't wield any other type of magic. This revelation left Gunnar confused and slightly concerned, and he was equally uncertain about how his fellow dwarves would react to his seemingly newfound abilities.

Navigating the labyrinthine network of underground tunnels that connected Fort Bjerg, Gunnar resolved to retrieve Karl before departing. That decision carried undeniable risk, he knew; returning to the barracks was a dangerous and potentially unwise thing to do. Nevertheless, Karl had been more than a comrade; he was like a brother, and Gunnar needed to protect him.

Gunnar took a sharp turn, choosing the less-travelled tunnels to approach the barracks discreetly. As he drew nearer, caution became paramount. He couldn't be certain who Wilfrid had managed to enlist as allies, and it was a safe assumption that any unit under Wilfrid's command would obediently follow his orders. He was under no illusions that anyone held any loyalty to him.

Drawing near to the barracks housing the Snow Wolves, Gunnar's keen ears picked up the muted echoes of heated shouts. His eyes widened as he watched a large group of armed soldiers converging around the building's sole entrance, a passageway masterfully carved into the ancient mountain by skilled Dwarven miners.

Remaining concealed and avoiding detection became his main focus as he inched closer, striving to understand the unfolding situation. It soon became clear that the Dwarven soldiers were demanding the surrender of the alleged traitors from the Snow Wolves, despite them knowing that Gunnar was surely not there. It was evident that his comrades were not complying, however.

As Gunnar surveyed the tense standoff, a mix of emotions surged within him. Pride swelled as he witnessed his unit standing resolute against the commands of a traitor. Yet, beneath that pride lurked a gnawing worry that Wilfrid might resort to extreme measures in response to their defiance. From the shadows, Gunnar silently weighed his options, considering how best to support his comrades from his concealed position outside. Amidst the tension, his admiration soared as Dreynas's elite warriors swiftly took down an entire squad, their efficiency a testament to their skill and training.

The operation unfolded with a stunning display of precision and professionalism that filled Gunnar with immense pride. It was executed with the finesse of a perfectly choreographed training session. Twenty warriors rushed out, clad in armor and wielding large shields to forcefully drive the soldiers back. Another group of twenty followed closely behind, wielding batons to incapacitate the soldiers. They swiftly subdued their opponents, efficiently grabbing them and escorting them back into the barracks as hostages. In a matter of mere minutes, the maneuver was complete, leaving no fatalities on either side. It was a breathtaking spectacle, completely catching Wilfrid's troops off guard.

Another team of soldiers replaced the incapacitated soldiers within minutes, and in the face of the Wilfrid's relentless reinforcements, Gunnar's mind raced with a surge of urgency. His heart pounded, a mix of adrenaline and fear coursing through his veins as he assessed the dire situation. The sheer disparity in numbers between his squad and Wilfrid's forces sent a shudder of urgency through him, a stark reminder of the daunting odds they faced.

Despite the overwhelming challenge ahead, Gunnar couldn't allow himself to stand idly by while his comrades faced such formidable opposition. His jaw clenched with determination as he wrestled with the weight of responsibility pressing down on him. The lives of his fellow Dwarves hung in the balance, and he knew that decisive action was imperative.

Recalling Karl's hints about manipulating time or enhancing his speed, Gunnar felt a faint glimmer of hope flicker within him. The memory of their previous encounter with the golem stirred something deep within him—a sense of untapped potential, a latent power waiting to be unleashed.

With a resolute resolve, Gunnar steeled himself for the daunting task ahead. Despite the odds stacked against them, he couldn't afford to falter now. The fate of his comrades and the future of their clan rested on his shoulders, and he was determined to rise to the challenge, whatever the cost.

Closing his eyes, Gunnar focused in an attempt to manipulate the flow of time. He concentrated on willing the surrounding Dwarves to slow down, but nothing changed. Frustration crept in, and he shifted his approach, this time attempting to accelerate himself beyond his normal limit. He took slow, deliberate breaths, desperately wishing for unnatural speed. However, as he opened his eyes and moved his hands in front of him, there was no discernible difference. His surroundings and movements remained locked in the normal flow of time, in sync with the Dwarves encircling the barracks.

He let out a heavy sigh. In frustration, he wondered at his own sanity. Did he truly believe that he had magical powers? No dwarf in Dreynas could manipulate time magic, so he had no right to think that he could, surely. He knew what Karl believed, but maybe Karl had been wrong. Had confusion and fear overtaken his rational thinking? Surely not. Karl was a seasoned warrior experienced in maintaining his composure in dire situations. Despite his current frustrations, Gunnar couldn't shake the feeling that something important *had* occurred, even if he couldn't grasp the full extent of it.

Shifting his focus back to the entrance, Gunnar's determination persisted, and he tried to catch a glimpse of an ally within. He considered the possibility of creating a distraction to allow the Snow Wolves to fight their way out. While his unit bore undoubtedly the kingdom's finest fighters, possessing superior training, experience, and skills compared to Wilfrid's troops, their numerical disadvantage and reluctance to harm fellow Dwarves made the plan exceedingly risky. It would more than likely lead to substantial casualties among the Snow Wolves. Recognising the urgency of the situation, Gunnar knew he needed an another plan quickly.

Gunnar scanned the rocky terrain which surrounded the barracks. Jagged crags and rocky outcroppings jutted out at irregular intervals, casting shadowed recesses from the lamps and torches below. Although the mountain wall rose almost vertically, Gunnar's keen eyes noticed several locations in the rock wall that would pose significant problems for Wilfrid's troops if a well-placed landslide were to occur. In his mind, he weighed up the advantages of creating a small avalanche somehow.

Turning his attention to the base of the rock wall, he began searching for a way to climb up to the first outcropping of rock. Although he spotted some holds and nooks which would lead up to his desired destination, the climb was exceedingly dangerous, and, more importantly, the risk of being spotted was far too high. He would be in complete view of Wilfrid's troops. A heavy sigh escaped him as he wished for the rock to simply fall and provide the cover he needed.

As Gunnar stood dejected looking at the mountain wall, an unusual sensation overtook him, starting as a subtle tingling but quickly escalating into a full-body tremor. His legs grew weak, and he struggled to maintain his balance. Panic surged within him as an inexplicable pressure built up, seeming to originate somewhere deep within him, somewhere in his chest or stomach. He couldn't quite discern exactly where.

Attempting to steady himself, Gunnar leaned against the mountain's rugged surface. The moment his hand made contact with the stone, he felt an unexpected surge of energy course through him. Despite his disorientation, he sensed an unusual connection with the rock, as if veins of power ran through the very heart of the mountain itself.

Summoning his will, he followed one of these veins, tracking it through the mountainside. It shot away in the opposite direction of his desired outcropping. A vague outline of an idea began to form in his mind. Again, he exerted his will, tracking a vein of power and compelling it to obey him, redirecting its course toward the target. He had no idea what he was doing, or how he was doing it, but it seemed to be working so he continued. As he felt his power converge on the chosen location, he released it, envisioning an explosive rockslide.

Nothing happened. Well, that wasn't quite true, actually. Suddenly, instead of the landslide he was hoping for, he felt his power recoil, shooting back towards him, launching him backwards several paces into a large boulder.

When Gunnar found his senses again, his head was groggy, the muscles in his body ached, and his arms were completely numb. He had a sharp, metallic taste in his mouth which threatened to make him vomit. He pulled out his waterskin and downed a quarter of it in an attempt to rid his mouth of the foul taste.

Painstakingly, he massaged some feeling back into his arms and shook his head vigorously to clear his mind. Slowly, he inched his way back to his vantage point overlooking the barracks. Despite the physical discomfort and disorientation, a sense of relief washed over him. This time, he hadn't lost his memory as he had during his previous, inadvertent use of his newfound abilities.

Gunnar carefully surveyed the scene once more, noting that not much time seemed to have passed since he'd been thrown into the stone wall. The same team of soldiers remained positioned outside the barracks, still in approximately the same locations as they had been before.

His eyes shifted to the outcropping he had attempted to dislodge. Reluctance washed over him as he recalled the painful and fruitless outcome of his first attempt. Gunnar hesitated to try again, wary of the potential consequences and the unknown limits of his newfound abilities.

Gunnar's recent experiences had led him to the conclusion that he must possess some form of magical ability – either that, or he was, in fact, losing his mind. Although these abilities remained beyond his control or comprehension, he couldn't help but wonder at the extent of this power and its limits.

A Potential Ally

The mere thought of commanding abilities similar to those of the formidable Elves filled him with a hint of excitement. He had studied the Elves enough to know that they were renowned for their mastery of magic. The mere thought of tapping into such powers ignited his imagination, envisioning the things he could achieve for Dreynas if he could master and control these abilities. He even considered whether his father would allow him to abdicate from becoming chief., a role he had always secretly dreaded.

Gunnar's thoughts turned to the Elves and their unparalleled affinity for magic, a fact he had learned during his extensive studies. Unlike the other races in Vellhor, the Elves possessed a unique ability to seamlessly utilize every known type of magic. In contrast, humans, for instance, typically had an affinity for only one aspect of magic, and even then, their powers paled in comparison to those of the Elves.

Gunnar struggled to recall the intricate details of the Vellhorian magical systems he had once studied. To be honest with himself, although he had possessed a firm grasp of the information, he had never encountered a practical need to apply it. Dwarves and the Drogo, his primary concerns until now, were not known for their magical prowess. Consequently, he had largely let the knowledge slowly slip away.

Gunnar's thoughts led him to the notion of manipulating time, a form of magic he recognized as time magic. He recalled that time magic involved the intricate manipulation and alteration of the flow of time itself. Gunnar also recalled that mastering time magic was notoriously challenging. Most instances of success in this domain were often purely accidental and fraught with unintended, often perilous consequences – he knew the truth of that first-hand. Only the elves had truly mastered the magical manipulation of time, cementing their reputation as unparalleled across Vellhor.

Gunnar thought more about the elemental magic he had inadvertently tapped into when connecting with the rock in the mountain. Elemental magic involved the manipulation of the fundamental elements—air, fire, earth, water, and aura. It was regarded as one of the simplest forms of magic to master, with many humans exhibiting an affinity for at least one element.

Considering the elements, Gunnar tried to devise a plan. Water and air were impractical deep within the mountain's confines. Fire was too hazardous and could lead to unintended consequences. He was adamant about not causing harm to the Dwarven soldiers. He was not a murderer, and it would only add weight to Wilfrid's accusations of treason. As for the aether, he didn't really understand what it was, effectively ruling it out as a viable option.

As he crouched there, deep in thought, Gunnar's instincts kicked in with a split-second warning. He realized only moments before it occurred that his hand had been forced. A crossbow bolt hurtled toward him, and his lightning-quick reaction allowed him to dodge it by a mere inch, narrowly avoiding a potentially lethal blow. Gunnar cursed himself for being seen, swiftly adjusting his position to secure better cover while maintaining a clear line of sight to Wilfrid's soldiers.

Gunnar peered out from behind the rock, a sense of impending doom settling in as he observed the soldiers swiftly organising themselves into formation, their determined gazes fixed upon him. Fifteen fully armed soldiers, arranged in three formidable rows, broke away from their duties at the barracks' entrance and began marching purposefully toward his position. The odds were stacked against him, and he understood the grim reality—he couldn't engage these Dwarves in combat and hope to emerge victorious. Gunnar needed a new plan, and he needed it quickly.

A Potential Ally

Gunnar watched as the soldiers halted their advance just ten paces away from him, their synchronized weapon strikes against their shields, reverberating with a deafening boom inside the mountain. In a well-practised maneuver, they transitioned into a defensive formation, raising their shields protectively before them. From their ranks emerged a lone dwarf who stepped forward, his voice firm.

"Gunnar Eriksson," the dwarf called out. "Step forward and surrender for questioning. Refusal will leave us with no alternative but to engage in combat, and we shall not hesitate to use lethal force." The gravity of the situation hung heavily in the air, and Gunnar knew he had to make a decision. He hoped against hope he had made the right one.

Reluctantly, Gunnar emerged from behind the protective cover of the rock. He dropped his weapons to the ground with a clatter and raised his hands high above his head to signal his lack of threat. With each slow, deliberate step forward, he approached the waiting soldiers, making his intention to surrender clear.

Gunnar was shocked to recognize the dwarf who had stepped forward as the same one who had permitted him to leave Wilfrid's office earlier. Gunnar would have sworn that he saw the dwarf smiling at him, but when he did a double-take, all he saw was his somber face. A moment of optimism and hope briefly kindled within him. However, the moment was cruelly brief. Without warning, a fist-sized rock hurtled toward him, striking him with brutal force and causing him to collapse to the ground unconscious like a sack of potatoes.

11

Prophecy Unbound

'As the seasons change, so do the fortunes of family; the return of a long-lost kin is the blossoming of an overdue spring.'

Anwyn

Once Anwyn awoke from her sleep, she felt invigorated, which shocked her somewhat given the events of the previous day. Her body thrummed with a raw energy, a power so strong that it was almost difficult to contain within her. She swung her legs over the side of her bed and stood up, expecting the weariness and aches from the previous day's battle to show their signs. However, she felt nothing other than a renewed strength in her limbs. Her muscles felt stronger than they had ever felt before.

When Anwyn left her room and entered the kitchen, she immediately noticed the absence of her parents. She walked outside and wondered around the clearing where the battle had taken place, pleased to see that her mother had cleared away the bodies. Although there was little to be done about the blood-soaked grass and broken tree branches scattered all over the place, she supposed that the forest would deal with that in her own way, given time.

After not being able to find her parents, a pang of worry stabbed at her chest and she hurried back inside the cottage to have a better look. Racing into the kitchen, she saw evidence they had recently been there, the smell of broadleaf tobacco and herbal tea still fresh in the air. Her mother's shoes were under the table, her father's shirt crumpled and thrown into the corner.

She burst into the bedroom and immediately regretted her decision. Her cheeks turned a fiery shade of red as she stumbled upon one of the most awkward and disturbing scenes she had ever witnessed in her life.

Caught off guard by their daughter's sudden intrusion, Laoch and Eira hastily disentangled themselves from their intimate embrace and flailed in opposite directions. Her mother tumbled to the floor, completely naked. Laoch, in a bid to assist his wife, only managed to make matters worse. Struggling to get out of bed because of his injuries and embarrassed by his own nakedness, he stumbled and ended up falling on top of Eira.

Anwyn didn't attempt to help either of them. Instead, she spun on her heels and fled the room, closing the door behind her, wondering whether her mother had a memory alteration potion hidden away somewhere in the cottage.

Anwyn was sitting at the kitchen table with a pot of freshly brewed tea in front of her, attempting to read a book when her parents emerged from their bedroom. Their faces sported expressions of sheepish guilt, much like two children caught red-handed in the middle of a prank. Eira, the first to sit down, greeted Anwyn with a warm smile, while Laoch struggled to find a comfortable position to sit. Anwyn, ever the dutiful daughter, stood and offered her assistance. Once they were all seated, she turned her gaze to her father.

"I hope your injuries are healing well, father," she began, a hint of playful sarcasm in her tone. "And that you two haven't made them worse with your bedroom *physiotherapy*..." Eira sputtered in astonishment, while Laoch couldn't contain his laughter at Anwyn's comment. He looked at his daughter, who was doing her best to maintain a stern expression, though a mischievous smile threatened to break through at any second.

"Anwyn, my dear," Eira began, "your father and I... well, we thought we had lost each other. I'm sorry you had to witness that, but we were so caught up by our emotions and passion that we, well, I suppose you know the rest..."

"Mother!" Anwyn cried, "alright, I understand, and I've heard enough. Can we please move away from this subject now?" She pleaded.

Eira nodded, her cheeks still slightly tinged with embarrassment. "Yes, of course dear, I just felt that we owed you an explanation."

"Explanation fully received and understood. Now, can we please move on?" Anwyn begged.

Laoch spoke again after recovering from his bout of laughter. "How are you feeling love, has your spirit recovered somewhat? You looked drained a few hours ago, but now your spirit looks restored."

"Surprisingly, I feel better than I have ever felt before. My spirit feels stronger, my strength increased and I have more energy than ever!"

"That's truly remarkable, my dear. As Seishinmori, these qualities are almost a given, yet since no living elf has ever crossed paths with one, the true scope of your abilities remains a mystery. The legends about the Seishinmori's extraordinary powers are plentiful, but alas, legend is all they are." Laoch replied.

Eira pressed on, "Anwyn, when your grandfather left us, he left behind something intended for the Seishinmori, should they ever be found. To be honest, we weren't certain if his prophecy would ever come true, and he's been missing ever since. If you can't decipher or even unlock it, our assistance will be limited."

Anwyn nodded, "I understand, mother. What is it he wanted me to have?" She felt strange acknowledging that she had actually been named as Seishinmori. However, she knew that she would have to get used to the fact.

From the storeroom, Eira retrieved a cylindrical tube made of supple brown leather, typically used for storing scrolls, and presented it to Anwyn.

As Anwyn took the tube in her hand, her fingers brushed over the smooth leather, tracing the edges with a sense of reverence. Inside her mind, a whirlwind of thoughts stirred. Was this really it? The artifact she had been searching for, hidden in plain sight? The surface felt cool against her skin, yet beneath that calm exterior, she could almost feel a faint thrum of power, like a heartbeat echoing through the leather.

As she ran her thumb over the runes, a surge of excitement mingled with apprehension. Each delicate symbol seemed to pulse beneath her touch, as if awakening from a long slumber. What secrets did they hold? What ancient knowledge lay waiting to be unlocked? Anwyn couldn't help but feel a shiver of anticipation ripple down her spine, mingling with the tingling sensation in her fingertips.

Part of her wanted to delve deeper, to decipher the hidden meaning behind the arcane script. But another part hesitated, wary of the consequences that such knowledge might bring. For now, she contented herself with simply tracing the runes, committing them to memory with a sense of awe and wonder.

The rune system employed by Alden, her grandfather, had its roots based on the connection between the forest and the four seasons. It consisted of four distinct runes, each meticulously crafted to symbolise a specific tree and its associated season.

Once, this long-forgotten system bore immense significance to the high Elves of ancient times. These runes amplified their connection to the natural world, enabling them to better communicate with animals, plants, and other forest entities. Each rune would serve as a catalyst for specific spells or rituals, and by garnering an understanding of the trees and seasons, these spells and rituals were given unparalleled power.

Regrettably, with the passage of time, the knowledge of inscribing and deciphering these runes had been forgotten, deemed obsolete in the modern Elven era. Yet despite this, as if guided by some innate wisdom, Anwyn found herself with the ability to comprehend their intricate language, breathing life back into a long-lost language.

The first rune, intricately carved, seemed to whisper its tale as she traced its lines. It captured the essence of the spruce tree during winter's purest embrace. As she concentrated, the air around her felt cooler, almost as if she could sense the crispness of a snow-covered forest. The spruce rune radiated purity, clarity, and unwavering focus, much like a landscape cloaked in pristine snow.

She moved to the second rune, its symbols more robust, reflecting the venerable oak tree basking in the warmth of summer. As her fingers brushed over the rune, she could almost feel the sun's golden rays warming her skin. The oak rune resonated with might, endurance, and steadfast protection, embodying the colossal oak tree, an emblem of unyielding strength.

Each rune, with its distinct story and powerful symbolism, drew Anwyn deeper into the ancient wisdom they held, their meanings unfolding before her eyes like a vivid tapestry of nature's cycles.

The next rune, etched with meticulous care, depicted the

holly tree, thriving in the midst of summer's embrace. As Anwyn studied the rune, she felt a surge of warmth, as if the summer sun itself were casting its protective light over her. The holly rune bestowed its protective mantle, emboldening her with courage and bravery, much like the resilience found in the holly tree's prickly leaves that withstand even the harshest elements.

The fourth and final rune heralded the spirit of the alder tree during spring's awakening. The symbols seemed to pulse with life, and Anwyn could almost sense the freshness of spring air and the scent of blooming flowers. The alder rune embodied growth, rejuvenation, and the boundless promise of fresh beginnings. Its energy mirrored the vitality of new shoots pushing through the earth's surface, embracing a new life with each passing moment.

Upon reading the final rune, the cap on the tube opened with a satisfying pop. The rush of stale air caught her off guard, and her nose wrinkled instinctively at the musty odour that escaped. In that moment, the vibrant aura of magic she had sensed moments before seemed to vanish into thin air, leaving behind only a sense of emptiness in its wake. Anwyn couldn't help but feel a pang of disappointment, as if a door she had been on the brink of opening had suddenly slammed shut.

But despite the absence of magical energy, her hands trembled with a mixture of anticipation and trepidation as she carefully unfurled the scroll within. Each movement was deliberate, as if she were afraid that any sudden motion might cause the fragile parchment to crumble to dust in her grasp.

Her heart raced with a fervour that matched the fluttering of the parchment beneath her fingertips. What secrets lay hidden within these ancient words? What knowledge had been preserved for generations, waiting for *her* to uncover its mysteries? Anwyn could hardly contain her curiosity as she laid the scroll out on the worn surface of the kitchen table, her voice steady but tinged with excitement as she began to read aloud, eager for her parents to share in the discovery.

> *"In a kingdom where anger's fires burn so bright,*
> *Beware the rage, a perilous blight.*
> *From fury's depths, a dragon king shall rise,*
> *His malevolent power, will reign from the skies.*
>
> *This prophecy warns of this dire fate,*
> *When anger's tempests unleash their hate.*
> *In the darkest hour, the world is in despair,*
> *Two pure spirits shall rise, beyond compare.*
>
> *This hope is a light in the darkest night,*
> *And a forbidden love, their spark will ignite.*
> *Two hearts entwined, their love concealed,*
> *Yet their union, a destiny revealed.*
>
> *From different lands, they'll hail and strive,*
> *Their love forbidden, yet they'll survive.*
> *In their union, a power untold,*
> *A story of love, forever extolled.*
>
> *In a world divided, torn by hate,*
> *Their love shall conquer, seal their fate.*
> *The prophecy tells, their love's embrace,*
> *Shall bring the world a lasting grace.*
>
> *In the hour of need, they'll rise to the fore,*
> *A beacon of hope, forevermore.*
> *With courage and strength, their power shall unfold,*
> *The chosen ones, their stories told."*

As the final syllables of her grandfather's prophecy fell from her lips, Anwyn felt a whirlwind of emotions swirl within her, each one vying for dominance. There was awe, tinged with a hint of fear, as the weight of those ancient words settled heavily upon her shoulders. It was as if the entirety of her family's legacy, their hopes and dreams, had been condensed into those few, powerful sentences, and now rested squarely upon her.

Yet amidst the tumult of emotions, a sense of clarity emerged. This was not just a revelation; it was a summons—an unmistakable call to action that resonated deep within her soul. The realization washed over her like a tidal wave, leaving her breathless yet exhilarated in its wake.

In that moment, Anwyn felt a fierce determination welling up from the depths of her being, a resolve to meet the challenge laid out before her head-on. The forest had chosen her for a purpose; she realized—a purpose greater than anything she had ever dared to imagine. And as that truth sank in, a thrill unlike anything she had ever known coursed through her veins, igniting a fire within her that burned brighter than any star in the night sky. It was as if the very essence of the forest had intertwined with her own, binding her to a destiny she couldn't ignore.

As each beat of her heart resounded, Anwyn felt the readiness to embrace whatever trials and tribulations awaited her. With each passing moment, her resolve grew stronger. She understood that her path had been determined, and she would encounter challenges and uncertainties along the way. However, the prophecy had bestowed upon her a precious gift: the knowledge that her actions would determine the fate of Vellhor.

Anwyn closed her eyes for a moment, taking a deep breath to steady her racing heart. As she exhaled slowly, she visualized herself in control, confident, and ready to take on this exhilarating challenge. With each breath, her heart began to steady, and she found a sense of peace within herself. Anwyn knew that this moment of tranquility would be crucial for her to gather the courage needed to take the plunge into the unknown Slowly opening her eyes, she remembered that her mother and father were sitting at the table, both of them looking at her, waiting for her to say something.

"I have to leave to find the Sacred Tree." she murmured softly.

In the realm of Luxyyr, the legend of the Sacred Tree, which was said to cradle the spirit of the forest within her, was known to every Elf. The Sacred Tree was said to be a conduit for ancient wisdom, allowing the Elves to tap into the collective knowledge of the natural world and the trees. Without any further knowledge of what she was to do next, finding the Sacred Tree seemed like the most prudent move.

The conundrum, however, lay in the fact that nobody possessed the knowledge of its precise location. This sacred entity had become an enigmatic tale, a myth, and for Anwyn, the elusive whereabouts of the tree could put a stop to her fated journey before she even left her cottage.

Laoch and Eira exchanged a knowing look, a silent understanding passing between them. Eira gracefully rose from her seat and turned her gaze towards the storeroom, the place where she safeguarded her cherished collection of books. As she delved into the cluttered shelves, her fingers danced lightly across ancient tomes and dusty scrolls, searching for the one she sought.

Moments stretched into minutes, but Eira's determination was unwavering. Finally, she let out a triumphant sigh of relief. Clutching a particular tome close to her chest, she made her way back to the kitchen table, her steps infused with purpose.

"Another of your grandfather's legacies," Eira began, her voice carrying the weight of familial history. "This book, Anwyn, may not unveil the exact whereabouts of the Sacred Tree, but it contains his theories and speculations. Within its pages lie several locations your grandfather believed could be the location of the Sacred Tree. It may take us time to narrow them down, but we will find it."

Anwyn's eyes sparkled with hope as she accepted the book from her mother. It was a precious gift, a glimmer of possibility in her quest.

"Thank you, Mother," Anwyn whispered, her fingers tracing the book's weathered spine. She hoped that within those pages, the answers she sought would be waiting to be discovered.

Laoch's voice broke the silence in the room as he cleared his throat, a solemn expression etched upon his face. "And what of the remaining words in the prophecy?" he enquired, his gaze shifting between his wife and his daughter. "It is clearly the same prophecy Alden spoke of before embarking on his journey. The prophecy that foretells of the greatest war Vellhor has ever borne witness to. But who, in the name of Vellhor, is this Dragon King? Dragons have not graced the skies of Vellhor for millennia; their whereabouts are lost to time itself, their disappearance a mystery that alludes even the High Elves of the Council."

Eira's focus seemed to be on the significance of the Sacred Tree rather than the illusive dragon king like Laoch's was. Anwyn, however, had picked up on a more alarming part of the prophecy which seemed to have escaped her parents' minds.

This hope is a light in the darkest night,
And a forbidden love, their spark will ignite.
Two hearts entwined, their love concealed,
Yet their union, a destiny revealed.

What in the name of Vellhor did that mean? Was she supposed to fall in love? It seemed integral to the prophecy, which mentioned this 'forbidden love' multiple times. She aired her question to her parents.

Whilst Laoch frowned at her, his scowl showing what he thought of someone trying to prize his only daughter away from him, her mother had a wistful smile on her face and responded lightly, "Anwyn dear, that can only mean one thing." Her smile widened, and she continued, "it looks as though you too will find someone who loves you as much as your father loves me!"

At that, her father's scowl softened ever so slightly for a brief moment before returning. "All I can say about that, Anwyn dear, is that this elf better show you the utmost respect! As Seishinmori, you are the rightful Queen of Elves. Do not forget that!"

Anwyn blushed and decided it was time to move the conversation forward and away from the prospect of her future love. However, she did briefly consider what – *'from different lands, they'll hail and strive'* – could have meant.

"We need to find the Sacred Tree" Anwyn pressed, "I will read through Grandfather's notes with mother, and we can try to discern our first location. Father, will you pack away as much as you can and prepare Honey, please? I would like to leave at first light tomorrow."

Unbeknownst to her, Anwyn's natural leadership had taken over, and she blushed as she added, "Um, please, Father, if it's not too much trouble."

Her father chuckled and responded, "A true Seishinmori! Issuing orders to your own parents!"

Anwyn's blush deepened further, and she continued to apologise to her father, who simply waved away her apology with his hand and a fond smile.

Anwyn

Laoch was seeing to the preparations for their departure, his earlier injuries still visible in his movements, when he came to an abrupt halt. His eyes fixated on the door, brows knitting together in apprehension. Anwyn, noticing her father's change in demeanor, swiveled her head to follow his gaze, and before she could react, a thunderous, echoing knock sent shivers down their spines, instantly drawing all of their attention.

Anwyn swiftly conjured a large fireball, cradling it between her palms, ready to unleash its fiery power at a moment's notice. Beside her, Eira summoned swirling masses of wind, each the size of a pebble, and took a vigilant stance. Meanwhile, Laoch hurried to the storage room to retrieve his weapons, his years as a warrior evident in his firm and steady demeanor.

Three more knocks resonated through the room before Laoch's commanding voice rang out, "State your name and the purpose of your visit!" His words were unwavering, a reflection of his seasoned warrior's resolve.

"My, my, what a welcome this is. I'd almost be inclined to guess that you didn't want to see me!" a soft, playful voice echoed from behind the closed door.

Laoch and Eira exchanged bewildered glances, their eyes wide with surprise and confusion. Eira's attack dissolved into the air, and she dashed toward the door, her heart pounding with hope. "Father, is it really you?" she cried out, her emotions in turmoil. Laoch, however, remained resolute, his sword still in hand, ready for any treachery.

With haste, Eira flung open the door and gazed up at the figure before her. Her father stood there, arms open wide as if ready to embrace her, a mischievous smile gracing his face. She hadn't seen him in nearly fifty long years, and after a brief moment of shock and disbelief, she fell into his waiting arms, tears of joy streaming down her cheeks.

After several heartwarming moments during which father and daughter shared an emotional embrace, they reluctantly broke apart. Alden, still wearing his beaming smile, strode into the room and walked up to Laoch, his warm disposition undeterred. With genuine affection, he enveloped Laoch in a tight embrace. Laoch, though his face remained impassive, hesitantly returned the gesture.

"Laoch, what a sight for sore eyes you are! It has been far too long!" Alden exclaimed with heartfelt sincerity. "I trust you have been looking after my daughter in my absence? Of course, you have! She had you well and truly wrapped around her little finger years before I left!" Alden chuckled to himself before turning his attention to Anwyn. Taking two steps toward her, he gracefully knelt on one knee and bowed his head in a display of respect.

"Seishinmori, please allow me to introduce myself. I am your grandfather, Alden," he began, his voice filled with warmth and a hint of playful mystery. "Recently returned from my... *travels*..." He paused, as if emphasizing the cryptic nature of his journeys. "If my predictions have been correct, and there is no reason they wouldn't be! I suspect you have recently found out that you are our Seishinmori, and you have recently also read the prophecy I left your parents?"

Anwyn stood there, still stunned by the revelation that her long-lost grandfather had returned at this pivotal moment. After fifty years of absence, she had secretly feared that her father's belief in Alden's demise had been accurate, and that he had perished somewhere on his travels. The reunion was a whirlwind of emotions and unanswered questions.

As Alden looked up at her, Anwyn couldn't help but take in the distinguished image he presented. His long silver hair was meticulously groomed and framed his face, bestowing upon him an air of elegance and wisdom that came with age. His eyes, though bearing the marks of time, still sparkled mischievously, hinting at the inner wellspring of a fun-loving spirit. Yet, it was his smile that truly captivated Anwyn.

Within his enchanting smile, she saw echoes of her mother's radiant grin, but Alden's was distinct, more playful, more mischievous. It invited intrigue and the promise of adventure, leaving her yearning to leave the isolated woods… In that instant, Anwyn realized that the Great Elven Forest could not have contained the boundless spirit of her grandfather. Alden was destined to be free, to roam the world, and Anwyn felt an undeniable longing to explore it by his side.

Apprehensively, she said, "Grandfather, please call me Anwyn. I am not yet used to the title of Seishinmori, and if I'm honest, I find it quite unsettling!"

Alden stood and barked a laugh, "Nonsense dear, you have the bearing of a true queen, and whoever does not call you by your formal title, should be executed immediately!" Alden paused then to briefly clear his throat before continuing, "however, my dear, I think I would rather like to call you 'granddaughter', if that suits you?"

Smiling widely, Anwyn embraced her grandfather and said, "of course grandfather, I too would like that."

12

THE SANDARAN FLOWER

'Like a delicate bloom with petals of poison, beauty veils danger in its embrace.'

KEMP

After the attack on the caravan, Kemp quickly fell into step with the guards, sharing their urgency to find shelter before nightfall. Eager to secure a safe location, they scoured the area until discovering a secluded spot. Unanimously, they agreed to set up camp there for the night. Nestled beside an imposing cliff, it proved to be an ideal refuge for their weary band. Towering rock walls rose skyward on one side, forming a natural barrier that shielded them from potential threats.

The ground here was uneven, strewn with large boulders and loose gravel, making it challenging for any attackers to approach stealthily. To further fortify their position, the guards had shown their experience and arranged a makeshift barricade of logs and boulders on the open side of their camp, creating a sturdy barrier that could be defended if necessary.

As the day drew to a close, the sun, a radiant orb of fiery gold, began its descent and painted the distant peaks of the Scorched

Mountains with warm hues of orange and crimson, the vibrant colors providing a sense of vivid reality to the name "Scorched."

The campsite now held an atmosphere of security, a place where the group could rest and regroup, knowing they had chosen a position that would be difficult for somebody to breach. It provided them with a sense of security which they all desperately needed after witnessing the tragic events from earlier.

As night descended, the group nestled into their makeshift camp, but sleep eluded Kemp. The haunting memories of the day played on a loop in his mind. The crackling of the campfire seemed to accentuate the weight of his thoughts. Kemp braced himself for a long night, the flickering shadows dancing in tune with the echoes of the day's harrowing events.

As Kemp gathered his belongings in the chilly morning mist, a heavy weight settled in his chest, matching the dense fog enveloping his feet. Despite the physical tasks at hand, his mind remained trapped in the shadows of his restless sleep. Each fold of his cloak and buckle of his pack seemed mechanical, his movements driven by a relentless need to keep moving forward, to outrun the haunting specter of Theodore's vacant gaze that lingered in the recesses of his mind.

Kemp was grateful that the final day of the journey to Lamos turned out to be uneventful. Some of the remaining guards had attempted to talk to him, but Kemp couldn't shake the nagging feeling that their words held a hidden mockery, their laughter concealed behind a polite facade. In response, he withdrew to the back of a wagon and sat in silence.

Kris had checked on him repeatedly throughout the day, offering words of encouragement and inquiring about the progress of Kemp's wounds and injuries. Despite considering his minor injuries as inconsequential, Kemp couldn't deny the warmth that enveloped him from the seasoned guard's gestures of concern. Kris's genuine kindness and their shared conversations provided a welcomed respite from the journey's tension and uncertainty.

As they drew nearer to Lamos, Kemp's gaze fixated on the intimidating view of the Scorched Mountains, which loomed ominously on the horizon, casting a foreboding shadow over the landscape. Towering peaks, sharp and jagged, reached upward as if attempting to pierce the very heavens. The sheer cliffs and craggy ridges formed an impenetrable barrier, a fortress of rugged stone that dared any who approached to challenge its might. This was a place where nature reigned supreme, where the elements ruled with an iron fist, and where only the most daring souls would venture to explore its treacherous heights. Kemp suddenly felt small and insignificant, the weight of his mission becoming apparent and shaking his resolve.

The group found themselves queued up, waiting in anticipation to enter the bustling city. City guards, clad in loosely flowing robes and armed with gleaming scimitars, meticulous in their duty, scrutinized each traveler's documents and examined their wagons, ensuring that the line inched forward at a frustratingly sluggish pace, testing their patience, and grating on the frayed nerves of the group.

The city gates stood as a testament to both architectural grandeur and practical fortification. Towering walls of sun-baked clay bricks, adorned with intricate geometric patterns and ornate carvings, loomed above the arched entranceway. The gates themselves were colossal, made from thick, solid wood reinforced with iron bands, and stood as a formidable barrier.

Guard towers flanked either side of the entrance, rising high above the walls. Kemp was somewhat grateful that he could see multiple guards armed with great longbows patrolling these towers, ever watchful for any signs of trouble.

Kemp, weary from the journey, wanted for nothing more than to step into the city's welcoming embrace. His stomach rumbled in hunger, his throat parched with thirst, and his body ached from exhaustion. All he wanted was to find a place to eat, get drunk, and succumb to the sweet embrace of sleep - ideally in that precise order.

As they approached the gates, Kemp observed a lively market scene unfolding beyond the walls, where merchants were energetically selling their products and travelers were busy finalizing their transactions before entering the city. The atmosphere was a vibrant tapestry of colors and sounds, with the tantalising scent of exotic spices hanging in the air.

Caravans laden with goods and travelers on horseback were a common sight, adding to the city's southern charm. The gates themselves bore inscriptions in flowing script, celebrating the city's rich history and its role as a crossroads of trade and culture.

Passing through these gates felt like entering a world where time had stood still, a place where the echoes of ancient stories whispered through the narrow alleyways, promising adventure, mystique, and the allure of Sandara.

As Kemp wandered through the labyrinthine streets of Lamos, he found himself entranced by the city's rich tapestry of cultural influences. The sight of meticulously positioned olive trees, their ancient branches casting soothing shadows against the sun-drenched streets, offered a comforting refuge to travelers like himself. Each corner revealed ornate water fountains, their crystalline streams beckoning to parched throats and weary souls, providing a momentary sanctuary from the relentless heat that enveloped the city.

Lamos was a living testament to the mingling of diverse cultures, and its Sandaran influence was unmistakable. Kemp's limited exposure to the outside world had not prepared him for this vivid mosaic of traditions and aesthetics. His awe was palpable as he marveled at the city's architecture.

Buildings adorned with gold and silver patterns lined the streets. Grand archways beckoned visitors into the heart of many buildings. Within their cool interiors, shaded courtyards with bubbling fountains provided a serene escape from the bustling streets. Kemp couldn't help but stare in wonder, captivated by the sheer beauty of it all.

Wandering into the bustling market square, Kemp found himself gawking at the maze of stalls draped in colorful fabrics. The sprawling square seemed to stretch endlessly, and Kemp marvelled at the myriad stalls that filled every conceivable space.

Compared to the markets in Tempsford, Kemp could only describe this place as "chaotic." Vendors and shoppers alike swarmed through the square, engaged in lively haggling over a dizzying array of goods. There was little semblance of order; stalls sprouted up haphazardly and seemingly randomly, giving rise to an endearing disorder that Kemp found rather captivating.

The energy pulsating through Lamos was undeniable, and Kemp found himself swept up in its irresistible currents. Despite the lingering unease from the recent attack, the vibrant bustle of the city drew him in like a magnet. The palpable excitement that filled the air was contagious, igniting a spark of enthusiasm within Kemp's own heart, momentarily eclipsing his apprehensions.

As Kemp meandered through the maze of rickety stalls, his gaze flitted from one enticing item to another. At one stall, a man negotiated for opulent silk fabrics, while another displayed finely crafted leather pouches. A woman presided over an assortment of broadleaf tobacco varieties, accompanied by intricately designed pipes. Nearby, a merchant showcased precious metals and gemstones, claiming their origins to be from the formidable Scorched Mountains.

Curiosity piqued, Kemp approached the gemstone vendor and inquired about guides who might lead him to the mountain range. However, he was met with a sharp and dismissive response. The vendor's curt words left Kemp taken aback, and he quickly retreated, slipping into a narrow alleyway to escape the vendor's rudeness and find a moment of solitude.

To Kemp's shock, an elderly lady, her leathery, sun-worn skin sagging loosely, suddenly reached out with a gnarled hand and clasped Kemp's wrist in a surprisingly firm grip. Startled, Kemp instinctively pulled his hand back, gazing down at the woman. She was seated in the shadowed recess of a building, adorned in an elegant pink shawl intricately patterned with golden leaves.

"A flower, sir? A flower for your love?" she inquired in the soft and exotic accent of Sandarah.

Kemp stammered, his gaze shifting to the beautiful pink blossom on a long, slender green stem that she held out to him. "Um, no thank you, ma'am. I'm alone here."

"That is a pity, young sir," she said softly, "I can sense you've endured some sorrow recently, so take this Sandaran flower. Offer it to a lady who catches your eye, and your fortunes shall take a turn for the better."

As Kemp pondered whether to accept the flower from the elderly woman, she deftly withdrew her hand. Her voice took on a solemn tone as she continued, "But be cautious, young sir, for this flower conceals more than meets the eye. It carries a poison that can be lethal when ingested. Nevertheless, if properly prepared, these wild blossoms can also be used to treat various ailments, from life-threatening infections to grievous burns."

She leaned in closer, her eyes gleaming with a knowing glint. "The flower holds the key for both life and death within its delicate petals. The people of Sandarah say that the flower is much like our women - both beautiful and perilous, yet also bestowing love and life."

With a sudden cackle, she extended the flower to Kemp once again.

Hesitantly, Kemp extended his hand and accepted the flower. As he grasped it, a jagged thorn scraped his thumb, leaving a faint mark but drawing no blood. He gasped in surprise and glanced at the elderly woman, whose raised eyebrow conveyed a sense of caution. "Careful, young one," she warned, "this flower need not be ingested to bring harm. A mere scratch would have given you a nasty fever!"

A bead of sweat trickled down Kemp's forehead, and he wiped it away with his free hand. "I'm not sure I want it, ma'am. It seems quite dangerous, and I fear it might cause more harm than good."

The old lady chuckled softly, her eyes twinkling. "Nonsense, dear. This flower can also save your life. Would you shun drinking water for fear of drowning? No, I didn't think so! Now, be on your way, sir. Enjoy my gift. I can sense that the woman you present it to will be something special indeed!"

Kemp, still unsure, asked, "But how will I know who that woman is?"

With a cryptic smile, the elderly woman replied, "You will know, young sir. That is all I can tell you."

As Kemp walked away, the weight of the flower in his hand left him feeling uncertain about the mysterious gift he had accepted. Suddenly, he came to a halt. His mother had always taught him never to accept a gift from someone without offering some form of payment or service in return. Turning to offer the old lady a coin from his purse as a token of his appreciation, Kemp was taken aback when he glanced back into the alcove, only to find the old lady had vanished.

Perplexed, Kemp looked down at the flower clutched in

his hand, confirming its tangible presence. With a sense of bewilderment, he retraced his steps to where he had been standing moments ago, discovering a tattered piece of paper lying on the ground. Carefully unfolding it, he found some writing scrawled inside, a singular word that read, "*RUIHA.*"

Feeling a mixture of confusion and disbelief, Kemp couldn't fathom what was happening. Half-convinced he was losing his mind and half-suspecting some enchantment had befallen him, he continued walking, searching for a place to stay for the night. After about ten minutes, his thoughts still consumed by the strange encounter with the old lady, he stumbled upon an inn.

Kemp examined the inn, noting the striking contrast between its ground floor made of the prevalent burnt orange stone found throughout Lamos and the upper floors constructed from a dark wood, appearing as if they were later additions. In the front courtyard, a massive olive tree stood tall, surrounded by benches. The windows were devoid of glass, instead featuring metal bars running from bottom to top, resembling prison bars. Hanging above the large double wooden doors, a weathered sign read, "The Olive Tree."

Kemp stepped into the inn and looked around. It was busy, and he wasn't sure whether there would be any rooms available. Chancing his luck, he walked up to the bar and a short man with grey hair stood there drying a glass tankard with a dirty rag. He was puffing on a large broadleaf cigar, which Kemp never saw leave his mouth once.

"Excuse me, have you got any rooms available tonight?" Kemp asked wearily.

The man, puffing on his never-ending cigar, scrutinized Kemp before gruffly responding, "Yeah, we've got rooms. Four silver coins a night, includes a bath and two meals—dinner tonight and breakfast in the morning. Ale or wine will cost you another silver, and spirits are an additional silver, as much as you want."

Never having been fond of strong spirits, Kemp deftly counted out five silver coins from his purse and firmly placed them on the counter. Looking at the grim man, he responded. "Food, ale and lodgings, please."

The man grunted in acknowledgment. "Find a free table and someone will come over and serve you."

Ruiha

The Olive Tree was a dump, plain and simple. The best part was the food, which barely passed as edible. The wine was diluted beyond recognition. The ale had the flavor of something brewed in a stagnant puddle, and the customers, no matter how many threats Ruiha issued, persistently harassed her. However, the worst part of it all was undoubtedly the coffee. She could only describe it as abysmal. Often, Ruiha found herself contemplating whether roasting and brewing mud would produce a more palatable beverage than what the Olive Tree dared to serve as coffee.

Still, she couldn't complain too much, she supposed. She had a roof over her head, two meagre meals a day, and as much abysmal coffee as she could drink. But, most importantly, she was away from the clutches of Faisal and his gang of murderers and thieves.

She was planning on staying at the Olive Tree for a few months until the heat died down a little. Afterward, she intended to venture out in search of thrilling and, more significantly, lucrative opportunities. Joining a guard team for a merchant caravan seemed like a good option. It was a role she believed she would be good at, and, most importantly, it offered a legitimate and lawful path forward.

As she was pondering her future, and trying not to taste the coffee which was swirling around in her mouth, she heard her name being called, by Klara, another of the servers who worked at the Olive Tree, who, shockingly, didn't mind the state of the coffee they served.

"Ruiha, Ruiha, your shift is starting. Leo won't be happy if you're late again!"

"Tell Leo he can wait, Klara. I'll grace him with my presence in five minutes, just as soon as I've endured the torment of this sorry excuse for coffee."

"I thought you hated coffee?" Klara replied.

"I don't *hate* coffee, Klara. What I *hate* is this crap you all seem to accept as coffee!!"

"So why are you drinking it, then?" Klara appeared genuinely puzzled as she asked the question.

Sighing, Ruiha responded, "Well, Klara, there's simply nothing better to drink in this bloody place. Besides, when you've downed coffee day in and day out for the past twelve years, it becomes a rather challenging habit to break... despite my best intentions." She mumbled the last part almost to herself.

As Ruiha finished her coffee, she slipped on her shoes and readied herself for her shift. Unlike the other women who worked at the Olive Tree, she applied none of the dark cosmetics around her eyes and never tinted her lips a deep crimson. The men downstairs needed no encouragement, and it genuinely baffled Ruiha why all the girls wore it. The Olive Tree wasn't a brothel. That was the first thing Ruiha made sure of, and by wearing the powders and paints, all they did was entice unwelcome attention.

As she walked into the common room, she walked through the clouds of broadleaf smoke and over to the bar, deliberately avoiding the wandering hands which reached out at her. They were so drunk, that it wasn't difficult to avoid them, the men were looking at her and it was almost like they were moving in slow motion, each one with a big stupid grin slapped across his face like they were the shiniest jewel in the king's crown. Idiots, she thought to herself.

"Leo, how are you, boss? I'm here and reporting for duty!" Ruiha mocked a salute as she greeted Leo, who only ever grunted in response to her.

"Full of conversation this evening, aren't we? Well, just letting you know that I'm here and ready for my shift. Catch you later boss, if you need me, I'll be out there avoiding the plague ridden bastards as best I can!" Winking at Leo, she wandered off into the crowd avoiding hands and collecting plates and cups as she did so.

Kemp

Kemp wandered over to a free table and sat down. He couldn't help notice the differences between the Olive Tree, and the Old White Horse that he'd stayed in when he was in Redbourne. There was no entertainment here, just the noise of people talking, drinking, smoking, gambling, and laughing in the background. The people here seemed gruff and unwelcoming compared to the people in Redbourne. Still, he had a room, and he needed sleep. He could always look for somewhere else to stay tomorrow.

After a few minutes, a woman approached to take his order. Her long, dark hair cascaded down her back in glossy waves, olive-toned skin radiated a warm and inviting glow. Although a scattering of small scars adorned her neck and arms, they only served to enhance her allure and imbue her with an air of mystery. Her eyes, bright and alert, were pools of rich, earthy brown and held a confidence which captivated Kemp.

Every movement she made seemed to carry the grace of a dancer, and her confident demeanor commanded attention wherever she went. Kemp marvelled at how she deftly dodged the gropes and stumbles of the surrounding drunkards without hesitation, always anticipating where a stray hand would land and subtly moving out of harm's way.

"Listen, are you going to order or are you planning on gawking at me all night?" Kemp jolted into the present and his cheeks flushed a deep crimson.

"I.. uh, I'm sorry," he spluttered, his words stumbling over each other in his flustered state.

A fleeting smile graced her lips, and Kemp observed a momentary softness in her enigmatic, dark eyes. But in the blink of an eye, her demeanor shifted as she whirled around and clamped her hand firmly around a man's throat, unleashing a low growl that reverberated in his face, "Listen, Deon, I've told you this before, so this really is your last chance, understand? Touch my arse one more time and I'll break every finger on your bloody hand. Then once I'm finished enjoying hearing your screams of pain, I'm going to find your wife, explain what you've done and together, we'll start on your second hand. Gottit?" Deon stared at her wide-eyed before nodding vigorously and stumbling off.

Turning back to face Kemp, the woman asked, "So what will it be, then?"

Kemp found himself utterly captivated by her, his gaze locked onto her with an intensity he couldn't explain. She possessed an aura of confidence and danger that left him spellbound. Without fully realizing his actions, he held out the Sandaran flower to her, his voice shaky as he spoke.

"I'd like to give you this flower, miss. It reminds me of you, beautiful but deadly."

The woman's reaction was far from what Kemp had expected. She examined the flower and then shifted her gaze to him, her expression unimpressed. With a sigh, she straightforwardly stated, "Listen, I don't have time for this. I'm not interested, okay? I'm here to do my job, and that's all. If you want a woman, there are plenty of brothels up the street. I'm sure they'll be more interested." Pausing and thinking about it, she then smirked and said, "just be sure to offer them more than a flower, okay?"

Kemp felt his cheeks burn with embarrassment, and he quickly withdrew the flower, mumbling an apology.

Kemp looked up at the lady again and saw the hint of a smile lingering on her beautiful face. Shakily, he smiled back, and explained, "Miss, truly, I am not interested in a brothel, and although I think you are wonderful, that was not my intention, the flower was given to me not an hour ago by an old lady down the street. She explained the Sandaran flower was beautiful, but deadly. She told me that once I found the right woman to give it to, I would know. And I am certain now that she spoke the truth, for this flower surely belongs to you."

The woman raised her eyebrow at Kemp then, "You're serious, aren't you?" Sighing, she sat down next to him. "Listen, I'll take the bloody flower, and I'll bring you your food and ale, alright? But you expect anything other than that, and my threat to poor little Deon back there will seem like a gentle scolding. Gottit?"

Kemp nodded and smiled, relieved that his gesture had been accepted. "Yes, ma'am," he replied. "My name's Kemp. It's a pleasure to meet you."

As she walked away with the flower in her hand, she called back, "My name's Ruiha."

Kemp sat there in utter astonishment, unable to make his mouth work.

Ruiha

Each night she worked, Ruiha had kept an eye out and paid attention to all the customers who were in the Olive Tree. She knew Faisal would send his people to look for her, and although she thought it unlikely that they would end up in the Olive Tree of all places, she knew not to be careless, so she scanned the patrons keenly, looking for anything unusual.

Tonight, there were a couple of new faces loitering about. The first she noticed was a big man who was clearly from somewhere up north, given his appearance and clothing. Although he didn't pay too much attention to Ruiha herself, he still gave her the creeps. He sat puffing on his broadleaf pipe, his hood obscuring most of his features. What struck her, however, was how he intently watched the second new face to the Olive Tree.

That second man sat watching everything around him, as if he'd never been into a tavern before, his eyes wide and guileless, gawking at the surrounding people. He would be described as handsome by most of the girls who worked at the Olive Tree, in a cute and innocent type of way. He was clearly new in town and by the way he acted; it was obvious he'd had little exposure to the real world. Distantly, she thought he would have been the perfect mark when she'd been a part of the Sand Dragons. She shook her head to rid herself of the intrusive thought and wondered over to him, deftly avoiding a grasping hand.

Their conversation left Ruiha even more intrigued. Despite all of her experience with people and the world, she couldn't shake the feeling that there was more to him than met the eye. Yes, he came across as shy and timid, lacking confidence and street smarts, but there was a spark in his eyes, a flicker of something that ignited a curiosity in Ruiha.

It was confusing. Had he been flirting with her? That whole story about the flower seemed like a cheap pickup line straight from the playbook of some thug back in Gecit. Yet, there was an undeniable sincerity in his words. He didn't strike Ruiha as the type to carry a flower around as a prop to pick up women. No, he felt genuine, and she sensed it in the way he spoke. There was no arrogance or overconfidence; his words were laced with authenticity.

She couldn't shake that spark she saw in his eyes, and the feeling that she had slowly been trying to push down as he spoke to her. She decided then that she would go back and talk with him later. She was determined to find out more about the intriguing young man who seemed clueless about the world.

13

The Hostage Situation

'A successful negotiation is a bridge built on trust, with each side crossing toward a shared understanding.'

Gunnar

As Gunnar gradually regained consciousness, he was greeted by a searing sensation in his head which dominated his entire awareness. The throbbing pain in his forehead, where the rock had made contact, made it nearly impossible to focus on anything else. He gingerly reached up, his fingers tracing the sizable lump that was tender to the touch. He winced in discomfort and silently cursed the mountain gods, realizing waking up without some form of searing pain seemed like a distant memory.

As the agony slowly faded, Gunnar's senses began to return to him, and he was grateful to discover he had no other injuries. While unconscious, the soldiers had refrained from further harm, which came as a relief to him. He had half expected them to take advantage of his unconscious state and beat him out of spite.

As Gunnar sat there in thought, his mind drifted to the dwarf who had beckoned him forward before he succumbed to darkness. The same dwarf who had permitted his departure from the General's office. Could he possibly have an ally among Wilfrid's soldiers? It was a fleeting hope, but one that lingered nonetheless, offering a glimmer of reassurance amidst the uncertainty.

After a few moments, Gunnar managed to sit up, surveying his surroundings with a critical eye. The stone bed he lay upon offered no comfort, lacking even the most basic amenities like a mattress or blankets. The dimly lit room provided minimal illumination, its sole source being a solitary candle flickering weakly in a corner. Gunnar's gaze wandered to the window, its thick iron bars both vertical and horizontal, rusted with age. It struck him as a futile attempt at containment, especially considering any dwarf proficient in craft magic could effortlessly dismantle them. Perhaps they were enchanted, he speculated, though he lacked the skill to confirm his theory. Craft magic was not a talent he possessed, at least not to his knowledge, leaving him unable to put his hypothesis to the test.

As he continued to survey the room, he noticed it was utterly devoid of any furnishings or adornments. It was a bleak, dark stone cell with nothing more than a large metal door and the barred window providing minimal external contact. Gunnar let out a sigh of resignation as he lay back down, closing his eyes and hoping the impact of the rock hadn't caused a concussion.

At some point, Gunnar was stirred from his sleep by the sound of loud voices shouting outside his cell door. He groggily sat up, realizing he didn't feel any better after the additional sleep. With a slight tilt of his head, he strained to listen to the words being exchanged, but the voices sounded distant and muffled, making it difficult to discern their content. However, he could swear he heard his own name being shouted several times.

A few minutes later, the metal door swung open, and the

dwarf who had granted him permission to leave Wilfrid's office stepped into the room.

"My name is Hansen. I have been ordered to bring you to the barracks so you can assist with some... *hostage negotiations*." Hansen's tone and movements seemed rigid, forced almost.

Gunnar stared blankly at Hansen then, not quite sure what he was expected to say to that.

With no response from Gunnar, Hansen continued, "Your unit, the Snow Wolves, have taken fifty-two Dwarven soldiers hostage within the barracks. It is estimated the number of hostages now actually outnumbers the remaining Snow Wolves. The General is not happy with the situation and has assigned me to restore control."

Gunnar maintained his steady gaze on Hansen. He kept the smile from his lips as he decided to garner more information before committing to anything. Observing Hansen, Gunnar noted the dwarf appeared relatively young, too young to have been entrusted with leading his own unit or squad. This observation, alongside the shouting he had heard earlier, led Gunnar to surmise that perhaps Hansen's current role was a form of punishment.

"Hansen," Gunnar inquired cautiously, "are we currently alone? What I mean is, can we speak without fear of being overheard?"

Hansen glanced around, then gave a discreet nod to indicate their privacy.

"Okay," Gunnar pressed, "I want to know... what you said to me in Wilfrid's office earlier. Did you mean it?"

Hansen nodded again, evidently not comfortable to put words to his answer.

Gunnar nodded in acknowledgment. "Thank you," he continued. "I didn't have the chance to say it earlier, but your help meant a great deal. Now, tell me. Why was Wilfrid shouting at you earlier?"

While Gunnar couldn't be entirely certain it had indeed been Wilfrid shouting at Hansen earlier, his educated guess appeared to be on the mark.

"General Wilfrid," Hansen began with a somber tone, "was... *disappointed* I granted you the chance to surrender. He holds a strong conviction you are a traitor and wanted you executed for treason."

Gunnar didn't realize how close he had been to death in that moment, the stark reality of it hitting home suddenly. "With no evidence or any form of trial?" he questioned.

Once more, Hansen nodded in solemn affirmation.

"But now it appears he requires my assistance in negotiating the release of the hostages," Gunnar remarked, a hint of irony in his voice.

Hansen's expression shifted to one of mirth, and he averted his gaze from Gunnar. The sudden change in demeanor puzzled Gunnar. "So if it's not General Wilfrid who needs my help in hostage negotiations," Gunnar inquired, "then who does?"

Hesitantly, Hansen replied, "Well, yesterday, the Hornbaeks arrived to initiate the personnel rotation. The first squadron of soldiers was eager to find out what was happening, and unfortunately, six of the Dwarves taken hostage are from Hornbaek."

Gunnar fell silent for a moment, carefully digesting this new information. This development could work to his advantage, however, involving another city's military had the potential for its own problems.

Although the General of the Hornbaek Army was unlikely to accept Wilfrid's accusations at face value. The situation involving the elite Snow Wolves going rogue would undoubtedly demand

The Hostage Situation

a thorough investigation. However, now warriors from his army had been taken hostage, it left Gunnar unsure as to how much patience the General would have with him.

Gunnar pressed further, his mind racing as the initial stages of a plan began to take shape. "So," he inquired again, more deliberately this time, "the Hornbaek General specifically asked for my help in the hostage negotiations, correct?"

Hansen nodded in confirmation once more.

Gunnar raised an eyebrow. "And what was General Wilfrid's plan for me, if you don't mind me asking?"

Hansen's response was delivered with a matter-of-fact tone. "General Wilfrid intended to execute you immediately and then launch an assault on the barracks in an attempt to rescue the hostages."

Gunnar couldn't help but shake his head in disbelief. "You do perceive how stupid that plan is, don't you, Hansen?"

There was a brief moment of hesitation before Hansen nodded in agreement.

"The Snow Wolves," Gunnar asserted with unwavering confidence, "would obliterate anyone who tried to breach those barracks through force. I've been personally responsible for their training for the past five years, and I can attest to that."

Hansen's voice carried a tone of resignation as he concurred, "I'm well aware of that, and honestly, I think the entire bloody squadron knows it too. There haven't been any volunteers willing to lead the charge, if you catch my drift."

Recognising a potential opportunity before him, Gunnar resolved to push his limits a bit further. Hansen was indeed an ally in this situation.

"Hansen," Gunnar began, carefully framing his request, "might I be able to arrange a meeting with the General of the Hornbaek Army before I begin negotiations with the Snow Wolves?"

Hansen nodded in agreement. "I've been informed the General is also interested in speaking with you."

Gunnar offered a polite, triumphant smile as Hansen left the cell and locked the door behind him.

Gunnar

After what felt like hours, Gunnar heard heavy footfalls approaching his cell door. To his surprise, the dwarf approaching halted and knocked on the cell door. Gunnar, somewhat taken aback by the unexpected politeness, responded, "Please come in."

The door swung open, revealing a short, barrel-chested dwarf with long, silver hair and an even longer, silver beard, both neatly braided into twin plaits. He had a large scar on his cheek, below his left eye socket, which suggested to Gunnar he was, or at least had been, a warrior himself.

The dwarf was old, surpassing even Gunnar's father, Erik, who had celebrated his two-hundred and fiftieth birthday a few years prior. Despite his age, this dwarf exuded the aura of a seasoned warrior, his confidence unwavering despite the distance of youth. His countenance remained stern, and his eyes held no discernible emotion as they surveyed the room, ultimately fixing their gaze on Gunnar.

Gunnar immediately straightened and offered a respectful bow of his head in acknowledgment. The gesture appeared to put the elder dwarf at ease, and he returned the nod before stepping further into the room, no longer seemingly concerned Gunnar might be unhinged.

"Gunnar, I presume?" the elder dwarf inquired, his voice carrying a weight of authority.

Gunnar inclined his head in acknowledgment. "Yes, sir. Gunnar Eriksson, eldest son of Erik the Blood of Clan Draegoor."

"Good," General Bjorn continued, his tone unwavering and matter-of-fact. "I am General Bjorn. I'm sorry, I don't have any other fancy titles to throw at you."

Gunnar couldn't quite discern if General Bjorn's remark was meant to be humorous or not. Unsure of how to respond, he opted for a respectful silence, his thoughts swirling with uncertainty amidst the formal exchange.

"Gunnar," General Bjorn began, his tone carrying no emotion in it, "I knew your father well, though that was many, many years ago, before he assumed the role of clan chief. I always thought he was a headstrong dwarf who gave too little thought to the consequences of his actions. Nevertheless, I also knew him as a good, loyal dwarf who would lay down his life for his friends, family, and soldiers. Unfortunately, I've never heard the same said of your uncle. Frankly, I don't hold him in high regard. Any dwarf who schemes and plots like Wilfrid cannot be trusted."

Gunnar was caught off guard by General Bjorn's directness. Despite Dwarves' reputation for plain-speaking and blunt demeanor, Bjorn's unvarnished words still managed to startle him. Taking a deep breath to steady himself, Gunnar prepared to respond, but before he could utter a word, General Bjorn interjected, cutting off any opportunity for Gunnar to speak his mind. The interruption left Gunnar feeling slightly disconcerted, unsure of how to navigate the conversation now that his chance to respond had been preempted.

General Bjorn continued, "However, he does hold the position of General of the Draegoorian Army, and I must treat his words with due gravity, irrespective of my personal opinions. As for you, Gunnar, beyond hearing the rumors of your dashing appearance, I possess very little knowledge about you. For all I know, you could be a traitor seeking to undermine your uncle and father."

Gunnar's heart sank upon hearing the General's words, but rather than engaging in an argument, he replied with measured respect, "I fully comprehend your standpoint, General Bjorn. I hold your authority in high regard, and I am more than willing to offer a detailed report and statement concerning the events of the past few days. I am committed to demonstrating my unwavering loyalty to my father, my clan and the Dwarves of Dreynas in any way I can."

Gunnar then executed a deep bow, awaiting the General's response before straightening once more.

"I happen to have had a rather interesting conversation with Hansen on my way over here, Gunnar." General Bjorn began, his eyebrow arching as he spoke. "The lad, although a pup still, seems to have his head screwed on tight and he seems to think you are innocent. In fact, he mentioned that you had the opportunity to kill three guards when they attacked you, but instead, you chose to incapacitate them instead?"

"Correct sir, I don't suppose he mentioned he was one of those three guards, did he?" Gunnar didn't want Bjorn finding that information out later and thinking that Gunnar had tried to mislead him.

Bjorn smiled, and finally Gunnar could see a spark in his dark, emotionless eyes. "Indeed, Gunnar," Bjorn affirmed. "Hansen is also under the impression the fifty-two hostages captured by the Snow Wolves are still alive."

Gunnar nodded deliberately, his conviction unwavering. "I would wager my life on the certainty they are still alive, sir. I've spent the last five years commanding those Dwarves, and I know without a doubt each and every one of them would hesitate to take the life of a fellow dwarf, even when their own lives are in jeopardy."

"Are you prepared to assist in negotiating the hostages' release?" General Bjorn inquired.

"Absolutely, sir," Gunnar replied firmly. "However, I would appreciate some guarantees that once the hostages are safely returned, every member of the Snow Wolves will be considered innocent."

General Bjorn considered Gunnar's request. "I would like to interview Sergeant Karl first, and the two of you will need to be escorted back to Draegoor for an official investigation. But I can assure you the rest of your unit will be deemed innocent, provided there are no fatalities among the hostages."

Gunnar recognized he wouldn't receive a better offer than this, and he understood that returning to Draegoor was his best chance to prove his innocence and initiate an investigation into his uncle's actions.

"I confirm that I am happy with your terms," Gunnar affirmed. "I will ensure the release of all the hostages within the hour."

General Bjorn regarded him with some uncertainty, but ultimately nodded in agreement.

Gunnar

Forty minutes later, the first hostages began filing out of the barracks entrance looking bruised and embarrassed, but in otherwise good health. General Bjorn had been true to his word and declared that the Snow Wolves were innocent of all charges. Karl currently stood beside Gunnar in General Bjorn's office, both Dwarves waiting for him to return from commanding the hostage release situation. Hansen was also there overseeing them so that they did not try to escape. He looked extremely uncomfortable with the duty, however, knowing full well that had Gunnar or Karl tried to leave the office, he could do nothing at all to stop them other than politely beg them to stay.

Eventually, General Bjorn arrived, his stern demeanor casting a heavy shadow over the tense gathering. His voice resonated through the stone room as he addressed Gunnar, "Gunnar, the hostages have all been released with no fatalities amongst them. It appears you have indeed kept your word."

Gunnar, a hint of relief on his face, replied, "Of course, sir. I had no doubt the Snow Wolves could be counted on."

Yet beneath his relief, Gunnar harbored a lingering unease. He worried about the fate of his men and he couldn't shake the feeling their troubles were far from over. A glance exchanged with Karl conveyed their shared apprehension. Both Dwarves silently steeling themselves for the challenges that lay ahead.

Maintaining a respectful tone, Gunnar pressed on, "Sir, I trust our agreement still stands? You will provide us with an escort back to Draegoor, where we can ensure a fair investigation is conducted?" His voice carried a note of hope, revealing his genuine desire to avoid any conflict within the General's office.

General Bjorn's genuine smile filled Gunnar with a renewed sense of hope. Yet, a nagging doubt lingered in the back of his mind, an unsettling feeling that something was amiss. As he gazed into the General's eyes, searching for any hint of deceit, he found none. There were no traces of malice, no veiled intentions. Reluctantly, he shrugged off his suspicions, only to find them replaced by another troubling thought.

The memory of Commander Wilfrid loomed ominously in the depths of Gunnar's consciousness. He knew all too well the Commander's thirst for vengeance and his relentless ambition. Try as he might, Gunnar couldn't shake the feeling that Wilfrid's shadow still lingered, plotting his next move with sinister intent.

Amidst the uncertainty, a troubling suspicion crept in—that Wilfrid's ambitions extended far beyond mere revenge, perhaps even reaching to the very heart of Draegoor itself.

"Gunnar, I will indeed keep my promise," General Bjorn affirmed. "As should be the nature of every dwarf in Dreynas, we should remember that a promise between kin is a bond that should not be broken." He shifted to a more serious tone as he continued, "However, I will need to keep you and Karl here imprisoned under my protection until we receive reports that the rest of your unit has reported back to Dreynas. I would be remiss in my duties as General of the Army of Hornbaek if I were to allow all of you to leave at the same time, only to discover that I had been deceived and that Wilfrid was correct all along."

Gunnar emitted a slight sigh, his nod acknowledging General Bjorn's decision. He understood if he were in the General's shoes, he might have made the same choice. Still, it didn't ease the frustration of not being able to depart immediately and resolve the entire matter.

"Understood, sir," Gunnar replied, a note of resignation in his voice. "May I inquire as to your plans concerning General Wilfrid's in the meantime?"

General Bjorn's gaze roamed the room, his eyes flitting around as if carefully weighing his words. "I hold no authority over General Wilfrid," he explained. "As the leader of the Draegoorian Army, he falls outside my jurisdiction. I cannot arrest or even question him without risking the wrath of the clan chiefs. Therefore, he will be permitted to stay here until our entire army arrives to relieve him. Whether he chooses to stay until the last of his Dwarves leaves, or leave immediately, however, is beyond my control."

Gunnar let out a weary sigh, fully expectant that General Wilfrid would attempt to seize any opportunity to eliminate Karl and himself, or perhaps even seek revenge on the Snow Wolves who had embarrassed him. He clung to the hope that General Bjorn would be able to provide the protection they needed.

"Fair enough, sir," Gunnar responded. "I understand the difficult position you are in, and I genuinely appreciate the protection you're offering. I have a feeling we'll more than likely need it." Gunnar allowed the weight of his words to linger in the air, hoping General Bjorn would grasp the gravity of their predicament and take their safety seriously.

"Very well," General Bjorn instructed, his tone businesslike. "Hansen, please retrieve my guards from outside and request that they escort Gunnar to a holding cell. He will remain there until I have concluded my interview with Sergeant Karl."

Hansen, somewhat startled by the sudden call to action, cast a swift glance at both Karl and Gunnar before hurrying out to carry out the General's orders. In that brief moment, Gunnar and Karl exchanged a knowing nod, a silent understanding that Gunnar expected Karl to fully cooperate during his discussion with General Bjorn.

Four heavily armed guards entered the room. In a stark contrast from the previous encounter when a General had called guards for Gunnar, these guards did not display aggressive postures, and their weapons remained sheathed. They efficiently and courteously escorted Gunnar out of the room while General Bjorn's voice echoed behind them.

"Karl, if you please," General Bjorn's voice boomed, "could you provide me with a detailed report regarding the patrol, the attack, and the loss of life over the past forty-eight hours?"

As Gunnar was led farther away, the words exchanged between Karl and General Bjorn became indistinct to him. All he could do was hope that General Bjorn would not dismiss their account as sheer madness.

14

Parting Ways

'A well-prepared traveler carries courage as a compass, determination as a map and the provisions of adaptability.'

Anwyn

After a few hours of catching up and sharing many hilarious stories with Alden, Anwyn relished the warmth of familial connection. Yet, beneath the surface of laughter, a weight pressed upon her, a reminder of the impending seriousness of their discussion. Each chuckle felt like a fleeting reprieve from the looming shadows of their reality.

As much as Anwyn could have continued listening to her grandfather's tales for many more hours, a sense of duty tugged at her heartstrings. She understood the gravity of the situation they were facing, the urgency that demanded their attention. With a heavy sigh, she steeled herself, knowing that the time for levity had passed. With a sense of reluctance, she finally broached the important question, her voice betraying the weight of the burden she carried within.

"Grandfather, please tell me, how will we find the Sacred Tree? We haven't had the chance to go through the tome you left."

Alden's brows furrowed in genuine confusion. "Tome? What in Vellhor's name are you talking about, dear?"

Eira passed over the large book containing Alden's notes and theories about the Sacred Tree, and Alden accepted them with a fond smile. He gently opened the tome, his eyes scanning over the pages with an affectionate nostalgia.

"Ahh, thank goodness I came when I did! These notes are nothing more than the ramblings of a mad old Elf! If you had followed these, you truly would never have found the Tree!" Alden chuckled heartily, shaking his head. "Luckily, however, I believe I have managed to locate our beloved Tree, and have a map will will guide you there."

The relief that washed over Anwyn was palpable. With Alden's guidance, their quest to find the Sacred Tree suddenly felt more attainable, and the journey ahead seemed filled with renewed hope and purpose. Anwyn's heart swelled with gratitude towards her grandfather, his wisdom illuminating their path like a beacon in the darkness. Yet, amidst the swell of optimism, a seed of doubt took root within her, a nagging whisper of uncertainty that refused to be silenced.

Anwyn initially smiled at the prospect of being able to find the Sacred Tree, her lips curving upwards in anticipation. But soon, beneath the veneer of enthusiasm, she felt a frown tugging at her face, a crease forming between her brows as her thoughts turned inward. Noticing the change in his daughter's expression, Laoch grew concerned and asked, "Anwyn, is everything okay? You seem troubled."

Internally, Anwyn wrestled with conflicting emotions, her mind a tumultuous sea of worry and determination. Despite the reassurance of their newfound hope, doubts lingered like shadows in the corners of her consciousness. She forced a small smile, masking the turmoil within, and replied to her father with a reassuring nod, "Yes, Father, everything is fine. Just lost in thought for a moment." But even as she spoke the words, she couldn't shake the sense of unease that gnawed at her soul.

Realization struck like a lightning bolt, and Anwyn felt a pang of disappointment wash over her as she lifted her gaze to meet her father's concerned eyes. "He won't be coming with us," she admitted quietly, her heart sinking. "He said 'guide you there,' not guide us there." The weight of those words settled heavily upon her shoulders, stirring a mix of apprehension and uncertainty within her. Despite her efforts to remain optimistic, a part of her couldn't help but feel a twinge of fear at the prospect of embarking on this journey without the knowledge or guidance of her grandfather.

Guiltily, Alden cleared his throat, acknowledging the truth of her words. "Um, well, yes, very perceptive of you. You are indeed correct. Unfortunately, I cannot come with you. However, I have information that is even worse." Alden raised his hand in a placating gesture, seeking to soothe their disappointment. "Now, please remember that I didn't make these decisions. These are ancient laws over which I have no control!"

Anwyn, eager to understand the challenges that lay ahead, encouraged Alden to continue.

"Although, you will indeed need to find the Sacred Tree eventually, Anwyn. As you are more than likely aware, the prophecy I left mentioned a forbidden love..." Alden began, watching his granddaughter closely.

Anwyn's cheeks tinged with a slight blush as she nodded, acknowledging the part of the prophecy that had piqued her curiosity.

"Well, yes," Alden continued, "the laws relating to the Sacred Tree do state that only the Seishinmori may seek her out. There are also allowances for the Seishinmeldo, however."

Anwyn's confusion was evident, and she looked at Alden as

if he were speaking a foreign language.

Seeing her befuddled expression, Alden decided to provide further clarification. "Ahh, well, what that means is that you must find this forbidden love and travel to the Sacred Tree with him," he explained, his tone grave yet tinged with a hint of excitement. "Together, you will face the Drogo in a battle that will determine the fate of our world. It's not a task for the faint-hearted, I must say."

Anwyn's heart skipped a beat at the mention of the Sacred Tree and the looming battle ahead. The weight of responsibility settled heavily on her shoulders as she realized the magnitude of the task that lay before her.

"Do you have any idea who he could be, by any chance?" Alden's eyes sparkled with curiosity as he posed the question, his eagerness to uncover the identity of Anwyn's forbidden love evident in his demeanor.

Anwyn sputtered in disbelief, her voice laced with incredulity. "Grandfather! I have never even left this forest. Where in Vellhor's name do you expect I would have met somebody?"

Alden nodded knowingly. "Right, well, as I had thought. Actually, that is rather good news. I have foreseen somebody in your life, and I was slightly worried in case there was somebody in Luxyyr who may cause complications." A flicker of relief washed over his features as he shared this reassurance with Anwyn.

"You have foreseen somebody in my life? Can you tell me who this is, grandfather? What is he like?" Anwyn asked eagerly, her curiosity evident.

Alden chuckled, his voice carrying a hint of amusement. "Are you telling me, Anwyn, that you are more worried about this forbidden love than you are of the battle with the Drogo?"

Anwyn met his gaze with steely resolve, her expression unreadable.

Alden smiled warmly, his eyes twinkling with affection. "Well, firstly, I can tell you he does not come from Luxyyr. In fact, he hails from the mountain realm of Dreynas! A prince, of sorts. A perfect match for the Queen of Elves, in my humble opinion!"

At this revelation, both Laoch and Eira exclaimed in unison, "A dwarf?!" The idea of their daughter, the Queen of Elves, being destined for a Dwarven prince from a distant realm was certainly unexpected, and they exchanged confused glances.

Alden chuckled in response. "Yes, indeed. And what a dwarf he is. However, I implore you to set aside any preconceived notions you may have about Dwarves and consider this for a moment. This particular dwarf has been revered for centuries as the savior of the Dwarven race. He has been blessed, or as some Dwarves might see it, cursed, with a drop of Elven Blood. This has bestowed upon him a rather unique set of characteristics, to say the least."

Laoch shook his head in disbelief, struggling with the idea. "It's impossible, Alden. Dwarves and Elves, they cannot... they can't, erm... they simply can't be together. It's just impossible!"

Eira chimed in to clarify, "What Laoch means, Father, I think, is that Elves and Dwarves, being from different races, cannot marry and reproduce." The gravity of this situation weighed heavily on their minds, challenging their beliefs and the traditions they had held dear.

Anwyn remained silent, her face flushed with embarrassment, feeling like an invisible bystander in the conversation that revolved around her as though she wasn't there.

Alden persisted, eager to emphasize the significance of this unique dwarf. "Did neither of you hear what I said? *Elven* Blood, dear. He has inherited a bloodline thought to have been lost over five thousand years ago! He only has a drop, mind you, but that drop has given him the ability to practise magic beyond what any other dwarf can achieve!"

Anwyn suddenly recalled an old legend or myth she had come across in her readings, one that suggested a distant connection between the Elves and the Dwarves. She voiced her recollection to Alden, who looked at her with keen interest, asking, "Where did you come across that information? I wonder?"

Sheepishly, Anwyn admitted, "I believe it was in some notes you left here, grandfather."

"Excellent, well at least I don't need to explain that much to you then!" Alden responded with a pleased smile. "You are indeed correct. Five thousand years ago, the Elven race and the Dwarven race were almost considered kin. We lived and traded closely together, and some families even intermarried, although that was a rare occurrence. Dwarves have always looked and acted as they do now, but back then, they could use magic similarly to how Elves can use magic today." The history lesson shed a new light on the connection between the two races, and all three elves were listening to Alden intently.

"What changed?" Anwyn implored, her curiosity and eagerness shining in her eyes.

Alden sighed and recounted the history. "Well, first there were the humans... They arrived from the south and claimed the land known as Fenmark, effectively driving a wedge between our people. Then came the Drogo, who emerged as the dragons disappeared, and they've been in a state of perpetual war with the Dwarves for centuries, which has kept their attention away from the Elves. But perhaps most significantly, when the Dwarves migrated from the Scorched Mountains to the Frost Mountains, their magic simply disappeared. No one knows why, and the Dwarves, being Dwarves, didn't seem to care and just went on with their lives. Since then, our two races have had very limited interactions indeed." The tale painted a picture of the forces that had reshaped their history and the rift that had grown between Elves and Dwarves over the millennia.

The four Elves sat in contemplative silence, processing the weight of the information. After a thoughtful pause, Anwyn couldn't help but inquire, "grandfather, what is he like, this dwarf?"

Alden's expression turned thoughtful as he replied, "Well, dear, I wouldn't actually know. I haven't met him in person. I have merely seen glimpses of him through my visions. I do know that his name is Gunnar, and like you, granddaughter, his spirit is also pure." The mystery surrounding Gunnar deepened, leaving Anwyn with a sense of anticipation and curiosity about the dwarf, who was destined to play a pivotal role in her life.

Anwyn's thoughts swirled like a hurricane of emotions, a chaotic blend of eager anticipation and nagging unease that set her heart pounding and her mind on edge. She was caught in a whirlwind of emotions, a wild dance between excitement and trepidation.

The thrill of the unknown tingled in her veins. Yet, beneath the surface, anxiety gnawed at her. The curiosity she felt over this dwarf, who destiny had foreseen her to fall in love with, tempered by the fear of the unknown, casting a shadow over her anticipation.

Alden, once again cleared his throat and somberly stated, "Ynfortunately, this first bit of information isn't all I need to tell you. Besides finding this prince of Dwarves, you will also need to convince him to journey with you to the Sacred Tree. Once you are there, however, I haven't seen anything more." Alden looked worried, the uncertainty of what lay beyond causing him evident concern.

Anwyn's voice was tinged with dejection as she voiced her concerns. "How am I supposed to find him? Am I to travel to

Dreynas alone? And once there, how will I be able to reach him?"

Alden's smile brightened slightly as he responded, "I have it on good authority that this prince will soon be leaving Dreynas and heading towards Luxyyr, through the Eldrakar Divide mountain range which divides us."

Anwyn's excitement was palpable as she asked, "Is he searching for me?"

Alden clarified, "Erm, not exactly. He has been involved in some unrest in Dreynas and falsely accused of treason." Alden smiled brightly to soften his words.

"And whilst I am out there trying to find the dwarf of my dreams, what may I ask will you three be doing with yourselves?" Anwyn muttered.

Alden responded with a mischievous glint in his light blue eyes, "Well, Anwyn, dear, I have been meddling in fate for the past fifty years to ensure that all the stars align perfectly. I have been busy down in Fenmark and within the Scorched Mountains themselves, and I plan on bringing your parents with me on my continued journey of meddling." His playful tone hinted at a sense of adventure and mischief that seemed to be a hallmark of his character.

Laoch and Eira shared a resigned, sorrowful look. Laoch, despite knowing the likely answer, felt compelled to ask, in a futile hope he was wrong. "Is there no way at least one of us could accompany her?"

Breathing out heavily, his shoulders sagging slightly, Alden said, "Unfortunately not, dear Laoch. This journey is one that only Anwyn and Gunnar can undertake. It is their destiny, and if any of us were to interfere, I fear it would do more harm than good."

As the weight of Alden's words settled upon them, a heavy silence enveloped the room. The only sounds that punctuated the stillness were the gentle tinkling of the stream outside and the distant chirping of birds, a stark contrast to the somber atmosphere within.

Breaking the silence, Anwyn raised her head and addressed her grandfather. "Grandfather, could you explain the rest of the prophecy, please? Who is this Dragon King, and where is he from? I assume that this is the war which you spoke to my parents of?"

Alden nodded solemnly. "Indeed, it is dear. The war is coming, and it will begin in the Scorched Mountains. The barbaric Drogo are seeking to resurrect their god, Nergai. They do not currently possess the knowledge needed to complete the ritual, nor where the tomb is located. However, I believe they are getting closer to discovering these secrets." His words conveyed the gravity of the impending threat and the urgency of the situation.

Alden contemplated her query again before responding, "I have not foreseen this war occurring within the next five years, but do not let that lull you into complacency. There will be many challenges and battles, and the coming months and years will be arduous for all of us."

He continued with a plan of action, outlining the daunting tasks ahead. "Your parents and I will need to petition the High Elven Council to have you officially instated as Seishinmori. Laoch, you must rekindle the relationship with your brother. His assistance would be greatly advantageous. Furthermore, we will need to navigate the complex challenge of having a dwarf accepted as the Seishinmeldo. Gunnar will have to convince the clans of Dreynas to commit to the war effort. As for you, my dear, you will need to push your skills past mastery and beyond the rank of High Elf. But that is only the beginning of your journey. Once you reach that level, there is additional room for your spirit to grow, allowing you to access the full strength and power of a Seishinmori. This alone is a formidable task, given the limited timeframe. And as for the humans, well, I have plans for them, but ultimately, they will need to choose a side or risk being swept up and annihilated in this war."

 Anwyn felt a surge of panic welling up within her. The enormity of the tasks ahead weighed heavily on her, but her resolve ultimately prevailed. Her grandfather believed in her, her parents had prepared her, and she had become a master of the arts. She knew she could do this; she had to do this. The fate of Vellhor rested upon her shoulders. However, amid all her worries about the challenges ahead, one thought nagged at her more than any other—meeting Gunnar. What if there was no attraction between them? What if he didn't feel the same way? Her mind spiraled into a relentless loop of "what-ifs," and she found herself more afraid of meeting Gunnar than the prospect of saving the world itself.

Anwyn

Anwyn, with her father's unwavering support, had meticulously prepared for her travels, cherishing every last moment they could share together before her departure. Together, they ensured that Honey was equipped and ready for the journey. Her grandfather had provided her with one of his maps, which found a secure spot in her pack, while her katana was safely nestled at her hip in its intricate black sheath.

 While Anwyn and Laoch were getting ready for the journey, Eira and Alden were in the kitchen, reminiscing and catching up on the events of the past five decades. Simultaneously, Eira was preparing food for travel, filling water-skins, and brewing a variety of elixirs specifically designed to aid Anwyn on her upcoming journey.

Her collection included vials of Swiftfoot, expertly crafted to grant both Anwyn and Honey enhanced speed and agility. In addition, she had carefully prepared bottles of Lifewell elixirs, designed to quicken the body's natural healing processes. Moreover, a stock of Stormcloak elixirs stood ready, offering protection against elemental hazards—ranging from the biting chill of extreme cold to the scorching intensity of heat and even the perilous blaze of magical fire.

Despite the preparations already undertaken, Eira's dedication to her daughter knew no bounds. She continued to labour tirelessly in the kitchen, deftly mixing ingredients and reciting arcane incantations to conjure forth more elixirs. Amidst this frenetic activity, she attempted to entertain her father, who sat contentedly, puffing on a pipe of broadleaf, his face adorned with an expansive grin that spoke of fond memories.

As Anwyn walked past, she marveled at the way her mother's fingertips effortlessly summoned the threads of spiritual power, weaving them delicately into the glass bottles around her. Anwyn, knowing that she possessed the innate ability to harness her own spiritual power, which could easily replicate the effects of the elixirs her mother worked so hard to create, explained, "Mother, I possess the power to replicate the effects of these myself. I don't wish to see you exhaust your strength for my sake."

Yet her mother's unwavering response remained the same each time Anwyn broached the subject. "A wise traveler carries provisions for both the expected and the unexpected journey." The wisdom in those words resonated within Anwyn; she wholeheartedly agreed. Still, a silent desire lingered—to spare her mother the effort incurred on her behalf.

After Eira had completed her preparations, she secured a

canvas sack onto Honey's sturdy frame. The sack emitted a faint jingling and jangling sound with every movement, making the once-majestic Elven horse appear more like a utilitarian beast of burden. Honey's expression clearly conveyed her discontent with the situation. Observing this, Eira swiftly muttered an incantation, casting a protective spell over the sack. Instantly, the vials within ceased their tinkling as if they had been enveloped in a layer of sand. With a somewhat contented expression, Eira remarked, "Hmmph, that should see you through most of the emergencies I can think of!"

Anwyn approached Honey with a gentle touch, her fingers caressing the sleek curve of her loyal steed's neck. She offered a crisp apple, the sweet scent mingling with the earthy aroma of the stables. As she gazed into Honey's eyes, pools of warmth and understanding, she whispered soothing words, her voice a soft melody in the quiet of the barn, a silent promise that all was well in their world. Over the years, amidst countless rides and shared adventures, they had woven a tapestry of trust and companionship, a bond unspoken yet deeply felt. In response, Honey snorted softly, the sound a symphony of affirmation, before nuzzling Anwyn's hand in eager acceptance of the offered treat. Anwyn's smile, tender and full of unspoken love, mirrored the reassurance she sought to convey, a silent affirmation of their unbreakable connection.

Turning towards her family, Anwyn couldn't help but notice the tears glistening in her parents' eyes. Their emotions were laid bare, a testament to the depth of their love and concern for her. Alden, once sporting a cheerful grin, had adopted a solemn, somber countenance, an acknowledgment of the gravity of the journey that lay ahead.

Alden spoke first, stepping towards Anwyn and embracing her gently. "My dear," Alden whispered in her ear, his voice comforting, "as you embark on this journey, I have some words of guidance for you, born from the lessons that my long life has taught me. Listen closely, for they may serve as a beacon in the darkest of times." Alden broke the embrace, but kept his hands firmly planted on Anwyn's shoulders as he looked intently into her eyes.

"Within you, there flows a wellspring of intuition," he continued, "a compass to navigate the treacherous unknown. If ever your heart senses disquiet, honor that whisper of caution. Your instincts are a gift, my child."

"In the face of adversity, remember the strength that flows through your veins," he advised. "The resilience of our Seishinmori is unparalleled. The path may be fraught with challenges, but know that you have the spirit to endure."

"Seek wisdom wherever you go." Alden implored. "Knowledge is a light that can pierce the darkness of ignorance. Learn from both the pages of books and the stories whispered by the wind, for they are the keys to understanding the world."

"Never underestimate the power of kindness. In a world often marked by cruelty, your compassionate heart will be your greatest weapon."

"Above all, my beloved granddaughter," Alden concluded, his voice trembling with heartfelt emotion, "promise me you will return safely."

As Alden concluded his speech, tears flowed freely down Anwyn's cheeks, and she turned her gaze briefly to her parents, who were also overcome with emotion. With a futile attempt to wipe away her tears, she responded to her grandfather, her voice tinged with gratitude, "I will etch your words into my very heart, grandfather. Thank you for your advice."

Alden, noticing the emotional impact of his words, stepped away with a touch of awkwardness, nodding to her before her parents approached to offer their comfort and support.

Instead of exchanging words, they embraced for several minutes, allowing their tears to convey their emotions in a way that mere words could not.

Eventually, their heartfelt embrace came to an end, and Laoch cleared his throat, his voice laden with love and concern. "I love you, my daughter. Be vigilant and always carry with you the lessons we've shared. They will undoubtedly prove invaluable on your adventure."

Eira followed with another warm embrace, her voice a soft, whispered reassurance. "I love you, my daughter. Stay safe."

Anwyn mustered a brave smile, her determination shining through, as she expressed her love and gratitude to her parents for all they had done. With a deep breath, she turned and gracefully mounted Honey, who responded with a soft snort.

Facing her family one last time, she called out with all the love in her heart, "I love you!" Her words hung in the air for a moment, a poignant farewell, before venturing forth into the unknown.

15

The Olive Tree

*'Like a well-brewed coffee, a delightful conversation with
a new friend warms the heart and awakens the spirit of
companionship.'*

Alden (a few days ago)

In the shadowed recesses of the Olive Tree, Alden observed with satisfaction as his carefully laid plans unfolded before him. The human mage and the dark assassin had now met, and their futures were now intertwined. Both were completely oblivious to Alden's presence, the puppeteer orchestrating their meeting and destiny; he thought.

A muffled chuckle escaped him as he recalled Kemp's bewilderment when Alden had seemingly vanished after offering him a flower. In truth, Alden had remained, concealed within the alcove. Had Kemp ventured a few steps further, he would have unwittingly trodden upon Alden's hidden form.

As Alden contemplated his next move, a wistful smile touched his lips at the thought of the reunion awaiting him back in Luxyyr. With little time to spare, and the images of his beloved family filling his mind, he finished his ale and stood to leave.

Outside the tavern, he slipped into an empty alleyway, allowing his magical disguise to dissipate. The ability to morph his appearance was a rare skill, one that even the esteemed High Elves of the Elven Council would undoubtedly envy, he mused with a grin.

Shaking his head to dispel the amusement, Alden retrieved a crystal, its surface glinting in the moonlight. Inside the crystal, the ethereal flame flickered magically. Though he hadn't completely mastered his mentor Thalirion's spell, the power he'd infused into the crystal would be sufficient for his journey to Luxyyr. He thought absently that Thalirion would be proud of his progress.

Kemp (present day)

Kemp pushed his plate aside, having barely touched his meal. The relentless assault of red chili peppers had turned his dinner into a culinary inferno that even a dragon might hesitate to devour. As he sat there thinking, he couldn't help but wonder two things: first, how anyone could consume what amounted to a blazing fire on a plate, and second, whether he might get to speak to Ruiha again before the end of the night.

Once the flames in his mouth had died down somewhat, Kemp's thoughts continued to swirl around his head. His mind meandered from Ruiha, considering her confident beauty, to the elderly woman who had given him the Sandaran flower and the note bearing Ruiha's name.

He couldn't wrap his head around how the old lady knew he would meet Ruiha, but not only that, but how could she have known he would instinctively offer her the flower? He thought back and realized that he hadn't known her name before he had offered her the flower. He had heard of people who had the gift of prophecy before, but it was a rare and unique talent. Could the old lady have been a prophet? Kemp mused to himself. Her actions seemed to hint at some form of magical ability, with her vanishing act, as if evaporating into thin air, only deepening the intrigue.

With no answers forthcoming, Kemp sighed. Giving up on Ruiha coming over and talking to him, he decided it was time to go and get some sleep. He needed to start tomorrow with a clear, fresh head. He wanted to get his trip to the Scorched Mountains sorted. As he stood, Ruiha approached him with determined strides. Her expression left Kemp uncertain whether or not she was angry. Her determined strides and her demeanor initially suggested a glare, causing him to startle briefly, but as she moved closer and much to his relief, he soon realized that she was, in fact, wearing a wry smile.

"And where are you off to?" Ruiha asked.

Kemp responded, a hint of fluster showing in his voice. "Erm., I'm off to bed now. I'm tired after a long day of travelling."

Ruiha glanced down at the uneaten plate of spiced lamb with rice. The food was one of the few bearable things about the Olive Tree and she was somewhat surprised that he hadn't touched a thing on his plate.

"You'll be hungry too if you don't eat your dinner." Ruiha said, an attempt at making small talk.

Kemp's cheeks tinged with a touch of embarrassment as he glanced at the plate and then back at Ruiha. "Ah... It's not really, uh... I'll be honest with you." He admitted with a sheepish grin. "I don't understand how anyone can bear the heat from the spices!"

Ruiha eyed the plate of lamb and rice, her brow furrowing in amusement. She leaned closer and gestured to the mild seasonings. "Are you serious?" she quipped. "This is practically a baby's first taste of spices in Sandara. You haven't even tried it, have you?" Her voice held a hint of playful incredulity.

Once again, Kemp glanced down at the plate. This time, his eyes hovered over the piece of lamb he'd made a valiant attempt to sample. "Well, you see, I did give it a shot," he began, feeling the need to explain, "but it had quite a spicy kick to it."

Ruiha let out a small, amused chuckle. "My, my, Kemp. I've heard rumors about you northerners and your fear of herbs and spices, but I honestly thought they were just tales!"

Kemp's embarrassment tinged his cheeks as he idly nudged the lamb around his plate with his fork, grappling with the idea of giving it another shot. Yet, almost as quickly as the thought crossed his mind, he dismissed it and set the fork aside.

Seemingly observing Kemp's hesitation, Ruiha attempted to suppress a small chuckle. He watched as she settled gracefully across from him, spearing a succulent piece of lamb with practiced precision, savoring its flavors. "It's rather delightful," she remarked, "though a dash of chili sauce could undoubtedly elevate it." Kemp simply stared at her in stunned silence.

As they conversed, Kemp couldn't help but be aware of the tantalizing scent of the meal wafting through the air, mingling with the soft glow of candlelight that bathed the table in a warm, intimate ambiance. The flickering flames cast dancing shadows, adding an extra layer of depth to their exchange.

In the midst of their conversation, Kemp found himself drawn to Ruiha's presence, her easy confidence and genuine warmth putting him at ease in a way he hadn't expected. Despite his initial hesitance, he felt a growing sense of comfort in her company, as if they were two pieces of a puzzle finally falling into place.

But beneath the surface, a whirlwind of thoughts churned within him. He couldn't shake the feeling that there was something significant about this moment, something that transcended mere conversation. Was it the way Ruiha's laughter seemed to light up the room, or the way her eyes sparkled with genuine interest as she listened to him speak? Whatever it was, Kemp couldn't deny the magnetic pull he felt towards her, a connection that seemed to grow stronger with each passing moment.

"So, where do you call home, Kemp?" Ruiha asked, her tone warm and inviting.

Kemp stammered slightly at first, but as he spoke, his confidence gradually returned. "I'm originally from a small village in Tempsford, but when I was about fourteen, my mage powers emerged, and my parents sent me to the Lakeview Arcane Academy. Have you ever heard of it?" His words flowed more smoothly now, and he felt a newfound comfort in the conversation.

Ruiha considered the question, for a moment and Kemp assumed that she was reflecting on her knowledge of Fenmark.

"I've heard of Tempsford," she responded slowly, "but the Lakeview Arcane Academy is new to me."

"It's perched at the northern tip of Fenmark, still within Tempsford. It's located on a vast lake nestled between the Great Elven Forest and the Eldrakar Divide."

Ruiha's eyes briefly flickered with recognition, her fingers fidgeting nervously. "I think I know where that is. So, anyway," Ruiha continued, "you're a mage, then? Used to know a few back in Gecit. They weren't formally trained or anything. Mainly used for high-end tasks, things us mere mundanes weren't any good at. Good ones were expensive, though, so we rarely used them."

As Ruiha spoke, a flicker of hesitation crossed her features, her gaze briefly darting away before returning to meet Kemp's. It was subtle, but Kemp couldn't help but wonder if her hesitation was directed toward magic itself or whether she was avoiding discussing her home, Gecit, which Kemp found she had been reluctant to talk about previously.

Kemp nodded in response. "Yes, that's right," he affirmed. "I'm an elemental mage in my final year of training. I can't wait to finish and get it over with."

Ruiha's curiosity was evident as she leaned in slightly. "That's interesting. What element do you have an affinity for?"

Kemp was initially taken aback. Mundanes rarely understood that mages typically only had an affinity for one element. However, she had mentioned working with mages in the past. Perhaps her knowledge stemmed from there. "Actually," he revealed, "I have an affinity for all of them."

Ruiha let out a low whistle. "You must be powerful and in high demand if you can manipulate all of the elements," she observed.

Kemp, however, remained humble. "Well, my power isn't necessarily stronger," he admitted. "But I've dedicated a lot of time to studying and perfecting the mastery of each element." His pride still resonated in his voice, though he remained grounded in reality.

Ruiha couldn't help but chuckle as she inquired, "and why in Vellhor's name are you down here in the arse end of nowhere? Somewhere you can't eat the food, nor drink the drinks served?"

"As part of my final thesis," Kemp went on to explain. "I aim to prove the theory that the dragons practiced a form of divine magic or ritual that bestowed them with immortality."

Ruiha looked at him blankly, as if working out whether he was joking or not. When he didn't respond, and it was clear he wasn't winding her up, she responded simply. "The dragons?" She asked, hesitantly.

Kemp cleared his throat to emphasize his point. "Well, yes, the dragons were last known to inhabit the Scorched Mountains."

Ruiha responded with a wry smile. "Yeah, about a million years ago!"

Kemp corrected her with a more precise timeline. "Actually,

there are records that state dragons were last seen in Vellhor, just over a thousand years ago."

Ruiha waved her hand dismissively, her humor evident. "One thousand, ten thousand, a million years ago. It doesn't really matter, does it? It was still bloody ages ago!"

Kemp conceded, "Well, that is true, I suppose. However, I disagree it doesn't matter. If my theory is correct, and we can find even the smallest bit of evidence to back it up, then our whole viewpoint and everything we know about divine magic could be completely wrong!" There was a palpable excitement in Kemp's voice, a passion he hadn't exhibited to Ruiha before.

Ruiha offered him a warm smile. "I hope you find the answers you're looking for. Although, I'm not entirely certain you'll find anyone willing to act as your guide. There are rumours that those mountains are deadly. Not many adventurers return, if you catch my meaning. So whatever you do, make sure you're careful!"

Their conversation flowed now, and Kemp had managed to find his confidence around Ruiha. Her laughter was melodic, and the lines of her face softened as she listened to Kemp's stories and dreams. In those moments, Kemp noticed that her guard lowered, and her eyes sparkled with genuine interest.

Ruiha

As the evening drew on, Kemp and Ruiha were oblivious to the world outside. Each carried the weight of their recent hardships — Kemp, burdened by the shame and cowardice stemming from the recent attack, managed to forget; while Ruiha, fleeing the clutches of the Sand Dragons, escaped her life on the run – if only for a short time.

As they discussed their dreams and aspirations, Kemp and Ruiha found a genuine connection, marked by shared smiles and laughter. Their conversation flowed effortlessly, surprising them both with the ease of their bond. Ruiha, trusting Kemp, shared the secret of her illegal arrival in Lamos, yet she kept the shadows of her past in Sandarah safely concealed for now. Meanwhile, Kemp, fueled by youthful ambition, expressed his longing to rise to the esteemed position of a court mage serving an important noble of Fenmark.

The atmosphere abruptly shifted, and Ruiha's once animated expression contorted briefly into a mask of alarm. With a rapid shift, she averted her gaze, a silent warning etched across her features. Leaning closer to Kemp, she spoke urgently, her words laced with a sense of impending danger.

"Apologies, Kemp," she whispered, her tone urgent yet rushed. "I don't mean to sound rude, but you need to be quiet. Do not draw attention to us, and, whatever you do, do not say my name."

Kemp regarded the top of her head, now lowered to obscure her face, and nodded in understanding. She was glad to see that he had taken her words seriously, maintaining a vigilant silence, taking her warning to heart as he met her lowered gaze with a subtle nod of acknowledgment.

Noticing Kemp's gaze trailing in the direction she had glanced moments before, Ruiha observed a hint of anxiety and caution in his tone as he leaned in to whisper, "there's a big man coming over to us."

Ruiha sighed in exasperation and responded in a hushed tone, "Did you see him with anyone else?" Her question hung in the air, a hint of concern in her expression.

Kemp's eyes darted around the room, scanning for unfamiliar faces, and he replied, his voice tinged with growing fear, "No, but there are definitely four or five new faces that weren't here earlier this evening. Is everything okay? Should I be worried?" His apprehension was palpable as he turned to Ruiha, seeking guidance.

Ruiha's response was blunt, her tone grave. "Unfortunately, everything is not okay, and yes, you should probably be worried. Although they are here after me and not you, so they may simply leave you be." Her words bore the weight of harsh truth, signaling a sudden and perilous shift in the situation.

The dimly lit room was buzzing with energy. The clinking of glasses and the hum of conversations and laughter echoed throughout the common room. The mood shifted abruptly when suddenly Ruiha stood, fork in hand, and spun, stabbing the fork into the large man's neck. He screamed, his hand reaching for where the fork had pierced him. Ruiha pulled the fork out, and a spurt of blood followed. She repeated the attack several times before the large man fell to the floor, writhing and screaming.

Ruiha looked up calmly, her eyes methodically sweeping the room for any additional threats. And there they were, confirming Kemp's earlier warning. Accompanying him were five gang members, easily identifiable by the distinctive dragon tattoos adorning the sides of their necks.

She knew of the big man she had just dropped. He was known in the underworld of Gecit as 'Bear'. He was an enforcer, but a fairly low level one. That meant Faisal had probably sent a lot more resources after her, and this thug and his five cronies were simply the ones lucky enough to wonder into the Olive Tree and spot her.

Before the five thugs reached her, she leaned down and snapped Bear's neck. She couldn't leave any of these men alive to report back to Faisal.

She scanned the room and saw patrons standing aside. A few had ducked behind tables or chairs, not wanting to be caught up in whatever was happening.

Interestingly enough, Kemp had stood and was facing the five men stalking towards her. The fear was evident in his eyes, yet he set his jaw with a determined resolve. Although she appreciated his show of support, a part of her secretly wished he had opted for the safer choice of hiding behind furniture. She didn't want him being caught up in this, and a twinge of guilt tugged at her for involving him in the first place.

As the five men closed the gap, nearing Ruiha and Kemp, she raised her voice. "You've really got yourselves screwed here, lads. I know you've all seen me, so I can't be letting any of you walk out of here alive now."

The men exchanged a glance, and Ruiha couldn't help but wonder if Kemp caught the fleeting flicker of fear that briefly crossed their faces.

Even as the gang members closed in, their intentions dripping with malice, Ruiha couldn't help but sigh inwardly. They clearly recognized her, aware of her capabilities. Yet, despite the looming threat, her gaze remained steady, devoid of any trace of fear.

Inwardly, she steeled herself for the inevitable confrontation, the taste of blood lingering on the fork clenched tightly in her hand. With each passing moment, the tension in the air thickened, anticipation coiling in her chest like a tightly wound spring.

Her muscles tensed as she shifted into a defensive stance, a silent acknowledgment of the violence about to erupt. Though the prospect of bloodshed loomed before her, Ruiha's resolve remained unyielding, her mind focused and her senses heightened, ready to meet the imminent chaos head-on.

A brute with a shaved head, lunged menacingly at Ruiha with a growl. Quick as a striking snake, Ruiha caught his wrist, twisted it with surprising strength, and plunged the fork into his thigh, ensuring she struck an artery. He would bleed out within ten minutes.

The second thug, a wiry and tattooed man, swung a glass bottle at Ruiha's head. She ducked, letting the bottle smash against the wall. With a swift and powerful kick, she sent him staggering backward, disoriented. She immediately followed up with an upward thrust; the fork piercing the underside of his jaw.

The third member of the gang, a burly figure with a menacing sneer, aimed a punch at Ruiha's face. She deftly dodged his attack, seizing his arm and leveraging his momentum to send him crashing into a nearby table. The sound of shattering bottles and glasses echoed as he fell, blood oozing from the glass shards embedded in his face, a gruesome sight that did little to faze Ruiha. Without hesitation, she grabbed a broken wine bottle and swiftly drove it into the man's throat, ending his life in an instant.

As the fourth thug, his face marked by scars, lunged at her with a knife, Ruiha reacted with lightning speed. She grabbed his wrist, her grip unyielding as she disarmed him with a swift twist, wrenching the weapon from his grasp. Meeting his gaze with a cold determination, she drove the blade into his chest without a word, leaving him sprawled on the ground, his intentions extinguished.

Meanwhile, the assailant who had targeted Kemp found himself facing unexpected retaliation. With great concentration, Kemp conjured a fiery ball that swiftly engulfed the attacker, leaving him writhing in agony. But the sudden display of power seemed to take its toll on Kemp, who doubled over in a violent bout of retching, his body trembling with the aftermath of his spell-casting.

Despite the chaos surrounding them, Ruiha wasted no time in rushing to Kemp's side, offering him support as she helped him to his feet, her voice urgent with concern. "We've got to leave, now," Ruiha urged softly. "These won't be the only thugs after me."

Kemp stood frozen, his gaze locked on the twitching figure before him. Then, with a suddenness that startled Ruiha, he bent over, his body wracked with violent retching again. The acrid scent of bile filled the air as Kemp continued to empty his stomach, his breath ragged and labored.

Ruiha watched him with a mix of concern and urgency, knowing they couldn't afford to waste any more time. She gently placed a hand on his back, offering a small measure of comfort amidst the chaos. "Kemp, we have to move," she whispered, her voice steady despite the turmoil around them.

Kemp nodded vacantly, allowing Ruiha to lead him towards the exit. But as they passed the staircase that led to his room, he suddenly snapped out of his stupor.

"My pack," he exclaimed, a hint of panic in his voice. "I need my things."

Ruiha took a moment to consider the situation before giving a curt nod. "Hurry, but keep it quiet. Those men are likely to have reinforcements on the way. We're running out of time," she cautioned.

Kemp acknowledged her advice with a nod, and he hurried up the stairs with Ruiha right behind him. Upon reaching the door to his room, Kemp moved to push it open. However, Ruiha, ever vigilant, halted him. She pressed her finger to her lips, and pointed to the door, which was slightly ajar with its latch visibly broken. Kemp's eyes widened in realization, understanding the potential danger that could have awaited him if Ruiha hadn't detected the breach.

Ruiha gently nudged the door open with her foot before tentatively walking in, scanning the room intently as she entered. The room was located on the upper floor, accessible by the creaky, winding staircase that they had just run up, so Ruiha knew that if the intruder was still in the room, he would have definitely heard their approach.

The room was dark, with low ceilings, and it seemed undisturbed. So not a robbery then, Ruiha noted. As she walked further into the small room, her eyes adjusted to the dim light, and she saw a man sitting on Kemp's bed against the far wall. She also noted that he was the same hooded man who had been staring at Kemp earlier on that evening. Ruiha frowned, speaking slowly as she asked. "Who are you? And what do you want?"

The man looked at her with disinterest, before his focus turned toward Kemp. "Harald!" Kemp exclaimed as his eyes adjusted to the dark room. "What in Vellhor's name are you doing here?"

Harald responded matter-of-factly, "Kris has disbanded the guard unit for a season. Now I'm stuck down in Lamos with no work."

Clearly still uncertain why Harald was in his room, Kemp responded, "Oh right, that's a shame. How come he's disbanded the unit?"

"Need to find more guards to replace the ones we lost on the road." Harald explained, his voice gruff.

Kemp shifted awkwardly and asked, "Oh, right, okay. That makes sense. But why are you here, Harald? How can I help you find work?"

Harald's gaze held determination, and he spoke with a clear purpose. "I know you're looking for a guide into the Scorched Mountains. I'd like to help—for a small fee, that is." A brief smile touched Harald's lips before vanishing.

Ruiha had encountered men like Harald many times before, and her instincts screamed at her not to trust him. She had spent years reading people for a living, a skill set she hadn't lost since leaving the Sand Dragons. Her intuition told her that something about Harald wasn't right.

His presence exuded an air of untrustworthiness, and his brief, sly smile hinted at hidden motives, calculations, or schemes. His hooded appearance seemed a deliberate choice to maintain a low profile, an attempt to fade into the background and evade scrutiny. The earthy, muted colors of his clothing reinforced the impression of someone seeking to remain unnoticed, concealing his true intentions. His voice was smooth and persuasive, yet it harbored an undercurrent of insincerity. It was the kind of voice that could convince you of anything while leaving you with a nagging sense of doubt.

"He's good," Ruiha mused inwardly, recognising the adeptness of the man before her. She understood the necessity of caution when dealing with someone of his type.

"And what do you know about the Scorched Mountains then, Harald?" she queried, her skepticism palpable in her tone.

Harald barely spared Ruiha a glance before responding. "I've travelled the Scorched Mountains several times in the past, albeit not from the south, but from the west in Fenchester," he explained. His focus remained on Kemp before he continued, his tone darkening. "The mountains are teeming with lizard folk. They're barbaric and won't hesitate to end you in the most gruesome manner for their own amusement."

At least he was being honest about that much, Ruiha acknowledged. In the Sandaran city of Ostium, located in the southern region of the vast Scorched Mountains, she was acquainted with numerous individuals who had embarked on a quest for wealth. However, none of them had ever returned.

However, she quickly intervened, asserting, "He's already secured a guide. Thank you, Harald. Your services won't be required." Her tone was firm, making it clear that his presence was neither wanted nor needed.

Kemp looked at Ruiha in confusion. Ignoring him, she deliberately stood with an air of guarded caution, her posture was rigid, her shoulders squared and slightly hunched, as if she was preparing for a confrontation.

Harald's intense gaze locked onto Kemp as he spoke in his honeyed tone, the air almost humming, "no harm in taking additional protection, is there Kemp?" His eyes flickered to Ruiha, and she saw the irritation in them, before he continued, "plus, the fee won't be much. I'm desperate for the work, so just need enough to tide me over until Kris reforms the unit in a couple of months."

Kemp, seemingly in a daze, nodded and gave a flat response. "Okay, Harald, I suppose you're right."

Ruiha, though unhappy with Kemp's decision, accepted it, knowing it was ultimately his choice. They had to leave Lamos as swiftly as possible, and there wasn't time for a lengthy argument. She quickly interjected, "Right, we'll sort out the details of this arrangement later. For now, our priority is to put as much distance between us and the Olive Tree as quickly as possible."

As if snapping awake again, Kemp shook his head and the fear of their situation seemed to fill his eyes. He looked at Ruiha and nodded. "Let's go," he agreed.

Ruiha felt troubled. Despite their need to move swiftly, her mind couldn't help but dwell on Kemp's swift acceptance of Harald. She found herself questioning why he couldn't see that the man wasn't to be trusted.

16

Between a Rock and a Hard Place

'When standing at the edge of the unknown, taking the plunge is the bravest step one can take.'

Gunnar

After General Bjorn had thoroughly interrogated Karl, the two Dwarves found themselves in a holding cell, sharing their evening meal while discussing the events of the past few days.

"What a shit show," Karl remarked, the frustration of their unjust imprisonment evident in his voice.

Gunnar nodded in agreement, his own irritation simmering just beneath the surface. Karl continued, "we haven't done a thing wrong. We've witnessed our comrades die right in front of us, and this is how they bloody treat us!" Gunnar sensed Karl needed to vent, so he let his fellow dwarf continue his rant. "I'll tell you, Gunnar, once all of this is sorted out, I'm leaving the army. I'll go work with my dad and my uncle in the mines, doing honest work where I'll be paid a fair wage and treated right!"

"Aye," Gunnar replied, his gaze distant as he considered Karl's words. Memories flickered in his mind, of shared triumphs and hardships, of the unwavering loyalty Karl had shown time and again. "I think that's your decision to make," he continued, his voice tinged with a hint of melancholy. "And if it's what you truly want, then I won't stand in your way."

Yet, beneath his outward support, Gunnar couldn't shake the nagging doubt that whispered in the depths of his thoughts. Was he truly being a good friend, encouraging Karl to settle for a life confined within the depths of the mines? Or was he inadvertently stifling his potential, denying him the chance to pursue greater aspirations?

"But I've seen your skills in action," Gunnar added, his tone softening with genuine admiration. "And I know you're capable of much more than just mining." He hoped his words conveyed the belief he held in Karl's abilities, a belief that transcended the confines of their current circumstances. "Regardless of what path you choose," he concluded, a flicker of uncertainty betraying his stoic facade, "I'll support you, my friend."

"Thanks, boss," Karl muttered, his gratitude laced with a hint of uncertainty. He then looked up, his gaze searching, and asked Gunnar hesitantly, "What about you, Gunnar? What are your plans, if you have any?"

Gunnar's gaze softened as Karl's question pulled him back to the present moment, breaking the spell of his introspection. He met Karl's searching gaze with a small smile, though a shadow of uncertainty lingered in his eyes. He had given little thought to his future beyond resolving their current predicament and returning to lead the Snow Wolves. However, the emergence of his newfound powers had made him pause and think. Could he hide them, or should he even try? Should he reveal them to his father and potentially use them for the benefit of the clan?

"To be honest, Karl, I haven't really considered it much,"

Gunnar admitted. "There's a chance my father will ask me to come back and continue leading the Snow Wolves, or he might want me to take on a larger role in managing clan affairs. I'm not entirely sure."

Karl nodded slowly, his expression thoughtful. "Aye, that's all well and good, but what do *you* want, Gunnar? Have you thought about that at all?"

Gunnar managed a forced smile, attempting to inject a bit of humor into their conversation. "Thinking about what I want? I barely have time to catch my breath, let alone think about what I want. The luxury of making choices has never been mine, and I fear it may never be."

Gunnar's gaze seemed to go through Karl, his eyes fixed on a future that he had grudgingly accepted long before this conversation with Karl. As the heir to his father's legacy and the inevitable successor to the mantle of clan chief, Gunnar bore the weight of responsibility with a heavy heart. The prospect of leadership, a role thrust upon him, was always a distant, and unwanted, presence in his thoughts. Despite the honor that accompanied his impending position, Gunnar had never sought the role of chief, finding himself caught between his duty to his clan and his family and his personal desires. His duty won each time he contemplated it.

Karl sighed and shook his head, his expression sympathetic. "It's a shame, Gunnar. Maybe once you become clan chief, things will change for you."

Gunnar's heart sank at Karl's well-meaning words. The prospect of assuming his father's mantle brought forth a storm of conflicting emotions within him. While it was an honor to be considered for such a position, he couldn't shake the nagging doubt that it would only serve to further tether him to the expectations of others.

As Karl's hopeful sentiment hung in the air, Gunnar couldn't help but doubt its validity. Would ascending to the role of clan chief truly offer him the freedom he sought, or would it only serve to entangle him further in the intricacies of clan politics?

Suppressing a sigh, Gunnar kept his inner turmoil hidden behind a mask of resignation. Rather than voicing his concerns, he offered Karl a small, resigned smile, the weight of his duty settling back onto his shoulders as he returned to his meal. It was a burden he had grown accustomed to carrying, one that seemed to grow heavier with each passing day.

Following a period of silence, Karl finally found the courage to address Gunnar's recently discovered magical talents. Gunnar could sense that Karl had been wanting to inquire about this for a while, but had seemingly struggled to find the appropriate moment to broach the subject.

"Hey, Gunnar," Karl began cautiously, "have you started remembering anything from our patrol, especially the encounter with that, well, the golem?"

Gunnar regarded Karl, recognising the curiosity and concern in his friend's eyes. He appreciated Karl's straightforwardness and decided it was time to open up a bit about his unusual experiences.

"No, I haven't," he said. "I'm hoping that some memories will come back to me, though. I didn't have time to tell you before, but during the siege of the barracks, I inadvertently did something similar. I think I may have tapped into some elemental magic. I tried to cause a landslide to block the soldiers."

"Really? And what happened?" Karl asked curiously.

Gunnar coughed slightly before responding sheepishly. "Well… It didn't go as I'd hoped. Let's put it that way."

Karl laughed, "Well, I suppose I didn't recall any rocks or rubble around the barracks when we were leaving. So what happened then?"

"Well, I thought I could feel something. A vein or tendril of power in the rock. It was like a root and I could force it to grow. Eventually I forced it to grow towards the right place, but when it got there. Well, let's just say I ended up on my arse again!"

Both Dwarves shared a brief moment of laughter as they pictured Gunnar sprawled out flat on his back.

"You've had more moments of unconsciousness in the past few days than most dwarves experience in an entire lifetime, Gunnar!" Karl teased, his lighthearted voice reminding him of the jovial dwarf Gunnar knew he was.

"Aye, Karl, that's not too far from the truth of it! However, some good news from that failed attempt, I suppose. I can fully recount what happened. I didn't lose any of my memories this time."

"Aye, I suppose that is good news. Perhaps your tolerance, or your skill, is improving." Karl mused.

Gunnar wasn't sure about that. He knew little of what was happening to him, having not studied the intricacies of a mage coming into their abilities before. But he knew that he would need to find a way to control his powers, otherwise, he could cause serious damage to himself, or somebody else. He said as much to Karl, who grunted and said, "if you inadvertently do what you did to that golem again, we could all be in trouble, that's stone certain."

The unease in Gunnar's eyes mirrored his inner turmoil. He knew Karl's assessment was accurate, even if it was disheartening. At present, there was little he could do to control his abilities effectively. His best chance lay in acquiring guidance and training in the arcane arts, and his mind gravitated toward one potential source—the Elves. However, his hopes were clouded with uncertainty.

Long ago, the Dwarves and Elves had shared a close kinship.

Dwarves, with their affinity for earth, stone and the mountains, and Elves, with their bond to trees, wildlife, and the forest. Over time, the two races had drifted apart, but Dwarves had retained some of their ancestral traditions, including reverence for the mountain goddess and her four sons. Elves, on the other hand, had seemingly forsaken their ancient ways, save for their continued spiritual connection to the forest.

Gunnar knew from his studies that the High Elves, in particular, wielded power and authority through a combination of strategies and tactics. Their dominance stemmed from their unparalleled magical abilities and strength, surpassing most other Elves in Luxyyr. These undemocratic, power-hungry leaders deployed methods of repression, manipulation, and propaganda to cement their control, leading to a growing chasm between the Dwarves and Elves.

Now, Gunnar faced an arduous challenge—he would potentially need to seek the aid of the very Elves from whom the Dwarves had distanced themselves. The prospect weighed heavily on him, and he knew there would be no easy path forward.

"Once all the dust has settled from this nightmare, maybe I'll request permission from the Council to travel to Luxyyr. Once the clan chiefs know about my magic, surely they will want me to learn how to control it?" Gunnar mused, his gaze fixed on an uncertain future.

"Maybe," Karl stated, his voice laced with skepticism. "Although they're just as likely to lock you up out of fear, Gunnar."

Gunnar's stomach churned at the truth in Karl's words. The weight of his newfound abilities bore down on him like an anvil, a constant reminder of the precarious position he now found himself in. Dwarves were renowned for their craftsmanship and resilience, not for wielding arcane powers beyond the realm of their understanding.

As Karl's cautionary words echoed in his mind, Gunnar couldn't help but envision the repercussions of his actions. He could almost feel the weight of judgment settling upon him, the disapproving glares of those who would see him as a threat to their established order, a deviation from the norms they held dear.

With a brisk nod, acknowledging Karl's insight, Gunnar bid his companion a good night. Yet, as he settled into his bed, the shadows on the walls seemed to dance in tandem with his troubled thoughts. Sleep remained elusive, stolen away by the looming specter of an uncertain future, one fraught with challenges and consequences he was ill-prepared to face.

Gunnar

Gunnar's much-needed slumber was a bittersweet respite. Just as he had settled into a deep sleep, the clamor of battle erupted outside his cell, violently tearing him from his dreams. Startled, he jolted awake, his eyes wide with alarm. Beside him, Karl was similarly roused from his sleep, his fiery red hair disheveled and a bewildered look on his face.

The noise of the ongoing fight reverberated through the stone walls, a cacophony of clashing weapons and shouts of fury that seemed to encase Gunnar in a suffocating grip of dread. He knew that beyond these walls, Wilfrid's troops would be gathering, their swords thirsty for blood, their minds consumed by vengeance.

As the tension in the cell thickened, Gunnar felt a surge of adrenaline course through his veins, his muscles tensing in anticipation of the impending onslaught. With each passing moment, the weight of uncertainty pressed down upon him, a heavy burden that threatened to crush his resolve.

Bracing themselves, Gunnar and Karl stood in grim silence, their senses heightened, their nerves stretched taut like bowstrings ready to be released. After what felt like an eternity, the sounds of fighting gradually faded, replaced by an eerie stillness that hung in the air like a shroud of impending doom.

Then the door to their cell began to tremble, its rusty hinges groaning in protest. Gunnar's heart pounded in his chest, his breath catching as he stared at the door, willing it to stay shut. A sharp crack echoed through the dim room, and with a resounding thud, the door burst open, slamming against the stone wall, revealing a bruised and battered Hansen. Relief flooded through Gunnar as he beheld the dwarf's weary yet determined visage, a beacon of hope amidst the darkness that threatened to engulf them.

Winded and panting for breath, he spoke urgently. "Gunnar, Karl. You need to leave immediately. General Wilfrid's troops have attacked the holding cells. We managed to stop the first wave from getting through, but we only have minutes before we are overrun."

Not being allowed weapons or their packs in the cells with them, Gunnar found himself uncomfortably empty-handed as they hastily left the cell, their footsteps echoing far too loudly for Gunnar's liking. Each step seemed to reverberate through the corridor like a thunderous drumbeat, amplifying the sense of vulnerability that gnawed at his nerves.

As they approached the exit of the corridor, Gunnar braced himself for the inevitable confrontation. His muscles tensed, ready to spring into action at the first sign of danger. Yet, to his surprise, no adversaries lurked in the shadows, no swords awaited them at the threshold.

As the realization dawned upon him, it felt like a welcome reprieve—a momentary respite from the relentless tide of adversity. In this moment, there was no fight to be had, no clash of steel to test their mettle. Instead, as he reached the end of the corridor, he discovered an exit that opened onto the side of the mountain. It offered a breathtaking view of the sprawling river below, truly a sight to behold.

Gunnar's brow furrowed in confusion as he exchanged a puzzled glance with Karl, uncertainty flickering in his eyes. What was this? What new challenge awaited them beyond the confines of their imprisonment?

Hansen's gesture drew his attention downward, towards the rushing waters that churned with untamed ferocity. A surge of apprehension tightened Gunnar's chest as he contemplated the perilous descent that lay ahead, uncertainty mingling with determination as he prepared to face whatever trials awaited them beyond the safety of the mountain's embrace.

Karl's massive bushy head swivelled around, his eyes widening with shock as he fixed his gaze on Hansen. "You've got to be fucking kidding me if you think I'm jumping down there! I can't fucking swim!" His fear was palpable, etched across his face in unmistakable lines of distress.

Honestly, even though Gunnar could swim, albeit not one of his strongest skills, he too was dreading the jump.

"Is there no other way, Hansen?" Gunnar asked.

Hansen shook his head vigorously. "No, this is the only way out. Unless you fancy going back and fighting your way through Wilfrid's troops."

Gunnar watched as Karl seemed to be giving that grim alternative some serious thought. He could see Karl's eyes darting between the perilous jump and the path ahead, clearly weighing the risk of leaping against the danger of charging headlong into an unknown number of enemies without a weapon. Karl's furrowed brow and tense posture spoke volumes, revealing the intensity of his internal struggle.

Before Karl could make that decision, which would no doubt lead to his certain death, Gunnar grabbed him by the shoulders and tackled him off the side of the mountain, the two of them plummeting through the air. They hurtled through the sky, their screams lost to the whistling wind as they plummeted downward. His stomach churned with the sensation of the sickening drop. His eyes caught the glistening river occasionally, and each time it came into view, it was startlingly closer than it had been before. Gunnar decided a quick prayer to Dreyna would be a good idea, but he didn't have time before he plunged into the water with a sickening slap.

It was like crashing into a wall of cold, liquid force. The river engulfed them both, momentarily disorienting Gunnar with its icy embrace. Strong currents seized his body, pulling him under, then up again, and then under once more.

Panic set in as he struggled to regain his bearings. He fought against the river's relentless pull, gasping for breath when his head surfaced briefly. His limbs flailed as he tried to swim towards the riverbank, but the powerful current swept him downstream with an unstoppable force.

As he was carried away, the world blurred and his surroundings turned into a chaotic blend of swirling water, rocks, and spray. Karl was now lost to him, and fear surged through every fiber of his being as he frantically sought any chance to break free from the river's relentless hold and reach the safety of the shore. Yet, just as land came into view and his hope flickered, everything plunged into an abyss of darkness.

Gunnar

Waking up on a shore after being dragged downstream in a violent river was disorienting and harrowing. As Gunnar's senses returned, he felt the cold, damp ground beneath him, sending a shiver through his body. The gritty, uneven earth pressed against his aching limbs. The thunderous rush of water echoed in his ears, a relentless symphony that filled him with awe and dread. Slowly, he forced his heavy eyelids open, the harsh daylight seeping through his lashes.

What greeted him was a verdant landscape alive with vibrant hues. Tall trees towered overhead, their leaves shimmering with moisture, and their branches swayed gently in the breeze. The air was filled with birdsong, soothing his battered soul. Despite his suffering, Gunnar marveled at the beauty around him. The sun hung high overhead, casting dappled shadows across the shore and bathing everything in a soft, golden light. He guessed it must be close to midday, though the passage of time felt surreal, distorted by the tumultuous events that had led him here.

It had been at least six hours since he had leaped into the river, driven by desperation and the hope of escape. Now, as he lay upon the riverbank, battered and bruised but alive, Gunnar couldn't help but wonder how far the river had carried him before depositing him onto this unfamiliar shore. The journey had been perilous, but somehow, against all odds, he had survived. And as he gazed out at the vast expanse of wilderness that stretched before him, Gunnar knew that his struggle was far from over.

Gunnar attempted to move, in order to sit up, but his body protested with aches and pains, so instead he remained lying there on the riverbank, trying to make sense of his location. It was pointless; he realized. He could be anywhere in Dreynas.

A sudden surge of fear and guilt clawed its way through Gunnar's chest as he remembered the desperate act that had led to Karl's fall from the mountainside. The haunting question loomed large in his mind: had he inadvertently caused the death of his friend?

The memory played out before him like a vivid nightmare, each detail etched into his consciousness with painful clarity. The desperation of their escape, the chaos of their pursuit, the split-second decision that had changed everything.

He tried to rationalize his actions, to convince himself that he had no other choice. Wilfrid's soldiers had been closing in, their swords poised to strike, their orders clear. In that moment of panic, he had acted on instinct, driven by the primal urge to survive at any cost.

But even as he clung to this justification, doubt gnawed at the edges of his resolve. Had he acted too hastily, too recklessly? Could there have been another way, a path that didn't lead to such a dire outcome?

The weight of guilt settled heavily upon him, a burden too heavy to bear. He couldn't shake the nagging feeling that he had failed Karl, that his actions had sealed their fate in ways he couldn't begin to comprehend.

Yet, even amidst the turmoil of his thoughts, one thing remained certain: Wilfrid's ruthless pursuit left no room for second chances. If they had been caught, there would have been no mercy, no opportunity for redemption. In the face of such relentless brutality, Gunnar had done what he believed necessary to survive. He just hoped he could live with the consequences.

A soft groan emanated from somewhere behind Gunnar and a flicker of hope arose within him. "Karl," he croaked. "Is that you? Are you okay?"

Gunnar managed to get himself into a sitting position, forcing himself through the pain and agony of the movement. He scanned his surroundings, desperately trying to locate the source of the groan. After only a few more agonising seconds of searching, he noticed a ragged body with red hair lying limp a hundred paces away.

With a supreme effort, Gunnar summoned the last reserves of his strength, forcing himself to stand. He wobbled unsteadily at first, like a puppet on strings, but gradually, he steadied himself. One step at a time, he staggered towards Karl's prone form, a surge of hope coursing through him as he prayed his friend was okay.

As Gunnar approached Karl's motionless form, the gruesome state of his friend's leg came into sharp focus. It was contorted at an unnatural and agonising angle, the bone gruesomely piercing through torn skin and soaked fabric. A wave of despair crashed over Gunnar as he knelt beside his injured friend, the direness of Karl's condition settling heavily on his shoulders.

Karl, opened one eye ever so slightly, a blood-red hue visible through the matted locks of his hair. Despite the alarming sight, a flicker of relief washed over Gunnar. Karl was alive, and Dwarves were renowned throughout Vellhor for their legendary resilience. Gunnar clung to the hope that his friend would recover.

The distant sounds of the raging river echoed in the background, underscoring the gravity of their predicament and the air carried the metallic scent of blood, and Gunnar knew that eventually it would attract the predators of the Frost Mountains.

Gunnar's hands hovered uncertainly over Karl's injured leg, a mix of helplessness and determination etched across his face. He had to do something, anything, to aid his friend.

Without wasting any time, he ripped a piece of fabric from his shirt and quickly made a makeshift splint to immobilize Karl's injured limb. Using another scrap of relatively clean cloth from his shirt, he gently cleaned the gruesome wound using the fresh water from the river. As he carefully applied pressure to stop the bleeding, Gunnar's focus shifted to minimising swelling. He elevated Karl's leg with a rock, providing a semblance of comfort.

Several more hours passed as Gunnar painstakingly crafted a makeshift stretcher. He selected two sturdy branches, their bark rough against his hands, and intertwined them with smaller, flexible branches. His fingers worked deftly, weaving the pieces together and securing them with thick vines he had carefully stripped from nearby trees. Each knot was tied with precision, his muscles straining with the effort. Gunnar's brow furrowed in concentration, beads of sweat trickling down his face.

Once the stretcher was complete, he gently lifted Karl, mindful of his every groan and wince. Gunnar placed him onto the stretcher with the utmost care, adjusting the bindings to ensure Karl's injuries wouldn't worsen during the upcoming journey. He stepped back to assess his work, his heart heavy but determined as he prepared for the upcoming journey.

As the sun dipped below the horizon, casting the world into darkness, Gunnar made a decision. It was not wise to remain exposed on the open riverbank, especially with Karl's condition. He decided to find a more secluded and sheltered spot within the thick forest of trees that bordered the bank, where they could safely camp for the night.

With determination, Gunnar grasped the makeshift stretcher's handles and began towing Karl deeper into the woods. The stretcher dragged along the uneven ground, rustling leaves and snapping twigs under its weight. Gunnar's muscles strained with each step, his breath coming in measured, steady puffs. He moved carefully, navigating around roots and rocks, the dim light making every step a challenge.

Karl lay motionless, his face pale and drawn, but Gunnar

pressed on. The canopy of trees overhead grew denser, the air cooler and more still. Shadows danced around them, the forest alive with the sounds of nocturnal creatures. Gunnar's senses were heightened, his focus unwavering as he searched for a suitable place to rest.

Finally, he found a small clearing, shielded by tall ferns and thick underbrush. Gunnar gently lowered the stretcher to the ground, his hands trembling from the exertion. He knelt beside Karl, adjusting the bindings once more to ensure his friend was as comfortable as possible. The forest provided a natural cocoon of protection, and Gunnar felt a small measure of relief as he began to set up their camp for the night.

Fully aware of the risks involved, Gunnar decided to start a fire. He knew the temperature could drop dramatically during the night, and with Karl's clothes soaked from the river, the dwarf's well-being was a top concern. The warmth of a fire would also help replenish their strength and energy, which they both desperately needed. It was a calculated gamble, but one Gunnar deemed necessary for their survival. With a sense of resolve, he set to work, gathering dry wood.

Gunnar knew hunting for food would be essential in the days to come, so he crafted some deer snares. Using strips of vines and roots, he twisted and braided them together to ensure the cord was strong and flexible. He then fashioned a large loop with a slipknot, designed to encircle a deer's neck as it passed through, tightening when the deer pulled against it. A thin, flexible branch held the loop open, anchored to a tree to prevent the deer from escaping. He placed the snare on a game trail leading to the river, probably the only water source around. Gunnar planned to repeat the process, strategically placing snares in areas likely frequented by deer.

As Gunnar set about crafting the snares, his mind drifted back to simpler times. Hunting had once been more than just survival; it was a cherished bond between father and son. Memories flooded his thoughts, transporting him to a time when the weight of responsibility had yet to burden his shoulders. He could still feel the crisp mountain air on his skin, hear the echoes of laughter as he and his father ventured into the wilderness together.

In those moments, the forest had been their playground, a vast expanse of untamed beauty waiting to be explored. His father had been his guide, teaching him the ways of the hunt with patience and wisdom. Gunnar's hands moved with practiced precision as he fashioned the snares, each knot tied, each trap set, a testament to the lessons learned in those idyllic days of his youth.

But amidst the nostalgia, a pang of anxiety tugged at his heart. He couldn't shake the fear that his father's rule was under threat. Worries about Wilfrid's ambitions gnawed at him, convinced there was a plot to overthrow his father's rule of Draegoor and claim dominion over their lands.

With a determined shake of his head, Gunnar pushed aside his worries, focusing on the task at hand. Hunting for food was essential for their survival, and he would do whatever it took to ensure that he and Karl made it through the challenges ahead.

After finishing the snares, he returned to Karl, who lay motionless next to the fire. Gunnar stoked the fire, adding a few more dried logs, then lay down on a bed of dried leaves. He closed his eyes, hoping the weather would hold for the evening.

17

Friendship with a Fae

'To commune with the Fae is to open your heart and spirit to the whispers of nature, where the wind carries the secrets of the forest.'

Anwyn

Anwyn, atop Honey, galloped through the familiar forest enveloping her home, a sense of melancholy washed over her, mingling with the anticipation of the journey ahead. The towering ancient trees seemed to sigh and creak, their branches swaying in a mournful dance that mirrored her own bittersweet emotions. Each step forward felt like a silent farewell to the familiar comforts of home, a departure from the safety of the known into the unknown.

Having pored over the map countless times, Anwyn was acutely aware of the path that lay before her. Her journey would lead westward for at least three days before the need to consult the map again arose. It was a route she had traced in her mind's eye, envisioning each twist and turn of the winding trail that would guide her towards her destination.

But it was upon reaching the river that flowed northward toward Coetyr that the true challenge would begin. The terrain would transform into uncharted territory, a vast expanse of wilderness waiting to be explored. Anwyn's heart fluttered with a mixture of excitement and trepidation at the thought of what lay ahead. She knew that the journey would be fraught with obstacles and dangers, yet she also felt a stirring sense of purpose, a calling that beckoned her forward into the unknown.

The first three days of her journey slipped by in a blur of quiet moments and steady progress. Anwyn urged Honey forward, their pace steady and measured, a silent understanding passing between them. Never did she demand more than her companion could give, mindful of Honey's limits, and grateful that thus far they had not required any of her mother's potent elixirs. As the sun dipped below the horizon, casting the world in hues of gold and amber, Anwyn would lead Honey to a halt, her hands gentle as she eased the saddle from her loyal steed's back. With practiced care, she would inspect every inch of Honey's sturdy frame, her fingers tracing over muscle and sinew, seeking out any hint of strain or discomfort. And when she found it, her magic would weave through the air, a gentle whisper of power as she healed and comforted, her touch a balm to soothe away any lingering ache. Each evening became a ritual of care and affection, as Anwyn tended to Honey's needs with a tender devotion born of years spent in each other's company. With a soft brush in hand, she would set to work, the rhythm of her strokes a familiar cadence, a silent conversation between them as she gently coaxed away the sweat and dirt from Honey's luscious coat. In these quiet moments, as she tended to her cherished companion, Anwyn found solace and purpose, her love for Honey glowing bright in the fading light of day.

Despite her accustomed solitude in the wilderness, Anwyn couldn't stave off the occasional yearning for her family. In these moments, it was Honey, a constant companion since Anwyn's earliest memories, who provided solace. The mare stood as her steadfast companion in this adventure, a silent presence offering comfort and reassurance amidst the vast expanse of the unknown.

As the sun began its slow descent on her third day of travel, Anwyn arrived at the tranquil bank of the meandering river. A sense of serenity washed over her, the gentle rustling of the leaves and the soothing murmur of the water welcoming her.

With deliberate and graceful movements, Anwyn dismounted Honey. After the day's arduous journey, both horse and rider seemed to welcome the opportunity to rest. Honey's sides rose and fell with each slow, calming breath, her gratitude for the pause clear in the softening of her expressive eyes.

Anwyn cast her gaze over the surroundings, her eyes scanning the lush greenery until they settled on a secluded spot beneath the protective canopy of an ancient willow tree. Its gnarled branches reached out like protective arms toward the water's edge, offering a sense of shelter and security amidst the vast wilderness.

With practiced ease, Anwyn set about readying her makeshift camp, her movements fluid and efficient. Yet, amidst the busyness of her tasks, her attention never strayed far from her faithful companion, Honey. The bond between them ran deep, forged through countless hours spent traversing the rugged terrain of their homeland.

As Honey grazed on the tender grasses that bordered the riverbank, Anwyn watched with a fond smile, her heart swelling with affection for the gentle mare. Having been together for so long, their spirits intertwined like the roots of the ancient trees that surrounded them.

With each step of her evening routine, Anwyn's movements were accompanied by the soft nicker of her beloved horse, a reassuring presence in the midst of the wilderness. She brushed

Honey's coat with gentle strokes, the rhythmic motion a comforting ritual that spoke volumes of their bond.

Once Anwyn had completed all of her evening amenities, she felt the pull of weariness tugging at her. Through small gaps in the canopy above her, she could see the emerging stars, which began to twinkle in the darkening sky. She reclined and closed her eyes, finding respite in the gentle sounds of the nearby river and the rustling leaves.

In her dreams, Anwyn found herself amidst a world of surreal beauty. A glimmering light danced above the tranquil waters, its radiant allure beckoning her forward. With a sudden start, she awoke, her heart pounding in her chest. It was as though an instinctual force guided her to venture towards the riverbank. As she approached the gently lapping water, the mysterious light grew brighter, and from its radiant glow, a diminutive figure began to materialize.

Before Anwyn stood one of the mystical Fae, an ethereal and captivating presence. She shimmered with a resplendent shade of green, a creature of pure energy, her form ever-shifting and dancing like a green candle flame in a gentle breeze. She hovered gracefully just above the ground, leaving delicate, undulating trails of green in her wake.

The Fae's form, ever-shifting and otherworldly, bore a delicate semblance of human-like features. Her hair, a mesmerizing cascade of emerald flames, flowed down her back like a fluid ribbon of light, shimmering and flickering in the moon's gentle embrace. Her large, expressive eyes, luminescent orbs of enchanting green, were locked onto Anwyn, holding her gaze with a captivating intensity. The Fae's delicate lips, glistening like morning dew on a tender petal, curved upward in a soft and welcoming smile.

The Fae's melodious voice filled the night with a cheery,

tinkling sound, a lilting cadence that felt like an enchanting conversation. Even though Anwyn couldn't comprehend the Fae's words, somehow, through an unspoken connection, Anwyn understood that the Fae was attempting to communicate with her, trying to bridge the gap between their worlds somehow.

With a sense of fascination, Anwyn ventured further into the water. Drawing closer to the Fae, who continued her sweet chattering, the frigid river water lapped against Anwyn's ankles. In the midst of the sparkling river, she stood directly in front of the radiant being. Anwyn couldn't decipher the Fae's words, but the unmistakable connection between them seemed to convey a profound message—a role as a guardian of the forest's heart, a protector and guide on Anwyn's journey.

With a warm smile playing on her lips, Anwyn whispered, "My name is Anwyn. What is yours?"

In response, the Fae moved with a palpable excitement, her tinkling melodies growing distinctly louder than before. A mesmerizing dance unfolded, a series of twirls and spins that mirrored the excitement in the air. It became clear to Anwyn that they had found a way to communicate, and Anwyn gathered that the Fae's name was 'Lorelei.'

'Well, Lorelei,' Anwyn acknowledged, 'it's a pleasure to meet you. Am I correct in assuming that you are here to guide me from this point onward?'

Lorelei nodded vigorously, her enthusiasm evident not just in the pronounced movement of her ethereal form but also in the melodious chirps that resonated like a joyful symphony, affirming their newfound partnership. Anwyn's face lit up with delight. Without hesitation, Lorelei fluttered gracefully, her ephemeral wings creating a soft, iridescent glow as she settled atop Anwyn's head. The feathery touch of Lorelei's presence made Anwyn chuckle softly. In that moment, beneath the stars,

Anwyn felt a deep contentment, grateful for the addition of another companion on her journey.

Anwyn

Anwyn awoke to the gentle morning light filtering through the leaves, casting a golden glow over the tranquil forest. She stretched languidly, the warmth of the new day seeping into her bones, chasing away the lingering traces of sleep. With a small yawn escaping her lips, she savored the peacefulness of the moment, relishing the promise of a new beginning.

As she scanned her surroundings for Lorelei, a flicker of confusion danced in her mind. Where had the ethereal Fae disappeared to? For a brief moment, doubt crept in, whispering that perhaps their encounter had been nothing more than a figment of her imagination, a dream born of the magic of the forest.

Yet, that uncertainty dissolved into thin air when a distant tinkle and a melodious chirp reached her ears, echoing through the stillness of the morning. Anwyn's curiosity piqued, she followed the sound, allowing it to guide her to where she had secured Honey for the night.

Approaching the gentle mare, Anwyn felt a surge of warmth in her heart at the sight of her faithful companion. She reached out, patting Honey's sleek coat with gentle affection, her touch a silent reassurance of their unbreakable bond. "Good morning, girl," she murmured softly, her words a tender greeting whispered into the crisp morning air.

In response, Honey nickered softly, her eyes alight with a sense of familiarity and trust. Anwyn couldn't help but smile, her heart swelling with gratitude for the steadfast presence of her loyal friend.

Another tinkle brought Anwyn out of her reverie. Curious about the source of the sounds, Anwyn continued her search, only to discover Lorelei rummaging through her pack. Anwyn stood with her arms folded, a bemused expression on her face, and inquired, "Lorelei, what are you doing?"

Lorelei's melodious twittering and tinkling conveyed her intention, and Anwyn understood that the Fae was searching for her map. With a small shake of her head, Anwyn walked back to the tree where she had set up camp, retrieved the map, and unfurled it. As the map unfolded, Lorelei's excitement was apparent, her tiny form hovering and clapping her hands, creating delicate tinkling sounds reminiscent of tiny bells.

After securing the map's corners with some nearby stones, Anwyn watched as Lorelei floated to the center of the map and gradually lowered herself down until she stood beside the river, mirroring their current campsite.

Anwyn inquired, "Are you trying to give me directions?" Lorelei responded with a tinkling, "yes."

Anwyn had an inkling that she was supposed to close her eyes, and she followed that instinct. As her eyelids sealed out the morning light, it felt as though she was drawn into the map itself. An initial rush of sensation washed over her, momentarily disorienting but far from uncomfortable. When she opened her eyes again, she found herself the same size as Lorelei, ready to enter the map.

Deep down, Anwyn knew that her physical size hadn't actually changed. She felt the ground beneath her feet in the same way, her hands still grasped objects with their usual strength, and her clothes fit just as they always had. But when she looked around, everything seemed different. The grass towered over her like trees, and the pebbles on the path looked like boulders. Lorelei's ethereal influence had altered her perception, making her feel as though she were the same size as the tiny Fae.

Anwyn tried to steady her breath, reminding herself that it was only an illusion. She pressed her hands together, feeling the reassuring solidity of her own skin. Yet, the disconcerting sensation of being "shrunk down" persisted, a testament to the Fae's powerful magic. It was as if her mind was being tricked, the world around her shifting and warping in a way that made her question her own senses.

Lorelei's joy was evident as she took Anwyn's tiny hand, and together, they followed the path she had set on the map. Crossing the river on the map, they continued their journey in a northwesterly direction. When Lorelei halted, Anwyn opened her eyes and returned to her normal state of perception, her next destination clear in her mind, guided by the magical connection she shared with her Fae companion.

After tending to her own needs, Anwyn moved with purpose, her movements efficient as she packed up her belongings and ensured that Honey was prepared for the next leg of their journey. Each item was carefully stowed away, each strap secured with practiced precision. Yet, amidst the practicality of her actions, a sense of anticipation simmered beneath the surface.

As she approached the riverbank, it marked a significant milestone in their travels, a point of no return that filled Anwyn with both excitement and trepidation. In all her fifty years of life, she had never ventured beyond this threshold, never explored the uncharted territories that lay beyond the safety of her homeland. It was a journey into the unknown, a leap of faith into the depths of uncertainty.

As she dismounted Honey and guided her through the rushing waters, Anwyn couldn't help but feel a flutter of nerves in her stomach. The water shimmered before them, a barrier to be crossed, a gateway to a new world. Yet, with each step forward, she felt a sense of determination settle over her, a resolve to embrace whatever challenges lay ahead.

After the crossing, with Lorelei settled contentedly on top of her head, her tiny presence providing a sense of comfort amidst the unknown, Anwyn urged Honey forward, her heart pounding with anticipation. As they ventured northwestwards, their path illuminated by the soft glow of the morning sun, Anwyn couldn't help but feel a glimmer of excitement at the prospect of what lay ahead.

About half a day passed before Lorelei awoke from her peaceful slumber. The tiny Fae emitted a yawn, a delicate noise which sounded like a gentle whistle, before hopping down and taking her seat atop Honey's head, facing Anwyn. Anwyn sensed that Lorelei might be hungry, but was unsure about what the Fae could eat, considering her otherworldly nature.

Anwyn's curiosity about the Fae's unique dietary requirements led to a captivating revelation. From their bond, she discovered that Fae couldn't digest physical food or water; instead, their nourishment came in the form of magic from the spiritual world. Eager to learn how to provide this ethereal sustenance, Anwyn found out that, under normal circumstances, Fae were nurtured by the Sacred Tree. When far from the tree, Fae could coax a drop of spiritual magic from an ordinary tree or plant by singing to it, although this method was time-consuming. Some fortunate Fae inhabited areas naturally rich in magical aura, allowing them to obtain sustenance as easily as if they were near the Sacred Tree.

What Anwyn discovered made perfect sense to her. When Elves sang to the trees and plants of the forest, this enchanting practice served a dual purpose: not only did it nurture the flora, but it also played a crucial role in revitalizing the Elves' own spirits. The melodic communion with the forest mirrored the effect achieved through meditation, fostering a profound connection between Elves and their woodland surroundings. As this understanding unfolded within Anwyn, it resonated deeply, weaving another layer into her knowledge of Elven lore and the relationship she shared with the magical realm around her.

Lorelei conveyed to Anwyn that, without the proximity of the Sacred Tree or an area with a high magical aura, the most efficient way for Anwyn to help nourish the Fae would be to create a small drop of energy and offer it to Lorelei.

Anwyn concentrated, channelling her magic to conjure a small, radiant drop of energy in the center of her palm. When it materialized, Lorelei responded with a twinkle in her eyes and a series of joyous chirps, leaping up and down as though she were cheering on Anwyn's effort. Anwyn couldn't help but laugh. Addressing her companion, she remarked, 'Lorelei, that was quite easy. I could do that for you every day if you like.' Lorelei's excitement only intensified, and she danced even more exuberantly than before.

Once her excitement had tempered slightly, Lorelei gracefully hopped down from Honey's head and with a series of fluid somersaults that seemed to defy the very laws of gravity, she pirouetted through the air before landing nimbly on her feet. An elegant bow followed, executed with a flourish that spoke of both grace and showmanship. Anwyn chuckled, thoroughly enchanted by the Fae's display. Lorelei, having concluded her airborne ballet, eagerly pounced on the conjured drop of energy, her enthusiasm undiminished. Anwyn couldn't help but laugh at the delightful spectacle, finding joy in the camaraderie they were building.

For the following four days, Anwyn and Lorelei continued their northwesterly journey, Lorelei's presence proving to be a constant source of amusement and companionship for Anwyn. In the three days leading up to their encounter with the Fae, Anwyn had shouldered the weight of her quest, the looming prophecy, thoughts of her family, and her fear and anticipation of meeting Gunnar. However, with Lorelei by her side, the burden lightened significantly, and time seemed to accelerate. She felt a great deal of gratitude for the company sent by the forest, which had transformed her solitary journey into something far more heartwarming and enjoyable.

While it was evident that Lorelei possessed the ability to understand Anwyn's thoughts, Anwyn found comfort in physically speaking to the Fae. Verbal communication served as a reassuring reminder that she was not alone on her journey.

"Do you ever get tired of hearing my thoughts all the time?" Anwyn asked aloud, glancing over at Lorelei with a faint smile.

Lorelei tinkled softly, her internal voice like the chiming of distant bells. "Not at all, Anwyn. Your thoughts are a melody to me, ever changing and full of life."

Anwyn laughed, feeling a warmth spread through her chest. "Still, it's nice to talk out loud. Makes me feel… more *normal*, I guess."

Lorelei nodded, her eyes sparkling with understanding. "And it reminds me of the beauty in spoken words. Each one carries weight and meaning, a bridge between our worlds."

Anwyn sighed contentedly. "Thank you for helping me, Lorelei. I don't know what I'd do without you."

Lorelei's gaze softened. "We are companions, Anwyn. Together, we will face whatever comes our way. You are never alone."

As Anwyn and Lorelei continued their journey through the untamed wilderness, her heart quickened with anticipation as she caught her first glimpse of the looming mountains of the Eldrakar Divide far off in the distance. The rugged terrain and dense forest had concealed the majestic peaks until now, but a break in the trees finally revealed their grandeur.

The mountain range stretched endlessly across the horizon, its peaks touching the heavens like ancient sentinels guarding the secrets of the land beyond. After a few days at ease, enjoying the company of Lorelei, the sight of the mountains filled Anwyn with a renewed sense of purpose and determination. With renewed vigour, she took a deep breath, and urged Honey toward the distant peaks.

Anwyn

As Anwyn and Lorelei journeyed further toward the Eldrakar Divide, Anwyn's connection to the forest deepened, and a profound sense of sorrow began to weigh heavily on her heart. This connection allowed her to sense the distress within the very soul of the forest. She glanced down at Lorelei, who had chosen to use Honey's head as her perch, and couldn't help but notice the small Fae's melancholic demeanor.

Anwyn observed that Lorelei's magical sparkle had dulled considerably, and the Fae appeared to be in a state of quiet sadness. The typically vibrant and playful Fae, who had brought so moments of joy and chatter to their journey, now remained motionless and silent. Anwyn couldn't ignore the dramatic shift in Lorelei's mood and couldn't help but feel a growing concern for her.

A single tear welled in the corner of Anwyn's eye, tracing a silent path down her cheek. The sorrow that emanated from the forest and radiated from Lorelei had a way of seeping into her very being. It was as if their melancholy was contagious, and Anwyn's own spirit had become subdued, drenched in a profound depression that tainted her thoughts.

As they approached the forest city of Gwydir, a knot of anxiety twisted in her chest, adding to her distress. It was here that the tensions between the city's elders and Anwyn had first taken root. The people of Gwydir believed Anwyn was responsible for the recent blight that had devastated their once-thriving groves. They saw her as a threat to their way of life, blaming her lack of a sibling for their misfortunes. The distress Anwyn had initially felt twisted and turned into a seething anger at the thought of what they had done to her father.

As their journey led them north of the city, they passed by some of the more distant groves that had once teemed with life and enchantment. These groves now stood marred by withering trees and rotting flora. On the breeze, Anwyn could smell the pungent and musty stench of decay. She wondered why the blight had taken this part of the forest, and whether, if she was successful in her part in the prophecy, would she be able to help heal the forest?

Continuing their westward journey, the mountain range loomed in the distance, only visible in small patches through the forest canopy. Anwyn's exhaustion weighed heavily upon her, a result of the profound sadness that had been tugging at her heart throughout the day. Gwydir lay off to the southwest, and the last desolate grove they had passed marked the boundary of the blighted forest. With a sigh, Anwyn believed it was safe to halt for the evening, her heart heavy with the weight of the forest's sorrow.

Anwyn and Lorelei began searching for a suitable place to make camp. In a secluded glen nestled within a grove of ancient trees, Anwyn found a sheltered spot which was hidden away from the path they were following. Thick, gnarled branches overhead formed a protective canopy, shielding them from the elements and any wandering eyes.

As evening descended, Anwyn set about preparing their campsite. With practiced movements, she unfurled their blankets and spread them over the mossy ground, arranging them just so to ensure maximum comfort for the night ahead. As she worked, her gaze frequently drifted to where Honey stood nearby, tethered to a sturdy tree trunk. The horse nickered softly, her presence a steady and reassuring presence in the gathering darkness.

Anwyn paused in her task, crossing the short distance to Honey's side. Without a word spoken between them, she reached out a hand to stroke the mare's velvety muzzle, her touch gentle and affectionate. In response, Honey leaned into the caress, her eyes closing in contentment.

With a gentle exhale, Anwyn leaned her forehead against Honey's, their breaths intermingling in the crisp evening breeze. In that fleeting moment, enveloped by the sights and sounds of the wilderness, their connection appeared to dissolve the melancholy that had surrounded her, if only for a short while.

Once their camp was ready, they kindled a small fire that crackled to life, casting a warm and comforting glow. Silently, Anwyn forged a small drop of magical energy for Lorelei, who slowly began absorbing it. Anwyn then began preparing her own modest meal of travel rations. The forest's silence, save for the whispering leaves, seemed to heighten the melancholy that had plagued Anwyn throughout the day.

As the fire flickered, casting elongated shadows across the campsite, a figure emerged from the darkness, looming like a specter. Anwyn tensed, her hand instinctively reaching for the hilt of her sword as she rose to her feet, her heart pounding with a mixture of apprehension and curiosity. The newcomer stood tall and imposing, nearly seven feet in height, his features obscured by the heavy cloak that enveloped him.

"I mean you no harm," his voice grated through the night, gravelly from misuse, yet carrying a resonance that sent shivers down Anwyn's spine.

Anwyn exchanged a wary glance with Lorelei, her mind racing with questions. "Who are you?" she demanded, her voice steady despite the unease churning in her stomach.

The stranger lifted a hand, the faint glimmer of a staff visible beneath the folds of his cloak. "I am but a messenger," he replied cryptically, his words carrying the weight of prophecy. "The sickness that plagues these woods is but a harbinger of greater darkness to come. A battle looms on the horizon, and you, Anwyn, are destined to face it."

Anwyn's breath caught in her throat at his words, her pulse quickening with a mixture of fear and determination. "What battle?" she asked, her voice barely a whisper.

The stranger's gaze bore into her, though his features remained hidden in the shadows. As he towered over them, his presence seemed to suffocate the very air. "A battle for the sacred tree," he cackled, the sound echoing like the twisted laughter of a malevolent spirit. His words dripped with venom, heavy with foreboding, as if each syllable carried a curse. "And though you may fight with all your strength,' he hissed, his voice a serpent's whisper, 'you will not emerge victorious."

Anwyn and Lorelei recoiled at the sinister tone of his words, a chill creeping through their bones despite the warmth of the fire. The stranger's ominous laughter lingered in the air like a lingering curse, leaving them paralyzed with fear and uncertainty. As they watched him fade back into the shadows, a sense of impending doom settled over the campsite, casting a pall over their hopes and dreams.

Anwyn felt a chill creep down her spine at the stranger's

ominous warning, her mind reeling with the implications of his words. They stood in stunned silence, feeling the weight of the stranger's words hanging heavy in the air. As the fire crackled softly, casting dancing shadows across the forest floor, Anwyn couldn't shake the feeling that their journey was about to take a perilous turn.

As the night wore on and the embers of their campfire dwindled to a dim, flickering glow, Anwyn's exhaustion began to take its toll. She had been unable to shake the heavy weight of sorrow that clung to her heart throughout the day, and with the mysterious stranger's warning, her eyelids grew heavy with the burden of her emotions.

The day's journey had been arduous, more emotionally than physically, and the forest's mournful atmosphere had been a constant companion. The whispering breeze seemed to carry the lamentations of lost souls, and the rustling leaves sounded like mournful sighs.

Finally, the relentless pull of fatigue overcame her, and she drifted into a restless and uneasy sleep. The forest's eerie symphony echoed in her dreams, intertwining with visions of shadowy figures and ominous warnings. Each rustle of leaves and distant howl of a nocturnal creature intensified her sense of unease, until sleep became a refuge from the haunting echoes of the forest's sorrow.

18

Herald of the Gods

The dragons' will is as unforgiving as the inferno that consumes all in its path'

Dakarai

Six months had passed since the attack on the Fang K'Bala. And, as promised to him, for the past six months, Dakarai had been a slave within Junak's household.

Junak lived in a huge fortified estate in the mountain city of Claw. It was built in an elevated position compared to the surrounding buildings, and from the higher windows where Dakarai worked and lived, it seemed to look down on them in the same manner that Junak looked down on everybody around him.

Such was Junak's arrogance and self importance, it seemed to Dakarai that he had forgotten about Dakarai, and what he had done during the attack. They had crossed paths on more than one occasion in the past six months, and Dakarai would have sworn that there was no recognition or recollection in the Chief's face whatsoever.

Although hopelessness and anguish had long replaced the anger and rage initially felt by Dakarai, the painful memories of losing his family were still there, wrenching at his heart every so often.

As each hopeless day passed, Dakarai would lose himself in the monotonous pattern of servitude and try to fade away into the background. He rarely, if ever, had thoughts of escape, knowing that any attempt would be futile, since Junak's estate was guarded by his warriors day and night.

He would also have nowhere to go. His home had been destroyed and from some of the brief conversations he had overheard, the Fang K'Bala had been completely decimated, with any survivors being no better than feral animals scraping to stay alive deep in the mountain.

"Dak, time to go! If we're not up in the kitchens by dawn, it'll be your scaly arse they'll be cooking up! I'm not covering for you again!"

From his lying position in his hard and flea-bitten cot, Dakarai looked up at Corgan and gave a weak grunt of acknowledgment.

Corgan was from the Strong K'Bala. He had been a slave for Junak for at least five years, having been abducted while on a hunt with several friends from his K'Bala. His friends had all been slaughtered.

Despite Dakarai's despondent character, Corgan always acted like they were both at a celebration feast and not slaves to a cruel and sadistic arsehole. Corgan's constant pleasant nature, despite their circumstances, was a source of constant bewilderment and annoyance to Dakarai. He supposed, however, that had Corgan witnessed his son tortured and burned alive and his wife raped and murdered, his cheerful demeanor may have also changed.

Corgan had welcomed Dakarai into the household on his first day as a slave and had shown Dakarai how to get by without drawing any unwanted attention. He constantly said, "the secret is to work hard without being seen. If they catch you not working, they'll beat you. If they see you, they'll beat you. If they hear you, guess what? They'll beat you. Just do your job and don't get seen. Simple."

Truth be told, Dakarai couldn't care one way or the other whether he was beaten. In the past six months, he had endured dozens of beatings. Each time they occurred, he would relish a break from the numbness he felt. The problem was, though, each time they beat him, they also took it out on Corgan too. And Corgan hated the beatings. Dakarai had spent the past few months listening to Corgan's advice and avoiding the beatings, simply to protect Corgan.

The kitchens were located right on the bottom floor of the estate, five floors below where Dakarai and the rest of the slaves lived, and like everywhere in the estate, it was accessible via servants corridors and stairwells, so that they did not interfere with the important members of the Skull K'Bala.

As they made their way down the narrow stone stairwell, they crossed paths with several other slaves making their way from one chore to another. Each time he saw them, he looked into their empty eyes and saw that the spark had left them. 'Like him then', he mused. Corgan, with his optimism, was certainly a rare Drogo indeed.

As they entered the kitchens, it was mayhem. The head chef was shouting and raging at anyone and everyone he saw. Pots and pans were thrown at slaves who weren't working hard enough and food was being prepared at every workstation.

Dakarai eyed Corgan questioningly, the unspoken words understood by Corgan immediately. "Ah, yes… the carnage here is because of our beloved leader's successful return from his latest mission. He has demanded a feast fit for a god, apparently!"

"His latest mission?" Dakarai questioned.

"Indeed, Dak." Corgan explained. "Junak claims that he is the herald of the gods! He has been searching for Nergai's tomb for years. You know this, we have spoken of it many times! Anyway, apparently, he has now found it."

"How do you know all of this?" Dakarai wondered aloud.

"Ah, Dak… when you have been here as long as me, and you actually learn to pay attention to your surroundings, you can actually learn a thing or two!" Corgan chuckled.

Dakarai simply grunted in response and went to pick up a broom.

Junak

In the haunting realm of his dreams, Junak once again found himself in the divine presence of his god. The colossal dragon materialized before him, scales weaving a hypnotic tapestry of black and gold, shimmering with a brilliance that threatened to blind Junak. The fiery amber orbs that served as Nergai's eyes locked onto him with an intensity born of ages past, their wisdom burning brightly. Ghostly tendrils of smoke snorted from the god's nostrils, twisting and curling into the air. As the ancient dragon spoke, the very air quivered under the weight of his authority, each word echoing like the distant rumble of impending thunder. With an urgency that struck terror into the deepest recesses of Junak's soul, Nergai delivered his dire warning, each syllable carrying the weight of an impending storm. "Hunt down the dwarf and Elf. It is imperative to thwart the prophecy they seek to fulfil. Fail, and the full extent of my wrath shall be unleashed upon you." With those words, Junak's vision shifted. He now witnessed a majestic tree and a battle unfolding beneath it.

Startled, Junak awoke to a world shrouded in the lingering shadows of his dream. Cold sweat clung to his body, and his heart raced with the echoes of Nergai's words. The command, "hunt down the dwarf and Elf," reverberated in his mind. The urgency in Nergai's tone left no room for doubt – there was a battle looming on the horizon. Junak knew that he had to find the Sacred Tree, the ancient Elven tree where the final confrontation would take place.

Throwing off his dampened sheets, Junak rose with a sense of purpose that cut through the lingering tendrils of sleep. Without hesitation, he summoned Shon'anga, his chief shaman. The old Drogo priest would surely possess knowledge about these two adversaries and the cryptic prophecy that now loomed over Junak's fate.

Shon'anga arrived promptly, his eyes betraying a flicker of fear upon hearing the urgency in Junak's voice. The chief shaman bore an ancient staff adorned with feathers and bones, a symbol of both his connection to the spirits of the underworld, and a token of his senior position.

Seated in the dim glow of flickering torchlight, Junak recounted the haunting dream, the divine warning from Nergai echoing in his bedchamber. Shon'anga listened attentively, his weathered face not betraying his thoughts.

"Prophecies are difficult things to predict accurately master, however, I believe there is a way in which we can navigate the intricacies of fate," Shon'anga murmured, his eyes darting left and right nervously. "We must travel to the Forgotten Realm and seek the crystal of Chronos. Legend has it that this crystal holds the power to unveil the threads of fate and guide those who possess them through the tangled web of prophecy."

Junak absorbed Shon'anga's words, his focus fixed on the path ahead. 'Crystal of Chronos,' he repeated in a quiet murmur, the weight of his divine orders settling upon his shoulders. 'How do we find this crystal, and what challenges await us in the Forgotten Realm?'

Shon'anga's eyes danced with unease as he spoke. "The journey is fraught with danger, my lord. We must travel southward to the city of Hammer, nestled in the southern expanse of your domains. From there, braving The Cimmerian Strait—a tumultuous sea draped in ceaseless mist, veiling indescribable ocean monsters—we must make our way to the mountainous Forgotten Realm in the southwestern reaches of Sandarah. Once we arrive, we must uncover the hidden valley where Chronos dwells and implore him for one of his crystals."

Understanding the gravity of Nergai's command, Junak made the decision to embark on this quest personally. 'Prepare a small band of shaman and warriors. We depart in three days,' he commanded, his eyes reflecting the burning resolve within. 'We shall face the challenges of the forgotten realms together.'

Bowing his head in reverence, Shon'anga responded. 'Of course, my lord. I will make the preparations immediately.'

"Before you do, Shon'anga, announce to the people that in celebration of our recent successes, I decree tournaments in the arena, in honor of Nergai. I seek the mightiest warriors from every Drogo city spanning the Scorched Mountains to partake as gladiators. Recruit the captives from our recent raids and scour the depths of the Scorched Mountains for every conceivable type of monster."

Shon'anga bowed his head once more and replied, "As you wish, master." Then he turned and shuffled out of the chamber, his staff held proudly in his weathered hand.

19

A Journey with the Enemy?

'In the echoes of misguided trust, each step bears the weight of a traveler led astray.'

Ruiha

The three unlikely companions, Kemp, Ruiha and Harald, had pressed on throughout the night, and much of the next day. And true to Ruiha's word, they had put as much distance between them and the Olive Tree as possible.

It was now late afternoon and Ruiha had finally allowed the weary travelers to set up camp, much to Kemp's obvious relief. She could tell that he had drained his magic in an attempt to keep up and heal the multitude of minor injuries he'd received on the long and arduous trek.

As the sun set to conclude for the day, the fire crackled and hissed, casting eerie shadows on the faces of the exhausted group. They had been on the run together for almost a whole day, and the tension between Ruiha and Harald had only grown thicker with each passing mile.

Occasionally, they would exchange a few terse words about their journey, their destination, or the path ahead, but the

A Journey with the Enemy?

bitterness that laced their voices was palpable. Their truce was hostile, a fragile agreement based on necessity rather than any type of trust or friendship.

As she sat, her gaze fixed on the dancing flames of the fire, Ruiha couldn't shake the feeling of unease that settled like a heavy cloak around her shoulders. Tonight, sleep felt like a distant dream, elusive and fleeting, overshadowed by the looming presence of Harald.

With a sigh, she acknowledged the futility of even entertaining the idea of rest. How could she sleep with the weight of suspicion bearing down on her? Her doubts about Harald and his true intentions had only intensified with each passing moment spent in his company. Yet, despite her reservations, she knew that voicing her concerns would only serve to sow discord within their already fragile group.

So, she made a silent vow to herself to keep her suspicions to herself, to maintain a watchful eye on Harald without escalating tensions unnecessarily. Kemp's trust in him gave her pause, a begrudging acknowledgment that perhaps there was more to Harald than met the eye. And so, for now, she resolved to give him the benefit of the doubt, even as her instincts screamed at her.

Reflecting on their journey out of Lamos, Ruiha's lips curved into a small, appreciative smile as she observed Kemp's resilience. Despite the challenges they had faced, he had proven himself to be a steadfast traveler, his determination matched only by his unwavering spirit. She felt grateful for his presence, his presence a source of strength amidst the uncertainty of their travels.

In contrast, Harald's demeanor spoke volumes of his background as a professional guard. His disciplined bearing and unwavering focus betrayed years of rigorous training and unwavering dedication to his craft. Ruiha couldn't help but admire his professionalism, even as she harbored lingering doubts about his true motives. It was clear that their pace posed no challenge for him; he moved with the ease and precision of a seasoned soldier, his every step calculated and purposeful.

Ruiha, too, had a history of intense training, spent in combat and evasion. She had spent years honing her skills, whether in pursuing her targets, evading her enemies, or fleeing from city guards. And now, once again, she found herself on the run. She threw the twig she had been fiddling with into the fire in exasperation, and a sigh escaped her lips as she wondered when, if ever, she might find respite from this life of constant running.

"Kemp, get some sleep," Ruiha instructed. "We'll be leaving at first light. Harald and I will handle the watches."

Harald grunted in acknowledgment, while Kemp nodded wearily and shifted to his side, using his pack as a makeshift pillow. After a few minutes, the soft sound of his snores filled the campsite as he finally succumbed to a much needed sleep.

She turned to Harald and said calmly, "I'm going to take first watch if you want to get some sleep."

Harald simply nodded, his expression inscrutable. Lying down with his head on his pack, he closed his eyes. After a while, Ruiha could see his chest rising and falling in a rhythmic motion. However, she doubted he was truly asleep. There was a tension in the set of his jaw, a subtle alertness in his posture that betrayed his feigned slumber.

After a few hours had passed, Ruiha made the decision to rouse Harald and inform him it was his turn to take over the watch. She extended her foot and gently nudged him. Harald's eyes fluttered open, and he promptly assumed a seated position. "Your turn," she whispered to him, to which he offered a nod in acknowledgment before taking a sip of water from his flask.

As Harald shifted position to face away from the fire in the center of their makeshift camp, Ruiha silently approached him from behind. As she crouched down beside him, she noticed his hand clench around his sword hilt. She couldn't help but smile.

"Harald," she begun, her voice steady. "It's clear I don't trust you. I'm not as bright eyed and bushy tailed as Kemp here. I've known men like you before, and I know you're up to something."

Harald interrupted her. His harsh voice was so quiet that it was barely audible. "I'm here looking for a paycheck, nothing more, nothing less." Strangely, his words brought a tingling sensation to Ruiha's skin and made the hair on her arms and neck stand up. She shuddered, and the feeling dissipated.

Ruiha knew his words weren't true. A man as skilled as Harald could have found numerous jobs in a city like Lamos. The city guard was crying out for skilled former soldiers, rich nobles would have protection work for him, bars would have security work available. Financial institutions would have paid him a fortune to protect their wagons of gold being transported. No, she knew he was lying.

"Shut up and listen for a minute." Ruiha growled. "Kemp seems to trust you. I have no idea why, mind you. But I don't. I know you're lying. I'm just warning you that the moment you try anything, I'm going to kill you. I won't give you a chance to explain yourself. I won't bother investigating matters. No. I'll simply end you and walk away. Gottit?"

Harald gave her a threatening smile as a response, and once again, Ruiha saw his irritation at her in his eyes. She merely smiled to herself and walked back to her spot to lie down and watch Harald for the rest of the night.

Kemp

As the morning sun rose above the horizon, casting its warm glow over the landscape, Kemp's muscles ached with the strain of their journey. Despite the weariness that threatened to weigh him down, he pressed on, his determination unwavering as they made headway on the road. The rhythm of their footsteps echoed in his ears, a steady cadence that carried them ever closer to their destination.

Having risen before dawn to pack up their belongings and break their fast, Kemp found himself grateful for the routine of their journey. It provided a sense of structure amidst the chaos, a semblance of order in the midst of uncertainty. Ruiha's words lingered in his mind, her assurance that they would reach the foot of the mountains by early afternoon serving as a beacon of hope in the darkness.

He clung to that hope like a lifeline, allowing it to become his anchor as they trudged onward. The promise of reaching their destination fueled his determination, dragging him through the pain and torture of the journey. Each step forward brought them closer to their goal, each mile travelled a testament to their resilience in the face of adversity.

Despite the physical toll exacted by their travels, Kemp refused to falter. He drew strength from the companionship of his fellow travelers, from the shared purpose that bound them together. And as they pressed onward, he allowed himself to believe that, perhaps, there was light at the end of the tunnel—that their journey, fraught though it may be, would ultimately lead them to safety and sanctuary.

As he looked up, the landscape stretched out before him, an arid and unforgiving expanse where the earth seemed to yearn for rain. The sun blazed in the sky, its scorching rays bearing down on them. Sparse, twisted shrubs dotted the landscape, their pale, withered leaves barely clinging to life. The parched earth crackled underfoot, a mosaic of fractured clay and coarse pebbles.

Kemp sighed silently to himself. He dug deep to find his resolve and muster more energy to finish the journey. He didn't want to be the reason to make them lag behind, and he wanted to prove his worth to Ruiha.

Ruiha

Ruiha glanced back at Kemp, her heart swelling with a strange mixture of pride and concern as she watched him navigate the treacherous terrain. With each step, he stumbled over dead roots and jagged rocks, his movements hampered by the unforgiving landscape that stretched out before them. She could see the weariness etched into the lines of his face, the tension that lingered in his every step.

But despite the difficulties they faced, a smile tugged at the corners of Ruiha's lips. Kemp had exceeded her expectations. She had set a grueling pace, pushing them to their limits, and he had risen to the challenge with unwavering determination.

Turning her gaze toward Harald, she observed his stoic expression as he skillfully navigated around obstacles. His face bore no sign of struggle, and Ruiha recognized that this pace would have posed a challenge for most of the soldiers she had encountered in her time.

Not for the first time since meeting him, she mused silently that he must have undergone exceptional training to effortlessly keep up without breaking a sweat.

As the sun climbed its way toward its zenith, the oppressive heat became nearly unbearable. Ruiha could see that even Harald now had to remove his outer layers of clothing and shove them into his pack. Recognising the need for a brief respite and a chance to take on some water, Ruiha called for a quick stop under the shade of a few trees which were clustered together.

The looming mountains were so close now that Ruiha could distinguish each individual crag and crevice. She knew they only had an hour's hard march and they would be there.

After a short break, the weary group set off once again. As predicted, after an hour, they approached the base of the mountain. The landscape transitioned from the flat, desolate terrain to the rocky and uneven terrain of the mountain's foothills. The temperature had dropped slightly, offering a welcome relief from the searing heat, and a cool breeze rustled through the stunted vegetation that clung tenaciously to life in this harsh environment.

The group moved in silence, their faces displaying a mix of exhaustion and determination. The mountain, an imposing and jagged silhouette against the cloudless sky, was a bittersweet sight to Ruiha. On one hand, she saw an end to the first part of their journey and an opportunity for respite, on the other hand she knew the dangers which lingered within, and she knew that their journey only truly began once they reached the mountains.

Kemp

As they gathered at the foot of the mountain, Kemp's eyes cast upward, taking in the enormity of the challenge that lay ahead. The mountain's slopes were rugged and treacherous, its peaks hidden in a hazy distance. He could see waterfalls cascading down from high crevices in the distance and he couldn't help but imagine swimming in the cool mountain streams to wash and refresh himself.

As the group took a moment to rest and recover, a sense of accomplishment washed over Kemp. He had survived the trek through the harsh terrain and the sweltering heat, and now he stood at the threshold of a new challenge. He couldn't help but think the mountain's majesty and beauty were a stark contrast to the barren landscape they had crossed, and it filled him with a renewed sense of purpose.

After a long rest period, collectively, they agreed it was time to begin the ascent up the mountain. As they trekked higher into the mountain range, the air grew thinner, the jagged peaks offered a shady respite from the sun, and the temperature dropped significantly, offering the group a much needed reprieve from the sweltering heat. They passed a small stream and decided that it would make the perfect place to set up camp for the evening.

Ruiha bathed and washed her clothing first, while Kemp and Harald explored their surroundings. Harald shot down two large birds with his bow, the variety of which Kemp had never seen before, but Harald ensured him they were edible. On their way back to camp, Harald foraged mountain mushrooms, plants and roots, which would make a nice accompaniment to their meal.

When they returned to their camp, Kemp's gaze was drawn to Ruiha, who sat before the crackling fire, her travelling clothes billowing gently in the mountain breeze. The sight of her exposed skin revealed a network of faint scars that crisscrossed her body and limbs, possibly, a testament to the trials she had faced before their paths had converged. Kemp wondered about the woman before him, about the life she had lived and the battles she had fought.

Kemp, caught in his contemplation, was startled when Ruiha looked up and met his gaze. Despite the faint smile she offered, he felt a flush of embarrassment creep up his cheeks at being caught staring once again. Quickly averting his eyes, he mumbled a sheepish "hello" as he busied himself with the tasks at hand.

As Ruiha rose and stretched, a playful glint danced in her eyes, her demeanor lighthearted despite the weight of their journey. With a teasing tone, she remarked on their need for a wash, her words carrying a hint of amusement. "Gentlemen, it's your turn to wash. I have a feeling that before long, your scent will attract a variety of curious predators, mistaking you for a couple of wild boars I've been travelling with." Kemp felt his embarrassment deepen at the gentle ribbing, while Harald simply grunted in acknowledgment.

With a sense of relief, Kemp took his leave, Harald following behind him as they headed to the nearby stream to wash away the grime of the day's travels. As they made their way through the forest, Kemp couldn't shake the image of Ruiha's scars from his mind, each mark a silent reminder of the resilience and strength that lay within the woman who had become his unlikely companion.

Once at the stream, Kemp relished in the cool embrace of the mountain stream, washing away the grime and sweat of the journey. The refreshing waters revived his spirit, offering him a brief and well-warranted moment of respite.

After a few moments of quiet solitude, Kemp found himself lost in his own thoughts, the rhythmic sounds of the forest providing a comforting backdrop to his introspection. So when Harald broke the silence with a sudden question, Kemp couldn't help but feel a sense of surprise wash over him. In the time they had been traveling together, Harald had rarely spoken, let alone initiated a conversation.

"The Sandaran," Harald began, his voice gruff from disuse. "Is there anything between the two of you, then?" The abruptness of the question caught Kemp off guard, leaving him momentarily speechless. Yet, despite his initial unease, he couldn't deny the sense of calm and trust that emanated from Harald, reassuring him that he could be open and honest in his response.

As Kemp stumbled over his words, attempting to articulate his feelings, he felt a surge of vulnerability wash over him. It was rare for him to divulge his personal sentiments, especially to someone he barely knew. Yet, something about Harald's straightforward demeanor encouraged him to speak his truth.

"Well, I do have some feelings for her," Kemp admitted, his voice betraying a hint of uncertainty. "But I don't believe she feels the same way about me." He paused, surprised at himself for divulging such personal sentiments to Harald, a man he had only recently met.

Harald responded with a grunt, his expression unreadable as he absorbed Kemp's confession. Then, with characteristic bluntness, he delivered his assessment of Ruiha. "I don't think she's to be trusted, Kemp."

The directness of Harald's words caught Kemp off guard, prompting him to consider the implications of his warning. Despite his initial instinct to defend Ruiha, the intensity in Harald's gaze gave him pause, as if the older man was peering into his very soul.

As he mulled over Harald's words, Kemp felt a sense of doubt gnawing at the edges of his mind. Could there be truth in what Harald was suggesting? It was a notion that unsettled him, forcing him to confront the possibility that Ruiha might not be as trustworthy as he had believed. After a moment of contemplation, he gave a brief nod of agreement before returning his focus to the task at hand, the weight of uncertainty lingering in the air around him.

Back at their camp, Harald set about preparing the birds for cooking, while Kemp took a seat on a log across from Ruiha. She was occupied with mending her boot, her attention fully absorbed by the task at hand. Her tongue peeked out of the side of her mouth in concentration, and Kemp couldn't help but be struck by her beauty. His mind drifted back to his earlier conversation with Harald, and he rubbed his face, hoping to find some clarity in the midst of their tangled situation.

"Kemp," Ruiha called from across the camp. "Chuck over your boots. I'll see what I can do with them."

"Thanks Ruiha," Kemp responded, "but there's nothing wrong with them that I can tell."

"Your left boot is splitting along the side. I noticed it a couple of hours ago."

Kemp looked down at his boots, which he had taken off and left to the side. Immediately, he noticed the fraying edges of his left boot.

"Thanks, Ruiha. But honestly, you don't need to do that. I can do it."

Ruiha offered him a smirk in return, before saying, "did you fix many boots in your days at the academy? I'm dead certain that you haven't got a needle and thread in that pack of yours, either. If you do, I'll eat my own boot!"

Kemp glanced at his pack, knowing full well he hadn't had the foresight to bring a needle and thread, before admitting to Ruiha, "you are, in fact, correct. However, you still don't need to mend my boots, Ruiha. I can't expect you to coddle me the whole time!"

Ruiha stood and sauntered over, and Kemp's heart nearly skipped a beat as she sat down on the log next to him. "Fair enough, Kemp. But... at least let me teach you how to fix them. Here, you can borrow my needle and thread for now."

At a loss for words, Kemp simply nodded and took the offered needle and thread. Together, they began repairing his boot, with Ruiha identifying the best places to thread the needle, and explaining how to stitch properly so that the repair would last. Eventually, they finished, and Kemp felt a small surge of triumph as he looked down at the repaired boot.

As Ruiha made her way back to her log, Kemp felt a familiar sense of conflict gnawing at his conscience. Caught between the palpable tension that simmered between his two travelling companions, he couldn't shake the feeling of being torn in two directions. It was evident they didn't trust or like each other, and he was caught in the middle.

Recalling a story his father had once shared with him in his youth, Kemp couldn't help but draw parallels between their current situation and the tale of the guide and the two travelers. In the story, the guide faced a similar predicament, caught between travelers who doubted each other's sense of direction. Each traveler handed the guide a map leading in opposite directions, forcing the guide to navigate a path of compromise between the conflicting courses.

As Kemp reflected on the story, a glimmer of hope sparked within him that their journey would ultimately lead them to find common ground. Perhaps, like the guide in his father's tale, he too would discover a way to navigate through the uncertainty that lay ahead. With that thought in mind, he resolved to seek clarity in the morning, once he had rested and regained his bearings.

Ruiha

As the sun dipped behind the jagged peaks, painting the sky in hues of orange and pink, Ruiha couldn't shake the sense of unease that settled over the campsite. The fading light cast long shadows across the rugged terrain, amplifying the rugged beauty of their surroundings. Despite the weariness that weighed heavily on her limbs, Ruiha remained vigilant, attuned to the slightest hint of danger lurking in the darkness.

The crackle of the campfire provided a semblance of warmth and comfort, its flickering flames dancing hypnotically in the cool mountain air. Yet, beneath the surface tranquility, an undercurrent of tension simmered, palpable in the silence that enveloped their camp.

Suddenly, the peaceful night shattered with a deafening roar echoing through the trees, causing Ruiha's heart to lurch in her chest. In an instant, her senses sharpened, every muscle in her body coiling with anticipation. With practiced ease, she sprang to her feet, her gaze sweeping the surroundings with calculated precision, searching for any sign of danger.

Beside her, Kemp's eyes widened in terror, his fear mirroring her own. Even Harald, typically stoic and composed, faltered for a moment in the face of the unknown threat. But where others may have succumbed to panic, Ruiha remained steadfast, her training kicking in to override any hint of fear.

Then, like a nightmare made real, a huge brown bear burst through the undergrowth, its massive form silhouetted against the fading light. Ruiha's instincts kicked in, her body moving before her mind could fully grasp the danger. She dodged to the side, narrowly avoiding the bear's slashing claws as it lunged towards her.

As she regained her balance, Ruiha's gaze flickered to Harald, expecting to find him springing into action to defend them. Instead, she was met with a chilling sight — Harald remained eerily still, almost as if he were waiting for the bear to strike, his eyes no longer betraying any hint of fear or concern.

As the tension in the air thickened, Ruiha's mind buzzed with a whirlwind of questions and suspicions, each one more ominous than the last. Why was Harald not reacting to the looming threat? Was his apparent indifference genuine, or was he concealing something more sinister beneath his stoic exterior? The uncertainty gnawed at her, fueling a sense of unease that simmered beneath the surface of her composure.

But before she could dwell further on her doubts, the bear's attention abruptly shifted, its predatory gaze zeroing in on Kemp, who stood frozen in terror, a picture of helpless vulnerability. Ruiha's heart lurched with dread as she realized the imminent danger her friend faced. Panic surged through her veins, but she knew she was too far away to intervene in time. In that agonising moment, she felt a surge of helplessness wash over her, her instincts warring with her inability to act.

In the chaotic flurry of action, Ruiha's mind raced as she watched Harald spring into action, his movements deft and purposeful as he positioned himself as a barrier between Kemp and the charging beast. A surge of astonishment and disbelief washed over her as Harald fearlessly confronted the rampaging bear, his strength and skill on full display as he fought to drive the creature back.

Amidst the chaos, a whirlwind of conflicting emotions swirled within Ruiha's chest. Gratitude mingled with confusion as she witnessed Harald's bravery, his selfless act of protection sparking a glimmer of hope amidst the turmoil. But beneath the surface, doubt lingered like a shadow, whispering insidious questions that threatened to unravel her trust.

Was Harald truly their ally, risking life and limb to shield them from harm? Or was his sudden heroism merely a facade, a calculated maneuver to obscure his true intentions? With each blow exchanged between man and beast, Ruiha grappled with the uncertainty that gnawed at her core.

As the bear finally retreated into the darkness, leaving behind a scene of carnage and chaos, Ruiha knew that her doubts would linger long after the echoes of the night had faded away, leaving her torn between loyalty and suspicion, her perception of Harald forever altered by the events of this harrowing night.

20

A God Amongst Dwarves

'The gods carve fate with the chisel of time, shaping destinies in the stone of existence.'

Gunnar

As the morning sun filtered through the dense forest canopy, Gunnar awoke to the realization that Karl's condition had not improved as he had hoped. It was becoming clear that the wounds, raw and agonising as they were, demanded the attention of a healer. With a heavy heart, he attended to his friend's wounds, cleaning and re-bandaging them as best he could, but there was a lingering sense of helplessness in the face of Karl's suffering. Gunnar knew that with no supplies or help, there was little more he could do to ease his friend's pain.

Despite his forlorn demeanor, Gunnar set out with determination to check the traps he had set the previous evening, knowing that their survival depended on him securing food. With no success so far, desperation gripped Gunnar as he approached the final snare, realizing that its outcome could determine Karl's life or death. As he reached it, a single deer, caught as if fate had granted a reprieve, awaited him. Gunnar, filled with a mix of gratitude and resolve, secured the precious meat and chose to keep the remaining snares for his uncertain future.

As he walked back to Karl, Gunnar contemplated the prospect of persuading him to consume a portion of the meat, knowing that it would aid his friend's recovery. The gravity of their situation bore down on him, and the absence of a clear plan left him grappling with uncertainty.

Approaching the camp with cautious steps, Gunnar's senses heightened as he took in the unexpected scene before him. Another dwarf, standing near Karl's stretcher, hovered over his injured friend with an air of familiarity. The weight of the deer carcass slipped from Gunnar's grasp, the soft thud of its impact lost amidst the tense silence that enveloped the camp. Without a word, he moved stealthily around the perimeter, his every movement calculated to avoid detection. With each step, he strained to gain a clearer understanding of the situation unfolding before him.

As he drew nearer, recognition dawned in Gunnar's eyes, mingling with disbelief at the sight before him. It was Hansen, standing before him unscathed despite the perilous circumstances they had faced. Gunnar's brow furrowed in confusion, his mind racing to comprehend how Hansen could emerge from the ordeal unscathed. Determination etched into his features, Gunnar resolved to confront Hansen and unravel the mystery of his miraculous survival.

Hansen turned, wearing a knowing expression that suggested he had been aware of Gunnar's presence the entire time. His smile was warm and welcoming. As Gunnar's gaze extended beyond Hansen, disbelief gripped him anew. There sat Karl, upright, cradling a cup in his hands while puffing on a broadleaf pipe. The surreal sight left Gunnar utterly dumbfounded, struggling to reconcile the reality before him with the injuries he had witnessed earlier.

Just an hour prior, Gunnar had feared the worst for Karl's

survival, yet now he watched in disbelief as Karl not only sat up but also partook in drinking and smoking. Gunnar's jaw hung agape in astonishment, his mind reeling with incredulity. How, in the name of Dreyna, had Karl managed to acquire a drink and tobacco in their current circumstances? The question echoed in his thoughts, a testament to the bewildering turn of events that were unfolding before him.

Hansen's smile shifted into a mischievous grin, heralding the onset of an enchanting transformation. A radiant, ethereal aura enveloped the dwarf, casting a warm and comforting light that glowed with a soft, golden hue. Almost imperceptibly at first, the dwarf's stature began to change. His previously stout and sturdy Dwarven frame expanded, growing taller and more imposing. Limbs elongated, muscles bulged with newfound strength, and his once stocky body seemed to stretch, almost doubling.

His skin took on a stony texture, mirroring the rugged, weathered surface of the mountains. It was as if his flesh seamlessly merged with the earth, becoming an integral part of the mountain itself. Hair transformed into a cascade of earthy hues, ranging from deep browns to rich mossy greens, flowing like waterfalls down broad shoulders and merging seamlessly with the stony skin.

Gunnar stood in stunned silence, a tempest of emotions swirling through his mind — shock, fear, and awe clamoring for his attention. The air seemed charged with an otherworldly energy as he grappled with the overwhelming experience, finding it challenging to single out any one emotion amidst the tumult within.

After a few moments, during which he stood paralyzed by the astonishing transformation, Gunnar gradually managed to collect his thoughts and emotions. His attention momentarily shifted to Karl, who sat there, unmoving, with pipe in mouth and cup in hand. Despite these familiar comforts, Gunnar couldn't shake the uncertainty lingering in his mind. He questioned whether the dwarf was still recovering from his injuries or if he, too, was caught in the grip of shock.

With a mixture of reverence and humility, he knelt before this godly form, the soft earth beneath him grounding the reality of the incredible power and presence that now towered before him.

Hansen beamed with delight at Gunnar's reaction. Then, a deep rumbling, as if the very earth had awakened, emanated from the ground. Thunderous echoes filled the air, and Gunnar's initial alarm melted into realization as he looked around. The source of the sound was none other than Hansen, who laughed heartily, the vibrations reverberating deep within Gunnar's chest.

As the rumbling earth and echoes subsided, Hansen's voice gained clarity, its deep resonance akin to distant thunder. The figure before him addressed Gunnar, his words carrying a hint of mischief that danced within the rumbling tones. "Gunnar Eriksson," Hansen said, "have you figured out who I am yet?"

Gunnar had his suspicions and the mischievous glances directed his way only served to confirm them. This figure standing before him had to be none other than Draeg. The Draegoorian God, after all, was known for his inclination to engage in pranks, tricks, and sometimes even minor acts of disruption. In Dreynas, some Dwarves even went so far as to dub him the God of Chaos. Draeg's notorious ability to alter his form at will, concealing his divine nature and sowing mischief under various guises, was etched in the annals of Dwarven lore. The mischievous gleam in the god's eyes mirrored the tales of Draeg's unpredictable nature that Gunnar had heard from his clan elders.

Gunnar locked his gaze onto the towering figure before him, what was once Hansen, and answered with a tone of reverence and humility, "I believe so, Draeg, son of Dreyna. I am humbled to be in your almighty presence. I am here to serve and yours to command." His words were spoken with deep respect and an unwavering willingness to follow the will of the mountain god.

Draeg's smile stretched even wider, an eerie feat considering his teeth resembled jagged rocks.

"Good, good," Draeg rumbled with a hearty chuckle, the sound echoing through the air like distant thunder. His eyes, however, held a warmth that belied the powerful presence he exuded. The glow within them seemed to flicker with a wisdom beyond Gunnar's comprehension. "Alas, I am here, not to command, but to advise—a mere messenger boy for my holy mother!"

Draeg's laughter resonated, as if he shared some inner joke with the very essence of the earth beneath them. Gunnar, though still processing the surreal encounter, found himself drawn into the infectious mirth. The atmosphere, once charged with uncertainty, now bore the unmistakable touch of Draeg's charisma.

"Gunnar," Draeg continued, his tone more serious now, "you've been blessed with Elven blood. Do you comprehend the weight of that blessing?" His gaze bore into Gunnar's, seeking an understanding that transcended mere words.

The resonance of Draeg's laughter lingered, creating a divine ambiance that seemed to dance with the very essence of the surroundings. As if sharing an unseen connection with the elements, he continued, "Gunnar, my friend, in this life we all play our roles. Mine, for now, is that of a guide. A humble conduit for the whispers of the divine."

Gunnar gazed at Draeg, a mixture of curiosity and humility in his eyes. The concept of "Elven blood" was entirely foreign to him, and he didn't hesitate to admit his ignorance to the mountain god.

"I find it hard to fathom how the entire Dwarven race has

allowed one of the most ancient and important prophecies of our time to slip through the cracks," the god mused, shaking his head with a hint of mock resignation.

"Well, let me enlighten you!" he exclaimed with a booming voice. "But first, we should probably check on Karl here. He hasn't uttered a word since I made my grand appearance, and I'm genuinely concerned he might have keeled over in silent shock!" Draeg couldn't help but chuckle heartily at his own joke, the sound reverberating through the camp.

Gunnar

After carefully settling a shocked and confused Karl down for a rest, Gunnar and Draeg strolled towards the river. It was there, with the gentle rush of water as their backdrop, that Draeg began reciting an ancient prophecy to Gunnar.

> *"In the heart of the mountain's embrace,*
> *A dwarf with Elven blood shall grace this place.*
> *With veins of stone and heritage entwined,*
> *Magic's gift in their soul, forever to bind.*
> *They'll wield ancient powers unseen,*
> *A bridge between worlds, a mystical dream.*
> *Through earth and forest, their path will blaze,*
> *A destiny written in the magical haze.*
> *In unity, they'll mend what's torn asunder,*
> *dwarf and Elf, in harmony, shall plunder.*
> *Their love, a force, pure and bright,*
> *Unveils the secrets, restores the light.*
> *World trembling under a Dragon King's ire,*

Flames and darkness, a world caught in mire.
But in love's embrace, they stand through it all,
dwarf and Elf, united, answer the call."

"I'll be honest with you, Gunnar," Draeg boomed. "The Elves are better at writing this stuff than we are..." Draeg laughed heartily at his comment.

"The Elves have a knack for prophecy, mainly because they have the patience to write out those long, intricate scrolls. Dwarves? We're too busy hammering away at our forges, crafting mighty weapons and clinking tankards of ale. It's hard to make accurate predictions about the future when you're constantly surrounded by the clanging of hammers." Draeg continued with a big grin.

Shocked by the prophecy thrust upon him, and subsequently by Draeg's nonchalant demeanor, Gunnar regarded Draeg with a slow blink, a momentary lapse of disbelief settling over him. Had the mountain god just engaged in a conversation with himself? Gunnar couldn't help but silently question the state of Draeg's sanity, his eyes narrowing ever so slightly as he assessed the situation.

Abruptly, Draeg's gaze bore down on Gunnar, the humor vanishing, replaced by a seriousness that demanded attention. "Gunnar, do you grasp the implications of this prophecy?"

Gunnar continued to stare, caught in a swirl of conflicting thoughts. He comprehended the prophecy's meaning, yet disbelief clung to him like a shadow. The idea that he, a mere dwarf, could be the subject of such an ancient and profound foretelling left him in stunned silence. Draeg's inquiry lingered in the air, and Gunnar remained frozen, grappling with the weight of destiny until the silence shattered with the sound of Draeg's throat clearing.

Draeg's stone brows cracked into a frown, and he slowly began shaking his head as if confused before he mumbled, 'I realize it was poorly written, but I thought it was still pretty self-explanatory.' He raised his large rock-like hand to his jaw in contemplation. 'Maybe the prophecy was referring to another dwarf. I was expecting the chosen one to be able to grasp a simple prophecy…' he mused.

Gunnar cleared his throat and corrected the mountain god. "Excuse me, Draeg, your grace," Gunnar begun, "but I understand the prophecy. I apologise for my rudeness, however, I am slightly overwhelmed by everything that has just happened."

"Ahh, I see…" said the god, "well as long as you understand it, that is the main thing!" Draeg begun. "Now, the threat we talk about, this Dragon King, is none other than the revered god of the Drogo Mulik, Nergai! Unfortunately, I can only remain in the realm of Vellhor for another day, before I must return to Aerithordor."

Aerithordor, the heavenly Dwarven realm where gods and fallen warriors resided, was a place of deep spiritual significance to the Dwarves. Believed to be situated amidst the craggy peaks of an impossibly high, unknown mountain range, this ethereal realm was a testament to both the Dwarven craftsmanship and their unwavering connection to the divine. The Dwarves held a deep belief that one day, should the gods deem them worthy, they too would take their place in the "Hall of Thordor," nestled at the heart of Aerithordor.

Gunnar's heart almost stopped. He reprocessed what the deity in front of him had said for a second time before asking, his voice tinged with a mix of urgency and hope, "Your grace, do you not intend to assist me with my role in this prophecy?"

Draeg chuckled and spread his arms out wide. "Gunnar, my friend. Why else do you think that I am here? Obviously, I plan on assisting you!"

"Thank you Almighty Draeg," Gunnar said, relief evident in his tone. "I am forever in your debt."

"Gunnar," Draeg said, whilst shaking his head. "Honestly, you have to stop with all the 'your grace's', and the 'almighty's' and any other nonsense titles you feel like calling me. Admittedly, I found it amusing at first, however, now it's beginning to get irritating."

Gunnar wasn't sure how to interpret that comment. As he glanced towards the deity, a huge grin adorned Draeg's face. However, the sight of the powerful god standing before him, capable of turning him into nothing more than rock dust with a mere thought, lingered vividly in his mind.

Conflicted, Gunnar decided to seek clarification. "What would you like me to call you?" He carefully omitted any 'almighty' or 'grace' from his sentence.

Draeg mused, a playful glint in his eyes. "Why... let me think... Just call me Draeg. I've always liked that name!" His big grin remained firmly in place.

"Okay then... Draeg," Gunnar said slowly, the weight of the god's power still fresh in his thoughts. "Thank you for assisting me in my part of the prophecy."

"Well, it won't be *me* assisting you as such." Draeg responded sheepishly. "Since, as I mentioned before, I will have to return in the morning. And, believe it or not, it is actually quite difficult for gods to travel to Vellhor. You would not believe the difficulties I had in getting here."

Draeg looked up, staring distantly into the sky, almost as if, should he look hard enough, he might see his home. For all Gunnar knew, he actually might be able to see it if he looked hard enough. He had no comprehension of the capabilities of a god.

Breaking the silence which had stretched out for a long moment, Gunnar cleared his throat. "So, Draeg. In what form exactly will this assistance be? If you cannot help me yourself, that is?" Gunnar asked.

Snapping back to reality, Draeg exclaimed, "Ahh! Yes, the assistance! Of course." He spent a moment mumbling something inaudible to Gunnar's ears before delicately pulling out a stone, its surface adorned with intricate patterns that seemed to shimmer in the light. Draeg handled it with care, as if it were a priceless gem that might crumble if held too firmly.

Holding the small stone out in front of him, Draeg blew gently across its surface. The stone seemed to come alive, emitting faint silvery sparkles that danced in the air, carried by the breath of the mountain god. Gunnar observed, captivated by the display, as the glinting sparkles scattered around them, adding a magical touch to the atmosphere.

Gradually, the stone started emanating a faint silvery light, which slowly gained strength, wrapping it in brilliance until it resembled a radiant gem cradled in Draeg's palm. A subtle, otherworldly hum resonated in the air as the glow danced like ethereal flames, creating a mesmerizing spectacle in Draeg's grasp. In the quiet clearing, by the riverside, the stone stirred to life, casting its silvery glow that seemed to illuminate the water and the surrounding trees. The glow grew steadily, turning the stone into a radiant orb, a beacon of magic nestled securely in Draeg's palm.

Then, a subtle vibration rippled through the stone, escalating until it cracked open like a chick breaking free from its shell. The outer casing disintegrated into dust, unveiling a small, stout, and sturdy being — a miniature dwarf. With rugged, earth-toned skin mirroring the appearance of stone, and wild, unruly hair shimmering in a deep purple hue reminiscent of amethyst, the miniature creature emerged into the quiet clearing by the riverside. As the outer casing dissolved, a faint scent of ancient earth lingered in the air.

Gunnar focused on the being, discerning distinct facial features — purple eyes beneath an expressive brow that peered up at him with a curious gaze.

Draeg began, "This little fellow is a Stonesprite. You've probably never seen one, nor even heard of one, as they are typically found only in Aerithordor. Gunnar, his connection to the earth and profound understanding of magic, will make this Stonesprite an invaluable ally in any threats you face against Nergai. His unique abilities can unlock ancient secrets, offering crucial guidance on your journey."

As Draeg had suggested, Gunnar had never heard of a Stonesprite before. It had never come up in any of his readings or studies, and he couldn't recall a single story, tale, legend, or myth that mentioned them. By the look of the tiny creature in front of him, he could understand why they had been omitted from the Dwarven epics. With skepticism, Gunnar observed the small creature as it tried to attack one of Draeg's fingers.

Draeg's laughter resonated, a deep and hearty sound that served as a potent reminder of his divine stature as a mountain deity. Gunnar, despite appreciating the joviality, felt compelled to express his thoughts, choosing his words carefully to avoid any semblance of rudeness or ingratitude.

"Apologies, Draeg," Gunnar began, "I don't want to come across as sounding rude or ungrateful. However, I'm curious—how exactly will this 'Stonesprite' be able to assist me on my journey?"

Draeg's gaze softened as he looked down at the Stonesprite, a compassionate expression crossing his features before returning to meet Gunnar's eyes. His words carried a sense of reassurance and wisdom.

"Gunnar, I understand your skepticism, especially considering the Stonesprite's current size and demeanor. However, let me assure you that as he grows and gains strength, you will develop a bond that serves as a gateway to a profound understanding of magic—an understanding beyond that of any existing dwarf, elf, or human. Stonesprites are divine creations, fashioned by the gods themselves. This little one is composed of my spirit and soul, akin to a child to me."

Gunnar took pause at that. His thoughts filled with the weight of the responsibility that came with the Stonesprite's divine origins. Concern surged within him, recognising that any harm befalling the Stonesprite might invoke the wrath of a god. Despite the palpable fear that gripped him, Gunnar swallowed it down, resolving to shoulder the responsibility and care for the Stonesprite with unwavering dedication and capability.

Draeg carried on with his explanation, a reassuring tone in his words. "As the Stonesprite grows and your bond deepens, you will witness the expansion of his sentience. He will evolve, becoming a source of insight beyond your wildest imagination." A playful grin crept back onto Draeg's lips, and he continued, "Given that he is intricately linked to me, you will essentially have the insight and power of a god at your fingertips!"

Gunnar found some reassurance in Draeg's words, a flicker of comfort amidst the uncertainty. Yet, his attention remained fixated on the Stonesprite, now displaying an energetic eagerness to explore, attempting to run and jump off Draeg's hands in a spirited bid to escape. Gunnar's initial reassurance wavered as he observed the Stonesprite's antics. Reflecting on his emotions, he realized his feelings regarding the Stonesprite were... *mixed*. He took a deep breath, resolving to keep a close watch on the unpredictable creature, knowing that their journey was far from over and the true test of their resolve was yet to come.

21

MOONLIT STRIFE

'In the cloak of night, the silent assailant tends to strike, for darkness harbors both secrets and danger alike.'

ANWYN

In the deepest hours of the night, as the moon cast an eerie, silvery light upon the glen, a faint rustling in the leaves overhead jarred Anwyn awake. Her senses sharpened, her Elven instincts keenly attuned to the slightest disturbances in the forest's stillness. Her heart raced as she assessed the situation — shadows flitted through the trees, and subtle but deliberate harmony of footsteps echoed from the darkness. Anwyn's mind began piecing together the evidence, and the unsettling truth became clear — she was clearly not alone.

Anwyn's worry spiked as she considered the source of the disturbance. Was it the towering visitor from the evening before, returning with perhaps more ominous intentions? Or could it be the Elves of Gwydir, known for their watchful and protective nature, but also capable of swift and decisive action when their domain was threatened? Her father's words of warning about them echoed in her mind, adding weight to her apprehension.

As the unsettling stalking sounds continued, it became increasingly clear that Anwyn was not being followed by a lone hunter. The footsteps and rustling indicated the presence of multiple pursuers, and their advance was unmistakable, each moment drawing them closer, their presence becoming more tangible with every passing second.

With the revelation of multiple trackers, coupled with her father's cautionary tales regarding the inhabitants of Gwydir and the city's close proximity, Anwyn swiftly pieced together the truth. It was undeniable: the stealthy figures trailing her through the darkness could be none other than the guardians of Gwydir, the city who sent the very assassins who had targeted her home and nearly claimed her father's life. Their keen awareness of her presence and their skilful navigation through the forest shadows left no doubt—they had detected her and were closing in with deadly precision.

Anwyn's frustration mounted. These Elves were testing her patience beyond its limits. Their initial assault had been a sinister plot aimed at her family. Anwyn's rage simmered, threatening to overwhelm her, but she channeled it into a steely determination, steeling herself to confront the elves who had surrounded her.

As she lay there, eyes closed, waiting for the attack to commence, she decided to meditate. She didn't need to. Her spirit was currently stronger than ever, but she found it calmed her racing heart significantly.

The glen she had chosen was quite small, so she knew that she would struggle to defend herself with her katana given the limited range of motion for a full swing. She would have to use her magic. *'I could use the practice'*, she thought to herself, as she continued harnessing the magical aura around her.

As the first elf swung down from the canopy, Anwyn's senses locked onto the unfolding threat. The elf's lithe form, clad in dark, leaf-patterned armor, moved with the grace of a panther. His eyes, sharp and calculating, glinted with malevolence. She opened one eye, her deep connection with the forest offering her an intuitive insight into the elf's intent. Without a moment's hesitation, Anwyn called upon her magical abilities to respond. With a mere thought, she unleashed a devastating pulse of energy, a searing blast that surged outward and enveloped her. She writhed and convulsed on the forest floor, utterly incapacitated by the overwhelming force of her magic.

The second elf, his eyes ablaze with power, faced Anwyn and Lorelei. His sleek, silver hair flowed in the wind, and a wicked grin played upon his lips as he raised his hands, weaving the threads of air and storm into a deadly symphony of chaos. His robes, adorned with shimmering sigils, billowed dramatically as he summoned his power.

With a flick of his fingers, he summoned a turbulent gust of wind that swirled and howled, a tempest of unrestrained fury that threatened to shatter everything in its path. The swirling winds whipped at Anwyn and Lorelei, threatening to disorient them, tearing at Anwyn's hair and clothing. Anwyn braced herself, expecting Lorelei to be blown away by the force. To her surprise, Lorelei stood firm, her presence unwavering amidst the storm.

It was a force that should have brought them to their knees, but he had severely underestimated Anwyn. As she stood there, holding back his attack, she almost smiled at the surprise that flickered in his eyes. With her honey-colored eyes blazing with determination, she began her counter-attack, ready to turn the tide.

With a whispered incantation, Anwyn harnessed the power of the ancient forest surrounding her. The trees and flora, enchanted by her profound connection to the natural world, responded to her call. Roots squirmed and branches twisted, weaving into a protective barrier that shielded them from the relentless assault of the wind. Leaves and flowers swirled around them in a mesmerizing display of power. Anwyn delved into her own elemental magic, surpassing that of her adversary. With focused intent, she overcame him, wresting control from his grasp, and expertly redirecting his own attack back upon him.

The elf's conjured tempest, now turned against him, became a maelstrom of chaos. The wind howled, battling the very hand that had summoned it. The ground trembled beneath their feet as the elf struggled to regain control. His once confident smile twisted into a mask of desperation and fear. With a mighty surge, the storm lifted him off his feet, carrying him high into the sky.

Anwyn's eyes blazed with fury as she extended her hand toward the soaring elf. The winds obeyed her command, swirling around him in a vortex of unrelenting force. Thunder cracked, and lightning arced through the storm, illuminating the elf's broken body, which was whipping around violently amidst the furious winds.

Lorelei, gleaming with ethereal light, skipped forward, and Anwyn briefly felt the courage coursing through her tiny companion. Anwyn's connection to the forest had granted her a power beyond imagination, and alongside Lorelei, they were poised to bring down the arrogant Elves who had dared challenge them.

The third opponent gripped a staff adorned with powerful runes that pulsed with dark energy. His hooded cloak billowed as he moved, shadows clinging to him like a second skin. With a flourish of the staff, he wove intricate illusions that unfurled like a shadowy tapestry, shrouding the ancient forest in a bewildering mist. Like sinister serpents, the mist twisted, creating an eerie labyrinth that restricted Anwyn's vision. The elf then began launching a series of magical attacks through the writhing mist towards Anwyn and Lorelei.

Initially, Anwyn assumed that her opponent's vision must also be affected by the mists, leaving him to guess where to direct his attacks, as none had successfully landed. It soon dawned on her, however, that Lorelei had woven a magical sphere around them, skillfully deflecting the oncoming assaults. Anwyn could sense that Lorelei's power was waning rapidly, however, and she could see that the protective sphere was gradually weakening. Each time an attack made contact with the sphere, it was successfully deflected, but with every deflection, the barrier flickered and blinked out of existence momentarily, only to reappear slightly weaker than before.

Anwyn tapped into her spirit and summoned a brilliant burst of radiant energy. She knew that this energy would feel like boiling water being poured onto the skin as it made contact. She didn't hold back. The brilliance of her magic was blinding, searing through the illusions. The adversary's illusions fell apart, leaving him exposed and vulnerable.

As her conjured energy enveloped him, his staff clattered to the ground and he let out an ear-piercing scream before he fell onto the floor, writhing and convulsing in pain until he no longer moved. With the bewildering mist dispersed, the battlefield was once again revealed, and Anwyn caught sight of her final foe.

The fourth and final elf raised his arms, calling upon the very essence of the forest itself. His dark eyes glinted with malice, and his intricate tattoos glowed with ancient power. From the earth, ferocious vines shot forth like angry snakes, their thorny tendrils weaving around Anwyn. The vines constricted her with an iron grip, threatening to drain her life force and restrict her every movement. Anwyn felt the oppressive weight of the vines leaching her power, the strength of her magic weakening with every passing moment.

As the vines threatened to crush her spirit, Anwyn realized

she needed to summon a power greater than her own. She reached deep within herself, seeking the connection she shared with the forest. However, instead of the expected connection, she felt Lorelei's presence. In this desperate moment of panic, their two souls linked in a way she couldn't explain. The Fae's ethereal energy merged with Anwyn's, creating a bond so intense it threatened to overwhelm her.

Suddenly, a surge of vitality enveloped Anwyn, coursing through her with newfound vigor. Her spirit radiated a power so intense that it almost emanated light, and the enchanted vines that had ensnared her quivered under the might of their combined power. With a triumphant scream, Anwyn channeled the newfound strength into her limbs, and the vines, now unable to withstand the overwhelming force, began to relent. They unwound, their thorny grasp loosening as they gently released their hold.

In that moment, amidst the fierce battle, Anwyn began to understand the true potency of their unity. She had tapped into the unbreakable bond between herself and Lorelei, realizing the immeasurable power that had emerged when their connection was at its strongest. With renewed determination and an indomitable spirit, she faced the fourth elf.

Unleashing the full extent of her newfound power, Anwyn directed an overwhelming torrent of energy toward her enemy. A brilliant, searing beam of light enveloped him, consuming his essence as he cried out in anguish. The elf's form dissolved into shimmering motes of energy until there was nothing left but a profound silence.

The battle had left Anwyn drained, and she sank wearily to her knees, feeling as if she had weathered a storm. Every muscle protested, and exhaustion weighed heavily upon her spirit. Lorelei fluttered nearby, her presence a comforting balm to Anwyn's weary soul. Gratitude swelled within her, but her energy was spent, and she could only offer a silent thanks. With each breath, she felt herself sinking further into exhaustion until she could do nothing but lower herself onto her side, eyelids heavy with weariness.

Amidst her fatigue, a flicker of thought danced in her mind—a vision of what she thought Gunnar might look like. A faint smile graced her lips as she surrendered to sleep's embrace. Her eyes closed gently, and Anwyn drifted into slumber, finding solace in dreams of those who had aided her journey and those she had yet to encounter... and perhaps, fall in love with.

Anwyn

Anwyn's eyes snapped open, and as her senses sharpened, she discovered herself in a fiery, nightmarish cavern. The air hung heavy with a pungent scent of sulphur, and a fiery haze enshrouded the entire space. The ground beneath her radiated searing heat, and sinister crimson flames flickered ominously, casting eerie shadows throughout the chamber.

Before her stood several Drogo Mulik, their imposing figures casting long shadows in the eerie glow of the flames. Anwyn's breath caught in her throat at the sight. Though she had never encountered one before, she had pored over countless descriptions and illustrations during her studies with her mother. The grotesque blend of draconic and lizard-like features was unmistakable, just as her research had shown.

Transparent scales adorned their bodies, gleaming like smouldering embers in the flickering light. Wickedly curved horns protruded from their heads and shoulders, casting unsettling shadows. Anwyn's heart raced as she took in the nightmarish sight before her. The twisted bumps and ridges that formed their noses, or snouts, and the contorted slits of their nostrils sent shivers down her spine. She knew she had to remain calm and composed in the face of this terrifying encounter.

Attired in ceremonial garb, the gathering of Drogo Mulik surrounded a colossal coffin sculpted into the likeness of a huge dragon. Most of its imposing form remained concealed within the shadows and ash, but Anwyn's gaze remained locked onto the malevolent eyes of the dragon, whose cruel sneer appeared to fixate directly upon her.

The dragon-shaped coffin bore intricate engravings of ancient runes, and the very atmosphere vibrated with the ominous intonations of a haunting chant. These were the vile blood shaman of the Drogo Mulik, known for their fixation on using blood and death to power these horrific rituals.

In the depths of the ancient chamber, Anwyn bore witness to a scene both horrifying and surreal. The lifeless bodies of four Drogo floated eerily above an ornate coffin, suspended by some arcane force that defied natural laws. As she watched, a sense of dread settled over her, amplified by the sinister ambiance that permeated the chamber.

Droplets of viscous, darkened blood dripped from the suspended forms, staining the coffin's surface with a deep crimson hue. The air crackled with an unnatural energy, sending shivers down Anwyn's spine. Despite her growing unease, she remained a silent observer, her senses keenly attuned to the malevolence that seemed to seep from every corner of the chamber.

With ritualistic precision, the blood priests moved with purpose around the coffin. Each incision they made into their own scales sent rivulets of obsidian blood cascading onto the ancient runes below, where they sizzled and hissed, filling the chamber with an ominous sound that echoed off the stone walls. Anwyn could feel the weight of the ritual in the air, a dark presence that seemed to coil around her, suffusing the chamber with an aura of ancient power and foreboding.

As the ritual reached its crescendo, the fiery landscape itself seemed to convulse and the very ground trembled beneath Anwyn's feet. The colossal coffin shuddered violently, as if its inhabitant fought to be freed.

But then, just as the chanting reached its zenith, a deafening, anguished roar echoed through the fiery expanse. The ground ruptured, and the lid of the coffin was forcefully hurled into the air. Anwyn witnessed the specter of a colossal dragon, its ethereal form spiralling in a vortex of ghostly fire and fury.

The ritual had failed, it seemed, igniting a storm of fury within the dragon's spirit. Panic gripped the Drogo Mulik shaman, causing them to scatter in terror. Anwyn, transfixed by the horrifying spectacle, could do nothing but watch in a state of dreadful fascination as the dragon's fiery form began being forcefully drawn back into the confines of the coffin.

She witnessed the spirit's colossal jaws snapping in rage, and in its seemingly last acts of defiance, it seized one of the shamans by the head and cleaved another in half, leaving behind a gruesome spectacle of blood and severed bodies strewn across the chamber floor. It was only after this grotesque display that the spirit was at last pulled back into the confines of the coffin.

Without warning, her surroundings blurred and swirled, and the nightmarish realm dissolved like mist before her eyes. Anwyn's heart raced as she was ripped from the fiery land, leaving her gasping for breath and drenched in a cold sweat. She found herself back in the familiar embrace of her own world, safe from the tormenting visions that had plagued her sleep. Yet, the chilling weight of what she had witnessed clung to her, its echoes fading but leaving a sense of impending doom.

As Anwyn opened her eyes, the soft hues of early morning filtered through the dense canopy above, casting a gentle glow upon the scene before her. The aftermath of the recent attack sprawled across the glade, a stark reminder of the violence that had unfolded. Broken branches littered the ground, and the earth bore the scars of fierce combat, churned and disrupted by the clash of forces. Debris lay scattered around, a testament to the chaos that had ensued.

Beside her, Lorelei fluttered anxiously, her delicate wings quivering with concern. "Anwyn, are you alright?" she asked, her voice like that of a tinkling bell, filled with genuine worry.

Anwyn turned, her eyes widening with surprise as she registered the source of the voice—Lorelei. The tiny Fae had never projected her voice before. Typically, Anwyn would only receive 'impressions' of Lorelei's thoughts or intentions. The initial shock of hearing the Fae's voice flickered briefly, but it was soon engulfed by the lingering shadows of her haunting dream.

Anwyn slowly rose to a sitting position, the weight of the night's distress still heavy upon her. She took a moment to gather her thoughts, the details of the dream still vivid in her mind. "I don't know, Lorelei," she admitted, her voice barely above a whisper. "I had a dream… or nightmare, or vision. I'm not quite sure what it was." She admitted. "It felt so real, though, like a warning of what's coming."

She rose to see the devastation strewn across the glen, Anwyn's heart plummeted as she stumbled upon the lifeless body of her loyal companion, Honey. The vibrant, honey-colored coat that had once gleamed in the sunlight was now marred by the cruel scars of the merciless attack. Anwyn's throat tightened as she choked back a sob, her vision blurred by tears. With trembling hands, she knelt beside her fallen friend, her fingers brushing over Honey's still form as if hoping to awaken her from this nightmare.

The silence that surrounded them was deafening, broken only by Anwyn's ragged breaths and the soft rustle of leaves in the breeze. Memories flooded Anwyn's mind: the countless rides through the forest, the shared laughter, the unspoken understanding between them. Honey had been more than a horse; she had been Anwyn's confidant, her steadfast companion, and the only friend she had ever had.

Anwyn's grief was profound, shattering sorrow, threatening to consume her whole. Each breath felt like a struggle, each heartbeat a painful reminder of the emptiness that now filled her soul. In that moment, she felt the weight of loss bearing down upon her, crushing her spirit with its unbearable weight.

But despite the darkness shrouding her heart, a flicker of determination ignited within Anwyn's spirit. With tear-streaked cheeks and a voice thick with emotion, she whispered her final farewells to Honey, promising to carry her memory with her always. In that solemn vow, Anwyn found strength, a resolve to honor Honey's legacy in her mission to protect Vellhor.

Looking up, Anwyn's gaze swept across the desolation. She was acutely aware of the wounds inflicted upon the land and her own soul. The recent battle had exacted a toll that extended far beyond the physical realm. With the memory of Honey's loss still fresh, Anwyn reached out to the diminutive Fae, Lorelei, finding solace in the tiny creature's steadfast presence.

"We must prepare," Anwyn declared, her voice unwavering despite the pain that lingered within her. "A storm is approaching, and we must be ready to face it." With a solemn nod, Lorelei offered a reassuring smile, her resolve matching Anwyn's as they embarked on their journey into the unknown, their unbreakable bond and shared courage serving as their most potent defenses against the challenges that awaited them.

22

A Timeless Tomb

'In the realm where magic prevails, she strides untouched, an enigma immune to its enchantments.'

Kemp

When Kemp awoke with the first light of morning, his gaze swept across the makeshift camp, and the silhouette of Ruiha caught his eye, delicately outlined by the soft dawn glow. As memories of his conversation with Harald from the previous evening resurfaced, a twinge of doubt and uncertainty flickered within him, like a flame dancing in a gentle breeze.

He tried to shake off his suspicions, but they clung to his thoughts like mist on a mountain ridge. Despite their shared trials and the unspoken connection between them, an elusive whisper lingered, suggesting that Kemp could not trust her. Kemp furrowed his brow, grappling with an inner conflict that defied reason. He couldn't pinpoint a single act or word that cast doubt upon her, yet the seeds of mistrust persisted.

Unbeknownst to Kemp, the tendrils of Harald's words had insidiously woven their way into the fabric of his consciousness, and now they were tugging at the very foundation of his trust, attempting to fracture his bond with Ruiha.

As they pressed on through the treacherous trails of the Scorched Mountains, the connection between Kemp, Ruiha, and Harald felt as fragile as the cliff edges they carefully negotiated. Hardly a whisper passed among the three, intensifying the unease that lingered in the air.

As the three travelers ascended the rugged slopes, the distant murmur of cascading water reached Kemp's ears. Intrigued, he followed the sound into a deep cavern until he stood before a majestic waterfall. The cool mist enveloped him as he stepped inside, and to his surprise, he found Ruiha accompanying him. Meanwhile, Harald lingered at the cavern's entrance, a silent observer.

At the edge of the pool, the roar of the waterfall echoed throughout the cavern. The cascading waters plunged from high above and reverberated through the cavern's walls. The sound, a powerful rhythm of nature, filled the air with an awe-inspiring energy.

Beside Ruiha, Kemp felt a mix of emotions swirling within him. The misty spray from the waterfall dampened their faces, creating an intimate moment amidst the grandeur of nature. The play of refracted light painted a spectrum of colors on the cavern walls, adding a magical quality to the scene. As they gazed upon the breathtaking spectacle, an unspoken tension lingered in the air, adding to the thunderous roar of the waterfall.

Desire warred with uncertainty within Kemp's heart. He yearned to reach down and clasp her hand, to bridge the gap between them in this moment of shared wonder. Yet, a hesitancy held him back—a mixture of not knowing her well enough and an underlying trace of distrust that cast a shadow over his emotions.

As Kemp struggled to divert his focus from Ruiha, her presence seemed to pull him in like an invisible force. He couldn't deny the magnetic draw she had on him, a mixture of curiosity and something deeper he couldn't quite name. His gaze fixated on the cascading water, where he noticed a peculiar pattern emerge. His mind buzzed with questions, wondering if Ruiha felt the same sense of anticipation that tingled in his veins.

Ruiha's voice, soft yet insistent, broke through his thoughts. "Do you see it too?" she asked, her eyes reflecting the shimmering waterfall. Kemp's heart quickened. He pressed closer, his fingertips grazing the cool spray. It was then that he noticed a subtle heat beneath his touch, an arcane resonance echoing through the water.

He marveled at the sensation, his thoughts racing. What was this heat? Why did it feel so… alive? Kemp's analytical mind struggled to rationalize the experience, but the deeper part of him, the part that longed for discovery, urged him to press on. With each passing moment, the waterfall seemed less a barrier and more a veil, designed to hide something.

Ruiha stepped forward, her fingers brushing the water alongside Kemp's. "This is no ordinary waterfall," she murmured. Together, they felt a rush of anticipation mixed with awe as the water parted like a curtain, leaving them completely dry. Their astonishment grew as they found themselves in a cavern adorned with captivating murals. Each brushstroke wove tales of a bygone era when dragons graced Vellhor. Yet, these murals went beyond mere stories; they revealed the intricate symbology of Draconic power, ancient rituals, and the destinies of long-forgotten dragon dynasties in vibrant detail.

As Kemp and Ruiha beheld the murals, they unfolded like a tapestry, showcasing the presence of ancient dragons who once walked and flew amongst humans, elves, and dwarves. Their colossal forms radiated power and wisdom, depicted amidst age-old rituals that highlighted the sacred connection between dragons and the magical world.

Entranced by the scenes surrounding them, Kemp and Ruiha ventured deeper into the cavern. The very air seemed to hum with an arcane energy as they marveled at the murals that adorned the walls. A particular masterpiece seized Kemp's attention, and he stood in silent awe, captivated by the portrayal of a singular Draconic deity overseeing the fates of not only dragons but all the other races of Vellhor as well. However, as they examined the depictions more closely, a troubling realization dawned upon them: the other races appeared enslaved, their forms bowed in submission before the mighty dragons.

The cavern walls pulsed with the divine essence of magic, each mural weaving tales of a time long forgotten—or perhaps, Kemp couldn't help but wonder, tales yet to come. There had never been any history of dragons enslaving the other races, leaving Kemp and Ruiha to ponder if these murals were prophetic visions of a future yet unwritten, a grim reminder of the power that dragons could wield over all of Vellhor. As he shook off the thought, the reality remained: dragons hadn't been seen for millennia.

Ruiha ignited a torch, its flickering flames cast dancing shadows on the cavern walls. As the torchlight revealed the intricacies of the ancient carvings, Kemp's eyes widened with realization. His heart quickened, and an electric thrill coursed through his veins. This wasn't just a collection of old depictions; it was a confirmation of his theory.

The story etched in stone detailed the mythical journey of Nergai, a dragon ascending from the fiery breath of its Draconic form to the divine stature of a god. It was the evidence Kemp had long sought, a profound confirmation of his belief that dragons, through a mystical process or divine ritual, achieved, or attempted to achieve, a transcendent state bestowing them with immortality.

Kemp's excitement ignited, leading him to delve deeper

into the mysteries concealed within the ancient cavern. As he ventured into the chamber, Kemp found himself standing in the middle where an enormous coffin, carved into the depiction of a giant snarling dragon, rested. With a sense of reverence, he extended his hand and touched the cool stone coffin, wiping away a thick layer of dust. As he did so, runes beneath his fingertips were exposed, a patchwork of ancient symbols etched into the stone. He couldn't help but feel the weight of history pressing against his senses.

As he made contact with the coffin, a strong scent of sulphur filled his nostrils, and the room seemed to pulse with heat. Distantly, the faint crackling of a fire echoed in the background. As soon as he broke contact with the coffin, the overwhelming sensations ceased.

Studying the giant coffin further, Kemp noticed that the complex array of runes covered the coffin in its entirety. Although he couldn't decipher their meaning, the power emanating from them was palpable. It carried a heavy aura of death and blood magic, causing Kemp to shudder involuntarily as his spirit scanned over the mysterious symbols.

"What is this place?" Ruiha asked, her voice barely above a whisper.

"I can't decipher all the runes," Kemp replied with reverence, his gaze still fixed on the coffin. "But from what I can understand, this appears to be a tomb used in some kind of blood ritual." He continued circling the coffin, his hand hovering just an inch away from the cold, engraved stone, as if feeling the residual magic lingering in the air. He knew that some of the runes he had seen were meant for evil, but he decided to keep that to himself.

"A dragon named Nergai, deified and turned into a god." Kemp's face reddened as he hastily brushed away a tear tracing a path down his cheek. Finally, he had uncovered the truth he sought, evidence that would silence the mockery and laughter that had haunted him for so long. The weight of triumph filled his chest, proving them all wrong.

As he dwelled on the faces of those who had mocked him, seething anger bubbled within. The rage surged like a torrent, threatening to drown reason and decency. His face twisted into a sneer, and a growl of anger escaped his lips. Vengeful thoughts infiltrated his mind, and a sinister smile played on his lips at the prospect of inflicting pain upon those who had doubted him.

Standing there, his features contorted, an unseen force seemed to bind him in the clutches of darkness. The room grew oppressive, with an aura emanating from the mysterious coffin. Dark thoughts clouded his mind, whispering insidious notions foreign to his typically gentle personality.

Just as the shadows threatened to consume him, a soft voice cut through the malevolent haze. "Kemp, what's come over you?" Ruiha's concerned tone pierced the sinister fog. She approached cautiously, her eyes searching his troubled face for a glimpse of the kind and timid man she knew.

Kemp struggled against the dark thoughts that held him captive, his inner turmoil clear in his eyes. Ruiha, sensing something amiss, reached out and gently touched his arm. Distantly, he realized his hand was resting on the coffin. The moment their connection was made and his hand left the coffin, Kemp felt a sudden jolt, as if awakening from a nightmarish dream.

His eyes widened with realization as the fog lifted. "Ruiha, I don't know what came over me. Those thoughts... they weren't mine," he confessed, confusion and remorse etched on his face.

Ruiha studied him intently, her concern deepening. "It's this coffin, Kemp. There's something dark about it."

Kemp nodded, gratitude replacing the shadows in his eyes.

Together, they took a step back from the ominous coffin, the malevolent influence gradually fading. As they distanced themselves, Kemp felt the return of his true nature, the warmth of friendship overpowering the unsettling thoughts that had briefly plagued him. The atmosphere lightened, leaving only lingering echoes of the dark encounter with the mysterious coffin.

As Kemp's mind continued to clear, a perplexing thought crossed his mind, his face contorted in confusion as he considered. "Why didn't it affect you?" he wondered aloud.

Ruiha studied his face for a moment. "I don't know, Kemp," she began. "Maybe because I didn't touch the coffin. I only touched you."

Kemp pondered her answer, bringing his hand up to his face and squeezing the bridge of his nose. He slowly shook his head, his brow furrowed. "No... that can't be it. That's not how magic like this works. You touched me. You should have been affected equally."

Before he could continue, Ruiha stepped over to the coffin. She reached her hand out and touched the stone.

"Ruiha!" Kemp cried, his voice filled with urgency. "No!" The air crackled with tension as Kemp watched in horror, his mind racing with fears of the consequences that might follow Ruiha's brash act.

But she removed her hand, the coffin having no ill effect on her whatsoever. Kemp's confusion lingered, but Ruiha wore a confident smile as she walked back over to him. "See, nothing to worry about!" She reassured him.

A Timeless Tomb

Ruiha

Alone in the chamber, Kemp and Ruiha stood before Nergai's tomb, their gazes fixed intently on the imposing structure. The air crackled with the ancient dragon's magic, but Ruiha remained unaffected. A chill ran down her spine as she observed Kemp's reaction to the potent energy radiating from the tomb, unsettling in its intensity. Suddenly, Kemp's eyes widened, and he instinctively took a step back, as if struck by a sudden realization. "Ruiha, something's off. I can sense the magic, but you seem... you must be *immune!*" he said, his voice tinged with disbelief.

She winced inwardly, her fingers tightening around the hilt of her dagger. "I'm not immune, Kemp. I'm a survivor, that's all." She whispered.

As her words hung in the sacred chamber, Ruiha's gaze drifted into the abyss of her memories, back to the unforgiving streets and shadowed alleys of Gecit, where her journey began.

Alone in the treacherous alleys of Gecit, Ruiha moved with the stealth of a hunted prey. The scent of her desperation hung thick in the air. Much like the soiled, tattered rags she wore and the bones visible through her taught undernourished flesh, it was a haunting reminder of her desperate struggle for survival.

With no family, Ruiha was barely surviving the treacherous labyrinth of slums and backstreets of Gecit when Faisal found her. At first, the sanctuary of the Sand Dragons provided her with a semblance of security amidst the chaos. And it was in the grimy underbelly of Gecit that she first tasted the bitter sting of magic.

In one of the many turf wars fought by the Sand Dragons, their rivals had hired a sorcerer. Most gangs didn't like using sorcerers for revenge hits, it was simply too expensive when mundane thugs could achieve the same effect for little cost.

She recalled how the air crackled with energy as spells were cast, killing or injuring most of her gang, but amidst the chaos, Ruiha stood untouched. Spells that should have obliterated her seemed to dissipate like smoke before reaching her. She knew, though, it was not any immunity that had saved her, but sheer luck. Even Faisal agreed with that, afterwards always referring to her as 'his lucky charm'.

Back in the sacred chamber, Kemp's realization echoed in the air. "It's not immunity," she confessed again, her voice carrying the weight of a history Kemp could never understand. "It's survival." She affirmed, quietly.

Although Kemp appeared to harbor reservations about her statement, he didn't dwell on it or press for further explanation. Instead, he gravitated toward the cavern wall, drawing Ruiha's attention along with him. As they approached the intricate carvings etched into the stone, Ruiha trailed behind, her gaze wandering over the mysterious symbols. Despite her inability to decipher their meaning, she sensed an air of reverence in Kemp's demeanor as he studied them, prompting her curiosity to deepen.

Her attention shifted as Kemp approached a darkened recess within the rock. She watched with curiosity as he extended his hand, hesitating briefly before reaching into the shadowed space. Memories of the magic that had gripped him earlier flashed through her mind, and she couldn't help but feel a twinge of apprehension.

She held her breath as he withdrew a crown from the darkness, the gemstone at its center pulsating with an inner fire. She had to admit that it was indeed beautiful.

As Kemp fastened the crown securely to his pack, Ruiha's mind wandered to what lay ahead. She couldn't shake the sense that this discovery would propel them onto an unforeseen journey, one fraught with unexpected challenges.

Harald

Outside the cavern's entrance, hidden from Kemp and Ruiha, Harald carefully retrieved a magical diviner from his cloak pocket. The small, ornate artifact, crafted from onyx and adorned with cryptic runes, pulsed with power, its surface emitting a faint glow. Crafted by ancient Elven hands, the diviner held immense value to Harald. With the discovery of the tomb entrance, Harald recognized that this was the opportune moment to relay his findings to Duke Cahir. Closing his eyes, he immersed himself in the surrounding arcane energies, deftly weaving threads of magic with practiced skill. The currents responded to his command as he wove them into the diviner, creating an unseen conduit linking him to his master.

"Master," Harald began, "the boy has uncovered the tomb. I have memorised the location, which I have imprinted ready for magical transmission."

Harald began channelling his memorised knowledge of the hidden tomb into the magical currents surrounding him. The process was complicated and had taken him several years to master under the strict tutelage of his mentor, Leopold. It involved converting the mental image and coordinates into a complex imprint in his mind. He would then send the imprint via magical pulses through the diviner. Harald knew that on the receiving end, Duke Cahir was in possession of a second diviner, which was magically attuned to his own, and he would now be deciphering the location of the tomb.

"Excellent work, Harald," Duke Cahir praised. "Now, ensure that there are no loose ends!"

Duke Cahir's issued command, marking his unsuspecting companions for death, was music to Harald's ears. Embracing his mission with a wicked smile, Harald let out a contented sigh. After his plans to kill Ruiha once already had failed, the opportunity to now eliminate both her and Kemp promised to be far easier, filling him with a sense of eager anticipation. Finally, his chance for revenge had arrived.

23

A Story of Stonesprites

'Bonds are the treasures mined from the richest veins of the mountain, more valuable than Frosteel, for they enrich the spirit and the soul.'

Braem (Draeg's brother)

In the divine forges and workshops of Aerithordor, skilled Dwarven artisans, having transcended the mortal realm of Vellhor, crafted powerful artifacts resonating with divine energy. They weaved the legends of heroes and gods into every creation… '*and Draeg gave him a bloody Stonesprite!*' Braem fumed.

Braem sat with a tankard of ale, the size of a small tree trunk, grasped tightly in his muscular stone hand. He couldn't believe Draeg had stolen his place to go to Vellhor. His little brother infuriated him most of the time. However, this stunt of his could cause the entire realm of Vellhor to fall. This was no joke. Lives were at risk and if Vellhor fell, how long would it be before the divine realms were targeted?

His mother's lack of concern surprised him; he had anticipated anger and worry mirrored in her eyes. Instead, she had shrugged it off, seemingly familiar with Draeg's nature, as if accepting his recklessness as part of who he was. His other brothers would be angry by Draeg's actions though. They would help him hold Draeg accountable for his actions, he was sure of it. Although, that depended on the outcome of Gunnar's quest, he supposed. If Gunnar was successful, Draeg would be hailed as a hero, and Braem would simply just have to accept it.

Frustration etched across the rugged contours of his stone face, he sighed, the expression chiselled into the stoic features of the god. Downing a lengthy swig of ale, he realized its inability to intoxicate him, even if consumed by the lake-full. Yet, somehow, the ritual somehow granted him a semblance of ease with the situation.

Yes, he thought, he'd wait here at the Gatestone for Draeg's return. And when that moment arrived, Braem was determined to unleash his frustration, and he was going to throttle him.

A small smile tugged at his lips at the thought of his brother's strangled pleas for help as Braem choked him.

Draeg

Draeg knew that Braem would be annoyed. In fact, he would be beyond annoyed. Draeg pondered whether the word 'furious' would be too tame a word to describe how his brother would be feeling right now. It was inevitable, his older brother was the God of War, Strategy, Oaths, Protection and Judgement, and he was also a complete control freak. He wouldn't have let anyone else go to Vellhor and give Gunnar the advice and guidance he needed, even though Draeg was better equipped to help him as the God of Fate… admittedly, he had also earned the nickname of 'God of Chaos' too. But in his defense, when you knew how the pages of fate would unfold, life became tedious, and he had to do *something* to break the monotony of knowing absolutely everything!

In fact, he didn't even need to read fate to know that Braem would be waiting at the Gatestone, ready to pounce on him. He chuckled at the naivety of his older brother. When would Braem learn that he couldn't catch him off guard?

Draeg understood the source of Braem's irritation, of course, and he acknowledged that tricking him and taking his place at the Gatestone might not have been the wisest move. Yet, when he had discovered Braem's plan to gift Gunnar an enchanted axe, of all things, he felt compelled to intervene. A bloody enchanted axe, for Vellhor's sake – Draeg couldn't fathom why Braem would choose such a potentially disastrous gift, convinced that Gunnar would be doomed to falter at the first hurdle.

No, Gunnar didn't need a weapon like that. Well, he did, just not yet he didn't. Something like that could wait until Gunnar was ready. He'd need to advance his spirit and train in the arcane arts first. Hence why a Stonesprite would be essential for his current stage. Once he had enough knowledge and full control of his spirit and his magic, that's when he could be armed to the teeth with enchanted weapons. Doing it now would be like giving a child a sword and expecting him to slay a dragon with it.

He needed to build his foundations first, and the best and fastest way to do that was by gifting him a Stonesprite. Apart from his mother, of course, nobody realized, but a Stonesprite created by Draeg – the God of Fate - had the unique ability to swiftly gain sentience and would evolve into a knowledge bank, providing Gunnar with insight into magic, combat, knowledge from eons past and could even provide a slight insight into the future. Providing that Gunnar could bond with the sprite. Now that was an argument he didn't want to have with his brother.

There was a slim chance that the Stonesprite might not be able to bond outside of Aerithordor.

Well, he thought to himself. He had almost a full day left with Gunnar. He would try to help form the bond and control whatever chaos was inside the little guy.

Before resuming his conversation with Gunnar, Draeg couldn't suppress a chuckle at the mental image of Braem seething beside the Gatestone. A hearty laugh escaped him when he envisioned Braem's impending disappointment upon realizing that Draeg had crafted a key to a different Gatestone, making his wait pointless. Wiping a stray tear from his eye, Draeg met Gunnar's bewildered gaze, realizing that the young one probably thought he had lost his mind.

Gunnar

Though Gunnar had grown accustomed to Draeg's occasional lapses in conversation and his sudden fits of laughter, he still found them disconcerting when they occurred.

Draeg had been in the midst of explaining how the Stonesprite would grow and soon communicate with him, when his expression suddenly went blank, his eyes losing focus. Minutes passed before he erupted into deep laughter. Gunnar remained silent, patiently waiting for the god to return to the conversation.

When Draeg's eyes cleared, he resumed with an infectious grin. "So… where were we?" Draeg paused, attempting to recall their topic. "Ah, yes, the Sprite's communication abilities." He continued, surprising Gunnar with his renewed focus, emphasizing that the Stonesprite would not only communicate but also provide insights into mastering magical arts, refining combat skills, and offering knowledge from the realm's most intellectual minds.

Gunnar hesitated before posing a question to Draeg. Sometimes, his inquiries derailed the deity, leading to lengthy detours before returning to the original topic. However, Gunnar's curiosity outweighed the risk of diversion; he needed answers.

"How?" Gunnar asked, his curiosity piqued. "How does he possess such knowledge? How can he offer such insights? He's only just… hatched?"

Draeg responded with a hint of amusement. "Ah, Gunnar," he replied, his tone laced with jest. "I assumed you grasped that detail during our earlier conversation. It seems I overestimated your attentiveness."

Reflecting on their prior discussion, Gunnar couldn't recall Draeg explaining how the Sprite would impart information. "My apologies, Draeg," Gunnar admitted, his voice humble. "I don't recall you mentioning that part to me."

In his attempt to address Draeg informally, Gunnar grappled with the urge to use a more formal title. He had managed so far, but the fear of slipping up gnawed at him. What would Draeg's reaction be if he did? Would he laugh it off, or perhaps not even notice? One thing Gunnar had learned about Draeg was his unpredictability; his actions and responses seemed to defy any pattern or logic.

Draeg's clarification interrupted Gunnar's thoughts. "Ah, but I did mention it, Gunnar," he asserted. "I spoke of the spiritual link between the Sprite and myself, imbuing him with the insights and power of the God of Fate."

Contemplating Draeg's words, Gunnar vaguely recalled a similar sentiment being expressed. However, the mention of the God of Fate left him skeptical. Raised with a belief in free will, Gunnar, like many Dwarves, clung to the notion that personal choices rather than predetermined paths shaped destiny. Yet, he couldn't dismiss the fact that a god had spoken to him about the prophecy, which had the potential to challenge his beliefs about free will.

Reluctant to offend the god, Gunnar chose to withhold his personal opinions regarding fate for the time being. However, another question lingered. "Apologies, once again, Draeg. But you called yourself the God of Fate? I have never heard you called that before," he inquired.

Draeg mumbled something inaudible before meeting Gunnar's gaze. Gunnar couldn't help but notice a subtle battle between irritation and amusement playing out on the god's countenance.

"Mortal Dwarves, with mortal memories," muttered Draeg. "I am the God of Fate and Chaos." Raising his hands to prevent Gunnar from interrupting, he continued. "I know, I know… most Dwarves expect me to be shrouded in robes, with my face veiled in shadow, symbolizing the mystery of fate! Bah, what a load of rubbish! Shaping destinies is a stressful job. No need to take everything so seriously all the time!" He asked rhetorically. "No, exactly! May as well have some fun with it!"

As Gunnar grasped more about Draeg's circumstances, a subtle understanding blossomed within him. Recognizing the responsibility they both bore, Gunnar found a common thread between his own role in the prophecy and the deity's burden. This shared experience fostered a modicum of sympathy within Gunnar for the god.

If he were to embrace the concept of fate, he reasoned, it would naturally clash with chaos. Fate symbolized order and predestination, while chaos stood for disorder and randomness. When he shared this perspective with Draeg, the god chuckled heartily, shaking his head.

"Firstly," Draeg began, "both fate and chaos carry

unpredictability. Secondly, both can significantly impact outcomes. Fate shapes events in a predetermined manner, while chaos disrupts or alters them through randomness." Sensing Gunnar's confusion, Draeg added, "Think of me as representing the balance between order and disorder. Fate and chaos are interconnected, essential for the universe to function."

As Gunnar delved deeper into understanding Draeg's complexities, he began to see the god's playful side in a new light. Recalling the tumultuous days in Fort Bjerg, he questioned whether Draeg could have shared details of the prophecy more gently. Yet, upon reflection, he realized that the chaos surrounding his final patrol had paved the way for the emergence of his magical talent.

The firsthand experience of Wilfrid's betrayal amid the chaos made Gunnar accept Draeg's words as truth. His escape, marked by perilous leaps and near-death moments, left Gunnar contemplating different courses of action Draeg could have taken. Yet, uncertainty lingered; he couldn't be certain of their effectiveness.

Connecting the dots, Gunnar started to see the relationship between fate and chaos, as Draeg had explained. Draeg's personality mirrored the balance between order and disorder. The once seemingly unpredictable methods of the god now made sense, though Gunnar couldn't help but humorously wish for a less cliff-hurling approach.

Having delved into Draeg's words, Gunnar now felt an insistent curiosity to know more about the Stonesprite. A tiny creature with a spiritual connection to a god seemed like a potent ally, reigniting Gunnar's interest.

"Draeg," he began, locking eyes with the god, "you mentioned forging a bond with the Sprite. How do I achieve this?"

Draeg's gaze, fondly fixed on the slumbering Stonesprite

nestled in his colossal palm, met Gunnar's inquiry. "A bond between a dwarf and a Sprite," Draeg rumbled, "is built on a profound mutual understanding. Despite their differences, they share a telepathic connection that allows them to communicate without words, extending to emotions, thoughts, and intentions."

Intrigued by the prospect of this bond, Gunnar couldn't shake his reservations about privacy and potential intrusions into his mind. When he voiced these qualms, Draeg dismissed them with a casual shrug, assuring Gunnar that the bond would be robust enough to prevent such minor inconveniences. Despite Draeg's assurances, Gunnar remained uncertain, the weight of his concerns casting a shadow over his curiosity.

Draeg continued, providing further insights into the potential bond. He explained how their magical abilities would complement each other, creating a formidable synergy. Gunnar's newfound physical strength and abilities would find a counterpart in the Sprite's ethereal wisdom, drawing from the magical energies of nature.

"To fulfill your role in the prophecy," Draeg emphasized, "you'll rely on the knowledge and insight the Sprite brings. The synergy of your magical abilities will elevate you to new heights."

Draeg painted a vivid picture of their future collaboration. "When you and the Sprite combine your magical prowess, you'll become an unstoppable team. Take time manipulation, for instance," Draeg pointed out, referring to Gunnar's inadvertent use of time magic against the golem. "The Sprite, with its connection to nature, will offer insights into the natural cycles of Vellhor. This knowledge will enhance your understanding of how time flows, allowing for seamless manipulation."

Pausing to let the information sink in, Draeg continued, "Moreover, Sprites possess a unique connection to magical energies. They can infuse your spells with additional vitality, making them more potent and effective."

Gunnar, slowly grasping the potential benefits, began to see the Stonesprite as an invaluable ally. However, Draeg wasn't finished.

"The Sprite's tie to the natural world," Draeg explained, "can aid you in crafting potent healing and restorative spells. Your combined magic holds the potential to accelerate the healing of wounds, cure ailments, and restore vitality much more effectively."

Absorbing Draeg's insights, Gunnar's initial skepticism waned, replaced by a growing sense of awe. He started to feel a sense of shame for doubting the Stonesprite. If even half of what Draeg described was possible, the tiny creature would indeed be an indispensable asset, unlocking a realm of possibilities for Gunnar. As his mind buzzed with questions, one clamored for immediate answers. His voice, tinged with both intrigue and excitement, almost quivered as he asked, "Draeg, can you guide me in the process?"

Draeg, once again casting a fond gaze at the sleeping Stonesprite in his hand, began to explain the intricacies of nurturing this newfound connection. "To bond with a newly hatched Stonesprite," Draeg intoned, "you must forge a connection with it in your mind."

Gunnar, listening with rapt attention, absorbed Draeg's wisdom. "This bond you seek," Draeg continued, "is one of tenderness and trust. As the Stonesprite grows, it will share its unique magic and insights. Nurturing the bond requires care, respect, support, protection, and understanding. Attend to its well-being, considering its unique nature as you would your own needs."

Draeg's words painted a vivid picture in Gunnar's mind. He envisioned himself cradling the newborn Stonesprite, akin to caring for a baby. However, a realization dawned upon him — he had always been uncomfortable around infants. The prospect of looking after a newborn brought forth memories of awkwardness, fearing he might inadvertently cause harm. Now faced with this responsibility, Gunnar sighed. This was going to be challenging.

As he looked back at Draeg, the god's gaze had grown serious. "But know this, Gunnar," Draeg cautioned, "Stonesprites are creatures of chaos. Their magic can be unpredictable. To bond with them, you must learn to harness and control the chaos within. Be a steady and grounding force. Encourage harmony between their wild energies and your steadfast nature."

Gunnar nodded, understanding the weight of this responsibility. Draeg continued, "To control the chaos, guide the Stonesprite in focusing its magic. Be patient as you find balance and purpose within the swirling energies. As you learn to coexist, the Stonesprite will become a trusted ally, unlocking the true potential of your bond."

With Draeg's final words, he extended his hand, offering the sleeping Sprite to Gunnar. As Gunnar cradled the Stonesprite, it woke and, with a sudden burst of panic, bit down on Gunnar's thumb. Gunnar cried out in pain, nearly dropping the Sprite, as Draeg erupted in laughter, tears streaming down his stone like face.

24

Friend or Foe?

"In the whispers of destiny, a powerful soul emerges to become a guiding light. A rising sun casting its golden glow, their wisdom illuminates the paths of those seeking strength and knowledge."

Anwyn

After what felt like an eternity, Anwyn and Lorelei stood at the base of the imposing Eldrakar Divide. Anwyn embodied grace and strength, her cascading blonde hair framing honey-colored eyes that had beheld the beauty of the forest and, more recently, its darkest depths. With her katana gleaming at her hip, she exuded prowess as a warrior.

Beside her, Lorelei, the diminutive Fae, shimmered like a delicate beacon of beauty. Her wings glistened with an ethereal luminescence, defying the shadows cast by the foreboding mountains. Emerald hair flowed behind her, and gemstone-like eyes sparkled with unwavering strength and resolve.

With purposeful breaths, Anwyn and Lorelei entered the foreboding Eldrakar Divide. Anwyn's boots echoed softly against the rocky terrain as the mountains, shrouded in mist, loomed like ancient sentinels, their peaks disappearing into the clouds.

Luminous mosses clung to the stone, casting an enchanting glow on the narrow, winding trail. The air grew cooler, carrying the scent of pine, enveloping the path in a comforting embrace, a stark contrast to the foreboding peaks surrounding them.

Venturing deeper into the heart of the mountains, Anwyn and Lorelei remained vigilant, their sights set on finding Gunnar. Anwyn's fingers tightened on the hilt of her katana, and she exchanged a knowing glance with Lorelei, their silent communication echoing their unspoken determination. The mysterious Eldrakar Divide held both beauty and danger in equal measure, and the path ahead would undoubtedly challenge them more than just physically—it would also be a further test of their bond and resilience.

Anwyn had been preoccupied lately, her thoughts consumed by the recent attack outside of Gwydir, and her disturbing vision of the Drogo Mulik ritual. So amidst the challenges and uncertainties that lay ahead, the mere thought of Gunnar brought a rare smile to her face, and strangely, a little flutter in her heart. To her surprise, these emotions seemed to transmit through their shared bond, which was clear in Lorelei's cheerful response. The Fae glanced up from her perch atop Anwyn's shoulder, chirping happily and bouncing with infectious excitement, as if attuned to Anwyn's newfound hope and determination. Anwyn was pleased to see the Fae returning to a semblance of her former happy self after the misery of the forest.

"Soon." Anwyn whispered with a smile. "We'll find him soon, and the next part of our journey will begin."

As the duo continued their journey into the mountains, they noticed subtle changes; as they ascended higher, the air slowly became thinner, making it more challenging to breathe. It became a lot cooler the higher they got, and Anwyn wondered how low the temperature would get once the sun set. The plants and trees

Friend or Foe?

changed with the increased elevation, the once lush and leafy trees replaced with sparse coniferous trees and alpine shrubs, and as Anwyn peered up at the snowy peaks, she noted that little vegetation grew at all. The thought of not being surrounded by trees brought a heavy ache to her heart.

Anwyn pressed forward, her footsteps firm against the unforgiving terrain of the Eldrakar Divide. The looming mountains, like ancient sentinels, observed their progress with a silent, unyielding gaze. The journey had turned grueling, with harsh winds slashing through the air and biting cold gnawing at their resolve. Yet, it wasn't the elements that troubled Anwyn the most. A distinct sensation of being watched clung to her, unseen eyes tracking their every move. Unable to shake this eerie feeling, Anwyn tightened her grip on her weapon, her unease mirrored in Lorelei's delicate form. The ethereal Fae quivered nervously on Anwyn's shoulder, as if sensing the same unseen gaze that sent shivers down their spines.

"Did you hear that?" Anwyn's hushed words hung in the frigid air. Lorelei tilted her delicate head, her ears twitching in response to the mysterious presence. Anwyn's brow furrowed as she strained to catch faint echoes of something that shouldn't be there—soft footfalls, the rustling of leaves. Yet, when she whirled to investigate, there was nothing but the dance of shadows cloaking the towering peaks, their silence as inscrutable as the mountains themselves.

With every step, the ominous sensation of being watched remained their relentless companion, a weight that settled upon their shoulders like a shroud. Anwyn stole furtive glances over her shoulder, her instincts honed to a razor's edge. Her fingers tightened around the hilt of her katana, her heart echoing the eerie sense of pursuit.

As the days turned into a relentless blur of uncertainty, the feeling of being followed refused to relent, gnawing at her nerves with every step. There was no longer any room for doubt—they were being stalked. The dread of it clawed at her, making her more vigilant by the hour.

One afternoon, as the sun cast long shadows amidst the sparse pines, Anwyn's eyes caught a fleeting silhouette among the branches. Her heart skipped a beat, uncertainty gripping her as she tried to make sense of the mysterious figure that seemed to materialize from nowhere. Before she could react, the enigmatic form disappeared, leaving only the whispering wind in its wake. Anwyn's breath caught in her throat.

Hissing a warning to Lorelei, her voice hushed and urgent, Anwyn said, 'We're not alone. Be ready.' Her eyes darted between the shadows, searching for any sign of movement, the tension in the air palpable.

The Fae's luminous eyes widened in alarm, casting a faint glow as they continued their relentless ascent up the mountain. Their senses remained on high alert, their anticipation tinged with trepidation as they awaited the inevitable appearance of their pursuer.

Their tension reached its peak when, in a rare moment of rest, a cloaked figure, just over four feet tall, emerged from the shadows. Stepping into the dim light, although the hood of their robe obscured their features and the depth of their intent, the figure was distinctly Elven.

Anwyn's right hand twitched, before slowly inching toward the hilt of her katana and her left began thrumming with magic, her voice steady but cautious. "Who are you? Why have you been following us?"

The Elven stranger remained shrouded in silence, their hidden gaze offering no answers, and their concealed presence causing uncertainty to flicker through the eerie ambience. Lorelei's

Friend or Foe?

ethereal glow dimmed slightly, echoing Anwyn's unease.

Anwyn's acute senses detected an undercurrent of energy that clung to the stranger, a potent magic that sent shivers down her spine. She hesitated, attempting to summon her own power, but it felt feeble and insignificant in comparison to this elf opposite her. Her bond with Lorelei surged with protective instincts, yet even their shared strength seemed insufficient.

As the tension escalated and the stranger's powers grew stronger, Anwyn's mounting frustration led her to make a bold move, an attempt to physically restrain the stranger. Her hands trembled with effort, but she was swiftly and effortlessly repelled by the Elf's overpowering strength.

After what felt like an eternity of strained silence, the Elven stranger spoke, his voice a low and raspy whisper, as if it hadn't been used in centuries. "I mean no harm," he croaked. "I've been watching you, Anwyn, and I have questions of my own."

Anwyn's heart raced, her mind flooded with a plethora of unanswered questions. Why was this elf following them? How did he know her name? How was he so strong? And was he friend or foe?

Despite her apparent vulnerability compared to the stranger's strength, Anwyn stood her ground. She knew that if the elf intended harm, he could have effortlessly overpowered her. His lack of aggression brought a flicker of reassurance. Yet, an unsettling doubt lingered, leaving her wondering what she could do if the Elf's intentions suddenly changed. In that moment, she faced the unsettling realization that she might be utterly powerless if he decided to shift his stance.

Anwyn's honey eyes remained fixed on the Elven stranger as she took a deep breath, her hand subtly inching toward the hilt of the katana at her hip. Magic was clearly not an option, but the reassuring touch of the cool steel in her grip offered a modicum of comfort. Though deep down, she understood the futility of defending herself against this elf with her blade.

Her voice quivered ever so slightly as she responded, "You have my attention, but you'll have to excuse my caution. Who are you, and what questions do you have?"

The Elven stranger acknowledged her with a solemn nod, his voice still a low, raspy murmur. "I am Thalirion. I have been following you for days now, to ensure that you are indeed the one I seek," he began. "As for my questions, they concern a prophecy that speaks of Anwyn, the Seishinmori."

Anwyn's brows furrowed at the mention of the prophecy. "How do you know of this prophecy?"

Thalirion's eyes gleamed as he continued, "I have travelled far and wide, seeking fragments of knowledge and piecing them together. I believe that our destinies are intertwined, Anwyn."

Anwyn hesitated. Her grandfather had set her on this course, however, he had never mentioned a Thalirion. She was torn between her duty to find Gunnar and her curiosity about the stranger's cryptic words. She needed to know more; she decided. "Why should I trust you, Thalirion?"

Thalirion sighed, his gaze never leaving hers. "I understand that trust is earned, Anwyn. I can offer you answers and assistance on your quest, but the choice is yours. Are you willing to allow me to earn your trust? And, more importantly, do you embrace this prophecy?"

Lorelei fluttered on Anwyn's shoulder and telepathically said, "Anwyn, his power is potent, however, I sense a strong familiarity with it. It feels connected to the forest somehow. I believe that we can trust him."

Feeling slightly more at ease with Lorelei's reassurance of Thalirion, Anwyn considered his words, knowing that her path was about to become much more complicated than she had ever imagined. But she couldn't deny the allure of discovering more about her own destiny, and if he spoke true, surely this knowledge would aid her in her quest. With a determined look, she finally said, "Very well, Thalirion. I accept my destiny and will hear your words, then I will decide if I can trust you."

A small smile tugged at Thalirion lips. It was a sincere smile that reflected a small triumph. It did not feel malevolent in the slightest. It was as though, by hearing him out, Anwyn had merely saved him a great deal of time.

Before he began talking, Thalirion took a deep breath. "As I have stated already, Anwyn," he looked around then, and his gaze settled on Lorelei, "and your little companion." He smiled warmly at Lorelei, and instantly Anwyn lowered her guard slightly. Her suspicions of the stranger lessening somewhat.

"I have spent many years travelling to seek out the answers I require. I have travelled the length and breadth of Vellhor, and beyond," he said mysteriously, "in order to confirm my theories, and all pathways lead back to your name."

A smile tugged on his lips before he continued, "I did not, however, expect you to be as strong as you are. My role has been made somewhat easier and I would like to thank whoever trained you." He bowed his head slightly in respect.

At his words, Anwyn's thoughts raced back to her parents, and she wondered how their own adventure with her grandfather was going. She hoped they were safe.

"Despite your strength, you are still not prepared for the next steps in your journey. That is why I have been wandering the Eldrakar Divide searching for you."

Anwyn wondered what he meant by that. She suspected that now she had been named as Seishinmori, she was far stronger than any elf in Vellhor. She hesitated at that, before realization settled on her. She was nowhere near as strong as Thalirion. She doubted whether she could ever gain as much power as he had.

"Your strength greatly surpasses my own, Thalirion. How are you so strong?" She asked him, the intrigue and curiosity evident in her eyes.

He chuckled, and in that moment, she was reminded briefly of her grandfather, Alden.

"Anwyn, I am well over one-thousand years old now. I have been studying magic for longer than any being in this realm. The strength I attained in Vellhor was only a fraction of what I have learned elsewhere on my travels. As I once was, you are currently a big fish in a very small pond. That scenario is about to change significantly." He smiled confidently.

The way Thalirion spoke confused Anwyn. He gave the impression that Vellhor was just a small fragment within a grander realm, speaking as if he had traversed them all in pursuit of wisdom, honing his skills along the way.

Thalirion smiled knowingly as Anwyn's thoughts caught up, and she wondered whether the ancient elf could also read her mind.

"I have sought you out in order to train you. Along with another." He looked at Lorelei again before continuing. "Someone slightly bigger than your current companion, that is."

"Yes, well… we are currently seeking out a third companion, who has been named in my grandfather's prophecy."

"Ah, yes… the wise Alden," Thalirion smiled fondly. "He has played his part well, and he has ensured that the prophecy could come into effect. I owe him much for his attentiveness."

Once again, Thalirion gave a shallow, respectful bow of his head. Anwyn was surprised that someone with so much power would be so respectful of others. From what her father had told her, power usually corrupted. This Elf, however, wielded his power with a humble grace. She nodded back in respect.

"I am sure he would love to meet you," Anwyn began. "He is currently fulfilling some other part of the prophecy alongside my parents."

Thalirion merely nodded in response, prompting Anwyn to press on. "We are seeking out a dwarf named Gunnar. My grandfather believes we will meet him here, in the Eldrakar Divide."

"Hmmmm," Thalirion mused, his gaze fixed on a distant point. "Let us see where Gunnar is currently."

With that, the elf closed his eyes, and Anwyn sensed the aura around him thickening. Moments later, she marvelled at the tangible power emanating from Thalirion, almost visible in its intensity.

Thalirion reopened his eyes, the power around him dissipating. "The dwarf is currently on the western coast of Vellhor, in the lands of the Drogo Mulik," he said calmly.

Anwyn was stunned, both by the accuracy of Thalirion's revelation and his apparent lack of exhaustion. She wondered how he could have located Gunnar without any personal belongings or magical links. When she questioned him, Thalirion smiled and explained, "My knowledge of magic exceeds what you currently understand as your limits in Vellhor. The power I just used barely even made my fingers tingle, let alone exhaust me."

Still shocked, Anwyn asked, "and what type of magic did you use to locate Gunnar? I didn't see you use any of his personal items to locate him. Therefore, it must be a magic that I have yet to master."

Thalirion smiled widely, "Excellent, Anwyn! I am pleased that you have recognized that. But I am even more pleased to hear your determination to master a higher level of magic! The spell I cast was a divination spell, also known as scrying. The same spell I cast in order to find you, in fact! By concentrating my aura and focusing my intent, I am able to perceive the location of the person I am searching for. I can see glimpses of the target's surroundings and therefore gain an estimation of their location."

"But he is on the other side of Vellhor!" Anwyn exclaimed.

"Which is why you will need to become more powerful, Anwyn. I could find Gunnar if he was in Sandarah, or further!"

As she realized how far away Gunnar was, her face dropped. She had travelled so far and been through so much, only to be told that she had been travelling in the completely wrong direction.

Thalirion must have noticed her anguish, because he quickly interjected. "No reason to worry, Anwyn. Believe it or not, you are closer than you think."

With that, he reached into his robes and pulled out a glass marble. He rolled it between his thumb and finger before launching the marble over to her. Raising one hand in the air, she deftly caught it.

The marble, seemingly ordinary at first glance, felt smooth and cool to the touch. A bright flame burned within, vibrant and orange, defying gravity regardless of the marble's orientation.

Flickering flames cast an ambient glow, revealing intricate patterns pulsing with the heartbeat of magic. Tiny motes of light swirled around the flame, drawing power from the fire within. The glass marble, adorned with invisible glyphs and symbols, emanated an undeniable power.

As Anwyn studied the marble, she marvelled at the delicate balance between simplicity and enchantment. "This, Anwyn," Thalirion spoke, "is called an Endless Bridge."

In that moment, as she gazed upon the Endless Bridge, a veil fell, and Anwyn felt the full weight and power of the marble. Shocked, she nearly dropped it.

Smiling, the ancient elf explained, "This orb contains Spiritfire, a flame forged by my own spirit. It serves as a tether to the essence of space itself."

Anwyn's gaze locked onto the marble as Thalirion continued, "To activate the Endless Bridge, crush the stone and focus on your destination. Watch closely now." Thalirion stepped closer, reaching out and placing his forefinger and thumb around the marble. With ease, he crushed the marble, causing it to glow with a warm, ethereal light.

"The flame responds to intent," Thalirion explained. "It forms a bridge, connecting our location to the chosen destination."

Anwyn's eyes widened as a bridge materialized—a pathway of flickering flames emanating a comforting warmth. Thalirion cautioned, "Do not underestimate its magic. The Endless Bridge demands a deep understanding of both departure and destination. Manipulating it incorrectly may unleash consequences beyond reckoning."

Thalirion held out his hand. "Now, Anwyn, are you ready to travel the world with me?"

Hesitantly, Anwyn extended her hand. As she made contact with Thalirion's skin, the world vanished, replaced by a tunnel of fire. Remarkably, she felt no heat at all.

25

Bonded in Stone

'The strength of a true bond lies in shared trust and mutual understanding.'

Gunnar

It was now late in the day, and Gunnar still hadn't managed to open the connection with the Stonesprite. In fact, he could have sworn that the tiny creature was beginning to dislike him even more with each hour that passed.

"Patience!" Shouted Draeg, as he sat with Karl by the fire, both of them smoking broadleaf pipes. Draeg's pipe was double the size of Karl's and it took Gunnar some time to accustom himself to seeing his friend and a giant stone Dwarven god sitting there smoking tobacco, and laughing at his expense.

As the last rays of the sun painted the sky in hues of amber and gold, Gunnar felt a sense of frustration settling in. Draeg noticed Gunnar's growing frustration and chuckled, sending a ring of smoke into the air. "You're too tense, my friend. The Stonesprite can sense it. Relax, and let the connection flow naturally."

Karl, with his deep, rich laughter, added, "Aye, Gunnar! Even the stones need a bit of charm."

Gunnar sighed, casting an exasperated glance at the Stonesprite, perched on a nearby rock. It seemed to meet his gaze with a mischievous glint in its amethyst eyes.

Whilst Gunnar had been attempting to form the bond with the Stonesprite, Karl had formed his own bond with Draeg. The two of them were now sitting around the fire shouting useless advice and taking pleasure in mocking Gunnar's repeated failures.

In that moment, Karl couldn't resist chiming in, his voice carrying across the clearing like a boisterous breeze. "Gunnar, you've got more stubbornness than a mountain. I'll give you that. But you're about as successful as a Drogo trying to be polite! Why don't you give it a rest for a while?"

Draeg erupted in hearty laughter at Karl's joke, and Karl, beaming with pride, revelled in the praise. "The idiot," Gunnar mused to himself. Admitting defeat, he slowly shook his head and sighed heavily. With a sense of resignation, he wandered over to join Karl and Draeg, the Stonesprite on the ground cheekily taking a swing at Gunnar's shin. Both Karl and Draeg erupted in laughter at the mischievous attempt.

Gunnar had dedicated the entire day to opening the connection and forging a bond, but the Stonesprite remained steadfast in its resistance. There was a fleeting moment when he sensed a glimmer of connection, a spark opening in his mind. It held promise, a potential breakthrough. However, the Stonesprite growled and abruptly darted in the opposite direction, leaving Gunnar with a blinding headache. That fleeting moment had been the closest he had come, but it felt like hours ago. Since then, the elusive Stonesprite had defied all attempts at forming a bond.

Karl blew out a long stream of smoke, breaking the silence with a casual inquiry. "Have you thought of a name yet?"

Gunnar, seated by the warm glow of the fire, furrowed his brow in contemplation. The notion of naming the Sprite hadn't crossed his mind. Delicately, he reached down, lifting the Sprite in his hands with a gentle touch, wary of causing any harm. As the flames flickered, casting eerie shadows around the camp, he gazed deeply into the Sprite's purple eyes, pondering the choice of a name.

Gunnar mulled over the idea of naming the Sprite. In Dwarven culture, a name wasn't just a label; it was a profound connection to one's lineage, carrying the weight of ancestors and traditions. His own name bore the legacy of his grandfather's triumph over a Drogo Mulik horde. The tale was legendary—his grandfather had led the battle, defeating over a thousand Drogo with just a hundred Dwarven warriors. As he thought about his heritage, the significance of naming the Sprite suddenly held importance to Gunnar.

As Gunnar pondered a suitable name for the Sprite, as unpredictable as a violent storm, he reflected on the day's frustrations and moments of despair. A chuckle escaped him as he recalled his failed attempts. "A name," he muttered to himself, "it's more than a word; it's a reflection of who you are. You're a whirlwind of chaos and unpredictability, a burst of destructive energy in my life. Maybe I'll call you 'Havoc,' a name that captures the true essence of your spirit."

With that decision, Gunnar felt a sense of connection and purpose. Naming the Sprite was a declaration of their partnership, a recognition of the Stonesprite's unique qualities, and a celebration of the chaos that would become an integral part of his life.

As Gunnar committed to name his chaotic sprite 'Havoc,' a warmth and companionship seemed to envelop the camp. It was as though the Sprite itself sensed the significance of the moment, as he pulsed with a vibrant, purple light, and let out a mischievous laugh that echoed around the campsite.

"Havoc," Gunnar addressed his new companion, "with this name, I welcome you into my mind. Our fates are intertwined now. Welcome to my side, little one."

In response, Havoc jumped up and down, leaving traces of purple sparks in his wake. And as the sun finally dipped below the horizon, casting a warm, golden glow across the campsite, Gunnar felt a profound shift within him. The bond with Havoc, the small being with hair like amethyst and eyes that shimmered like purple starlight, deepened in ways he couldn't fully explain. It was as if a delicate thread of energy, invisible to the naked eye, wove itself into the very core of his being.

With each passing moment, he could sense Havoc's presence growing stronger, like a whisper in his mind. It was a gentle yet powerful sensation, a connection that transcended the ordinary world, and he began to feel Havoc's emotions as his own.

Gunnar closed his eyes and let his thoughts drift, seeking something deeper. In his mind's eye, he could see Havoc's form running among stones and rocks, a tiny guardian of the mountain's secrets. Their thoughts intertwined, and he knew that the sprite had accepted him as a kindred spirit. The bond had been forged.

Gunnar's thoughts were abruptly interrupted by a loud, rumbling voice. As he reluctantly opened his eyes, he tried his hardest not to show the irritation he felt in them for being disturbed from the intimate and personal experience of forging a bond.

"A name!" Draeg laughed, his booming voice in stark contrast to the silent surroundings of the wooded campsite. "Who would have thought? Amazing... That's a new one for me, I'll admit! But, whatever works, hey?"

"So," Karl continued. "The bond worked? You're welcome!" He chuckled.

Gunnar shut his eyes once more, drawn by a tugging sensation in his mind. It seemed as though Havoc had something to communicate. Concentrating on the thread of energy within his spirit, Gunnar endeavoured to grasp it, but it proved challenging, like trying to grasp smoke with your bare hands. Frustrated, he opened his eyes and gazed at the Sprite. "What is it, Havoc? What do you want to tell me?"

Havoc burst into laughter and dashed towards Karl. With an impressive leap, he landed on Karl's knee and, in another acrobatic display, managed to hop onto his shoulder. Perched there, he began rumbling something unintelligible before leaping and playfully smacking Karl in the face. Amidst fits of laughter, Havoc jumped back to the floor, rolling around in amusement. Karl stared at him in shock. Though Havoc hadn't caused any harm, the unexpected attack caught Karl off guard. Draeg erupted into laughter, his massive stone hand smacking on his knee, creating soft rumbles in the ground around them.

Havoc then ran up to Draeg, standing with his hands on his hips, radiating pride. Gunnar could tell that the Sprite was pleased with his achievement, and a smile began to tug at Gunnar's lips, unable to hide his amusement.

"Haha, you're a feisty little one, aren't you?" Draeg laughed. "Well, Gunnar, you have formed the bond, which has dampened the chaos within him somewhat." Draeg looked over to a stunned Karl and chuckled, before adding, "however, it seems that you have some work to do still to control it completely!"

Gunnar was relieved that the attacks, previously aimed at him, had ceased, and he couldn't help but wonder when he would be able to communicate with Havoc. Gunnar believed that speaking with the Sprite would significantly aid in controlling the chaos.

As if sensing Gunnar's thoughts, Draeg spoke, "It will not be long now before he can communicate." Draeg began. "Soon, he will be able to communicate with you verbally and telepathically. Once that happens, you will find it a lot easier to strengthen the bond and control the chaos in him."

Curious, Gunnar inquired, "How long do you think it will take?"

Draeg raised his hand, stroking his brown and green mossy beard, his brow furrowing in thought. "Well…" he mused, "No two Stonesprites are ever the same, so it's difficult to answer your question. There are quite a few variables at play. The strength of the bond—stronger bonds progress quicker, but even that isn't set in stone. The amount of chaos within the Sprite makes a difference. The personal qualities and attributes of each party… it is quite a challenging question to answer."

Draeg looked at Gunnar, a guilty expression on his face. Gunnar, sensing something wrong, asked skeptically, "What is it, Draeg? Why are you looking at me like that?"

Clearing his throat, Draeg's eyes shifted guiltily from Gunnar to Havoc before he responded, "Ahem, it's just that… a Sprite has never actually hatched outside of Aerithordor before."

Gunnar maintained a blank expression as he stared at Draeg. Uncertain of the implications, he pondered the potential effects on Havoc and their bond.

"Actually," Draeg continued, "a Sprite has never actually bonded with a mortal dwarf before either."

Gunnar, now thoroughly surprised, asked, "What?"

Draeg's smile returned, and he clapped his hands together, rubbing them with a noise resembling a small earthquake. "Well, Gunnar, that I can answer! As you know, I am the God of Fate…"

"And also the God of Chaos!" called out Karl, a smirk playing on his face.

Draeg briefly glanced at the dwarf, and Gunnar marvelled at how comfortable Karl had become with the God. Karl seemed fearless, unafraid of any reprisal from Draeg. Gunnar couldn't decide if Karl was remarkably brave or just plain stupid.

Ignoring Karl's comment, Draeg continued, "So, as the God of Fate, I have indeed witnessed several variations of your journey, and I can say that an extremely strong bond is definitely achievable and, in fact, probable, in most instances!"

Gunnar wasn't entirely confident, knowing that in some instances, at least, a strong bond wasn't achieved according to Draeg's insights into the fate of his journey. Despite his reservations, he pushed them aside and resolved to try his hardest to make the bond as strong as possible. He simply nodded to Draeg in acknowledgment and brought Havoc up to his chest as he maneuverd into a lying position, ready to get some sleep.

As Gunnar lay there deep in thought, Havoc gently snoring on his chest he suddenly remembered the prophecy, and a question briefly crossed his mind, "Who was this elf he was supposed to meet? And did the prophecy mention love?" He mused. Uncertain, he would have to ask Draeg again in the morning. With that thought, his eyelids drooped shut, and sleep overcame him.

Gunnar

Gunnar awoke with a start, his senses jolted into alertness by a sudden shout of alarm from Draeg. The air crackled with urgency as Gunnar's eyes snapped open, scanning the surroundings in a rapid sweep. He saw Karl lifting his head up in confusion and glancing around.

The campsite, bathed in the soft glow of a dying fire, pulsated with tension. Shadows danced wildly, driven by the flickering flames that struggled to maintain their feeble existence. Gunnar's heart pounded in his chest as he searched for the source of Draeg's distress.

And then, as if summoned by chaos, a portal of fire ripped through the air, tearing at the fabric of reality itself. The flames blazed with an otherworldly intensity, casting an eerie light that played across Gunnar's face. The very air seemed to shudder as the portal tore open, revealing glimpses of a distant, fiery realm beyond.

Emerging from the blazing flames, two Elves stumbled forward, their once-graceful movements somewhat disrupted by disorientation. The elderly male elf navigated the transition with stoic poise, his timeless gaze surveying the unfamiliar surroundings. In contrast, the younger, elegant female elf appeared shaken. Strands of her long, flowing blonde hair clung to her face, tousled by the fiery journey they had just undertaken. Her honey-colored eyes widened with a mix of surprise and fear as she struggled to regain her composure in the face of this abrupt change.

The air crackled with residual energy, as Gunnar's mind raced to make sense of the scene unfolding. The air thickened with a mix of tension, and Gunnar instinctively went to search for the haft of his axe, only to remember he had been forced to leave it at Fort Bjerg.

The portal continued to flicker and dance, casting an uncertain glow on the faces of the Elves before him. In that moment, Gunnar couldn't help but be captivated by the beauty of the female Elf. Despite her disarrayed appearance, her elegance shone through, accentuated by the golden hue of her hair and the warmth of her eyes.

Upon closer scrutiny, the female elf bore some species of fairy perched delicately upon her shoulder, her emerald green hue reminiscent of undulating waves or the flickering flames of a fire.

"Thalirion, you stupid bastard!" Draeg, exclaimed. "You know that I can't see you when you use those... *things!* You scared me half to death!"

The elderly elf nodded in response, a smile playing on his soft lips. "Draeg, you are lucky you are not a mortal then, aren't you?"

Gunnar noticed the tension between the two groups ease as it became evident that the Dwarven god and the older elf knew each other. And more importantly, there didn't seem to be any hostility between the two.

"Who in Vellhor are you two? And what in all that is holy was that thing you just stepped out of?" announced a still shocked Karl.

The elderly elf responded, "I am Thalirion. This is my companion Anwyn, the Seishinmori of the Elven people. And our *third* companion is dear Lorelei, a Fae representative from the forest herself."

"And what about that fiery hole of flame you just stepped out of?" Karl demanded.

"That is called the Endless Bridge, a unique piece of magic designed to transport people from one place to another."

"And completely undetectable to the Dwarven God of Fate!" Draeg exclaimed dramatically.

Upon hearing that the big stone dwarf, Draeg, was a god, Anwyn's eyes widened in awe. Karl must have noticed, because he chuckled and said, "oh don't be too awestruck Anwyn, you'll give him an even bigger head than he already has!"

At that moment, Havoc leaped out from behind Gunnar and imitated his head growing humongous and draping on the floor before rolling around on the floor laughing.

Lorelei hopped down and stared at the Stonesprite curiously. To Gunnar's surprise, Havoc froze. He glanced up towards

Gunnar nervously, as if to ask, 'what do I do?' Gunnar shrugged in response.

"Anyway," Draeg said, ignoring Karl's jibe. "It is lovely to meet you, Anwyn and Lorelei. This is my companion Karl, who is an idiot." Karl laughed before flourishing an intricate bow for the newcomers.

"And," Draeg continued. "This is Gunnar, the heir to Draegoor and his newly bonded Stonesprite, Havoc."

Gunnar noticed that Anwyn tensed at the mention of his name and narrowed her eyes on him, scrutinizing his every movement. As their eyes finally met, Anwyn nervously brushed a strand of golden blonde hair from her eyes and offered him a gentle, if apprehensive, smile.

They muttered a brief, awkward 'hello' to each other as Draeg and Thalirion looked at each other knowingly.

"Well, this is my final day on Vellhor." Draeg exclaimed. "I will pass you over to the care and tutelage of Thalirion, who will be responsible for your training."

"Training?" Asked Gunnar. "Apologies, Draeg, but you never mentioned training before. What exactly are we training for?"

"The upcoming war, of course!" Draeg boomed back. "If you are to command the armies of Dreynas, you will need to become a lot more.... I want to say *impressive,* but I don't want to be rude." Draeg stood with his stone finger and thumb stroking his chin. "...*powerful...* you will need to become far more powerful if you are to wrestle power away from the clans and control Dreynas as its rightful ruler!"

Gunnar stood dumbfounded, his mouth open in shock as he struggled to comprehend Draeg's words. Finally, he found a semblance of composure and sputtered out, "Rule? Dreynas? What?"

"That's right, Gunnar," Draeg continued. "You will need to

command the Dwarves of Dreynas, and Anwyn will lead the Elves of Luxyyr. Our two mighty races must join forces if we are to have any chance of winning this war." He glanced across to Thalirion and whispered, "He's strong and has a good heart, but he's not the sharpest tool in the box, if you know what I mean. I've had to explain things to him twice on most occasions!"

Karl and Havoc burst out laughing at that, and Gunnar glared at them until they eventually went silent.

"Draeg, do you understand how the political structure of Dreynas works? There is not one 'ruler' of the Dwarves. The clan chiefs would never allow it. For one dwarf to rule, there would need to be a unanimous decision to appoint one ruler over all clans. One king. And that will never happen."

"Ahh, but it must, Gunnar. The world is changing, forces are at play that will force the hand of the clan chiefs. If they refuse to accept fate, then they face being slaughtered by our enemies. Only by uniting the Dwarves and Elves will we have the strength to face what is coming."

Gunnar had spent time with all of the clan chiefs. He knew them well, and he also knew how pigheaded and stubborn they could be. He knew they would be unwilling to compromise their own power and accept one dwarf ruling over them all. The only exception would be his father, Erik. In his eyes, this would catapult Draegoor to sit on top of all of the clans. He would support this move, but not for the reasons Draeg had just explained.

Either way, ruling Dreynas—or even Draegoor, for that matter—was not what he had ever wanted, and the thought of it now made him feel sick. He took a deep breath, trying to steady himself. The weight of Draeg's expectations felt crushing.

"Draeg, you must understand," Gunnar said, his voice wavering, "I've never aspired to lead. I'm not sure I'm the one to unite the clans."

Draeg's gaze softened slightly. "Gunnar, true leaders are often those who least desire the role. It is your reluctance that makes you worthy. The strength and wisdom you carry within you are what we need. Trust in yourself, as I trust in you."

Gunnar looked around at his companions, seeing a mixture of uncertainty and hope in their eyes. The enormity of the task ahead loomed over him, but he could also feel a spark of resolve igniting within.

"I will try," Gunnar said quietly.

Draeg nodded, a glimmer of pride in his eyes. "That's all I ask, Gunnar. Together, we will forge a new path."

The weight of the responsibility still hung heavy, but Gunnar felt a newfound determination taking root. The journey ahead would be fraught with challenges, but he allowed himself to believe that perhaps, just perhaps, they could overcome them.

26

Alliances Forged

'Amidst the trials of the proving grounds, strength is forged, skills sharpened, and character tested—a place where resilience blossoms into true mastery.'

Anwyn

Anwyn stumbled out of the Endless Bridge, her senses reeling from the disorienting journey through the vast expanse of space. The weight of Gunnar's unexpected presence caught her off guard as she regained her bearings. Irritation bubbled within her, fueled by the lack of warning from Thalirion. Cursing under her breath, Anwyn felt ill-prepared and vulnerable, standing in silence like a voiceless child, unwittingly making a mockery of herself. As she grappled with these emotions, the distant echoes of her journey lingered, enhancing the surreal atmosphere around her.

Yet, as she studied Gunnar in stunned silence, she couldn't help but admit that he did possess a rugged handsomeness. His appearance, raw and untamed, held an undeniable allure. The fact that Elves were unable to grow facial hair, made Gunnar's long braided beard a captivating anomaly. Authenticity and strength radiated from him, and Anwyn found a certain rough-hewn appeal in these qualities.

Unable to shake the words of her grandfather's prophecy from her mind, she wondered about the forbidden love it had mentioned. The verses spoke of a love that would conquer in a world torn by hate. This dwarf, standing before her, was supposedly the object of this destined love, and she didn't even know how to talk to him. Whilst she had been educated in social etiquette by her parents and was supposed to be adept at navigating diverse social environments, talking to Gunnar in real life proved more challenging than any lessons with her mother.

As she reflected on her limited real-world experiences, Lorelei fluttered over to Anwyn, her thoughts tinkling like chiming bells in Anwyn's mind. "He seems pleasant," Lorelei conveyed to Anwyn.

Anwyn reciprocated with a smile, replying to Lorelei's thoughts, "Indeed, but I've already made a fool of myself. I feel like an anxious child."

"Anwyn, you are the Seishinmori. In your own right, you possess immense power and strength. You stand against the forces of evil, destined for remarkable feats! This dwarf should consider himself fortunate to even engage in conversation with you!"

Slightly taken aback by the strength of the Fae's encouraging words, Anwyn nodded in agreement, appreciating the solace of their telepathic conversation.

"Thank you, Lorelei," she sighed within her thoughts. "I'm just a bit nervous, afraid I might make a fool of myself."

"Relax, Anwyn," reassured the Fae in her mind, "everything will unfold smoothly. But I'm concerned about his companion."

"Karl?" Anwyn questioned. "He seems harmless. No need to worry about him."

"Not the dwarf. That stone creature, Havoc," Lorelei corrected.

"He's born from chaos and disorder. His spirit is in constant *havoc*." She chuckled, or tinkled rather, at her own playful remark.

"Draeg mentioned that they were newly bonded. Maybe as their bond strengthens, his spirit will even out a bit," Anwyn suggested optimistically.

"Perhaps, Anwyn, perhaps..." Lorelei responded, her tone indicating her lingering skepticism

Determined to prove to the group that she was not, in fact, a scared child, Anwyn decided that it was time they discussed their plans.

"So, where do we go from here, then?" Anwyn began turning toward Draeg with a determined glint in her eyes. "Draeg, your... holiness?"

Karl chuckled to himself, while Havoc rolled around on the floor in what Anwyn assumed was laughter. Even Thalirion had a small grin on his face. She was glad that Gunnar hadn't laughed at her, but he did have a bemused expression on his face. Unsure of what she had said wrong, she looked around in confusion.

"Ahem," Draeg exclaimed. "Please don't call me 'your holiness', Anwyn. I really do hate being idolised and revered. Merely calling me Draeg will suffice."

Karl's chuckle turned into a burst of laughter before he finally apologised. "I'm sorry," he said, wiping away a stray tear. "It's just the longer you get to know Draeg, the less godlike he really seems!"

"I'm still as powerful as one, Karl. Even if I detest being worshipped all day, unlike some of those self-absorbed gods and goddesses out there! So be careful, or I might decide to simply smite you!" A mischievous glint in Draeg's eyes accompanied his words, implying a jest. Yet, Anwyn couldn't help but wonder if Karl realized that Draeg might genuinely possess the power to smite him. Surely he knew? However, as she glanced over at Gunnar, the nuanced expression on his face prompted her to reconsider whether Karl was fully aware of this.

"'Apologies, Draeg," Anwyn began, "I'll avoid using godly titles from now on." Draeg responded with a simple smile.

"But please, enlighten me about our next steps," she continued. Thalirion took the lead in the conversation. "Firstly, Anwyn," he said, "you are formidable. You've mastered numerous arts and disciplines, and your magic holds remarkable potency, for a mortal, at least."

"But I am a mortal," Anwyn interjected, confused.

"Are you?" Thalirion countered. "Can the Seishinmori truly be considered a mere mortal? Your spirit now intertwines with that of the forest. You possess traces of immortality, granting you access to more power than an ordinary Elf!"

Anwyn considered Thalirion's words, realizing he had a point. She had accomplished the extraordinary feat of reviving her father, an act even her own mother deemed beyond the capabilities of a normal Elf. It was only after learning of her role as the Seishinmori that her mother comprehended how she had achieved it.

"And Gunnar, you've merely scratched the surface of the magical potential granted to you through your Elven Blood inheritance. I dare say you pose more of a threat to yourself and those around you than to our enemies at the moment! You'll need to refine your magical abilities and master your skills until you can stand toe-to-toe with even Anwyn here!"

"But how can I ever be expected to match Anwyn in magic? She is an elf who has been using magic her entire life. I only accidentally used magic a few days ago!"

"And this is precisely why our destination will be so crucial! Have you ever heard of Nexus, the Echo Realm?"

Anwyn, Gunnar, and Karl exchanged puzzled glances, indicating they had never heard of Nexus before.

"Nexus serves the purpose of creating a realm where time operates at a different pace, enabling prolonged periods of training and study without the limitations of the mortal realm," Thalirion explained. "Functioning as a bridge between dimensions, Nexus provides a distinctive environment for individuals to explore the full extent of their magical abilities. The trials and challenges within Nexus are specifically designed to test and refine not only one's magical skills but also their character and determination."

"And why is it called the 'Echo Realm', may I ask?" Karl implored.

"Ah," Thalirion exclaimed, "the name 'Echo' implies a reflection or reverberation. Within Nexus, the realm mirrors reality, capturing elements from both Vellhor and the realms of the gods. Essentially, Nexus acts as a reflection or echo of the magical forces at play in the mortal world."

"I might be dense, but I'm not sure I'm catching on," Karl responded.

"I agree, you're dense!" laughed Draeg. Anwyn began to see why Karl had become so accustomed to Draeg's humor.

Ignoring the interruption, Thalirion continued, "When a magical being dies in Vellhor, their Spectral Echo ascends to Nexus, but it becomes more... erratic, you could say. Meanwhile, the spirit of the deceased rises to the realm of the gods, where they can spend eternity feasting with their favorite deity." Thalirion looked up at Draeg, an amused glint in his eyes.

Suddenly, his expression darkened, the amusement replaced by a somber, almost foreboding look. "But beware," he added, his voice dropping to a near whisper. "This transition is perilous. The Spectral Echo, untethered and wild, often lashes out, causing disturbances in Nexus. Sometimes, these echoes become twisted and malevolent, haunting the living and spreading chaos."

"And you're proposing we venture there for training?"

Anwyn inquired, a shadow of concern crossing her face as she contemplated the possibility of the Elves she recently been forced to kill awaiting her arrival in Nexus, seeking revenge.

"Indeed," Thalirion affirmed. "You must have heard of the Sacred Tree, haven't you?"

Anwyn nodded in response.

"The Sacred Tree serves as the only known gateway, or portal into Nexus, fueled by the magic of the Forest. Rumor has it that there's another portal hidden somewhere in the Scorched Mountains, but that has never been confirmed." Thalirion explained.

Anwyn noticed that Gunnar, who had remained quiet for some time, had a solemn expression on his face before he asked. "Who exactly are our enemies? You have mentioned these enemies and spoken of preparing us for this war many times, yet we have not discussed our enemies any further."

Thalirion responded, "It won't shock you, Gunnar, to learn of an alliance between the Drogo Mulik shaman and certain high-ranking military officials from Dreynas."

As Gunnar and Karl exchanged glances, Anwyn pondered the challenges the two might have encountered in Dreynas. Her grandfather had spoken of being falsely accused of treason.

"Surprisingly, the Drogo Mulik have also forged an alliance with the humans, striking a deal that extends their influence across Vellhor. Moreover, their machinations now extend even into Luxyyr," Thalirion disclosed with a grave tone.

Despite prior warnings from her grandfather about the Drogo's impending war plans, Anwyn was taken aback to discover their schemes unfolding in Luxyyr. Determined to uncover more, she confronted Thalirion.

"Tell me, Thalirion. What exactly is happening in Luxyyr?" she demanded.

"You would have sensed it yourself, Anwyn. The blight and

disease of the Forest. With your connection, you surely would have felt it?"

Anwyn recalled the sorrow and pain she experienced passing Gwydir. The Elves from Gwydir had targeted her, holding her responsible for the blight and attempted to kill her father.

"I felt it," she admitted sorrowfully. "However, the High Elves of Gwydir, and possibly the entire Elven Council, blame me for that."

"Why?" Karl interjected.

Anwyn looked at Karl, and although she assumed that Dwarves would not think that being born without a twin was strange, let alone a reason to be cursed and shunned, she couldn't shake the embarrassment she had carried her entire life for lacking a sibling.

"Because I was born without a twin." Anwyn replied flatly. Karl, unsure if she was joking, found himself caught in an awkward silence. As the pause lingered, he realized she was serious. "What?" he exclaimed. "I've never heard of anything so bloody ridiculous in my entire—"

Thalirion raised his hand, halting Karl's words. He then explained, "Karl, the Elves have different beliefs than Dwarves. Anwyn here is the first elf born in Luxyyr without a twin sibling in many centuries. Luxyyr's Elves are quite superstitious. Anwyn's future role, once she's strong enough, will be to educate and unite the cities of Luxyyr, ultimately leading them."

Just then, Lorelei began fluttering excitedly on Anwyn's shoulder, her vibrant green hair swaying with each movement. Suddenly, Anwyn's gaze snapped up, a spark of realization igniting in her eyes. "That's right," she murmured, "I'd nearly forgotten!" Her intense gaze met Thalirion's, conveying the urgency of her revelation. "We were visited, by a Drogo, I think. On our way out of Luxyyr."

Thalirion nodded, prompting Anwyn to continue.

"He warned us of a battle. At the Sacred Tree."

Thalirion's expression tightened in contemplation, his brows furrowing as he weighed the gravity of the situation. After a few moments of solemn silence, he finally spoke, his voice tinged with concern.

"That does not bode well," he murmured, the weight of his words hanging heavy in the air. "You are not yet ready for a battle."

His statement echoed with an ominous certainty, a stark reminder of the challenges ahead and the perilous journey they faced. Anwyn's heart sank at the realization, the enormity of the task before them weighing heavily on her shoulders. With each passing moment, the shadow of the impending battle loomed larger, casting a pall of uncertainty over their once hopeful quest.

Gunnar, determined not to be manipulated by the strings of prophecy and fate, voiced his thoughts. "Surely, there must be a way to avoid a battle. Diplomacy is a far more effective tool for crafting a peaceful future than war."

"Unfortunately, Gunnar," Thalirion sighed heavily. "The Drogo Mulik are desperately attempting to raise their god, Nergai, from the depths of the underworld. Their leader is a fanatic who cannot be swayed. Once he succeeds, it will become evident across Vellhor that Nergai is filled with one thing and one thing only: the will to destroy everything on Vellhor."

Thalirion's words lingered in the air, casting a somber shadow over the group. The gravity of the situation settled upon them like a dense mist, and Anwyn could feel the weight of responsibility pressing down on her. As she reflected on Thalirion's words, she found herself revisiting the ominous dream she had recently had — a dream that now felt more like a glimpse into the threads of fate.

"Thalirion," she began, her voice carrying the echoes of

uncertainty, "before our paths crossed, I also experienced what I believe was a vision. In my dream, I witnessed Drogo Mulik shamans enacting a ritual, and I feel it may be linked to Nergai."

"Tell me of it, Anwyn," Thalirion urged, his gaze steady and inquisitive.

With the dream, or vision, still vivid in her mind, Anwyn began describing it for the group. "Several Drogo shaman encircled a large coffin fashioned into the likeness of a huge dragon. They were each chanting in a steady rhythm. Although I could not understand the language, I got the impression that they were enacting some form of dark magic. They had sacrificed two of their own whose blood slowly dripped onto the coffin, sizzling each time a drop landed. As their chants grew louder and louder, they stopped and each of them sliced through their own skin and let their blood flow onto the coffin. As the ritual reached its peak, the spirit of a huge dragon emerged from the tomb, snarling furiously. Even though it was only a dream, I could feel the rage emanating from the dragon. The ritual seemed to falter, however, drawing the spirit back into the depths of the tomb. In its retreat, the enraged dragon spirit managed to claim the lives of a few of the Drogo shamans."

Thalirion listened intently to Anwyn's account, his eyes narrowing with concern. "That is a disturbing vision, Anwyn," Thalirion mused, his voice low and thoughtful. "The connection to Nergai is evident, but it raises more questions than answers. The sacrifice, the blood magic, it all points to a ritual of considerable power."

His gaze shifted to the others, his expression grave. "Drogo Mulik shamans are known for their knowledge of blood and death magic. Both are potent forces. It is as I thought, however, they have not managed to find a way to raise Nergai. The ritual may require specific sacrifices, and if any of them are incomplete or improperly performed, it could disrupt the summoning process. The ritual you described involved the sacrifice of two individuals, and if the conditions for these sacrifices weren't met precisely, it would have led to failure."

Thalirion's words hung in the air, each syllable heavy with the weight of their meaning. An uneasy silence settled over the group as they processed the implications of his statement, their thoughts drifting to the challenges that lay ahead.

After a tense moment, Thalirion spoke again, his voice measured but grave, cutting through the silence like a blade. "We must proceed with caution," he urged, his words a solemn reminder of the dangers that lurked in the shadows. "The path ahead is fraught with peril, and we cannot afford to underestimate the forces arrayed against us."

His gaze swept over the group, his eyes reflecting the gravity of their situation. "Dreams can be cryptic, but they often carry kernels of truth. Your vision suggests that the Drogo are closer than I had presumed, and with the warning from this visitor. It is imperative now for us to get to Nexus as quickly as possible."

A long moment of silence passed as the group digested this grim news, Gunnar spoke up. "The question is now, what is the quickest route to the Sacred Tree?"

Thalirion pulled out a small marble before stating, "The Endless Bridge, of course."

Grimacing, Draeg looked upon the small marble and exclaimed, "Urgh, get that thing away from me! If I can't sense its magic, how am I supposed to trust it!!"

"Don't be so dramatic, Draeg," Thalirion admonished, holding the marble between his fingers. "This is merely my spirit condensed into an eternal flame. You cannot sense it, since during the forging process, I took measures to conceal the nature of the Spiritfire from other divine beings. Trust in my craftsmanship and our need for speed."

Despite Thalirion's reassurance, Draeg remained unconvinced. After a moment, however, realization dawned on him.

"As much as I would love to trust you, Thalirion, unfortunately, I must return to Aerithordor and confront my family. My mother will have advice and guidance which will benefit us greatly."

Thalirion nodded in acknowledgement. "So be it. Farewell, Draeg. We will no doubt see each other soon."

With a firm grip, Thalirion crushed the marble between his fingers. A portal of fire tore a hole in reality, creating a bridge of flames between the realms of Vellhor.

27

Betrayal

'When the whispers of doubt become the shouts of betrayal, the echoes are deafening.'

Duke Cahir

Duke Cahir paced up and down his chamber, sure that he would wear down the thick, lush carpet before his Head Shadowmancer, Leopold, returned. He knew that he was gambling with this venture, but he'd had assurances from Leopold that this turn of fate could lead to his rise in power. He also knew that should things go wrong, it would not only be the end of his reign as Duke, but could lead to the downfall of Fenmark completely.

Luthar, seated on Fenmark's throne, deceived Cahir's unambitious father into assisting in conquering Lamos and subsequently endorsing the 'Silver Crowns Alliance' under the guise of fostering unity. In truth, this maneuver served only to strip Cahir of his rightful claim over Fenmark and thrust Luthar into an even more formidable position of power. Following Cahir's father's demise, Luthar had capitalised on the ensuing instability, using his political and military strength to coerce the remaining Dukes and seize the crown for himself.

The mockery of a coronation unfolded, signifying Luthar's undeserved ascent to the throne and heralding a new era for Vellhor. As Cahir stood witness, bitter waves of resentment threatened to engulf him. Despite the internal storm, he maintained a stoic façade, biding his time for the moment when he could seize control. Despite the significant risks involved, Cahir couldn't help but smile, hoping that the impending opportunity for his calculated move was now approaching, a daring gamble in the face of uncertainty.

Duke Cahir embraced the looming risk, a constant companion on his journey to power. He staunchly believed that the path to greatness demanded facing challenges head-on, for, as the age-old saying goes; only by challenging dragons can one discover their hordes of treasure. Little did Cahir know the profound truth behind the old saying, as this venture held secrets beyond his imagination, where both dragons and hidden treasures lurked, waiting to reveal themselves in unexpected ways.

Eventually, a soft knock echoed at the door, and Cahir hoped it was Leopold, not his Chamberlain. In his current mood, he was poised to harm any unwelcome visitor, and Cahir certainly didn't have the time to find a new Chamberlain.

"Enter," Cahir called out, and a moment later, the door slowly creaked open.

Leopold, aged and weathered, stood before Cahir. He was possibly one of the oldest men Cahir had ever laid eyes on. His hair, a multitude of grey, hung limply down to his shoulders. Etched with countless wrinkles, his skin bore the sullen demeanor of one who had weathered life's storms a few too many times. Draped in an unassuming black and brown overcoat, like all members of his order, Leopold's weary and clouded eyes reflected a lifetime of dissatisfaction.

At first glance, Leopold seemed like a grumpy, old, insignificant figure. However, Cahir knew better. He had witnessed the man's power first-hand and hadn't elevated him to Head Shadowmancer out of kindness. No, Cahir thought, Leopold was likely the most potent mage in Fenchester, perhaps even in the entirety of Fenmark, and his unwavering loyalty lay solely with the Duke.

"Good Evening, Your Grace," Leopold rasped. His rough, low voice, almost a whisper, sent shivers down Cahir's spine every time he spoke.

"Leopold, tell me what you have learned." Cahir's response was sharp and business-like, concealing the worry that gnawed at him deep down.

Leopold's eyes shifted to the Duke before lowering once more in respect. "Your Grace, I realize you are probably feeling rather anxious, however please do not fear, I have been careful with my negotiations with the Drogo Mulik, and I would be able to determine whether there was any malice or ill intent on their behalf. They are not the most... *intelligent...* beings."

Cahir stared at Leopold, pondering once again if the old man could read his thoughts. He sincerely hoped not. Deciding the most prudent course of action would be to ignore Leopold's comments, he said, "Leopold, just tell me your report."

Cahir could have sworn he saw a ghost of a smile on the old man's lips for a split second.

"Yes, of course, Your Grace," he began, his voice still a harsh whisper. "As you know, Harald has managed to find the tomb of Nergai."

Cahir thought it was a bit of a stretch implying that Harald had found it. However, he stayed silent and waited for the old man to continue.

"We've shared the location with the Drogo shaman, and once they confirm it as Nergai's tomb, they have committed to providing enough troops for your upcoming campaign."

"And they'll unquestionably fight alongside our forces?"

"Certainly, Your Grace. I wouldn't doubt your strategic acumen in deploying the troops at your disposal. However, I propose deploying the Drogo as the initial wave of infantry, followed by our own forces. While the Drogo lack discipline, they excel as ruthless and effective killers."

"Obviously, Leopold." Cahir snapped. "What I'm asking is, can we trust them to remain loyal? Will they refrain from turning on us?"

"I don't sense any duplicity, Your Grace. Their leaders and shaman appear willing to sacrifice their own people for this cause. The loss of 500,000 of their soldiers doesn't seem to faze them."

"Well, they would find themselves caught between two human forces if they chose not to cooperate. Nonetheless, it's wise for us to have contingencies in place to prevent any potential betrayal."

"Your Grace, I agree that a prudent and cautious approach is warranted. However, attempting to deceive the Drogo might not be advisable. After we launch an attack on the other kingdoms, our nation will face internal fractures, Fenchester will experience instability, and we'll be in a weakened state. The Drogo might seize the opportunity to strike us while we are vulnerable."

Cahir dismissed the man's cautionary words. Having experienced the ravages of war before, he was well aware of the challenges the upcoming years would bring. Nevertheless, he was unwilling to expose himself to potential betrayal by the Drogo. Thus, he resolved to establish contingency plans in case they chose to turn against him. In his view, considering they were more akin to animals than civilised beings, caution was paramount.

Ruiha

Ruiha followed Kemp with quiet steps as he delved deeper into the tomb, a smile playing on her lips as she observed his awe and near speechlessness in the face of each discovery. Although his excitement brought a smile to her lips, she could not deny that an unmistakable tension loitered in the air, casting a sly shadow—a shadow that seemed to grow larger the more time they spent with Harald. More than once during their journey, she pondered the possibility that Harald, with his enigmatic aura, had been attempting to weave enchantments around them, a suspicion that clung to her consciousness like a whisper in the dark.

In the preceding days, Ruiha had detected subtle flutters in her surroundings—almost imperceptible shifts in temperature and atmosphere, coupled with a gentle tingle on her skin. Each occurrence coincided with the disapproving scowl of Harald directed at her, his gaze swiftly turning away when caught. Recognising the peculiar connection between these sensations and Harald's scrutiny, Ruiha couldn't shake the unsettling feeling that something sinister was at play. As she ventured further into the chamber alongside Kemp, she resolved to find a way to distance herself from him as soon as they left the tomb.

As Ruiha thought on her future, she realized that her options were somewhat lacking. A return to Lamos was swiftly dismissed; the city would be crawling with Sand Dragon henchmen, all desperate for whatever reward Faisal had put on her. Aligning herself with a mercenary or guard company surfaced once again—a prospect that appealed to her skills and training. The idea of travelling the world, safeguarding merchants, ignited a spark of excitement within her. However, as the prospect beckoned, a pause seized her. The thought of parting ways with Kemp, and walking separate paths, brought an unsettling hesitation into her considerations. Despite their short time together, the connection she felt with him surpassed anything she had experienced before, casting a shadow over the options that lay ahead.

Brushing away her conflicted thoughts, she focused on the now. Kemp traced his fingers along the dim cavern wall, completely absorbed in deciphering the details of the engraved runes. Just as she was about to ask Kemp about his findings, an unconscious alarm sounded in her mind. The hairs on her neck tingled, and an unsettling sense of someone's presence in the chamber enveloped her. In a flash, she switched to a defensive stance, raising her guard.

Cautiously, she tightened her grip on the hilt, taking a small step back to position herself behind a weathered stone column. Though not entirely obscured, the column's contours played with the dim light, making it a challenge to spot her in the shadow-laden room. This strategic placement not only shielded her from potential attacks behind, but also focused her attention on the imminent threat.

After a few steadying breaths, she discerned a flicker in the shadows. The dust particles in the air danced violently, signaling impending movement. Sharpening her focus, Ruiha witnessed Harald materialising a few feet away. His face twisted with malice, a cruel sneer distorting his features as he swung his sword towards where Ruiha had stood mere moments ago.

Adrenaline surged through Ruiha's veins, a ferocious tide that mingled with a grim satisfaction as she swiftly retaliated. Her blade sliced through Harald's outstretched arm, a decisive strike that sent his hand and sword crashing to the ground, accompanied by the unmistakable flow of blood from his severed limb.

Almost comically, Harald glanced from his severed stump to the floor where his hand and sword lay, then back at his maimed arm, before letting out a guttural scream of agony.

She raised her sword, the blade resting against Harald's throat, delicately grazing the skin and coaxing a small bead of blood. After a pause, as the pain and shock ebbed, Harald seemed to grasp the gravity of his predicament. Deprived of his hand and weapon, now faced with a sword at his throat, realization etched across his features.

Ruiha arched an eyebrow and locked eyes with Harald. "Not looking good for you, is it, Harald?" Her words dripped with sweetness, and a sly smirk played on her lips throughout.

"I warned you, didn't I?" Ruiha began, her tone shifting into a mix of anger and frustration. "You didn't bloody listen. No one ever bloody listens to me. I warned you, and now I'm going to have to kill you."

"Why haven't you already?" Harald asked, his voice hoarse.

"Oh, don't get your hopes up, Harald. You are definitely dying today. But first, I want to know. What the fuck are you doing? Why are you here, following a student mage around? And why, in Vellhor's name, did you just try to kill me?"

Despite the loss of blood and the pain Harald must be feeling, he still managed a triumphant smile. "You'll never know." He said defiantly.

Ruiha slowly shook her head in mock dismay. "Oh Harald, why would you say that? You're about to die, you have nothing left to lose. Now the last moments of your life can be as quick and painless as you'd like." Nonchalantly, she kicked a stone across the floor before adding. "Or it can be the most painful and excruciating experience of your miserable life. Believe it or not, torture is something I used to excel in."

A glimmer of fear flickered across his eyes for a moment before disappearing. He looked down at his wound, which was slowly pumping out his lifeblood. "I'll be dead in a few minutes, so you won't be able to torture me." Harald remarked stubbornly.

Ruiha only chuckled in response. "You think so? Kemp, can you come here, please?"

Kemp had witnessed the entire scene in utter silence. He seemed to be in shock, lacking any words to offer.

"Kemp, would you mind using magic to heat up my blade, please? I'd like to cauterize our dear friend Harald's wound, and keep him alive, *for a little longer at least...*"

Harald shot a pleading look over to Kemp. "Kemp, don't do it. She's tricking you. She's the one who attacked me, remember?" His gaze was intense and Ruiha felt the pressure in the atmosphere shift slightly.

Kemp shook his head, as if trying to clear his thoughts. He cast a quick glance at Ruiha before fixing his gaze back on Harald.

Ruiha noticed the moment the enchantment broke. Kemp's eyes cleared and his jaw firmed, and he responded, "You've been placing spells on me since I left the academy, haven't you?"

Harald must have realized the game was up, as he got angry and started yelling. "This bloody assignment. Babysitting a spoiled child. And now what? I'm going to die here?" He laughed manically, and Ruiha wondered if he had lost too much blood.

"No... No, I don't think so! I won't be dying here today." Harald laughed wickedly, and with that statement, as if from thin air, a long thin metal needle appeared in his one remaining hand and he lunged towards Kemp.

Ruiha sighed and swung her blade down again, severing Harald's hand and forearm at the elbow.

Gobsmacked, Harald glanced down at his two stumps and screamed in agony again before collapsing onto the hard floor, unconscious.

Ruiha looked up at Kemp, who was shifting his gaze between her and Harald, his mouth forming an open 'O'.

"You.. you saved me!" He finally managed to splutter. "Thank you, I will never forget this for as long as I live."

"I mean, you're welcome and all, but he had it coming. I won't lie. I actually enjoyed it a little too much." Ruiha quipped with a smirk.

"Is he dead?" Kemp asked.

Ruiha stared down at the body on the floor before looking back up at Kemp and saying. "Not yet, he's not got long though, maybe another minute or so."

"Shall we save him?" Kemp asked hesitantly.

"I reckon we should try, at least. We need to know who sent him, what he wanted, and I also want to know if we're likely to have any more crazy mages following us trying to kill us."

Just as they were about to attend to Harald's wounds, Ruiha and Kemp tensed at the unmistakable approach of footsteps. It wasn't a lone pair or a small group of travelers; the echoing sounds suggested a band of soldiers on the move. The steady, thunderous rhythm of marching boots resonated against the cold, stone walls of the cavern, creating an ominous symphony. Metallic clinks and the jingle of weapons added a layer of foreboding to the approaching sound.

As the marching drew nearer, Ruiha discerned a lack of synchronization in their movements—a disarray that hinted at chaos rather than discipline. Faint shouts and snarls in the distance heightened her concern. Brow furrowed, she scanned the dimly lit chamber, desperately seeking another exit or a hidden spot. The flickering torch light revealed only the ancient tapestries on the stone walls and a scattering of dusty crates, leaving the chamber feeling both ancient and claustrophobic.

The distant sounds of shouts and grunts grew louder, an

unintelligible noise that added to the urgency. Ruiha spotted the approaching group through the cascading waterfall obscuring the entrance to the tomb. Unable to see an escape route or hiding place, a growing sense of urgency gripped her.

Suddenly, five of the largest creatures Ruiha had ever seen entered the chamber. Towering at least seven feet tall, each one was heavily muscled and lacked clothing on their upper bodies, save for the occasional rag or strip of cloth tied around an arm.

Unnoticed by the intruders, Ruiha examined them more closely and noticed reptilian-like skin and scales covering their bodies and faces. Tiny horns protruded from their shoulders and heads, giving them a menacing appearance. Ruiha could feel her heart pounding in her chest as adrenaline coursed through her veins. Her palms grew sweaty, making it difficult to keep a steady grip on her weapon. The air around her seemed to thicken with tension, as if the very atmosphere recognized the imminent danger. These, she realized with an involuntary shudder, must be the Drogo Mulik, commonly known as lizard men or lizard folk.

After a brief pause, the Drogo turned their attention to Kemp and Ruiha, who stood near what Ruiha presumed was the now lifeless body of Harald. Kemp, on the other hand, appeared visibly shaken. His face had turned pale, his hands trembling uncontrollably. It was clear that the sight of these intimidating lizard men had rattled him to his core. Ruiha could see the fear reflected in his wide, darting eyes, mirroring her own unease. The lizard men snarled and gnashed their teeth, but maintained a cautious distance. Ruiha sensed they might be awaiting the arrival of their leader or captain.

The chamber continued to fill with more Drogo, their scales glinting in various hues, each displaying unique markings. Many directed aggressive gestures toward Ruiha and Kemp, while others circled the coffin or scrutinized the cryptic markings on the walls. The room buzzed with a palpable tension as the lizard folk explored their surroundings. Ruiha's mind raced, trying to calculate their next move, while the oppressive atmosphere pressed down on her, making each breath a struggle.

Eventually, a towering Drogo stepped forward, distinguished by three small curved horns on his head. His reptilian gaze hinted at a higher intelligence, and his muscular torso bore metal piercings and intricate dark tattoos spiralling around his arms and chest. Leaning on a colossal double-sided axe, he regarded them with a perplexed smile, a leader contemplating what to do with these unexpected intruders.

Gesturing at the three of them, he spoke in the common tongue, "This is the wrong way around. You are supposed to die. He is supposed to live."

After gently nudging Harald with her boot, Ruiha shrugged and calmly replied, "Oh, don't worry about him. He's just having a bad day."

The leader barked out a laugh. "I like you! I will keep you for entertainment!"

"Or... you could just let us go and pretend like we never saw each other here?" Ruiha suggested, grasping Kemp's hand as she began edging toward the only entrance/exit to the chamber.

This time, the leader laughed even harder, and some of the other Drogo around him nervously joined in, chuckling.

"You funny little girl. No, I will keep you," the leader declared, issuing orders in his own guttural language to the group around him. Three Drogo stepped forward.

As the trio advanced, their expressions remained unfazed by the fact that Ruiha held a sword, perhaps underestimating her resolve to use it. She promptly proved them wrong. With a swift, slicing motion, her blade swung through the air, decapitating one of the Drogo. The remaining two simply looked at their fallen comrade, grunted, and continued their advance.

Taking a step back with Kemp, she tightened her grip on his hand, bracing for another assault. Kemp raised his hands, unleashing a stream of fire that seared the flesh off one of the approaching Drogo. Without hesitation, Ruiha sprang forward, her sword piercing the final approaching Drogo through his heart.

She expected the leader to be angry, but instead, he regarded Kemp with what Ruiha interpreted as disinterest in his eyes.

"Magic," the leader grunted. "Capture them." He turned around and repeated himself in his own guttural language before walking away.

As the group closed in, some began hurling rocks at them. Ruiha scanned their surroundings, desperately searching for any glimmer of hope or escape. The grim reality gripped her heart, leaving Ruiha grappling with the dire realization that there seemed to be no way out of this predicament without a fight to the death. She clutched Kemp's hand, her fingers squeezing tightly in an attempt to provide him with an element of comfort amidst the impending chaos.

The air crackled with hostility as the jeers and the thuds of rocks landed around them. Ruiha's mind raced, her instincts urging her to find a solution. Yet, the confined space seemed to offer no solace, leaving her with a sinking feeling that their fate hung on the edge of a blade. Amidst the impending storm, she went to whisper words of reassurance to Kemp, steeling themselves for the inevitable clash that awaited them.

As she turned slightly, she noticed that Kemp had begun countering the onslaught by hurling projectiles of his own back at the crowd, employing wind magic. Simultaneously, he had erected an invisible barrier that deflected some of the rocks hurled their way.

Suddenly, a large, dark rock slammed against the side of Kemp's head, causing him to collapse to the floor. The force of the impact crushed the crown secured on Kemp's back, and Ruiha winced as the distinct sound of a crack filled the air. In response, an ethereal light erupted from the crown.

Before Ruiha could comprehend what was happening, Kemp was enveloped in a tunnel of light. She knelt down next to his unconscious body, but before she could reach out to him, he disappeared suddenly. She glanced around in confusion before she felt an excruciating pain in the back of her head, and then the world around her went black.

28

The Forgotten Realm

'With strength and defiance, evil forges its own path forward.'

Dakarai

Dakarai had been rounded up along with the rest of the male slaves. They were herded into a colossal carriage that carried them through the sprawling underground city, eventually reaching a massive stone arena. Upon arrival, they had been locked in the underground cells. Within the confines of that shadowed and foreboding space, Dakarai languished, his anticipation replaced by a numbing acceptance of the grim reality that had befallen him. The air hung thick with the oppressive stench of decay, a noxious cocktail of bodily fluids and the lingering remnants of despair that coated the cell floor. In the oppressive darkness, Dakarai, whose spirit had long ago withered away, found himself waiting for the return of his captors, harboring no illusions of mercy.

The cell seemed to absorb the light from the lanterns, leaving only the dim glow of hopelessness in its wake. He could almost taste the bitterness in the air, a palpable reminder of the merciless fate that awaited him. The walls, adorned with the scars of past occupants, stood as witnesses to the cruelty inflicted by his own people. Now, in the depths of this wretched pit, Dakarai, hollowed by the loss of his son and wife, existed as little more than a ghost, waiting for the evil that had already taken away all he cherished.

In the distance, Dakarai observed a slaver, a sinister figure draped in dark attire, leading a procession of Drogo slaves through the cold, stone corridors. The air thickened with anticipation and fear as the captives, eyes wide with trepidation, shuffled along in chains.

As they approached the cells, a hushed murmur filled the air. The slaver, a cruel smirk playing on his lips, raised a commanding hand to quell the uneasy whispers.

"Welcome to the pits of hell, you sons of whores!" he proclaimed, his voice resonating through the cavernous space. "In the heart of this arena, you shall entertain the masses and earn your pitiful right to exist."

He gestured expansively toward the battleground above. "Survival is your sole purpose now. Forget your former lives; here, strength alone commands respect. Fight, bleed, and die for the amusement of your betters."

Pacing before the captives, the slaver's reptilian eyes gleamed with sadistic glee. "Every move, every struggle, a spectacle for the pleasure of our city. Your lives now belong to the roar of the crowd and the whims of your masters."

He allowed a malicious pause to permeate the air before concluding with a chilling command: "Prepare yourselves, for the pits hunger for your blood. Only the strongest will taste the fleeting sweetness of survival. Welcome to your new existence, slaves. May Nergai reward those he deems worthy."

Junak

The perilous journey to the Forgotten Realm had exacted a heavy toll on Junak and his warriors, with half of their number lost to the murky depths of The Cimmerian Strait. The creatures they encountered seemed to have crawled from the very bowels of the underworld, a realization that lingered in Junak's thoughts.

Despite the dangers, Junak stood triumphant at the entrance to the concealed valley, Shon'anga by his side. Nestled between desolate mountain peaks, the valley was littered with mist-wreathed trees and thorny shrubs unfamiliar to the subterranean Drogo. The air whispered with the secrets of this untouched realm, beckoning him forth.

Gazing down at the diminutive Drogo shaman next to him, Junak demanded, "How do we summon this Chronos?"

"Master, Chronos is a se'er, an oracle. Do not fear; he knows we are here. He will summon us once he is ready," Shon'anga responded.

Irritation etched across his face, Junak snapped, "So we are simply to wait here until Chronos decides?"

"Yes, master, that would be the best course of action, I believe."

Gripping his enchanted axe, Junak stepped forward, feeling the unstoppable strength gifted to him from Nergai coursing through his veins. "No," he exclaimed firmly.

Shon'anga's eyes widened in shock and fear. Desperately, he begged, "My lord, my lord, please. You cannot venture into the valley without an invitation."

Ignoring the shaman and his warnings, Junak continued to step forward. After five steps, he stood, back straight, and yelled, "Chronos, Keeper of the Crystals. Nergai waits for no one. Come forth and speak with us, or I will unleash the full might of the God of Rage, Vengeance, and War upon your puny valley."

As Junak concluded his sentence, the very ground beneath him seemed to writhe and squirm. Swiftly adopting a warrior's stance, he stood ready. In mere moments, a serpent, as thick as his thigh and six feet long, vaulted into the air, hissing with furious intensity. Junak, unyielding, extended his bare hand, seizing the serpent in his vice like grip until a satisfying 'pop' echoed through the valley.

Two more serpents attacked simultaneously, and Junak, undeterred, wielded his enchanted axe with calculated precision. With a fierce whirl, he deflected their venomous strikes, each swing thrumming with unmatched power. The air crackled with the clash of scales and metal as Junak severed the serpents' heads.

"If you have more, send them now so that I may kill them swiftly. Otherwise, stop this and come down here. I wish to speak with you."

The ground immediately ceased its unsettling movements, and from the shadows emerged a hooded figure. Slowly and mysteriously, the enigmatic being approached Junak. Unfazed and defiant, Junak stood his ground, the haft of his axe tightly gripped in his hand, ready for whatever revelation or confrontation awaited him.

Draped in a dark, tattered cloak that swirled like mist and smoke, the hooded figure revealed little of their visage, leaving only a glimpse of what could only be a skull and a hollowed-out eye socket. A chilling silence enveloped the air as the stranger continued their approach, the heavy weight of uncertainty settling between them. Junak's eyes bore into the mysterious figure until, finally, the stranger came to an eerie halt in the shadowy expanse of the valley.

With a voice that seemed to carry the weight of ages, the

hooded figure finally spoke. "Junak, warrior of Nergai, your presence here was foreseen. I am Chronos, the Keeper of Crystals."

Junak's grip on his enchanted axe tightened, his eyes narrowing with suspicion. "If you knew that I was coming, then why did you attack me?" Junak asked.

Chronos stepped closer, the air humming with an arcane energy. From the recesses of his robe, he pulled out a large crystal globe. "The serpents were but a test to measure your strength and resolve, Junak," he explained.

Junak's gaze remained fixed on the crystal, as swirling images of an elf and a dwarf formed within the crystal. "And what of this elf and dwarf? What part do they play in all this?"

The hooded figure's eyes bore into Junak's. "The prophecy you seek foretells of their unity against the shadows that aim to engulf this realm. Their alliance is a beacon of hope, and your actions will determine whether that beacon shines brightly or is extinguished like a candle in a storm.

As Junak contemplated the weight of those words, Chronos continued, "If you wish for your master's plans to come to fruition, then you must prevent them from succeeding in their quest."

"Then you will help me," Junak said menacingly. At that moment, he stepped forward and grabbed Chronos by his throat, feeling the bones in the hooded figure's neck.

Chronos let out a fierce cackle. "You cannot harm me, Junak. I am not from this realm."

"Neither is Nergai," the Claw chief snarled, bringing the blade of his axe up against the Keeper of the Crystals' throat. "And you will help me."

29

BATTLE FOR THE SACRED TREE

'In the aftermath of sorrow, tears blend with ash. It was an anguish that spoke of loss and the bitter residue of pain.'

ANWYN

The group came tumbling out of the portal, arriving at a lake in the middle of the forest. Thalirion calmly readjusted his attire, seemingly unaffected from the journey, whereas Gunnar and Karl, experiencing this form of magical transportation for the first time, were on their hands and knees retching uncontrollably from the sudden plummet through reality. Anwyn hid a triumphant smile at the thought of controlling herself, with it being only the second time she had travelled the endless bridge before.

Anwyn stared out across the expanse of water and saw that in the middle of the magical lake, in the heart of a small, hidden island, stood a colossal tree. It was easily the largest tree that she had ever seen. It was a magnificent sight that almost brought a tear to her eye.

Its towering presence reached high into the sky, its ancient branches, twisted with age, stretched outwards like the arms of a giant. Leaves of vibrant emerald adorned each branch, shimmering in the dappled sunlight that filtered through its lush canopy.

As Anwyn stared in awe at the giant tree, Lorelei dived headfirst into the waters of the mystical lake and began swimming and splashing around. Anwyn couldn't help but chuckle at the display.

Once the Dwarves had recovered from the ordeal of travelling the Endless Bridge, Anwyn looked around at her surroundings. "This place feels so familiar." She mused out loud.

"It should," Thalirion began, "We are back in Luxyyr. In the Great Elven Forest!" Closing his eyes, he inhaled a deep breath, taking in the scent of the forest. A look of calm serenity washed over his face before he opened his eyes again. "We are located between Coetyr and Gwydir, believe it or not."

Anwyn struggled to conceal the look of skepticism on her face. "This lake is not on the map my grandfather gave me."

"Indeed, it is not. This lake is on no map. In fact, it is invisible to all but the Seishinmori and the Fae of the forest."

Gunnar had a puzzled look on his face. "Apologies, Thalirion. When we first met, you introduced Anwyn as the Seishinmori, but nobody has explained what that means exactly."

"It means that Anwyn is the rightful ruler of Luxyyr." Thalirion explained. "The forest has selected her to rule the Elven people… once she is strong enough." He added.

Anwyn looked around at Karl, who was now staring across the lake at the huge tree on an island in the middle of it. She then looked back at Thalirion.

"Are you telling me that Gunnar and Karl cannot see the Sacred Tree there?"

Chuckling, Thalirion responded. "No, no. They can obviously see the tree. I have allowed them to see it. Had I not, then no, they would not be able to see it."

Karl swivelled his head, his unruly red hair swaying as he did so. "What is to prevent someone from inadvertently stumbling into the lake and drowning if they cannot see it?" he asked, a sliver of fear in his eyes.

Anwyn observed Karl's uneasy expression, recognising the practicality in his question. She shared his concern, silently pondering the potential dangers of an invisible lake.

Thalirion, with an air of calm reassurance, responded, "Well, Karl, had you been a mile or so further away, the magic from the tree would have repelled you from coming any closer. It would have dissuaded you, ensuring you never reached the lake. The tree itself acts as a guardian, warding off those who aren't meant to approach."

Karl's brows furrowed as he absorbed Thalirion's explanation. The sliver of fear in his eyes seemed to ease somewhat.

Anwyn couldn't help but reflect on Thalirion's revelation, realizing that it explained the many failed attempts by Elves to find the Sacred Tree.

"You are not Seishinmori, Thalirion. How can you allow Gunnar and Karl to see the Sacred Tree? In fact, how can *you* see the Sacred Tree?" Anwyn questioned.

"Ahh, but Anwyn. I may not be Seishinmori... *now*... but that has not always been the case."

Anwyn gasped, "You were Seishinmori? That is impossible. My parents told me that a Seishinmori has not been selected for over a thousand years!"

"One thousand, three hundred and twenty-four years." Thalirion smiled in response.

As the weight of Thalirion's revelation settled over the group, a hushed silence enveloped the magical lake. The very air seemed charged with anticipation, and even the rustling leaves of the Great Elven Forest held their collective breath.

Thalirion broke the silence. "Indeed, Anwyn, I once bore the mantle of Seishinmori. A role that intertwines with the fabric of Luxyyr itself. But that is a tale for another time. Now, our focus should be on what lies ahead."

Anwyn nodded, her mind a whirlwind of thoughts and questions. She turned her gaze back to the colossal tree on the hidden island, wondering what awaited her.

Gunnar and Karl, digesting the newfound knowledge, exchanged determined glances. Their stout Dwarven resolve remained unshaken.

Anwyn's gaze shifted from the imposing silhouette of the Sacred Tree to Thalirion, her brow furrowed in uncertainty. "I do not see any Drogo forces here to oppose us," she remarked, a hint of doubt creeping into her voice. "Perhaps my visitor was wrong."

Thalirion remained silent, his keen eyes scanning their surroundings with a calculating intensity. Sensing his deliberation, Anwyn pressed on, her tone hopeful yet tinged with apprehension. "Or perhaps we are early and we could make it to the Sacred Tree before the Drogo arrive?" she suggested, her words hanging in the air with a sense of urgency.

As the weight of her proposal settled over them, Thalirion turned to face Anwyn, his expression unreadable. For a long moment, he said nothing, his mind undoubtedly grappling with the risks and uncertainties of their situation.

Finally, he spoke, his voice steady and measured. "If we move swiftly and cautiously, we may yet reach the Sacred Tree before the Drogo arrive. But beware, this could be a trap."

Suddenly, a distant rumble echoed through the forest, vibrating through the ground beneath their feet. Anwyn's eyes widened, and she turned to Thalirion for an explanation.

"A dark presence approaches." Thalirion declared, his voice heavy with urgency.

Before anyone could react, the tranquility shattered. The air crackled with energy as a portal opened nearby, and through it emerged a horde of Drogo warriors, their growls and shouts echoing in the clearing.

The Drogo, adorned in dark red cloths and carrying weapons, spread out like a swarm of locusts. Thalirion's eyes narrowed as he assessed the approaching threat.

"An ambush," he muttered, conjuring a staff adorned with ancient runes from thin air. "Prepare yourselves."

Anwyn felt a surge of energy coursing through her veins, an invisible link forming between her and Lorelei, the Fae at her side. The bond between them pulsed with their newfound strength, awakening the power within Anwyn.

Gunnar and Karl, despite lacking magical abilities, stood unwavering, their fists clenched in determination. Gunnar's cloak rustled as Havoc stirred within, the Sprite eager to help.

As the Drogo closed in, Thalirion channeled the essence of the forest, summoning nature's might to aid them. Anwyn unsheathed her katana, the blade humming with power, while Karl and Gunnar braced themselves for combat.

As the battle unfolded, the clash of weapons and the roars of the Drogo warriors reverberated through the ancient trees. Thalirion moved with an elegant ferocity, his staff a conduit for the very essence of the forest. Vines twisted and snaked around the Drogo, restraining their movements, while bursts of arcane energy erupted from the staff, sending foes staggering backward.

Anwyn's movements were a dance of lethal precision. Her katana sliced through the air, leaving trails of glittering energy. Each stroke was met with an uncanny accuracy, as if the blade itself was guided by an unseen force. She seamlessly transitioned from parrying attacks to launching counterstrikes, her every motion a testament to her skill and strength.

Havoc emerged from the folds of Gunnar's cloak. Although in his infancy, Havoc exhibited a remarkable control over earth and stone. His tiny form darted between the legs of the Drogo, causing the ground to tremble and shift beneath their feet.

Gunnar and Karl fought like a well-honed machine. Karl, using his formidable strength, grappled with the towering Drogo warriors, swinging them around like ragdolls, despite the difference in size between them. Gunnar, with Havoc manipulating the terrain beneath the Drogo, used the confusion to grab his adversaries and break necks and crush skulls with his undeniable strength.

The air crackled with magical energy as Anwyn's bond with Lorelei reached its zenith. The Fae, now surrounded by a radiant aura, emitted waves of magical power that enhanced Anwyn's every move. Together, they became an unstoppable force on the battlefield.

Despite the fierce resistance of Thalirion, Anwyn, Gunnar and Karl, the Drogo were relentless, wave upon wave of snarling warriors pouring out of the portal. Dark red cloths billowed around them as they pressed forward, determined to overrun the group. Thalirion, beads of sweat glistening on his brow, maintained a constant flow of magic, fending off the attackers with an unwavering resolve.

The forest, once tranquil and breathtaking, had transformed into a chaotic and treacherous battleground. Trees lay destroyed, and the once-moist ground had turned into churned earth, burdened by the weight of the relentless battle. The mingling scent of blood and sweat now intermingled with the fragrant aroma of the ancient trees.

Thalirion fought his way to Anwyn's side and shouted over to her. "We need to close that portal."

Anwyn deftly adjusted her stance, narrowly evading the

swinging axe that aimed to decapitate her. Swiftly pivoting on her heel, she retaliated with a precise slash, cleaving the Drogo attacker in half.

"How?" she screamed, her voice cutting through the chaos, as she skilfully parried two incoming strikes simultaneously.

Thalirion, uttering an incantation under his breath, slammed his staff onto the ground, sending forth a shockwave that targeted the Drogo attackers around them. The impact didn't prove fatal, but it left them momentarily stunned. In that brief respite, Anwyn, Gunnar, and Karl seized the opportunity to swiftly dispatch their disoriented adversaries.

"Pour your willpower into your spell and disrupt the flow of energy fueling it," Thalirion yelled over the tumult. "I will hold them off, giving you the chance to get close enough."

Anwyn nodded, her eyes flashing with determination as she carved through the Drogo warriors towards the portal. Thalirion, his staff crackling with arcane energy, forged a path by striking down a line of Drogo, aiding in clearing the way.

As Anwyn fought her way towards the portal, Gunnar and Karl covered her flank, their Dwarven strength proving invaluable. Thalirion's attack had bought them a precious moment, but the portal's energy continued to surge.

Closing her eyes for a fleeting moment, Anwyn centerd her focus on the portal. Channelling her willpower, she summoned the essence of the surrounding forest. Amidst the chaos of battle, the clamor fell silent, replaced by the serene rustling of leaves and the distant chirping of birds. In that moment, Anwyn felt her connection with Lorelei strengthen. The bond was more potent than ever, and she tapped into their combined power. The magical energies of the portal flickered under the strain as Anwyn's connection to the forest deepened.

Anwyn pressed forward slowly, the weight of magical pressure bearing down on her. With each measured step, she sensed the flow of energy between realms. The air crackled with magical tension as she approached the portal's epicenter. Amidst the fray, Thalirion, locked in a fierce battle, cast protective spells to shield Anwyn from the remaining Drogo, whilst Gunnar and Karl, who had picked up some rusty swords, fiercely cut down adversaries all around her.

As Anwyn reached the threshold of the portal, she thrust her katana into the air. The blade shimmered with newfound power as she uttered an incantation, pouring her will into the spell. The energy disrupting the portal's flow surged forth, creating a dazzling display of light and force.

Recognising the pivotal moment, Thalirion intensified his efforts to hold back the Drogo onslaught. Anwyn's spell reached its zenith, and with a final surge of determination, she brought her katana down, slicing the portal in half and disrupting its energy flow.

The portal, once a swirling vortex of magical energy, began to collapse in on itself, creating a distorted spectacle of fading light and imploding force. Through the unravelling portal, a Drogo shaman became visible, staff raised high in his scaled hand, which was reaching out through the diminishing gateway. Alongside him, snarling in fury, was a colossal Drogo wielding a giant axe.

From the disintegrating portal, the shaman exerted a strange force, momentarily arresting the process. It seemed as if the collapse had been hindered. Then the unthinkable happened—the process began slowly reversing, defying the laws of nature itself.

Amidst the chaos, the shaman unleashed a devastating assault on the Sacred Tree in the distance, his dark magic engulfing it in flames that roared with sinister intensity. The once majestic tree, a symbol of ancient power and serenity, now became a tragic inferno, its towering form consumed by flames that licked hungrily at its branches. Shadows danced in eerie patterns across the battleground as the tree became a beacon of destruction.

Red-hot embers floated off into the distance with the billowing smoke, carrying the essence of the once venerable tree into the air like spirits departing from a sacred place. The crackling of the burning wood mingled with the distant sounds of battle, a symphony of chaos and destruction that echoed through the land.

Witnessing the desecration of the Sacred Tree, Anwyn released an agonizing scream that pierced the air, her heart rending with grief as she fell to her knees. In that moment, all thoughts of protecting herself vanished amidst the overwhelming sorrow that engulfed her. The battlefield echoed with her cry, a mournful lament for the loss of ancient power and a sacred symbol.

Gunnar, moved by Anwyn's anguish, sprinted towards the remnants of the portal. Seizing an oversized axe from a fallen Drogo warrior, he swung it with unparalleled strength. The blade cut through the air, cleaving off the hand of the shaman in a single decisive stroke. The hand, still gripping the wooden staff, fell to the ground with a muted thud. The magical assault on the sacred tree ceased abruptly, the echoes of Anwyn's grief slowly dissipating in the sudden stillness that followed. The battlefield, bathed in the glow of the burning tree, bore witness to the profound cost of the struggle against these dark forces.

With the shaman incapacitated, the portal, now bereft of support, collapsed in on itself completely. The remnants of its magical energy dissipated into the air, leaving only echoes of the otherworldly struggle that had taken place. With the Drogo warriors now slain, the battlefield went quiet, the Sacred Tree blazing in the background.

Anwyn was on her knees, overcome with grief, her sobs echoing through the decimated forest. Thalirion, a usually serene figure, now wore an expression of pain and anguish, a stray tear tracing a path down his cheek in mourning.

Raising his staff high into the air, Thalirion summoned a colossal storm. An intense determination furrowed his brow as the swirling tempest whipped up water from the surrounding lake. With an indescribable amount of power, he directed the storm towards the Sacred Tree, using the elemental force to extinguish the flames that had ravaged its ancient branches.

"Hurry," he rasped, his voice carrying a weight of urgency. "We can still make it to the gateway. The way is still open, but not for long."

With those words, the water in the lake parted, creating a passage to the island. The weary group, fueled by a renewed sense of purpose, sprinted towards the Sacred Tree with all haste, determined to reach the gateway before it closed.

The acrid stench of smoke hung ominously in the air, making it challenging to breathe. The mystical island now lay in ruins, its sacred essence extinguished by the destructive flames. As they reached the tree, Thalirion called them to a halt. Pressing his hand upon the charred bark, the anguish he felt was evident on his face.

"Quickly, there is but a spark of power left. We must leave immediately, for reaching Nexus must be our main priority now."

With his words, the tree emanated a weak glow, faint runes lit up around an ethereal doorway. Thalirion muttered incomprehensible words of ancient magic, and the doorway flashed brighter for a mere second. Urging them forward, he guided them through the portal and into Nexus, the Echo Realm, where the next chapter of their training would truly begin.

30

Dark Places

'The art of escape lies not in fleeing, but in finding the hidden doors within oneself to navigate towards a brighter future."

Ruiha

Ruiha grunted as she parried an attack aimed at her head. Her opponent was at least two feet taller than her and she could see his muscles bulging through the torn and tattered shirt he wore.

"I don't know how you're still alive! You're so tiny and weak!" Dakarai laughed in the common tongue.

"You're not the first big thing I've fought, you scaly bastard!" As the words left her lips, Ruiha maneuverd gracefully within arm's length of her towering Drogo opponent. With an exotic flourish of her sword, she halted it mere millimetres from his neck. A triumphant smile played on her lips as she tapped the flat of the blade against his tough, scaled cheek.

In amazement, Dakarai asked, "how do you do that? Every time?"

Laughing, she turned on her heel. "Despite what you barbarians believe, it's not all about strength. Grace, speed and skill win more fights than brutality does."

After her capture, Ruiha found herself stripped of her belongings and chained to a cold, unforgiving wall under the fighting pit arena. One of her captors had taken great pleasure in telling her that she was to become a gladiator, a pawn in the cruel games orchestrated by Junak.

Since that day, Ruiha had been thrust into a relentless cycle of brutal fights and rigorous training. She had adapted to the relentless training regimen well and had shocked the larger Drogo with her prowess during the arena battles. Now, with each appearance in the gladiatorial arena, she could hear the name 'Shadow Hawk' being chanted in the stands which echoed alongside the cheers of the bloodthirsty Drogo, revelling in the spectacle of a human gladiator.

She had been nicknamed the 'Shadow Hawk' ever since her first fight in the arena, where she had faced an aged Drogo and a monster which she had never discovered the name of. The monster was spider like in appearance and about the same size as a large dog. She had used her speed and skill to deftly detach the spider's head from its body, before plunging her blade into the Drogo's heart. The stunned murmurs of the crowd echoed her swift triumph as she walked back to her cell.

As Ruiha's fame grew, so did the unlikely friendship between the former assassin and the large, subdued Drogo, Dakarai. Lost in the depths of melancholy, he found an unexpected solace in Ruiha's no-nonsense attitude and unyielding determination. Her unapologetic spirit seemed to breathe life into his world, lifting him from the abyss of his utter indifference.

During the grueling training sessions, Ruiha's relentless drive pushed Dakarai to rediscover a sense of purpose. Her resilience and refusal to succumb to the cruelty of their circumstances ignited a spark within him. Slowly but surely, Dakarai's stoic demeanor began to crack, revealing glimpses of his former self.

As they sat in the shadowy corner of their cell, they shared stories—of lost loved ones, of shattered dreams, of the people they missed, and of the relentless pursuit of survival. Ruiha, with her pragmatic outlook, chipped away at Dakarai's wall of indifference, replacing it with a flicker of determination.

As they faced each brutal challenge together, the cheers of the bloodthirsty Drogo were met with a silent understanding between the human and the Drogo. Through the trials of the pit, they found a shared purpose—the hope for freedom and the strength to defy their oppressors.

As they walked back to their cells after their training session, Ruiha lowered her voice and asked, "Dak, did you manage to speak with Corgan?"

Dakarai's eyes darted left and right, vigilantly scanning his surroundings before he responded. "Yes, he has managed to recruit seven more."

Ruiha nodded thoughtfully, her gaze fixed on the dimly lit corridor, absorbing Dakarai's information. "Hmmm, so that's nineteen of us in total," she mused. "Still nowhere near enough for what we need."

"Corgan is an influential Drogo," Dakarai began. "He's been a slave under Junak for over five years, mastering the art of survival and diplomacy. He'll find more, Ruiha."

In the dimly lit corridor, Dakarai's words carried hope that conflicted with the harsh reality of their existence within the pit.

"Look who's all sunshine and rainbows today!" Ruiha joked, a playful glint in her dark eyes.

Dakarai looked at her in confusion. "What are you talking about?" He asked.

"You know, sunshine and rainbows… *optimism*?" Ruiha responded.

"What does sunshine have to do with optimism? And what is a rainbow?"

Sighing, Ruiha retorted. "Sometimes I forget that you savages don't go up to the surface very often."

"I have never been." Dakarai said proudly.

"Well, Dak. I will tell you something. You're missing out. Nothing better than the sun warming your face and the wind in your hair," Ruiha said dreamily.

The look of disgust on Dakarai's face made her burst out laughing, drawing the attention of a couple of guards.

"Keep walking and shut up." One of them shouted, before the other one cracked his whip, emphasizing his power over them.

As they wearily settled back into the confines of their dimly lit cell, which was chilled by the perpetual dampness, Dakarai and Ruiha gravitated toward their refuge in the back corner. The small alcove they had claimed offered a semblance of privacy, shielded from the gazes and hushed conversations of the other inhabitants who shared the cramped space with them.

"Will the Shadow Hawk be fighting tomorrow?" Dakarai asked, jokingly using her nickname.

"Ugh, Dak, don't call me that." Ruiha protested. "You know how ridiculous that sounds, don't you?"

Dakarai laughed in response before saying, "But you are the Shadow Hawk, Ruiha. You realize that is the reason most Drogo are even interested in speaking to Corgan?"

Ruiha shifted uncomfortably before deciding to answer the original question and diverting the attention away from her infamous name. "Whatever, Dak. And, yes, I was told that I am fighting again tomorrow. How about you?" She asked.

"No, I have not been told that I am fighting. I'll be training again. There are a few slaves I haven't managed to speak to yet. I hope to broach the subject of our escape tomorrow."

"Sounds good." Ruiha responded.

"Yes well, I'm not all *sunshine and rainbows,* unfortunately!"

Ruiha burst out laughing, breaking the grim silence in the cell. "Dak, you're funny, you know that, right?"

"I'm serious, Ruiha. Nobody shows any interest. They're all too scared."

"They're idiots! There are what… fifty guards, at most? We currently out number them at least two to one. If we all fought together, we'd be able to overpower them." Ruiha complained.

"Yes, I think they know that. What I think they're worried about is what they will do after we escape the pit. Most of us don't have homes or family to go back to. Some have been slaves for years. Most of the nineteen of us who have committed to the escape, have only recently been enslaved. We remember what freedom is. The rest of them have forgotten, and now they fear what will happen once they are free."

"So, what? They're happy throwing away their lives in this shithole for the entertainment of those savages up there?"

"Ruiha, I am working on them. I will speak to those I haven't managed to speak to yet and see what they say. The longer we endure and the more we lose in the fights, the more who will realize the futility of inaction."

"Until there aren't enough of us left because we've killed each other or been fed to monsters." Ruiha muttered under her breath.

Their conversation was abruptly halted by a commotion echoing down the corridor. The guards' clamor pierced the air as they shouted and clashed weapons together, instigating a commotion that rippled through the enslaved inhabitants. The slaves clustered near the cell entrance, desperate to catch a glimpse of the upheaval.

Dakarai and Ruiha rose, crossing the cell to investigate the disturbance. In their approach, the throng of slaves naturally cleared a path for the Shadow Hawk, the nickname grating on Ruiha with each muttered utterance. Glancing back, she caught Dakarai grinning at her evident discomfort. Shaking her head in resignation, she reached for the cool metal bars, peering through the door to discern the source of the commotion.

The sight that met her eyes was nothing short of shocking. A procession of two dozen Dwarves, bound together by chains, was being herded toward the cell block, the guards' spears urging them forward. The guards, with sneers and taunts, poured hate and venom with every word directed at the Dwarves. Even Dakarai wore a frown, his disapproval evident as the Dwarves were marched into the cell block.

"What is that about?" Ruiha asked, as she turned towards Dakarai.

"Dwarves," the big Drogo responded. "Probably captured from the recent raids into Dreynas."

"What are the Drogo doing in Dreynas?" Ruiha asked.

"Corgan, as a trusted slave, was closer to Junak than anyone I've ever met. He once explained to me that Junak could commune with Nergai, and that he had been frantically searching for Nergai's tomb. Junak has been conducting raids across the Drogo Mulik lands, as well as the Frost Mountains in Dreynas, in order to find it."

Not that she didn't trust Dakarai, but unsure of who might be listening, she opted to keep her knowledge of the tomb close to her chest for now. In the pit, there was always someone willing to sell a secret to the guards for an easier life.

"What does he want with this tomb?" She asked.

"Believe it or not, Ruiha, the crazy fool thinks he can resurrect Nergai!" Dakarai scoffed.

Kemp

Kemp's eyes slowly fluttered open, his senses overwhelmed by an oppressive darkness that seemed to seep into his very soul. A bone-chilling mist hung in the air, its touch leaving an eerie coldness on his skin. He groaned as he sat up, the palms of his hands feeling the clammy embrace of the cold, damp ground beneath him. The surrounding air was thick and heavy with a strange dark mist, muffling any sounds that might have existed in this desolate place. He strained to recall the events that led him to this eerie realm, but his memories were fragmented and elusive, slipping through his grasp like the tendrils of the strange mist around him.

The last vivid image in his mind was the tomb of Nergai. Harald, his fellow traveler, had betrayed them, leaving Kemp and Ruiha vulnerable to the merciless onslaught of the Drogo. A shiver ran down his spine as he remembered the scaly creatures and their attack.

As his mind cleared and his recollection began to return, a pang of panic speared his heart as he remembered Ruiha and his eyes darted frantically, searching for her, hoping she was safe and close.

As Kemp surveyed his surroundings, he realized he was no longer in the tomb and Ruiha was nowhere to be seen. The landscape before him was a nightmare painted in shades of darkness. The ground beneath his feet seemed to writhe with unseen shadows. The air was thick with an otherworldly chill, and the sky above was a canvas of perpetual twilight, with no discernible source of light.

Strange, twisted trees with gnarled branches loomed over him like giant skeletal claws. Their leaves were a sickly shade of grey, as if drained of life by the very essence of this strange place itself. Kemp felt an unsettling presence all around him, as if the shadows were alive and watching his every move.

As he cautiously took a step forward, the ground trembled beneath him, releasing a low, mournful hum. Spectral figures made of smoke materialized from the darkness, and Kemp stumbled backwards in fear. They wore tattered remnants of clothing, their faces distorted masks of anguish. Kemp could feel their malevolent gaze upon him, their hollow eyes fixated on his every move.

Suddenly, the air erupted with a piercing cacophony of ghostly wails. The spirits, seemingly agitated by Kemp's presence, closed in on him, their ethereal forms gliding through the shadows. Panic clawed at Kemp's throat as he attempted to summon fire into his hands, his fingers tingling with the promise of power. Yet, the magic refused to materialize. The echoes of his spell faded into the chilling air, leaving him vulnerable and defenseless. The panic he felt moments earlier twisted into a deeper terror, the realization sinking in that his magical abilities had betrayed him in this forsaken place.

Desperation fueled his movements as he sprinted through the shadowy landscape, the spirits pursuing him with relentless determination. He could feel their icy touch as they reached out, trying to pull him into the darkness from which they emerged. Kemp's breath came in ragged gasps as he navigated through the twisted terrain, searching for an escape from this nightmare.

In the distance, a faint glimmer caught Kemp's eye—a feeble green light struggling to pierce through the oppressive darkness. With the spirits closing in, he sprinted toward the light, hoping it held the key to his escape from this shadowed nightmare. Little did he know that this realm of shadows had more secrets to unveil, and the echoes of his past would continue to haunt him in this twisted place.

Thank You for Embarking on The Vellhor Saga!

Your journey through *Elven Blood* is just the beginning. To show my appreciation, I'm offering you an **exclusive**, free short story that delves even deeper into the world of Vellhor. Each book in *The Vellhor Saga* comes with its own unique short story, available **only** to my mailing list subscribers.

Sign up today to get your first story and continue your adventure with the characters you've grown to love.

https://BookHip.com/FRBGJQW

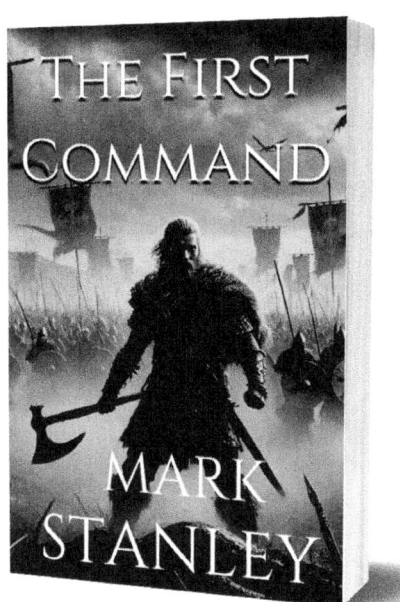

What You'll Get When You Sign Up:

- **Exclusive Short Stories**: Unlock new tales from Vellhor, not available anywhere else.
- **Insider Updates**: Be the first to know about upcoming books, special events, and more.
- **Early Previews**: Get sneak peeks at new releases before anyone else.
- **Special Offers**: Access discounts and offers available only to my mailing list subscribers.

Don't miss out on these exclusive extras

Join now and keep the adventure going!

Stay Connected!

I'd love to stay in touch with you! Follow me on Facebook and Instagram for the latest news, behind-the-scenes content, and to connect with other fans of *The Vellhor Saga*. Plus, be on the lookout for special giveaways and exclusive content just for my social media followers!

Facebook - https://www.facebook.com/profile.php?id=61561728111921

Instagram - https://www.instagram.com/markstanleywrites/

Afterword

A Sneak Peek at Book 2

Shon'anga struggled to suppress the whimper that threatened to escape his lips as the physician painstakingly cleaned and re-wrapped his severed arm. Despite his best efforts, the pain was unbearable, and a soft cry slipped out, betraying his agony. It felt as if every touch of the cloth was a dagger piercing his flesh.

As punishment for his failures, Junak had decreed that he was to receive no pain relief during the procedure. Shon'anga clenched his teeth, gritting against the torment as he remembered Junak's words echoing in his mind: "You live or die by the hand of Nergai. He will test the strength of your faith."

The weight of those words bore down on him like a mountain, testing not just his body, but his spirit. Shon'anga closed his eyes, his thoughts a whirlwind of pain and doubt, his faith wavering in the face of such relentless suffering.

Shon'anga's mind grappled with the grim reality of his situation. He knew that his chances of survival were slim at best. Among the Drogo, physicians lacked the advanced medical knowledge and surgical expertise of other races. The absence of an anaesthetic compounded the direness of his condition. Yet, despite this knowledge, Shon'anga had somehow endured the harrowing procedure and was now in the slow process of recovery.

During the operation itself, Shon'anga had drifted in and out of consciousness, each awakening accompanied by waves of excruciating pain. But with each return to consciousness, he found himself clinging to a glimmer of hope. The fact that he was now on the path to recovery, rather than descending into the darkness of the underworld, sparked a flicker of optimism within him. Could it be that his faith had been tested by Nergai and found to be steadfast?

As he reflected on his experiences, Shon'anga delved into the inner workings of shamanism. He pondered the stark contrast between those who wielded magic for personal gain and those who dedicated themselves to serving their god, Nergai. Until recently, he had dismissed the latter group as mere zealots, their fervour blinding them to reason. However, when Junak, the imposing ruler of the Claw clan and now all of Drogo Mulik, had approached him, emphasizing the importance of piety and devotion to Nergai, Shon'anga had found himself reluctantly playing along. After all, he knew that Junak would have sought another shaman had he not complied with the facade.

As doubts lingered in his mind, Shon'anga wrestled with conflicting emotions. Despite his reservations, he couldn't deny the possibility that aligning himself with Junak and embracing this newfound faith might have saved his life.

Now, gazing down at his missing limb, doubts gnawed at Shon'anga's mind like hungry beasts. Had he made the right choice in aligning himself with Junak and embracing this newfound faith? Despite his reservations, he reminded himself that he was alive, and in Junak's eyes, his survival would be seen as a testament to his unwavering devotion.

Shon'anga's thoughts drifted to the precious crystals he had

Afterword

obtained from Chronos, the enigmatic figure who had unlocked secrets of magic previously beyond his reach. Among them was the coveted 'fate crystal', a rare artifact capable of tracing the strands of destiny. With each use, it required replenishment of aura, a skill he had learned under Chronos's tutelage.

Despite being a Drogo shaman, notorious for their struggles with meditation and aura manipulation, Shon'anga had mastered these techniques under Chronos's guidance. Yet, he hesitated to share this knowledge with his fellow shamans, preferring to keep this advantage to himself, a secret reservoir of power in uncertain times.

The portal crystals shimmered with aura, their potential untapped yet palpable. Shon'anga couldn't help but marvel at their beauty and power. Once activated, they would fulfil their purpose, transporting warriors across vast distances with unmatched speed. The sheer magnitude of this magic defied everything he had ever known or learned about the arcane arts.

Keeping both a fate crystal and a portal crystal on a leather necklace, Shon'anga found himself subconsciously clutching and rolling them in his fingers, especially since losing his hand. The smooth surface provided a comforting distraction amidst his turmoil.

Along with his hand, Shon'anga had lost his staff in the attack on the Elven tree. It was a devastating blow, and he couldn't help but mourn its loss as much as his severed limb. While his hand was undeniably useful, his staff held immeasurable significance. It had amplified his magic, elevating him above his peers. Without it, he feared his abilities would diminish, rendering him vulnerable in a world wrought with danger.

With a heavy heart, Shon'anga sighed as he rolled onto his side, seeking solace in the embrace of sleep, if only to momentarily escape the weight of his losses and uncertainties.

Shon'anga awoke to a deep, gravelly voice calling his name. "Shon'anga... Shon'anga..." the voice called in its deep baritone. Shon'anga shifted his gaze in the darkness, which was absolute. It shocked him. Despite living underground his entire life, he was certain he had never before witnessed such absolute darkness. There was always a shaft somewhere in the underground world letting sunlight or moonlight in. If not, torches and lanterns were scattered everywhere across the Scorched Mountains, ensuring enough light for the Drogo to see. He searched for something that broke up the absolute darkness, a patch which was slightly lighter or darker than its surroundings, but he couldn't distinguish anything in the black.

"Shon'anga..." the voice called again.

"Who's there?" Shon'anga replied hesitantly.

Suddenly, fire erupted in the distance, a fierce burst of flame that illuminated Shon'anga's surroundings in a blazing inferno. For several heart-stopping seconds, the intensity of the light nearly blinded him, leaving him disoriented and bewildered. As the flames subsided, shock coursed through him as he realized he was back in the tomb of Nergai once again.

Briefly, a surge of panic gripped him as he wondered if he had inadvertently activated one of the portal crystals in his sleep. Hastily, he reached for his necklace, fingers fumbling in the darkness, only to find both crystals securely in place.

As the fire faded, torches lining the cavern walls flickered to life, casting eerie shadows and providing a dim illumination that allowed Shon'anga to maintain his vision. But the sudden appearance of light paled in comparison to the awe and terror that seized him as a massive, black-scaled dragon emerged from behind the gigantic coffin.

The dragon moved with a deliberate, almost regal grace, each careful step resonating with unimaginable power. Shon'anga's

Afterword

heart raced, his breath catching in his throat as he scrambled to his feet and instinctively prostrated himself on the cold stone floor. Every fiber of his being trembled in the presence of the colossal creature, feeling the reverberations echo through the chamber with each heavy footfall of the dragon's clawed feet.

"Master," Shon'anga said fearfully. "How may I be of service to the great Nergai?"

"Shon'anga." Nergai responded, and the shaman could see puffs of smoke coming from Nergai's nostrils as he spoke his name. He tried to suppress a shiver of fear, but he was unsuccessful. "Your failure has cast a shadow on our cause, but you will soon have the opportunity to redeem yourself. Make no mistake, however, I will be watching you closely, Shon'anga. Displease me and I will shatter the very foundations of your existence."

"What the master wills, his most humble servant will provide." Shon'anga said, his face still pressed against the hard floor.

"Excellent, Shon'anga," Nergai said with what the shaman took to be a smile. "Now, I believe it is time for you to earn a new staff…"

Firstly I'd like to say a big thank you to all you wonderful readers who have stumbled upon my writing and have stuck around to actually give it a read!

So, born in the amazing 80s (1984 to be precise), I'm Mark Stanley, and my life's been quite a journey, fueled by a mix of optimism and the occasional misadventure.

Following in my old man's footsteps, I did a stint in the British army where I saw some of the best and the worst the world has to offer, but, no matter where I was in the world, there would always be a book in my pack.

Then, I ventured into the world of international intrigue with NATO for a solid three years. Let me tell you, writing international policy is nowhere near as exciting as conjuring up fantasy realms!

Alongside my partner-in-crime (and life), Katie, we run a recruitment agency that's ticking along nicely, all while I'm secretly plotting my next epic fantasy masterpiece.

Family is my anchor in life. Three crazy kids—Luis, Ava, and Owen keep me on my toes, along with our crazy spaniel, Stanley, and the majestic feline queen, Tia.

About the Author

Fun fact: my love for the fantasy genre? You can blame my mum's creative disciplinary tactic of making me read as a punishment!

When I'm not crafting stories, you'll find me experimenting in the kitchen or sweating it out at the gym, trying (and often failing) to keep pace with Katie.

Now for some insight into my academic credentials: I've got a CIPS Level 3 Certificate in Procurement and Supply and an LLB Hons Law Degree from the University of Hertfordshire. But let's be realistic, formalised education and my ADHD? Let's just say they didn't always see eye to eye.

I am an avid reader and writer inspired by the captivating works of *Michael R. Miller, Philip C. Quaintrell, Davis Ashura, John Gwynne, Will Wight,* David Estes and *Jefferey Kohanek.* Drawing from the rich worlds and compelling characters created by these authors, I craft stories that blend fantasy and adventure, aiming to transport readers to realms filled with wonder and excitement. With a passion for storytelling and a dedication to the craft, I continually try and explore new narratives and share them with my growing audience.

So, that's me in a nutshell—full-time writer, full-time dreamer, family man, and eternal seeker of the next great adventure. Thanks for joining me on this wild ride called life!

And if you'd like to delve deeper into my world of writing and adventures, feel free to connect with me on social media or visit my website for updates and behind-the-scenes glimpses into my writing process.

Printed in Great Britain
by Amazon